IT IS WHAT IT IS

Karen Minors

Marie—
Enjoy this as
much as I enjoyed
writing it! Be ready
for book two!
♡ Karen

iUniverse, Inc.
Bloomington

It Is What It Is

iUniverse books may be ordered through booksellers or by contacting:

iUniverse
1663 Liberty Drive
Bloomington, IN 47403
www.iuniverse.com
1-800-Authors (1-800-288-4677)

ISBN: 978-1-4502-7620-7 (sc)
ISBN: 978-1-4502-7621-4 (dj)
ISBN: 978-1-4502-7622-1 (ebk)

Printed in the United States of America

iUniverse rev. date: 2/3/2011

For Nakia
For Pops

<u>My Angels of Music</u>

Teddy Pendergrass
Michael Jackson
Wayman Tisdale
Luther Vandross
Barry White
Lisa "Left Eye" Lopes
Aaliyah Haughton
Art Porter, Jr.
Phyllis Hyman
Marvin Gaye
Minnie Ripperton

Acknowledgements

I give thanks first to my Savior, the Author of my life, for blessing me and allowing me to use my talent and share it with others. It is through much prayer and supplication that I am able to bring forth my first love, the love of writing. I am grateful for being picked up out of the low valleys, and being able to shine. I am thankful to HIM for opening doors I could not see; Great is Your mercy towards me.

My biggest fan ever, my husband Nakia, for allowing me to hide off in my quiet space and just write. Thanks for giving me the view and place to start this project in Bermuda and for reminding me of the time when I am due at work in just three hours! (Once I start, I just can't stop!) Would you check out that book cover? Say what? Who would have thought you had all those hidden talents? Quit playing … do what you do! I LOVE YOU SO MUCH!

Jordan and Caleb, mommy loves you guys so much. Thanks, Jordan for making my favorite mango nut tea and sharing your daily stories with me, and for keeping your little brother entertained so I could get those last chapters in. You are my future author in the making! Caleb, you are too young to understand now, but as I continue to write, you will see how much it meant for me to spend time with you on those days I needed to get you to the park.

My entire family connection of Bushrods, from King George and beyond. (If it wasn't for Facebook, I would not have found so many of you. Even all the way in Germany!) Thank you all for the support and love. There are too many to name personally, but you know who you are. A special touch of love to Andrea and Tracey for ALWAYS sending me a message of encouragement. I am glad to have found you.

My Johnson family, for the many years of gathering at great-grandma Clara's house for Thanksgiving dinner. To Clara Ruth Johnson, the matriarch of the Johnson family, for 100 years of life. I love you and cherish your lemon meringue pie like nobody's business.

Grandma Hazel, thanks for loving me and giving me the understanding of so many different scriptures; for teaching me that "when you know, and you know that you know, then you know." And for always being ready to feed me when I come to visit. Grandaddy James "Jimmy" Bushrod, for your many life stories and for teaching me how not to "take [people] out back and show [them] what the good Lord has saved me from." I miss your old self and I wish that I could have your mind back to the way it was, even for one day, just so we could talk like before.

My dad, Robert, for giving me so much over the years. Your love and support is immeasurable and there is no way I can repay you for all you have done. Even when I didn't want to hear your lectures about life, money, school, and work issues (or anything I needed at the time), I listened and took your advice to heart. Thanks to you for everything.

My mother Linda and stepfather CJ, I am grateful for ALL you have done. Thanks for listening to me and for plugging my book to everybody at church!

My big sister Kisha, for being a friend and loving me not because you are obligated to but because you just love me! For the many, many, many things we have shared over the years and how we can still pick up the phone and leave crazy voice or text messages just to make each other laugh. (Is your foddy home? LOL) You are very special to me….always. Thanks to Mike for loving you and taking care of his family from day one.

Aunt Roshea, (who is more like a big sister than an aunt) for keeping it real with me, even when it may have hurt my feelings. You speak the truth and don't sugarcoat anything…at all! To uncle Roy for your wit and crazy [cuss] words of wisdom.

Aunt Doreen and Uncle Phil, for the many cookouts and pool parties, and for enjoying the Bermuda swizzle (a bit too much, maybe!)

Sandi, my bestest friend in the whole wide world, all the way back to fourth grade with Mrs. Lee at FWF Elementary School and through infinity and beyond! (Okay, Toy Story; it's from being around the children too much.) And to Craig, for being the best godfather to Jordan in the whole world. Remember how cute Jordan was in his tuxedo at your wedding? I love you both dearly. Thanks, Craig, for helping me understand Jordan and his ways when he was younger, as you could relate to my struggles.

Kismet, for your encouraging and spiritual words. There are many aspects of you in this novel. Thanks for taking the time to read my first draft during your [busy] day.

The Belles, Gerard and Jovohn, my brother and sister, for loving us and taking care of Jordan as if he were your own, for being there to keep him during the birth of Caleb. Thanks, girl, for the late nights at work when we were mad and laughing all at the same time to keep our minds in check. And for the excellent listening skills when I needed to vent. No more blizzards and being stuck when there was no room at the Inn, huh? (I will take the warm bed and cup of coffee for two hundred Alex!

LOL.) Gerard, thanks for spending Wii times with the boys. You guys needed it. (And so did I!)

Nathan Seven Scott, what can I possibly say? Taking it all the way back to UMBC until now, we have always kept our close bond. Our number seven being a coincidence…..I think not! It's just divine. Thanks for ALL of your support and words of encouragement and helping me and Nakia see that we can be the next Will and Jada Smith. I love you for all of your coaching and for not running up my tab for what you have given me! The sky is the limit, and I will meet you at the top!

Tandra, it has been a forever friendship. Thanks for sharing your family with me during our UMBC days. I am proud of you and love you.

Keesha, for checking in on me every blue moon to see how the book was coming along.

My nephews and nieces: Erik, Aaron, Jeremy, Christian, Ryan, Lindsay, Tariq, and Ari.

Frances and Charlotte Lee (aka Poppy and Sha Sha), and Glennis and Michelle Mitchiner, for always making me feel a part of your family. Nobody can throw down like the Lees.

Aunt Gloria, for loving me and my family as your own, and for constantly checking for me on Facebook and following my updates.

My GG, for all your craziness and stories over the past couple of years, and for loving me and welcoming me and Jordan to the Bermuda side. Thanks for sharing your family history with me and for making me feel a part of the family. Shirmelle, Taray, and Cody, my Bermudian sisters and brother, although we are not there with you all, you are with me in my heart. I love you Granny, and miss Pops, too.

"Shake it like that" Ally [Cat] Falby, for your positive energy and for taking the reigns and moving forward. I love your vision and I believe in you. I can't wait to be sitting on the Board and working along with you in reaching your dream. Thanks for being my manager and for sharing your time with me. I see great things in your future. ("What somebody say?")

The best editor in the whole wide world, Khadijah, for your expertise and feedback, for believing in me and for pushing me to give my all. You are an inspiration in all that you do. Liberated Muse Productions helped to put me out there. Words cannot express my gratitude. Thanks to Hook and Khari for sharing you with the world (and me). I will meet you at the top as well, and will love to work with you again on many more projects....a play maybe?

Dr. Acklyn Lynch, for believing in the shy, eighteen-year-old who was made to read her work in front of class *And the World Comes Tumbling Down*. You told me that I would be a good nurse, but that the writer in me would not sit still. She has come forth, and I thank you for leaving a mark on my life. You inspired me after all these years and I am living my dream. Thanks for believing in me.

Ananda, Tinesha, and B. Swangin Webster (that's her name, for real, y'all) for your mentoring and support. You ladies are the bomb, and I am glad to know you personally.

Paul Graves, for your expertise in photography. You always come correct!

Toni Lucas-Stallings of Joe Chisley's Hair Angels, for taking care of my hair for real, for real. I love you, cousin! Sashay, Shawntay....Miss Tré Chic.

Bryan Mills and the Secret Society for giving me music I can groove to.

Dionne, Teisha Marie, Kenny Wesley….for voices and music like no other. I love what you all are doing and I am playing your CDs to death! (No, for real; I am playing them to death!) I listened to your music as I put the finishing touches on this project.

My LaReine ladies who would come together for our "book club" eatings, I mean, meetings….Jenea, Nicole Allen, Nicole Willis, Monica. I love you for your words of encouragement and for plugging me. (We never discussed our last book, did we, Jenea?)

Anissa "Ni" Davis, for all the laughter and tears through the Army and Air Force Nurse Corps and for giving me stories for the next couple of books.

Jackie Weisberg and Zoila Suárez, for bringing my vision to reality without even knowing it. Zoila, you are my 'Maiya' whom I created in my mind and you helped bring my dream of this character come to life and feel so real.

Southern Maryland Hospital supporters….you all know who you are. Thanks for supporting me and for giving me fuel for the book….y'all just don't know….character development begins with your surroundings. Phyllis Whitaker, thanks for encouraging me to do a hardcover format; now you gotta help me sell them!

GWU Hospital and to the Transportation team (y'all thought I forgot, didn't you?), I said I would list you by name, so here it goes….Manager Renee Blake, Brenda Hill, Mark "Preacher Man" Johnson, Kelly Collins, Marquitta Mack, Marvin Stone, Charles "Challs" Coles (Friendly HS in the house!), Debbie Wade, Shanae Williams, Greg Jones, William Tate, Jayson Gibson, Joe Thomas (aka Fred), Chovia Rienne, Tesfaye Demissie, Paul Debruhl, Julia Graham, Jeff Sabbat. If I misspelled your name, I apologize…just blame it on Brenda, because she compiled the list for me. I miss you guys and hope to see you soon. Keep up the good work and treat my dialysis folk right! Thanks to Brenda and Amanda in the gift shop, for your kindness when I needed some sugar (y'all still have those Chuckles jelly candy that I like so well?)

Paula Moore, for giving me fuel for the fire in ways you have NO idea! Dr. Palmer for listening to my story pitch (and adding your own!); Dr. Donkor and Dr. Osman, for encouragement and support; Dr. Yazdani, for always asking if I needed anything, for plugging my name everywhere, even when I didn't know you were doing it, and for finding us a place to stay when we were told there was no room at the hotel during the snowstorm; thanks Dr. Shab Shab on behalf of the Metropolitan Nephrology group, for getting food for us when we were stuck at work with nothing to eat. Thanks Dr. Wyche for your beautiful personality and positive outlook; you made a difference when you came to work, in ways you can't imagine!

To my Facebook fans and supporters, I am ecstatic. Thanks for following me and patiently awaiting my project.

The METRO commuters every day of the week who stared at me as I danced my way to and from work, thank you for keeping me sane. I was able to build more character depth for future projects just by being in your presence. METRO rail operators for keeping me safe during my commute (especially my cousin Tara for telling me who to call when the crazy weekend freaks came out late at night!)

To the haters with all the negative vibes that I encountered, I am grateful because it was through the storm that I was able to push forward and birth this project. You cannot mess with a child of God and win!

Last, but certainly not least, to the readers of this book. I thank you for this journey you are about to take with me. So buckle up, hold on tight, sit back, and enjoy the ride….and feel free to leave your comments for me.

Karen L. Minors
www.karenminors.com
P.S. If there is anyone I may have forgotten, charge it to my head and not my heart; writing this book was a chore in itself.

It Is What It Is *— a cliché, popular within the circles of coaches, business execs, and those of us who just want to say "It's happened. I'm going to forget about it. I'm going to move on. There is nothing that can be done about it."*

In a nutshell, it means "this is the way it's going right now, and that's how it is." Kind of a way to say: don't over think the situation. A reminder to keep things simple, don't overanalyze things, or a way to put a definition on something that's hard to explain.

PART ONE

THE PAST TO THE PRESENT

If you always do what you always did, you will always get what you always got. ~Moms Mabley (Jackie Mabley)

Where do we go from here?
What do I do with these feelings?
Longing to have you near,
Knowing we shouldn't be dealing.

Why must the bad things always feel so good?
Why can't I just stay away?
Though our situation was understood,
Still does not mean it's okay.

Dealing, **Eric Robeson featuring Lalah Hathaway**

ONE

MILAN

I hung up my lab coat in my office. I needed to rush if I wanted to surprise Jackson at the Gaylord.

Jackson had called my house several times and sent about five text messages. He had been sweatin' me for awhile and I was playing the game he always loved to play--*Hide and Go Get It*!

This time I was "it", because, as always, I remained in control.

I decided against showering and changing at work, to avoid the suspicious looks and questions from my coworkers. They were some nosey folk, especially my assistant, Shane. He was always in everybody's Kool-Aid, telling you the flavor and all that!

Just as I was shutting down my computer and about to grab my purse from the bottom desk drawer, I heard a man clear his throat.

Without looking up, I said, "Whatever it is, it will have to wait until

3

later. Sorry but I am lea…" I stopped in mid-sentence as I stared at the one man whom I have loved all my life.

Jackson.

I found myself speechless and I almost cried.

It was like I couldn't move. I was in shock.

"You just gonna stand there, or you coming over here to show me love?"

I moved so fast that I almost tripped over my own feet. I grabbed him around the neck and kissed him deeply, as he used his foot to close the door shut. I held on to him so tight and didn't want to let go. All my control vanished.

"What are you doing HERE? I was just leaving to surprise you in your room."

"Oh, so you did get my messages?"

"Yes. All eight of them! I was busy all morning and Maiya called to say you were here. Why didn't you tell me you were coming?"

"I wanted to surprise you. Plus, coming to Texas now wouldn't be a good idea. You did say David was in Cleveland, right?"

"Yeah, he's gone for a week. What about Leesa? What did you tell her?"

"Don't you worry your pretty head about her. Let's just get outta here!"

* * *

At the hotel, Jackson and I went straight to the room. Before the door was shut all the way, we were undressed down to our underwear. I pushed Jackson on the bed and straddled him. He grabbed my breasts and unsnapped my bra, sucking and biting along the way. He sat up and pulled off my panties, and then rolled over on top of me. He removed his boxers and was ready for action. His penis stood at attention and he entered me immediately. I moaned in acceptance and gave in to him. Jackson was about business. He had wanted to see me as soon as he got to Maryland. The phone sex just wasn't enough for him, and he just had to have me.

All of me.

And I had to have all of him, too.

After Jackson sexed me real good, I ran for the shower.

He was right behind me, ready for seconds.

"Order some food. I'm starving," I demanded.

"I'm starving, too, but it ain't just for food!"

Jackson took me again, right there in the shower. My face was right up against the cold tile, while jets of hot water sprayed all over our bodies. Jackson knew he could have me any way possible.

Yet, although I loved him since we were kids, I knew in my heart that he would never leave his wife. So, I was willing to just accept the sporadic sexual encounters, enjoying the expensive gifts, trips around the world and clandestine getaways.

But, I knew that Maiya was right.

There wasn't going to be a way I could keep this up.

No way.

How could I when I was getting married in less than two months?

The future has not happened yet; the past is over; your eternity is right this moment. ~**Oprah Winfrey**

TWO

MAIYA

My name is Maiya Vaughn and I declare today that I am officially done with this whole love thing. I am twenty-eight years old and never been married nor had any kids. I am currently single, but, I'm not looking for love. I did that for the past six years, and it has landed me nowhere-- except in the land of the brokenhearted. My girlfriends say I have settled before, just for the sake of having a man, and, they are probably right. I just wanna be loved. But, not just by anyone. Not this time.

First, it would make sense to tell you a little about who I am. Look-wise, I have to admit, I'm not half bad. I am attractive, and I have a nice shape. Standing five feet, six inches tall, weighing one hundred thirty pounds, and wearing a size eight dress size, I got a little something going on. Don't get me wrong. I am not conceited or overly confident; just positive and love myself. So, at times, I will toot my own horn. Beep, beep!

But, as I'm sure you know, having it together on the outside doesn't guarantee that you'll get what you want in the love department. My past love life is proof of that.

For me, this current attitude about love started after a series of failed relationships that began about eight years ago, with the last one ending with a man who I thought would be my future husband. But, don't let me get ahead of myself. Let me start from the beginning.

First, there was Derek.

Derek was a homicide detective with the Metropolitan Police Department. Before he made detective, he was a beat cop and spent a lot of long nights at work. That's how we met; he was patrolling around the club I was leaving with my girls one night. At the time, I was in my third year in college and was home for winter break. He was Hershey-chocolate brown with dark eyes and was so sexy to me. We were together for two years, but there was too much BMD-- Baby Momma Drama. After awhile, I just couldn't take it. Between his ex-girlfriend with whom he had no children and his daughter's mother, I was living a soap-opera melodrama, resembling a character out of *The Young and the Restless.*

His ex would show up at his family's functions, and Derek always made an excuse for her presence. I guess I should have left his ass alone when I discovered the condoms missing from the pack and her number on caller ID. But, I just didn't get it. She would show up at his apartment and just sit outside waiting for him to come home. When he hit rock bottom with his finances and I couldn't help him out financially, he called his ex to bail him out. That was a wake-up call for me. I cut him off completely and blocked his number out of my phone. I remember one week I saw her car at his place every day and the two of them leaving out together in the morning. But, Derek wanted us both. He resorted to calling me from his sister's phone just so I would talk to him. He even had some of his police buddies try to contact me, so I had to change my number. He would leave notes in my door, and even called my best friend Milan to get her to convince me to take him back. He was pathetic, and I couldn't believe I let myself go there with him. He eventually moved away, after getting evicted and taking a job down south.

Then, there was Carlos.

Carlos and I were good friends who were really attracted to each other. He actually found me on BlackPlanet.com, and I was excited to reunite with him after all the years that had passed. We went to middle school together back in the day, and although he was a grade behind me, I always thought he was cute. The age difference just didn't cut it for me....at least not until I saw him all grown up. The cute little boy I remembered grew up to be a fine ass man! I really wanted to be with him, but after our relationships to others had ended, we didn't want to ruin our lifelong friendship and be on the rebound with one another. But, the feelings for each other were overwhelming. We shared some intimate moments but it never blossomed into a monogamous relationship before I met the man who would ultimately put a bad taste in my mouth when it came to love. Carlos would always have a special place in my heart, but I realized he was in my life for a season. He taught me how to have a friendship with someone you are attracted to, and if we were meant to be together, it would be. Our farewell was cordial, and I learned that love is a wonderful thing. It just wasn't our time.

My love life sunk lower after Carlos, but I didn't realize it at first because I got caught up.

It all began when I came upon this website, mochaluv.com after hearing about it from one of the girls at work. She mentioned how she had met a few nice men on the site, and enjoyed the dating scene. I was curious. By this time, I was twenty-two years old and in graduate school for a Master's degree and I thought I could meet someone to hang out with and have fun. When I read a few of the stories and how some couples had even gotten married, I was all for it. You see, even at 22, I was a sucker for romance. I think I am a good person and knew then that I would make a man happy one day. I felt it hadn't happened yet because I just keep running into the wrong men.

Anyway, I met this guy on mochaluv, and we connected instantly, sending each other IMs, until we finally exchanged phone numbers. His profile name described his smooth skin-- it was the color of toasted almond-- and I fell immediately in love with the words he put across his page. His love for the arts and poetry got my attention right away. He had posted to his homepage a poem he had written, *She Is*, where it described his soul mate. It gave me chills just reading it, and I had to get to know the man behind the words. I would gaze at the pictures on his page anticipating meeting him face-to-face, especially after our daily conversations that lasted until the wee hours of the morning. We shared common interests in travelling, the outdoors, and adrenaline-rushing daredevil activities such as bungee jumping and sky diving. After talking on the telephone for about two weeks, we decided to meet. We wanted to see if the connection would be there in person, especially since we had seen one another's pictures online, and we both liked what we saw.

His name was Joaquin and he was thirty years old when we met. He had never been married and had a preteen named Noah, whom he was raising on his own. I had to give it to him-- that was very admirable for a man to raise a child by himself. Joaquin was the oldest of three children and grew up in Upper Marlboro, Maryland but was now living in Crofton, Maryland where he worked as a part-time office manager. He went to school at night so he could study marine biology, and worked during the day. That impressed me even more. He had a huge aquarium in his home, and it was filled with exotic sea life from everywhere. When he talked about the fish in the tank and the stuff he learned in his courses, I could tell how into the subject he was.

Physically, he was even more attractive in person. His pictures on his webpage did him no justice. He had jet black wavy hair and was more handsome than I could have expected. He said he got his good looks from his parents. Joaquin's father was from the Dominican Republic and his mother, who spoiled him shamelessly-- even as an adult-- was African-American from Washington, DC. He was an admitted momma's boy, and he was very accustomed to being by himself. Him telling me this openly and early in our dating relationship should have been a red flag for me, but trust me, this didn't rear its ugly head until after I was way too deep into the relationship. I realized later that when he shared his desire to one day be married and have more children, he was only saying what he thought I wanted to hear. And, it worked.

We stayed together for six years.

Many of those years found me just going through the motions. But, let me slow down and lead up to all of that.

When we first decided to meet face-to-face off-line, I was very excited. We met at the restaurant Jasper's on a Friday evening, around five o'clock, just before the after-work rush. We shared appetizers of spinach dip, Buffalo wings and potato skins and more good conversation as he told me how he thought we could be good friends. I was fine with that, but knew that soon we would become more than just friends.

It happened sooner than later. The attraction was there, and I was happy to say that I finally had a man. We stayed online every night getting to know each other better. We eventually spent more time together, taking turns over one another's place. The first time he came to my place, we stayed up all night long. I listened to him read poetry to me. This man had mad skills, and I was falling for him quicker than I thought. His words spoke depth and they touched me to my inner core. Before we realized how late it was, we were both fast asleep on my living room couch.

I never felt like he tried to take advantage of me, and we soon decided to see each other exclusively. But I knew he was tryna get some. Hey, I was tryna give him some, too. OKAY! That's how men are anyway. I wanted to see if he could live up to the Latino side of him and show me the Latin lover. Unfortunately, our first time together wasn't exactly fireworks. He was only okay, but, hey, I thought, what's a girl to do? I was young and inexperienced, and thought that was as good it was going to get if you did it with someone you have feelings for. So, to me, it was a good start and after a while I got used to his lackluster performance in bed. For, ultimately he gave me something more than a gossip-worthy sex life.

Joaquin became like family to me.

See, I grew up without my momma. She died giving birth to me, and my daddy never remarried. Joaquin and his family became my family.

Joaquin has two younger sisters, Gabrielle and Leah. They are older than me by four and six years, and we really got along well. We are still pretty close. It was because of me that Joaquin came to more family functions because I got along so well with his sisters and dad. They told me how different he was when we were together, and they liked to see him happy. His sister Leah is married to an accountant, and has three children I fell in love with immediately. I just love them to pieces. They call me auntie Mai, and there were times when Leah and I would just take the children out to the park, swimming, or bike riding. One year we took a family trip to Disney World and I don't know who had more fun, me or the children.

Joaquin's sister Gabrielle is a different story, however. She is single, mostly because she is very picky. She is only interested in white men because she says they can give her the finer things in life. She is a very saucy woman with jet black hair cascading down her back and beautiful brown eyes. The three of us were like sisters, and Gabrielle and Leah just couldn't understand why their big brother hadn't proposed marriage. I knew the reason though, and I hated it. He was just comfortable with the way things were with us, and got caught up in the comfort zone. But every holiday I kept hoping for that ring, though it just never came.

I found comfort in the knowledge that despite Joaquin's reluctance to propose, his family loved me. Joaquin's father, who loved me like his own, said I was his third daughter, and he couldn't understand why his knucklehead son hadn't made me his wifey yet.

His mother wasn't too fond of me, but like I said, he was a momma's boy and she felt like no one was good enough for her boy. She did like the fact that I got him to go to church, on the few occasions that he went. But, she felt I was too much of a health nut when it came to eating. She said I was bougie! I can't help the fact that I don't eat pig's feet and head cheese. Ewww! That's just nasty! I would like to NOT clog my arteries. Please. Plus, high blood pressure ran through my family and I had to watch that. And I didn't wanna become a fat fat fatty!

No thunder thighs, Hostess Twinkies stomachs, or brelly for me. (What's a brelly, you ask? It is when you can't tell where your breasts end and your belly begins--it all blends into one.) I was not about to compromise my health just so some lady could like me. I wasn't trying to marry her. And if she didn't love me but her son did, I was satisfied with that. For the time being, at least.

So, how did I discover that Joaquin was not the one for me? One of the many deal breakers with us was the fact that Joaquin did not want any more children. He finally admitted his feelings about children after we had been together for more than four years.

"How can you change the rules in the middle of the game?" I had asked him.

"I'm sorry, but I just can't see myself raising another child. I changed my mind. At least I am being honest," Joaquin answered.

"This just isn't right. I thought we talked about this. I thought we wanted the same thing. You said you wanted more children, remember? You just said what I wanted to hear, right? This was all a game to you," I continued.

"We did want the same thing, but I just don't want it anymore. I do want to get married and it would be nice to have more children, but I just don't see that, at least not right now. It's been hard raising Noah all these years, and I just don't wanna start all over again."

I was devastated at this point. His words cut me like a knife.

I felt closer to Noah for all those years, raising him as my own child. When we first met, Noah was barely twelve years old. He was an impressionable preteen, and we had an instant bond. There were nights I stayed up late to give him nebulizer treatments whenever his asthma acted up. I helped him study while Joaquin was in class at night and even went to his soccer games. With his mother abandoning him and sporadically coming around once every blue moon, there was no other consistent woman in Noah's life as a mother figure besides his grandmother. She barely came around since she couldn't stand to be around me, so I spent every moment with him, as if he were my own child. I enjoyed my time with Noah, and dreamed of our life as a family one day. Having Noah in my life allowed me to embrace the desire to be a mother one day, and with Joaquin stripping me of that future possibility, I was bothered.

Our religious differences were also a problem for me, but it was my own fault, I guess. I went to church regularly and took my spiritual upbringing very seriously. Plus, my aunt Rocsi would have gone upside my head with her wooden spoon if I defied the rules set before me. There was no doubt that you would attend church if you lived in the Vaughn household! But, my desire to have a man outweighed the fact that I desired a saved man, though. Those differences caused problems eventually.

I recall weekends when he would stay with me and he refused to go to church. He would always say "pray for me" as I left for church, but that was the extent of his attendance.

I remember one particular evening when we were having dinner, and we were discussing the Bible. He claimed to have read it in its entirety. Not once, but twice.

"What did you learn? Any particular stories stick out or any lessons you can apply to your life?" I asked.

"No, I just kind of read it because I thought I should," he responded.

"Any favorite scriptures or prayers that you remember?"

"Not really, I mean, our religions are different so we didn't learn the same. Who can really decipher a scripture anyway? It's all in what the individual gets out of it. What you learn and what I learn may be interpreted entirely different."

"That doesn't make sense, Joaquin. Scriptures do have meaning, and how one learns because you grew up Catholic and I grew up Baptist has nothing to do with it. You just don't take spirituality seriously. Who cares what your religion is? We believe in a higher being. At least acknowledge that. But scriptures like John 3:16 and Romans 3:23 mean nothing to you?"

"Maiya, come on. Let's just drop it and enjoy the rest of the evening".

I thought maybe Joaquin would change his mind later on, and become more interested in exploring our spiritual beliefs together, but it didn't happen. At that point, I had no respect for the relationship. The differences just made things unhappy for me. I started seeing Carlos again before finally breaking it off with Joaquin. The affair with Carlos lasted the last two years of my relationship with Joaquin.

Yes, I cheated; I was wrong. And I am not proud of it. I wasn't ready to leave Joaquin completely, though. I really missed my friendship with Carlos, and I was being selfish. When Carlos began to back away from me, I made up my mind to let go of it altogether. The memories of Carlos and I are ones I would cherish forever--including a secret that I would never admit to Joaquin. I can remember the first time Carlos walked away, and it stung me. Carlos wasn't ready for what I wanted, and when he finally confessed his love to me, it was too late. I was already in too deep with Joaquin, and we were talking of marriage, despite our problems and different plans for the future.

My Aunt Rocsi prayed with me, and my girlfriend Kiana invited me to join her Singles Ministry at her church and challenged me to their fast. I agreed to do it, and I gained so much strength. But, it led me to take personal responsibility for my actions. Admitting how I was responsible for the choices I've made when it came to the men I decided to be with was upsetting. Ultimately, the Lord spoke to me, and I knew I had to give up my relationships with Joaquin and Carlos. They weren't healthy.

Joaquin didn't let me go so easily. For a solid month, I did not see him, and when we talked on the phone, it was very brief. I told him of my spiritual quest, and he accepted it at first. When he realized he wouldn't be getting his freak on, he blew up and said something about "being tired of waiting for you to go through your spiritual thang." I didn't want to accept the fact that I would be alone at first, but my spiritual growth and self-worth meant so much more to me.

But even after all my praying and fasting, I still couldn't let him go completely either. We kept in touch, allowing Joaquin to woo me again and promise that he would do better if we got back together. He even suggested going to church with me more and even wanted to visit different churches to find one that he would feel comfortable attending and maybe even joining. So, I took him back. We moved in together and tried to make it work. We finally called it quits, though, after spending a week in Miami shortly after we got back together. Our break-up was fueled by a simple exchange we had while attending my friend Kiana's wedding.

Joaquin is not a bad person, and his vices did not even include smoking or drinking. Although he did have a temper, and he would blow up over dumb stuff, he was still a good man. He just wasn't the man for me. "Always the bridesmaid and never the bride," Joaquin had said to me.

For some reason, those words stung more than they should have. All the years I felt I had wasted with him, for him now to ridicule me for not being a bride made me so upset. I fired back.

"Sweetie, I will be a bride some day," I remember saying back to him, insulted. "Just because YOU probably won't be the groom, doesn't mean my day won't come!"

And, that was the end. When we left Miami and got back home, I was now ready to finally tell him good-bye. While he was at work, I left him a "Dear John" letter on the kitchen counter along with my set of house keys, and never looked back.

The break-up was a mutual agreement, I later learned. Joaquin was tired of the relationship, too. We remained friends even after. Well, maybe not friends, but at least we were cordial to each other. His sisters and I are still very close, and we talk every few months. Joaquin doesn't come around like he used to, but he calls me and sends me an email every blue moon.

I wish I could say I learned my lessons once Joaquin and I were done, but I didn't. I still tempted fate. I decided to reconnect with Carlos who I had cut off after my spiritual reawakening before Joaquin and I got back together. I emailed Carlos around Christmas of that year after my final break-up with Joaquin. I just wanted to see what he was up to. Whenever I drove to work, I looked across the highway at the building where he worked and thought about him, wondering if he was thinking about me. I just wanted to say hello, but it brought back all of the feelings I had for him.

Apparently, I must have been on his mind, too. After reconnecting through emails, we reignited our physical relationship. The problem, this time, was that *he* was the one in a relationship. And though he decided to leave his girlfriend for me, I realized that this was no way to begin a new relationship—stealing someone else's man. Though I had wanted for sure for us to get it right and be together, it didn't happen. I walked away from each of my failed relationships realizing that beauty is only skin deep. All of these men were fine, no doubt about it. But a connection needs to be deeper than just physical attraction.

So, here I am, single and successful in my career. I have goals that I still want to achieve, and even though I am no one's wife, I know whatever God has for me, it is for me. I am no longer that complacent woman in search of her soul mate. When it happens for me, I will have to let go of the past and move on. I have accepted my single lifestyle and am happy for once. My girlfriends, including my best friend Milan, are still trying to hook me up, and I am open to dating. I know that this time around, I will not settle for less than what I expect. The man for me must first have a relationship with God, not already be in a relationship and, most importantly, he must treat me right!

* * *

Since breaking up with Joaquin, I have been working out regularly and focusing on myself health-wise. Today was no different. I arrived at the gym at seven a.m. for my early morning swim, loving that I had the pool all to myself. I swim three days a week, and run four to five times a week. I was determined to break the generational curse of obesity and hypertension which ran rampant in my family. Thus, I committed myself to a healthy lifestyle, which included eating right and daily exercise.

Exiting the pool, I was stopped suddenly by amazement when I saw a man standing on the pool deck. He was the finest thing I had seen in a while. His short-sleeved Polo shirt showed off his biceps and outlined curves on his body that made me want to jump on him! There was an emblem on the upper left breast pocket of his shirt. I couldn't quite make out what it was, but I knew it was a business logo.

He stood at six feet four inches tall, and weighed about two hundred and fifty pounds. I was good at gauging a person's body stature because I spent a lot of time at the gym and knew how to size up a body. I could tell that he worked out regularly, because he was cut up. Body chiseled and very defined. He had creamy, French-vanilla colored skin, and I thought *that man can be the cream in my coffee!* His eyes were blue-grey and his hair brownish-blonde and wavy. He had just enough facial hair that you could see his five o'clock shadow, and he had a neatly trimmed moustache.

I had to turn away so he wouldn't catch me staring. But, then I thought again. *Men always gawked at women, so it's all good for me to do the same!*

I have never seen this man at the Arena fitness center before, and I come here all the time. I always remained focused on my workout program at the Arena, but this man took my mind away for a few moments. Now all I had to do was get up the nerve to speak.

I walked over to my chair and grabbed a towel to dry off. I could feel this man staring at me. *Damn, I know he ain't coming over here to talk to me*, I thought.

Yep, here he comes.

The handsome stranger walked towards me, looking behind me at something.

He smiled and said, "Good morning."

I responded with a nod and a smile. "Good morning."

He rested his gaze on me. "You know, I was watching you swim and I have a suggestion. If you dig in just a little deeper during your crawl, you will get more out of the stretch all the way to the end, and cut your time by about 45 seconds."

Was this a joke? He walked all the way over here to criticize my swimming technique? I could feel my previously ecstatic attraction for him start to come down a few notches.

"Well, thank you, but I'm not trying out for the US Olympic team. I'm just tryna get my workout on, mister whatever your name is," I replied with a bit of attitude.

"Ooh, sorry. Didn't mean to strike a nerve," he laughed. "My name is Malachi. Malachi Taylor. Just thought I could help," he responded, extending his hand.

My attitude melted instantly. I shook his hand. *Mmm! Big hands, too!*

"My name is Maiya Vaughn. Nice to meet you, Malachi. Well, I better get going. And I'll think about what you said and try it the next time I swim." I rolled my eyes as I gathered my gym bag and started walking away.

"Excuse me, Maiya? I know this may seem a bit forward, but I was wondering if maybe we could get together for coffee or lunch sometime. If you are interested, that is."

A-ha. *Ok,* I thought. *So, he has game.*

"I think I may have some time to spare, I mean share, with you," I said, coyly.

He smiled. "Well, good. Take my card and give me a call when you find that time to spare."

"No, how 'bout you take my card and call me," I said with a smile.

"Okay, then, Miss Maiya. We'll exchange cards and I will call you this week. Until then, take care young lady."

Young lady? Ok, that was a bit weird, but who cares? I got the digits.

"Bye," I said, as I walked into the locker room.

When I walked past the mirror in the locker room, I gasped. I couldn't believe I stood there talking to that man with my swim cap squeezing the mess out of my forehead, making my eyes look all slanted.

I bet he is just laughing at me.

"Oh well. I'll just have to work it when we meet for coffee," I said out loud.

*   *   *

I showered and got ready for work. I love being my own boss. When Milan and I decided to open up the physical therapy office after I finished graduate school, I was unsure of what to expect. Now that the business is booming and we have a dedicated, professional staff, things are looking up. We are even planning on expanding to open up offices elsewhere in the United States. Our first big project will be New Orleans. We volunteer with Habitat for Humanity and have been helping rebuild Louisiana since Hurricane Katrina. Our goal is to bring back medical facilities and open up another outpatient physical therapy office.

As I walked into the building, I couldn't stop smiling. Douglass & Vaughn Physical Therapy Services, Inc. was located adjacent to National Harbor Medical Center. It was a four story brick building that offered extensive outpatient therapy services, to include occupational and physical therapy. There was a pool on the first floor, and three days a week we offered water aerobics. There was also a sauna, Jacuzzi, and massage suite for additional services. I was very pleased with what we had accomplished. This had been a good year for us. There was enough room for other business opportunities as well, and we hoped to expand sometime in the near future.

Though I adored my work place and seeing the fruits of my labor surround me, I still enjoyed getting away from my place of business to do my exercise. Plus, in the past, we had problems with employees abusing the facilities, so I wanted to lead by example to my staff and not use the facilities for personal use. Before I made this rule policy, somebody decided to throw a pool party and attempt to shoot a video and it turned out a disaster. I won't begin to tell you the nasty things people were doing in the physical therapy pool. Milan and I agreed that we would keep the area strictly for our clients. However, I thought maybe we would eventually ease up and at least allow the employees to use the facility before work for exercise. Until that happens, though, I still travel to the Arena for my own exercise needs. I'm glad I do. If I wasn't there this morning, I wouldn't have met Malachi.

As I walked into the office, my assistant greeted me with messages.

"Good morning, Ms. Vaughn," said Kari.

"Morning, Kari. How are you today?"

"All is well, thank you. There are two messages for you from Mr. Taylor. He sounds really nice. Anyone I would know?"

"I'm not sure, Kari. Are you familiar with Taylor Made Construction Company?"

"Oh, yeah, I have heard of them! That's the company that designed and built the Arena! How did you two meet?" Kari questioned.

Oh, I thought, *so that was why he was fully-clothed in a work polo on the pool deck. He was surveying the building.* I decided to dodge Kari's nosiness.

"Don't you have meetings to schedule?"

"Yes ma'am. I just think you deserve a good man, and I want to see you happy. We all do, that's all."

"Thanks, Kari, but I have a lot of work to do. Happiness and a man can wait for now. Give me thirty minutes and come into my office so we can go over this week's agenda."

Kari is a college student studying physical therapy at the College of Southern Maryland. She is perfect for the job, and I plan to keep her around so she can join the company as a full time therapist after graduating from the program. Kari is good with people, and she has trained the other office assistants. Milan plans to have Kari shadow her once clinical rotations start. That way, she can be better prepared and familiar with the daily patient schedule. Kari knows our business and she knows my personal business, too—particularly my new "No Love" rule. I must admit. Malachi Taylor made me forget my rule for a minute.

As I sat at my desk, I thought about what Kari said.

I want to see you happy. We all do.

I keep people out of my personal business, but everyone knew about my breakup with Joaquin. I got lost in my work, and my attitude changed for the better. I am happier now, whereas before, I was short-tempered with the staff, and a few times, Milan told me to take some mental health days. I have longed for someone to share my world with, but my track record with men and relationships was 0-3 in the last eight years.

Derek, Joaquin, Carlos.

I thought about Malachi. And I wondered what my girls would say about me dating a white man. I don't even know why I am getting worked up, because my friend Kiana's husband is white, and we all love him. Plus, who is to say that Malachi is going to even be more than just a one-date free meal? A million and one things crossed my mind, and I began to feel guilty. *Why am I trippin' about what they may say*, I thought. I want to be happy and I need to keep my options open. All of my girls are in love. Milan was engaged to be married this fall. Kiana got married two years ago. Tion was getting married this summer, and Jordan was close to an engagement any day now. I deserve to find my own love, too. I am worth it.

But it's all good though. *It is what it is*, I thought, chuckling to myself in the quiet of my office, remembering how Carlos used to say that to me all of the time.

I sat down at my desk and read the messages left from Malachi. The first one read 'it was so nice to meet you today. I can't wait to get together.' *Nice*, I thought, *but too personal to leave with my assistant*. Plus, he left them so soon after we met. The second one was just a number to call. I took out the business card he gave me earlier. The numbers are different. What is that about? Is he being sneaky? I had to stop myself.

You're doing it again, Maiya. Give the man a chance.

I laughed out loud.

I should just call the number.

There was a knock at the door.

"Come in."

"Good morning, Sunshine. Whatcha up to?" asked Milan.

"Hey, girlfriend. Just about to make a phone call and maybe set up a date, but I'm not sure. I don't wanna seem pressed."

"Okay, stop the press. Call who? Date? What's going on?" inquired Milan.

"I met a man after my workout this morning, and we exchanged numbers. Only problem is, I don't know if I should call him or wait for him to call me again. Or should I not call him at all until after he calls me two more times, or ..."

"Wait, wait, wait!" Milan cut me off. "You need to chill out and stop reading all those books. Last month it was *Brothers, Lust, and Love* and now it's *He's Just Not That Into You*. Maiya, girl, slow your roll. Stop playing the games, okay. Carlos isn't coming back and Joaquin you don't want to come back. And, ooh wee, who cares about what happened to crazy Derek-- cut the brotha some slack and call him. You'll never know until you give it a chance."

"That's just it. He's not a brotha," I said. I frowned up my face and added, "And shut up. I learned a lot from those books."

"I'm sure you did, sweetie. But, let's move on now. So what if he's not a brotha; we know you like the Latinos. No problema chica," Milan laughed.

"Um, no. Malachi is not Latino. He's white."

"Oh. Oh. Oh. Wow. And he got you thinking about calling back! Well, he must be fine then," screamed Milan.

"He is, but...I don't know. The whole interracial thing-- people can be so cruel, you know."

"Damn, girl. Let me find out you trying *Something New* like Sanaa Lathan's character in the movie. Get down with the swirl, Maiya! Do your jungle fever thing. You'll just be the chocolate chip all up in his vanilla ice cream! Ha-ha! No, but seriously, though. Who cares? Interracial dating happens all the time. You know it wasn't all that bad with me growing up with my German mother and mixed father. You're mixed, too, so why you trippin?" Milan asked, as she pulled a thermos out of her bag and took a sip.

She was right. "Yeah, ok, I hear you. Let me not keep you from your clients. Are you busy today?"

"Nah. My next client isn't until 10:30 am, but I have training to do with Sean to work that out. We are having a brief staff meeting before that," she said. She threw her head back to drink the remains of the thermos.

"Dag, what you got in there? Must be good," I said. She looked at me and grinned. Her eyes were shiny and mischievous.

"Let's not change the subject. Seriously, all jokes aside. This new guy you met could be a nice person, but you'll never know by holding on to fantasies of Carlos. You are blocking your blessings. You say you've moved on, but you haven't. Let go of what you had. Just call the man. Malcolm, Maxwell, Matthew."

"Malachi."

"Whatever. Call him." Milan got up to leave. Then she stopped. "Hold up. Is he the Malachi that works with Taylor Made Construction?"

"Yeah girl, why?"

"Girl, you are so crazy. That man is not white. You are lunchin'. His mother is mixed German and black, and his father is Afro-Latino. They just real light."

"And how do you know all this?"

"Remember when I sponsored the walkathon for my patients?"

I nodded yes.

"Well," Milan continued, "I met Mr. Jaime Taylor who is Malachi's uncle. He was a patient of mine after his motorcycle accident and he came to the walkathon after he finished his therapy. Fine brotha, too! Caramel skin, bluish gray eyes, and jet black wavy hair. Ooh, girl. Anyway, the construction company has been in the family for over 40 years. They even donated materials and money to reconstruct Ground Zero," explained Milan. "Like I said, I never met Malachi, but Mr. Taylor told me about the Arena that they designed and built. He wanted to introduce me to him, but saw that I had a man, so he didn't push it. He told me all the business, though, and said that Malachi's fiancée cheated on him and he found out about it a month before the wedding. He hasn't met anyone or even dated since then. It sounded so sad. That woman sounded so scandalous, too!"

"Wow, I remember Kari mentioned Mr. Taylor coming in for his appointments. I just never paid attention to the name. What a coincidence."

My phone rang. It was Kari reminding me of the agenda. We were supposed to meet in the conference room at noon. It was already nine o'clock, and I needed an hour to go over the agenda with Kari and to make adjustments to the schedule.

"I gotta go Lani. I'll see you tonight for dinner. Smooches," I said as I hugged her. I could smell the sweet scent of brandy on her breath.

"You've been drinking girl? It's the morning."

Milan waved me off. "Girl, I was just sipping on some brandy and honey. Sore throat."

"Oh," I said. I hope she wasn't getting sick. I tried to feel her forehead but she stepped back and laughed.

"Alright, *Mom*. Geez, you're so maternal. See you around seven. And you better call ole boy!"

"I will. Now go."

A good head and a good heart are always a formidable combination.
~Nelson Mandela

THREE

MALACHI

So, here I am doing a follow up visit to the Arena, a place that I originally designed, when I see the most beautiful sight before me.

I was watching her technique and form as she swam, and I noticed it was pretty much flawless. I had to play it off and find a unique way to approach her, so I decided to talk about her swimming, since it was obvious a sistah knew what she was doing.

She gave me attitude, and all I could do was laugh. I introduced myself to her, and even got her to smile. Since I spend a lot of my time staying busy between work and playing in a jazz band, I haven't really focused on dating anyone.

That is, since my ex-fiancée, Tia. She kind of broke a brotha down, so I have been out of commission for the moment.

But, this lady caught my eye. I was not about to pass up the chance to meet her and get to know her better. And, I figured momma would get a kick out of knowing her only child was getting his feet wet again.

To say I was hurt over my breakup would be an understatement. I was completely devastated, to say the least. But I continued to play my guitar, and manage my company, Taylor Made Construction, Inc. It was a family business that I took over once my dad passed away, and my uncles and cousins helped keep our family dream going. Our company is listed in the *Top Ten Family Businesses*, and I have been featured in *Black Enterprise* magazine twice. We are very successful, but success means nothing to me if I don't have someone to share it with. It's lonely at the top when you're single. But, maybe I won't be for long. I really sensed something special about Maiya.

Maiya Vaughn. That's her name--the woman I couldn't keep my eyes off of at the Arena. She had smooth light brown skin, and long, muscular-toned thighs. She had the cutest mole on her upper lip, and her eyes are a beautiful light brown. She probably didn't realize that her swim cap was so tight that it made her eyes look slanted, and I laughed to myself and would tease her about it later.

Seeing her in a full torso swimsuit was a turn on, and she had a small tattoo on her left breast. Don't get me wrong. I wasn't undressing her with my eyes, but I am a man, so I'm gonna look. I am not the type to hit it and quit it, and I was not looking for a booty call. I'm looking for quality. So, when I gave her my card for us to meet later and she flipped it on me and gave me her information so I could call her, I liked that. This woman had an air about her that let me know she had it together. She was a no-nonsense woman, both sassy and classy. With a bit of attitude, but it was cute.

I knew I would be calling her and looked forward to meeting her for coffee and conversation one day soon.

Real soon.

The office phone rang and interrupted my thoughts.

"Hello."

"Christian? How are you doing? I was just wondering when you were coming to visit. Lindsay is due any day now, and Benjamin is going crazy buying up everything in Babies R Us!"

It was my mother. She called me by my middle name, Christian, instead of by my first name, Malachi, which I preferred.

"I'm fine ma. I'll be there for a visit real soon, so tell them not to worry. I'll call Ben later tonight. Tell those guys that I miss 'em. I'll be busy the next two weeks finishing up another contract, but I promise to be there for my godchild. If I can knock this project out, I can be there by Tuesday. Tell Aunt Marie to have my place ready for me!"

"Christian, you make sure you take some time out to have fun. Don't always stay so glued to the job, now. Have you had any gigs lately? Met any nice girls?"

I had to laugh at that. "Ma, I told you. I'm doing fine. And yes, I do take time out to have some fun. As a matter of fact, I have a gig this weekend. We are playing at the Birchmere, opening up for Ledisi. I'll make sure to get you a copy of our CD. And no, I haven't met any nice girls. I'm not really looking, you know? But I am doing fine, ok? Stop worrying."

"You are my only child, so don't you tell me not to worry. After all that drama that triflin' girl put you through, you deserve to be happy. And I don't wanna be too old before you give me some grandbabies. So get to work on that for me. Listen to your mother; I know what I'm talkin' 'bout. Since you didn't listen to me when I told you not to marry that skank in the first place, it's time you take my advice. I knew she was no good."

"Ma, please, I am at work. We are not talking about that right now. I gotta go. Love you, bye."

"Christian, don't you hang up this phone on me."

"Seriously, ma. I gotta go. I'll call you next week."

"Bye, baby."

I had to laugh at my momma. You would not think she was German, with her thick, country accent which came from her being raised in Farmville, Virginia with her mother and grandmother. Her father's family was still living in Germany, and she went back every year to visit. She moved to Hampton with my aunt after they sold the farm. She and Aunt Marie were like sisters, and had married brothers; my father, Christian, and his twin brother Luke. Uncle Luke was pastor at Unity Baptist Church in Farmville. After he died, my aunt Marie moved to Hampton, and later my momma, Elisa, followed.

I had a lot more to finish up before I met with the fellas to rehearse, so I handled my business and made it home in time to grab something quick to eat.

I checked my voicemail.

Three messages.

All solicitors.

And a few missed calls that I knew were from Tia.

She kept calling me. And, to be real, I knew exactly why.

I had no business going over there to talk to her that night. We had ended up drinking and next thing I knew, we were butterball naked and getting down to serious business. I made a mistake. And even after all that she had put me through, I was not ready to deal with the consequences. I had been beating myself up over the booty call, because I was afraid of what we may have created.

I was very hurt with all that happened with our breakup, and seeing her that night and feeling her body again next to mine, well, it was familiar and it felt good. But, now, I know it was a mistake. I'm regretting it now, especially now that I'm trying to date and meet new people, like Maiya.

I can't stop thinking about all of the things that have led me here, though. It has been a pretty rough year. The breakup with Tia and the drama with my best friend Fred has been a lot to digest. It's been a lot to heal from. Men can't really talk out-loud about how much a broken relationship hurts. People start to think you are a punk or a whiner-- especially when you got played as bad as I did. So, I mostly keep it to myself. But, man, you can't hear a worse story than mine.

Tia had been seeing my boy Fred secretly behind my back for a long time before I was hipped to it. In hindsight, Tia did have a point, though. I worked entirely too much. But, the way I saw it, my work schedule was still no excuse to cheat. And, definitely not with my best friend. Though Fred has been a dog for as long as I've known him, messing with each other's girls was off-limits. I guess that was the rule until Fred decided he wanted Tia. Man, you can't trust anyone really.

I had been working on a really big project at the time, and I just wanted to meet the deadline so that we wouldn't have to worry about the costly wedding. Tia wanted a really big event, and I worked hard just to give her whatever she wanted. If it wasn't for Tia's best friend Jasmine calling to tell me to listen to the radio, I would have never known that my best friend from college was getting buck wild with my future wife.

Yes. Here's the deal.

I had been out of town on business, finishing up one of my latest projects to design an international bank in downtown Chicago. Jasmine, a friend to both Tia and me—and Fred's wife, happened to call me on the phone while on my way back home a day early. She told me to tune in to a syndicated talk show hosted by Wendy Williams. The topic was scandalous affairs. When I found the station, I couldn't believe what I heard! It was Tia. And she was going on and on about how her man works too much and is not home long enough to lay the pipe down like she wants him to. Now, I am no saint, and I can be a freak when I want to be. I ain't no punk about mine, trust me. I just wasn't into all the kinky mess that Tia liked-- bondage and dominatrix stuff. To hear her talk about me on national radio, about how I wasn't holding it down at home—justifying her infidelity to me, crushed something inside that is still broken.

Jasmine and I consoled each other on the phone. She said she was destroyed when she learned her best friend and her man were screwing around on her. She just couldn't let the lies continue without telling me what she knew.

"After I found out about the affair, I confronted them both and I told Tia that if she didn't tell you about the affair, I would," Jasmine had said to me. "Do you know that heifer just laughed in my face?"

"I know that was hard for you to do, Jazz, but I appreciate it," I told her. "I am sorry about Fred, too. I would have never known for him to do that to you, either."

Jasmine was like a sister to me, and we shared a lot over the years. I was godfather to her son, Freddie, Jr., and she was the one who had introduced me to Tia. That was years ago during our college days. Jasmine admitted that she felt bad for me, but sorrier for herself. She had a child with Fred, while Tia and I weren't even married yet. I felt sorry for us both, though.

I decided to drive to Hampton and visit with my aunt after getting myself together. I wasn't just going to visit, though. I was planning on moving out of the home Tia and I shared together. My aunt kept an upstairs condo vacant for family and I would enjoy the time away. I really needed it. Tia was planning on going away for a few days for a high school reunion, so I moved all of my things out and arranged for a thirty day notice to vacate the premises to be sent. Then I called the wedding planner and cancelled everything. She was not going to talk me out of leaving.

I took a hiatus from the business after learning about Tia's affair. I spent three months in my home in Aruba. I just kicked back beers day in and day out, spent time with the locals fishing and kayaking, and writing music for the band. Most of the music was melancholy, but it was my release and I felt free. There were days I stayed in bed until way past noon, and three weeks had gone by before I realized that I needed to shave. My family grew really worried about me and my cousin's wife Lindsay convinced me to seek counseling because she said I sounded like I was going through depression. I just killed time doing nothing. It felt like Tia killed a part of me. I vowed that if I ever had a chance to find true love, I would do things different the next time around.

Ever since I moved out, though, it's like something about Tia that still has got me hooked. I'm hoping that the last mistake I made with her won't come back to bite me.

There are years that ask questions and years that answer.
~Zora Neale Hurston

FOUR

MAIYA

I accomplished a lot in the meeting. We established a new contract with an agency to provide the company with therapists on an 'as needed' basis, to fill in on days that we offer water aerobics classes. Many of Milan's employees are trained in hydrotherapy but are limited in their time schedules because they have to see their daily assigned patients. With the agency pool, Milan would be able to book more appointments to those needing hydrotherapy and still keep the regularly scheduled patients.

While Kari and the others finished up, I asked her to hold all calls for the rest of the afternoon.

"Are you leaving for the day, Ms. Vaughn? And should I close out your schedule?" asked Kari.

"No. I just need to get these facts from the new agency emailed to Milan so she can begin scheduling more patients for hydrotherapy and other aquatics. Also, can you get your cousin Kendra on the phone? She is interested in renting one of the massage suites and I need to know when she is available for a tour."

"Sure thing. I'll get her right away and hold all other calls."

I walked into my office and saw a post-it note on the computer screen. It was from Milan. It read YOU BETTER CALL HIM in bold letters. I shook my head and laughed out loud and tossed it in the trash can. I reached in my gym bag and pulled out Malachi's card.

31

Taylor Made Construction Inc. – Malachi Taylor
Architect, specializing in graphic design and construction plans.

I looked at the message from this morning with the number. I picked up the phone to dial, and then hung it back up. Kari called in on the intercom, "Ms. Vaughn, I have Kendra on the line."

"Thanks. Put her through."

"Good afternoon, Ms. Vaughn. Thanks for getting back to me. I am really interested in the suite. It's been hard working from home."

"I do understand. When would be a good time for you to tour the facility? I can have Kari arrange everything for you."

"I am available the rest of this week."

"Okay, great. Then, I'll put you back to Kari and she will set everything up for you. I look forward to meeting you."

"Thank you, Ms. Vaughn. I will see you soon. Bye."

"Good bye, Kendra. Take care."

I paged Kari to pick up line one. "Kari, check my appointments this week and allot about two hours' time for Kendra. Thanks." I picked up the phone and dialed Malachi's number. He answered on the first ring.

"Malachi Taylor."

"Hi, it's Maiya returning your call."

"Ms. Vaughn. Well, well, well. I phoned you only about four hours ago," he said, laughing.

"Excuse me! I do have a business to run, and I try not to spend my work time on personal phone calls. I have to set an example for the young adults that work here."

Malachi laughed again. "Why you gotta be so serious all the time? Ease up, sistah. Just jokes here. Sorry if I struck a nerve."

"No. I'm sorry. Can we try this again?"

"Alright."

"Hi, it's Maiya, returning your call."

"Hello, Maiya. Glad you could get back to me. I see you got my message. I wasn't going back to the office until this evening, which is why I left this number with your assistant. It's my personal cell. The one on my card is my business cell. I didn't wanna play phone tag, so I gave her this number--just in case you were wondering."

I hesitated, and then sighed. "No, not really," I lied.

"You are not a good liar. I know you thought I was tryna run game. Admit it," he laughed.

"Okay, okay. I was thinking that, but only for a minute. I am trying to give people more of a chance." I got quiet.

"Hello?" Malaichi responded. "You still there?"

"I'm here," I laughed. "So, I was wondering, how about that coffee?"

"Ah, yes. Our coffee date. There's a place I know called Latté Dah. It's a quaint place to have quiet time, enjoy coffee or tea, whatever you choose, indulge yourself in conversation or read a good book. I know the owner. She's a real sweet person, and it's in the open so we can talk, get to know one another. I'd like to get to know you, Ms. Vaughn. Is that alright with you?"

I found myself smiling. "That's just fine with me, Malachi. Can you clear some time on your busy schedule for me tomorrow?"

He laughed. "Look who is calling *me* busy! You are a work horse I'm finding out. I will make time for you, pretty lady. How does eight o'clock suit you?"

"It suits me just fine. Where is the place?"

"It's located in Hanson Crossing, right on the corner. You can't miss it. I'll see you then, Maiya. Have a good day."

"I will. And you do the same. Bye now." I put the phone in its cradle.

Kari paged on the intercom. "Ms. Vaughn, I took a few calls and cleared your schedule for tomorrow. I booked Kendra for Thursday afternoon and Milan wants to have lunch Wednesday at noon."

"Thanks, Kari. I won't be in until ten tomorrow morning. Get with Milan and work out the hydrotherapy and aquatics classes for the next three months. We will need to redo the April and May schedule and make adjustments for the incoming agency pool of therapists. Also, delegate some duties to your comrades. I made a list of what I will need and sent you an email. This should keep them all busy for the next two weeks. If you run into any problems, let me know. Oh, and Kari?"

"Yes ma'am?"

"It's four o'clock. Don't you have class? Put the phones to voicemail and get to school. I'll see you in the morning. Oh, and send me a copy of your mother's recipe for egg rolls and pancit. Asian Pacific Heritage month is approaching and you know how we celebrate up in here!"

Kari laughed. "Yes, Ms. Vaughn. Good night."

I went through my emails. I got a response from Therapies R Us, an agency that wants to contract therapists and technicians with Milan. *Oh, hell no!* I wanted to respond. Milan told me to delete all emails from that company. Their last three candidates for hire were total disasters! They were unprofessional, uncouth, and just downright common. One guy showed up late while eating a bag of Funyuns with crumbs all over his hands and shirt. Another girl came dressed in a lace, hot pink bustier and miniskirt. And the last guy claimed he was overqualified, since he was a doctor in his country, but willing to take the job and then go back to the Philippines after he got trained! Milan gave them the boot, and began looking for other agencies. She asked me to handle the administrative details. All I could do was laugh. I wished I had seen Milan's face when they came to interview.

I closed out my emails and shut down the computer. Jeremy was finishing up with his last patient, and the cleaning crew had started their nightly ritual. They sure knew how to keep this place clean. It stayed spotless on a regular basis.

"Good night, Maiya."

"Good night, Jeremy. See you in the morning."

"No, ma'am. I am off to see my mother in the morning. I'll be gone for two weeks. You know its Carnival back home at this time." He was from Trinidad, and never missed going home in February.

"I forgot. Bring me back something special, and have a safe trip."

"I will. See you when I get back."

Surround yourself only with people who are going to lift you higher.
~**Oprah Winfrey**

FIVE

T he sun had gone down by the time I left my office at six pm. I only lived five miles down the street. That's what I loved about this place. Everything was on my side of town; my home, my job, my gym. And soon, I hoped, my man! I got home in a matter of minutes. The girls were coming over and it was my night to cook. Our lives were very busy, but we never missed getting together once a month.

Milan, Kiana, Tion, Jordan and I have been friends for a long time. Milan and I have been friends the longest. We are best friends who grew up next door to one another, and we are like sisters. And we have always been inseparable. People sometimes mistake one of us for the other, since we look so much alike. Yet, my hair is a bit more out of control than hers, and her eyes are dark brown. She also is a shade lighter than me, yet people who don't know us will still confuse us as being the same person or sisters when we're together. My dad always tells us we act just alike, even as young girls. We have a lot in common, including the fact that we are both only children. Milan's parents would always let Milan invite me over once they learned that my mom was dead. We had so much in common that we quickly bonded upon meeting. We share clothes, favorite foods, and interests so much so that people assume we like the same thing in men, too. But, that's where the similarities end.

Our taste couldn't be any more different. Milan dated my cousin Jackson when we were younger and after him, there wasn't anyone she got serious with until she met her current fiancé, David. She could not stand any of my former boyfriends, especially Joaquin. But, despite our taste in men, our similarities still outshine the differences. It made sense that we share the same girlfriends.

Our girlfriend Kiana went to church and high school with us. We met Tion and Jordan when we attended Grambling State University. Tion is from Louisiana, and Jordan is from Virginia. We stayed in touch over the years, and were committed to our monthly gatherings. It worked out since we were centrally located in the Washington DC metropolitan area that locals like us call the "DMV", which stands for DC, Maryland and Virginia.

Tonight's gathering was always a highlight and I grinned to myself as I thought about what my friends would say when I told them I may be dating again. I quickly prepared my shrimp and crab Alfredo with linguine, a tossed salad, and garlic breadsticks. That was one of my special 30-minute meals that the girls just adored. The wine was chilling, and I lit a few candles and turned on my *Feels So Good* CD by Chuck Mangione. It soothed me and put me in a different place. A relaxed phase. Growing up listening to jazz fusion while my Aunt Rocsi cleaned the house, I developed a strong love for instruments like the saxophone and guitar. There was just something about the improvisation of these two instruments that I could always relate to. It gave me a sense of peace, and my love for anything relative to this genre of music left me feeling loved in a sense. I closed my eyes and swayed to the music, and in my mind instantly appeared Malachi's face and body, so vivid as if he was really there. As the music played, I began envisioning Malachi's arms wrapped around me. In my imagination, I could feel the ripples of his muscles underneath my fingertips and the heat of his body near me, enticing me with lust. I could feel my nipples harden as the music swelled as Malachi's face danced through my mind. The loud knock from the door shook me out of my fantasy.

"Come on in," I called out, guiltily fumbling with the CD player as I turned down the music.

"Hey, Sunshine. Let me get that glass of wine," said Milan, throwing her keys on the sofa.

"It's on the counter, help yourself," I said. My face had to be crimson as I blushed at how deep I was fantasizing about a man I hardly knew.

Milan peered at me closely.

"What were you doing, Mai?" she asked.

"Oh nothing," I said. "I'm going to step in the shower, so let the girls in. All of the slippers and blankets are in the basket by the sofa. I'll be back."

Yes, a cold shower was in order.

Each girlfriend had her own pair of slipper socks that matched blankets that I crocheted. They teased me and called me the 'Black Martha Stewart'. They didn't know why I didn't own a craft business since I loved arts and crafts so much.

By the time I showered and changed, Milan was cracking jokes, holding her usual beer glass full of wine as the rest of the girls were laughing and egging her on. They all had their glass of wine except Kiana, which I found very odd. I had gotten Kiana's favorite wine, Six Grapes, and she never turned down a glass.

"Good evening ladies. Help yourselves to dinner. I hope it is pleasing to your palate. And leave room for dessert. Kiana, no wine tonight sweetie? What's up with that?" I inquired.

"I have some news ladies," Kiana said, smiling.

"Alright now. What's going on sistah?" asked Jordan.

"Jude and I are expecting a baby. So, no wine for me, thank you! I just found out yesterday." We all screamed in excitement and hugged her one-by-one.

Tion paused abruptly in the midst of our celebration.

"Hold up, heifer," she exclaimed dramatically. "This is all good and well, but don't go blowing up when you know my wedding is three months away."

We were appalled. We knew Tion could be a bit self-absorbed, but this was just tacky.

"Dag, Tion, chill out. It's not even about you! If she blows up, then she blows up. Let it go. It's not too late to have alterations. Stop being so stank," cried Jordan.

"Jordan's right. Chill out, Tee. It's all good. Just be happy. I am," said Milan. "You go girl," she said to Kiana. They gave each other a hug. I told Kiana that this was the best news I heard all week.

"Thank you, ladies," Kiana said, looking at us appreciatively. She turned towards Tion. "And I should still be fine for your wedding, Tion. My baby won't interrupt your special day. But I may not be fine for yours Milan, if you are planning a wedding this year. The baby is due in October," Kiana said proudly. We broke into shrill screams of excitement again, hugging her and rubbing her still flat belly. Tion, embarrassed, tried to save face.

"I didn't mean to sound like that, Kiana," she said. "I'm sorry. I am happy for you. I just really want all of you by my side, that's all."

Kiana was classy and was never one to hold a grudge. "It's okay. Just make sure y'all plan me a bangin' baby shower with the works. The party planner can't plan her own party, so make it happen. Do what you do!"

We talked about Kiana's pregnancy for a few more minutes before I stood up as I smelled the aroma of my food waft into the room. I saw that Milan had finished her glass of wine and was pouring another.

"Dag, Lani. Slow down on the booze. You have to eat," I cautioned.

"Girl ain't nothing but a little wine. Doctors say it's good for the heart," she said a bit too loud. I raised my eyebrow as she waved me off and guzzled back her third glass of wine. *Alrighty, then*, I thought. But, I soon forgot about Milan as I smelled my breadsticks. I didn't want them to burn.

"Alright, ladies. Let's eat and get caught up on our show," I said as I walked toward the kitchen. "Oh, and by the way. I'd like to share that I have a coffee date in the morning," I laughed as I darted into the kitchen. I could hear their cry of surprise.

"Okay, watch out now! Tell us more," screamed Jordan.

"Girl, you better get out here and tell us how that miracle happened," Kiana yelled.

While we ate dinner, I told them how I met Malachi and our plans to meet tomorrow. They were all pleased to hear that I even accepted an invitation, or even that I was bold enough to call back. I grinned as

I described Malachi, and laughed when I told them how I thought he was white at first.

"That's funny. But, you know what? If he was a white man, I say it would still be an interest worth pursuing. Race should not restrict you from finding love. Hey, you gotta do you, girl. It's all about how he treats you, not his skin color. And if he happens to be light bright and damn near white, it's alright. You feel me?" said Tion.

"Tee's right, Mai. Jude's parents dealt with the interracial and interfaith issues, with his father being Jewish and his mom a straight up Baptist sistah, ok!" Kiana added.

"Tee, you are crazy. But y'all are right. Race in this day and age should not be an issue like it is. And, let me tell you, when I thought he was white, that didn't stop me one second from being attracted to him. This man is not only fine, but also has such an attractive way about him. It was just a good feeling to be admired and to know he wants to get to know me. I thought I was checking him out, when all along he was having all eyes on me."

"Damn, that sounds so romantic," Jordan cooed.

"Yeah, I hope he turns out to be something special, Maiya. You deserve it girl," Kiana said.

"Girl, you know I will give you the 4-1-1 after we meet. We're meeting at Latté Dah over at Hanson Crossing. Anyone know the place?"

"Actually, I went there last week to see what they offer. It's a cute little place, nice and quiet. I thought about you Maiya, because of the chai tea that you like. I think you'll like it," said Tion.

"Well, I hope so. My fingers are crossed that he doesn't turn out to be a weirdo," I said as the girls laughed. I began stacking their plates as they finished one by one. "So, how was dinner? Ready for dessert yet?" I asked.

"Everything was delicious, Mai. I'll clear the table and get the dessert plates. Who's got the dishes?" asked Jordan.

"I got them," said Milan. "Maiya and I have the same dishwasher. All we have to do is stack the dishes in there and it handles its business. I'm ready for dessert."

"Me too," said Kiana. "What is the specialty tonight, Ms. Black Martha Stewart?"

"Lemon chiffon cheesecake with raspberry sauce," I answered with a sweep of my hand. "I hope you ladies enjoy it." I put my hands on my hips and paused. "And Tion, please, no critiques. You are always complaining 'bout something. Just be quiet and eat, got it?"

"Okay, I'll try girl," Tion said, pulling out a mirror and checking out her flawless make-up. "You know I'm picky though," she said absently as she dabbed at the corner of her mouth with a napkin, still peering at her reflection. "I was just gonna say, though, that tonight's dinner was divine. The only thing you needed to do was to add some more pepper in your Alfredo sauce." I didn't even have to respond. I could see everyone roll their eyes and suck their teeth at that comment. Milan was giving her the mean side-eye.

"Then use the shaker next time," yelled Jordan. She had little patience for Tion.

"Or don't eat next time," said Milan as she carried plates into the kitchen.

I sliced the cake and passed out plates and soon, we were eating cheesecake and continuing our conversation about Kiana's new baby and my upcoming mini-date with Malachi. I noticed at first that Milan had become unusually quiet while nursing yet another large beer glass full of wine. She didn't say much, especially when Jordan kept asking her questions about her upcoming wedding, but I didn't think much of it at first. I was too caught up in my own excitement to give it much thought. Malachi was the main thing on my mind, I admit, and I was caught up in sharing all that I knew about him with my closest friends.

* * *

The next morning, I was ready to go for my run by 5 a.m. I usually run three miles on the trail along the waterfront, but today I felt like doing the entire five-mile course. I would go to the Arena for a swim tonight. Running was such a stress reliever for me. I always made it a point to run every day, at least a minimum of 15 miles per week. Milan would usually tag along to ride her bicycle, catching up to me at the midpoint, but she had been sleeping later and later these past few months, often complaining of a hangover. This morning was especially cool for February, so I grabbed my fleece pullover, finished my protein bar, grabbed my water bottle, and headed out the door. The start of the trail was just at the end of the parking lot, with one side designated for runners and the other for cyclists and skaters.

I liked going over to the Arena, especially since the Olympic-sized indoor pool was in a glass building, so you still had the feel of the sunshine coming through and could enjoy the beautiful landscape as if you were outdoors. I smiled, thinking how my dad's company did an awesome job on that. I took off at an average speed of about 10-minute miles, but at the quarter mile mark, I usually picked it up to 8-minute miles to up the workout. At this rate, I would be finished by six, giving me enough time to shower and get a quick bite to eat before meeting Malachi. I had thought about him all night.

Malachi's beautiful smile and charm stayed on my mind as I started my run. I was happy about meeting a nice man, because I felt it was time to move on. With all the drama in my past, things had to get better, right? I couldn't help but feel like I was getting too hyped about this coffee date. Here I am, with my desire to be married, and want to have a family some day, and putting all of these hopes into this one date with a man I hardly know. I had to be cautious and take things slow. It only made sense. Rushing into things never worked. My past proved that. I was so tired of playing games-- the roller coaster ride of relationships was a game at which I was an expert. I had been there, done that, and bought a tee shirt.

I was so focused on my thoughts that I was startled a bit when Milan rode up next to me.

"Hey girl," yelled Milan.

"Hey, what's up? You workin' today?"

"Yeah, I have to go in to finish the orientation with Sean, and then I'm free. I got the email from Kari about opening up more hydrotherapy classes, so I plan to give her the available days I have. She's really good with admin details. I hope her replacement is just as diligent as she."

"I know girl, she's an excellent worker. We'll be lucky to find someone half as good as she is."

"You're right. Well, look, call me and tell me how 'tea' went. I haven't been on this thing all week, so I'm going to go ahead a bit. Pray for me that I don't fall out from overexertion. Ha ha! Later Mai," said Milan. She sped off on her bike and waved good-bye. I would have sworn that today would have been a day she slept in after all that wine she had been drinking last night, but, I sensed that there was something manic going on with Milan right now. She seemed unusually cheerful. Oh well.

I finished my run and did 50 pushups and 100 sit ups before walking back to get a shower. I ate a small bowl of Special K and a banana, drank some orange juice, and then got ready for tea and conversation.

By the time I arrived at Latté Dah, I was energized and ready to take on the world. I met the owner, who seemed to be expecting me.

"Hi, I'm Janet. You must be Maiya."

"Yes, ma'am. How'd you know that?"

"Malachi described you to a tee and said you'd be here around eight. He wasn't sure what your preference for hot drink is, so I put out my variety of teas and coffees for you, so let me know what may tempt your taste buds."

"Thanks so much. Do you happen to have chai tea in decaf? And any rice milk?"

"I have the tea in decaf, but no rice milk. Mostly, people ask for soy milk. Maybe if you like it enough here and come back, I will get rice milk and add it to the menu. How about a muffin or scone?"

"No thanks, just a medium cup of tea please."

"Make yourself comfortable. There are some books on the stand. Malachi likes the spot by the window," said Janet, pointing towards a lounge chair with a huge bouquet of exotic flowers resting on a table.

"Thanks."

I walked over to the chair and sat down. There was a card with my name attached to the vase. I took the card and read it. "A bouquet of flowers for the prettiest rose I've ever seen" I read aloud. *How sweet of Malachi to do that*, I thought. There was a book of poetry lying next to the vase, so I picked it up and began to read it. *That Which Awakens Me* by Ananda Leeke. I smiled. Ananda Leeke is a local celebrity who I had seen speak and perform readings at a couple of events I had attended this past year. I had been meaning to get her latest book, but never did. Malachi couldn't have known that, so I was impressed with his selection. When I looked up, he was coming towards me.

"Good morning, Ms. Vaughn. How are you today?"

"Fine, thank you. It is a lovely morning. Thanks for the flowers, Malachi. They are beautiful."

"I'm glad you like them, Maiya. You like the book?"

"I like it, how sweet. This place is really something. I can see why you enjoy coming here. And Janet seems really nice."

"Yes, she is. She's one of my favorite clients," he said. "And, I asked her to take care of you before I got here. I hope she did." He took off his blazer and laid it on the back of his chair before sinking into his seat. His muscled arms were covered by a collared shirt that matched the blue in his eyes. "So, now, Ms. Maiya. Tell me about yourself." Janet brought over his coffee and creamers and he thanked her before continuing. "I wanna know all about you. What you like and don't like, where you're from, what you do in your spare time, where is your man?" Malachi laughed as he spoke the last question.

"Wow, you wanna know it all, huh?"

I sipped my tea. It was nice to have a man interested in getting to know all about me up front. But, I had to admit. I wasn't used to this.

"Well, let me start with what I like. Ok. Hmm, well, I like chai tea with rice milk, and a good book. I like to watch the sunset, listening to jazz, and foot massages. I like rainy afternoons and board games, while eating a grilled cheese sandwich and tomato soup. I like to cook because I love to eat! I love arts and crafts. I like an honest person, which is why I cannot tolerate a liar! I like family gatherings and friendly get-togethers." I was on a roll. Getting self-conscious, I redirected the question. "I could go on and on," I said. "So, why don't you tell me what you like?"

"Well, first of all, I like watching you as you 'go on and on'. Your face gets so animated," he said. I blushed.

"But, if you're interested, I don't mind telling," he set down his coffee. "Let's see. I like cool mornings so I can sit by the fireplace and just reflect on life and my goals. I like tranquil, peaceful places, which is why I go away every year to my home in Aruba. I like to exercise and I also like to cook, like you. I love listening to jazz, and I play the guitar. Um, oh yeah, I'm very into my family, so I spend a lot of time with them. If you can't tell already, I love my job. I love to create the reality out of people's fantasies, which is why I love being in architecture and graphic design. And I also like the company of a nice young lady like you. I would like to like you, Maiya. And, I would like it very much if you liked me, too," Malachi said, smiling.

Damn, he's such a flirt, I thought.

I laughed. "Ah, I see. Well, you're making it easy. Flowers, poetry? A cozy coffee shop? You seem to be doing everything right so far. I also see we do have some similar likes. What about your dislikes? Do you have any?" I inquired.

"Actually, I do. I don't like closed-mindedness and I will have to cosign on the dishonesty. I don't like people who judge. Oh, and I don't like cats! You don't have a cat, do you?" he asked me, raising one eyebrow. I laughed and shook my head, trying not to spill my tea.

"So, tell me, where are you from?" he asked.

"I grew up right here in Fort Washington, but I went to school in Virginia, since my aunt was a schoolteacher there for twenty years. My mother died when I was a baby, so my dad's sister—my aunt helped to raise me. My dad says I look just like my mom. I don't have any brothers or sisters, but my aunt's sons are like my brothers and my girlfriends are like sisters to me. My best friend Milan and I are owners of a physical therapy outpatient clinic by the hospital. I run the Management and Administrative offices while she runs the physical therapy office. Oh, and I dislike cats, too, but I do have a dog named Chloe."

Malachi laughed. "Whew. That's good. Real good. I'm so glad you aren't a cat lady." His face grew somber. "I'm sorry to hear about your mother, though. I can imagine how it was tough growing up without a mom."

I appreciated his sympathy. Even though my mom died before I had a chance to know her, her absence has impacted me in ways I can't always explain.

"Thanks for that," I said. "Yes. Growing up without a mom was hard. My heritage from my maternal side seems to be lost to me in a way. My mother never knew her birth family and from what I am told, they are still in Portugal. She was raised in an orphanage in her country before she moved to DC and married my Dad soon after he got back from his tour in Germany."

Sensing my sadness, Malachi switched the mood.

"So, the Portuguese side from your mother blessed you with that beautiful hair," he said.

I couldn't stop the blush from spreading across my face.

"Thanks for the compliment, but it is a struggle to manage, I can tell you that much."

He reached up and gently played with a tendril of my hair. I could feel the heat from my blushing spread to other parts of my body.

"And how about your spare time, Maiya? What do you do for FUN when you're not working?" His hand moved from my hair to my chin as he guided my face to look him in the eyes. My eyes got lost in his for a moment.

"I read. A lot. A whole lot," I said. I casually brought my tea cup to my lips so he had to move his hand from my chin. I sipped on my tea and tried to gain my composure. "So the book was a good gesture. I'm an avid reader and I love to work out. I don't go out much, but that's been ok since

I enjoy time with my friends. My girls and I get together once a month to catch up on the latest, but our lives are so busy now that we don't get to go to Blues Alley or the Birchmere like we used to. There are two weddings coming up, so everybody is on a budget. I've gone a few times solo, and it was really nice, but I would have enjoyed some company. I am realizing that your relationships with your friends change when you start sharing your time with someone who is a love interest."

"So true. It's easy to get wrapped up. It sounds like you know how to keep busy, though. And it's interesting that you mention Blues Alley, since I play there sometimes with a local band."

Ah, a musician, too, I thought. He is too good to be true.

"That's right, I heard you say you play guitar, right?"

"I can play a couple of instruments, but my favorite is the guitar, yes. I play with a group of guys called SOUL. We usually open up for various artists. You will have to come to a set with me some time. I am sure that you will enjoy it." He paused. His beautiful eyes rested on me. "Maiya, I noticed that not once have you answered my question about your man."

I set down my teacup.

"Well, there is nothing to answer. I don't have one. I have been enjoying living the single life for the past year and haven't really met anyone that is worthy. Plus, I have had my share of enough drama to last a lifetime."

"What is it that you are looking for?"

I frowned. "Who said that I was looking?"

"Oh, excuse me. If you were looking, what would you be looking for in a man?"

Enough with the questions, I wanted to yell.

"How 'bout you tell me what would it be that you are looking for, if you were looking for a woman," I said. I was not going to be interrogated.

"Okay, okay. Let me see. I would like to be married one day, and I would love to have a family. I love children. My parents were married forever, and I learned growing up about true family values, and the man's role in the home. My dad was the youngest of four boys, and my uncles taught him a lot about life. They stayed together throughout the entire build up of the company and made sure when he passed away that I was well taken care of. So, I want that for myself, and I want someone special in my life to share it with. I guess I say all of that to say that first and foremost, I want a woman who wants a family and wants to be loved unconditionally."

"You sound like you know what you really want. So, you haven't met that person? Or do you not already have that special lady? I can't imagine too many women not being up for being loved unconditionally."

"Well, Maiya, you'd be surprised with how much of a tall order that is. I mean, I do expect loyalty in return. So, I guess there is a condition to my love." He smiled at me.

"And you have never been married? Any children?"

"No, ma'am. Never married, and no children. I was engaged eight months ago and we would have been married by now."

Oh no, I thought. *Rebound.*

"What happened? If you don't mind me asking."

"I found out that she cheated on me with my best friend."

"Wow," I said. *Yikes, this is worst than I thought.* "I'm sorry to hear that. How did you find out?"

"Believe it or not, a radio talk show. On Wendy Williams to be exact. They were talking about cheaters and the most scandalous cheating ever done. She called in to the show and shared with the whole world how she was in love with me, her fiancé, but was sex-crazed about my best friend, Fred who was also supposed to be my best man. She used another name, but I knew her voice. She knew I never listened to the show, but I got a phone call from our mutual friend telling me to tune in to the show that day. It was a Friday.

"I remember every detail of that day. I was planning on coming home early to surprise her before she was to go out of town. Can you believe it?"

As he recalled the story, I could see the vivid emotion being relived on his face. His eyes kind of got cloudy as he recalled the dreadful moment he heard his fiancée publicizing her infidelity on the live radio show. My heart broke for him as I listened.

I was spellbound by the story. I had never heard a man talk so openly about being played by someone he loved. I didn't know whether to be impressed or worried that something was wrong with him. The truth is, after listening to his story, I realized that he and I had a lot in common when it came to giving love to undeserving people.

"Wow, Malachi. That sounds terrible. That's too bad. But, you know what? I've been through a lot of the same drama. It makes you stronger, and you're able to learn from it and move on. I spent six years of my life in a dead-end relationship because I thought he would change. You live and you learn, Malachi, and eventually you'll get it right. And I will too!" I put my hand on top of his. He smiled back and put his other hand on top of mine, caressing the top gently.

"It's all good. It is what it is. I am glad that I found out when I did, instead of after we said 'I do'. My man Fred tried to explain, but it was not even worth the effort. That friendship is dead, and I let that go. But, I really want to find the right one, the love of my life. And I will one day."

Listening to Malachi, I couldn't stop comparing his story to my ill-fated relationship with Derrick. I understood how badly it hurt to be cheated on. Malachi could tell my thoughts were drifting. His question pulled me back.

"So are you gonna answer my question?" he asked again. "What are you looking for in a man?"

What could I say? I thought I knew each time I got in a relationship, but never got what I wanted. Right now, I was just happy to be sitting here gazing at his handsome face.

"You know what?" I said. "Most women want the fantasy story, the prince, big beautiful home and family. All I really want is a person who connects with me spiritually, mentally, and physically. I want an honest man; a man who will love me down to my stank ass drawls. You know what I'm saying? A person I can be myself around and not have to tiptoe around saying what I feel and just allowing me to do what comes naturally. I want someone who is not gonna cheat on me, or put on a front to get what he wants and then roll out. When you are in a relationship, you gotta be in it together. Otherwise, it just won't work."

"That's deep, Maiya. I truly understand where you are coming from. You sound like someone really hurt you, and I am sorry about that. Just do me a favor."

"What's that?"

"Just don't take your past out on all the brothers who may wanna get to know you. Not all men are scandalous. There are still some good men out there. And you're looking at one of them."

I paused for a moment to take it all in. "I hear what you're saying, and I will definitely try not to hold the next man accountable for the last man's mistakes. I say the same thing to you. I think you are so inspirational to not be bitter and negative after what you went through with Tia. I think most men could learn a thing from you about moving on."

Maybe it was me, but he seemed a bit uncomfortable when I said "moving on". I caught how he changed the subject.

"I could talk to you all day, girl. But I'm sure you've gotta go."

"Yeah, I do need to run. This was really nice. Thanks for inviting me."

"Sure thing. I just want to know before leaving if I can see you again. Can I call you sometimes? I would like to talk more. This was really nice and I am glad you came to meet me."

"Yes, this was nice. I will be done at the office by five, and then I'm off for a swim. Why don't you join me? Show me more of your technique that I soooo needed help with," I said, laughing.

"Okay. I'll just meet you there."

"I'll be on the deck. See you then." I stood up and turned to pick up my vase.

"Don't worry about those. I'll send them to your office. It's gonna be awkward trying to drive with them."

"Okay, thanks. See ya this evening," I responded, taking two peach tulips from the vase. I turned to the shop's owner behind the counter. "Bye Janet. Thanks for everything. It was nice meeting you," I called to her.

"Sure thang, sweetie. Don't be a stranger now. Come back and see me sometimes. I'll have that rice milk just for you."

"I will be back. I promise."

I walked out and got into my car. I could tell that Malachi watched my every move; I could feel him smiling. My body felt so warm and excited that I was looking forward to that cool swim after work. The fragrant flowers in my hands reminded me of his eyes staring at me and I couldn't stop blushing. What was I getting myself into?

* * *

I had to handle some business and run errands before going back to the office, so I didn't get there until a few hours later. Kari greeted me as usual.

"Good morning, Ms. Vaughn. Here are your messages. And this package."

"Thanks Kari. Is the conference still on as scheduled?"

"Yes, ma'am. We'll be setting up at noon. The mayor has already confirmed."

"Okay, thanks."

I skimmed over my messages. They were all from Malachi. One read 'thanks for this morning. You made my day.' Another read 'your flowers will be arriving soon'. *He must have left this right after I left the tea shop,* I thought. My mouth fell open at what I saw next. Not only did Malachi deliver the flowers from this morning, he brought me the whole floral shop. There were three delivery men each carrying a vase of two dozen roses in various colors.

I immediately called him. "You are too much! What am I gonna do with you?"

Malachi responded, "Just let me spoil you. See you tonight."

Kari paged on the intercom. "Delivery for you Ms. Vaughn. May I send it in?"

"Yes, Kari thanks." The guys brought in the flowers. One of them said to me, "You sure must be special, lady. This guy spent extra just to have this sent this morning."

"Thank you, sir," I said, handing him a tip.

"Oh, no thank you, ma'am. Mr. Taylor included our tip already. Have a good day and enjoy."

There were so many flowers that I had to arrange them around the sitting room that was adjacent to my office. I placed the rest of them along the window sill behind my desk.

When Milan saw the flowers, she immediately asked me if I had slept with him.

"Girl, you must have sprung something on him-- I ain't never seen a man this wide open sending flowers like this without there being some good loving going on behind closed doors," she laughed raucously and sipped from her thermos. I closed my door so Kari couldn't hear her guffaws. I assured her that this was all "pre-booty" behavior. I was incredibly flattered and dazzled.

"Aha, 'pre-booty'," she said. "That means you plan on giving him some real booty later to thank him for the flowers. Girl, with all these flowers, you'll be thanking him for days. Your poor booty is gonna be tired."

Trying not to laugh and encourage her, I shooed her out so she would stop teasing me and I could get some work done.

As hard as it was to focus, I spent the rest of the afternoon after the conference going over preparation for the upcoming inspection. Milan already had her office manager pull all the files and critique what needed to be corrected or adjusted. The newly hired individuals would be going to a newcomer's orientation, and that would be held at the Gaylord right across the street. Milan's uncle is one of the managers there and able to handle all the details. The new employees were excited just about being there on the waterfront and all the activities they had planned. As pleasant as the office day was, my mind drifted as I started to think about Malachi. I had already planned in my mind that if things went well with him and I, then he would be my date for the Christmas party.

Eventually, I got back to focusing on work and before I knew it, the day was over. Time almost got away from me as I got through the day's work. I was so ready for my evening swim and couldn't wait to see Malachi again. I really enjoyed his company and the flower delivery had really been one of the most romantic gestures anyone had ever done for me.

By the time I got changed, Kari paged to tell me Malachi was running late, but he would still meet me at the Arena. When I got there, Ramon had towels and water lying on my favorite lounge chair. I did a few simple stretches, then walked over to the pool and dove in. The water was very warm, and it consumed my body. I set my stopwatch and began my workout. I loved the fact that the indoor pool was just the perfect temperature. I only planned to do thirty minutes, but it felt so good that I decided to do an extra twenty minutes. When I got out and walked over to get some water, I noticed Malachi was still not there. My phone had two missed calls, and the message icon was blinking. It was a text from Malachi. The text read that something had come up at work and he needed to stay late, possibly all night. He promised to call me later.

I couldn't hide my disappointment.

I picked up the rest of my things, and went to shower and change in the locker room. My head started to hurt and I tried to fight back the tears that stung the back of my eyelids. I didn't like this feeling of being stood up and I wasn't used to this. I was so angry at myself for allowing myself to get caught up even if he has already shown me more romantic gestures in the mere days I've known him than in the years I've spent with other men.

I was home by seven, and fixed a grilled salmon salad. The only thing for me to do was some of the work I had brought home with me. I was going to focus on work so the thought of Malachi wouldn't consume me.

I went over the details from the video teleconference, getting absorbed immediately. The phone rang and interrupted my thoughts.

"Hello."

"Hey, Maiya, it's Malachi. Sorry I couldn't make it tonight."

"Oh, that's okay," I lied. I tried to sound cheerful to hide my disappointment. "I know how work can get crazy sometimes. Now you owe me," I continued. "And you'll have to deal with MY workout," I laughed. "What happened that made you have to miss tonight?"

I could sense his reluctance to share.

"Um, it was nothing. It's taken care of," he said. "But, I would love to take you up on your challenge. Just name the time and place, and I am there," Malachi responded. "I'm so glad you're not mad at me for not making it today. I promise I'll make it up to you."

"Ok, well we'll see. Tomorrow is not really my running day, but I'll make an exception for you. Do you know the park and trail by the waterfront?"

"Yeah, sure."

"Can you meet me there at 6 a.m. ready to run?"

"I'll be there."

"Then I guess I will see you in the morning."

"Maiya, wait. Before you go, I do have a question."

"What's that?"

"I know you said you love jazz. I was wondering if you would go with me to a concert in June. I know it's a few months away, but I figured I would ask you now. It's actually a weekend event, and I can arrange to have you stay overnight so we won't have to drive back and forth."

An overnight date? I hesitated before asking, "Who is on the lineup and where is it?"

Malachi ticked off a list of some of my favorite musicians.

"Boney James, Brian Culbertson, Eric Darius, Mike Phillips, Dave

Koz, Candy Dulfer, Rahsaan Patterson, Dwele, Heather Headley, Kim Waters, Acoustic Alchemy, Maysa, Down to the Bone, the Rippingtons, Ledisi, you name it. The list goes on and on. It's in Hampton, Virginia, but if you can only go for one day, that's cool, too. If this is a bit premature, just let me know."

My interest won over my hesitation.

"I love just about every single artist you named. I'm in. I just have to make sure I can take the time off of work; I'm working on a big project that I've been spending some weekends devoting time to. How 'bout you email me the details with the dates, and I'll check it out. I can let you know for sure by the end of the week, okay?"

"Okay, Maiya. I hope you find the time to swing it. It would be really nice getting away with you. And, again, I'm sorry about having to miss today. Can't wait to see you tomorrow. Good night."

"Good night, Malachi," I said, smiling into the phone. "See you at six sharp!"

His deep voice roared with laughter.

"Aye, aye, drill sergeant. See you at six."

I was brought up knowing that you don't let anybody get you down and you don't let anybody get the best of you. ~**Charlayne Hunter-Gault**

SIX

M alachi was warming up on the mini obstacle course when I walked up. I could tell from a distance that the brotha was built like a linebacker. *He is so fine, I can't wait to...* I stopped those thoughts instantly before they could finish. Rushing things before they started was my MO before. I had to strengthen my will to take things slow this time. I focused my attention on his face and called out.

"Hey, you! Ready to get your workout on?" I asked.

He looked up and smiled, waving me over.

"I'm here, so let's do this girl. I'm all yours. Show me what you got!"

"Okay, well. I see you warmed up. I was thinking we would run 3 miles, and then go over to the Arena for weight training."

"Let's get to it. Lead the way."

"Do you need some water? I have extra in case you need it."

"Nah, I'm good. Got it right here."

Malachi and I ran the course. He kept a good pace that I was able to handle. He was impressed. We talked a bit while we ran, and I commented on how in shape he looked which led to us sharing a bit about ourselves. Malachi shared with me his ethnic background, and I learned about his mom and dad. He laughed that his mother's German genes obviously were the dominant, but in the summer season, his skin color would be honey and not the creamy vanilla that showed up now. The blonde hair that he had was a mystery to his family, since most of them had dark brown or jet black hair.

"I was always teased in school. The white kids didn't know what to think of me, and the black kids just put up with me, but they all treated me different. I mostly hung with my cousins who are darker than me but don't make such a big deal about how I look. I hung with them and their circle. They were my crew when it came down to kids trying to punk me at school or in the neighborhood 'cause they thought I was white or just soft. Kids can be so cruel, you know," said Malachi. "It didn't help my case that my mother let my hair grow longer in the winter, so you could really see how thick and curly it is. Boys don't like having a kid, especially a boy, in their midst with pretty hair." He laughed at the memory. My heart warmed at his story. We had a lot in common.

"I dealt with the craziness because of my biracial heritage as well," I shared. "But, I must admit, I did think that you were white when I first saw you. Sad to admit it, but I was unsure if I could deal with it if you were white. Interracial relationships get so much negativity these days and I wasn't sure I could be strong enough to deal with it."

"At least you are being honest. What changed your mind?"

"My best friend Milan recognized you from your uncle's description when he was a patient at the clinic. He came to the walkathon, but you were out of the country. She explained to me your mixed heritage, and I felt stupid for even thinking the way I did. I'm sorry."

"So, Maiya, if there was no Ethiopian or anything 'of color' in me, would that make a difference? Would you still have a problem with me not being black enough? Would you still be hangin' out with me?"

"Being Black enough isn't the issue anymore. Society has us so caught up into thinking that interracial dating as being such a problem; I can say I am guilty of slipping there. I dealt with discrimination as a child because although I have the brown skin color, my hair and my eyes let others know there was something else there. I was never quite accepted, and I guess I am just doing to you what others have done to me all my life. I can admit to my ignorance in that, I guess." I couldn't believe I had told him all of that. "And yes, I would still be hangin' out with you if you weren't Black."

"Well, I'm glad you're hanging with me. Thanks for sharing with me how you felt at first. We're so programmed to only associate with those who look like us that we often stop things before they can start. I know that you admitting your reservations with me was difficult. So, thanks for being honest."

"No problem. I feel better now." I smiled.

We finished our run and made it over to the Arena. Malachi then offered to lead me through some light weight lifting exercises. He stood behind me as he spotted me and I could feel his body's heat intermingle with mine. It took all that I had to stay focused and not drop the weights. By the time we were done, I was feeling exhilarated. My body was stretched and exercised just right and my attraction to Malachi was building each minute I was around him. The idea of spending a weekend with him for the jazz festival didn't sound like the best plan now knowing how attracted I was to him. Going slow would not be an option. As I thought on this, I realized that Malachi was talking to me, warning me that my body may be achy tonight, so to be sure to take a warm bath tonight.

"That sounds like a good idea. Thanks for the workout and the talk. As usual, I had a nice time with you."

Malachi smiled and walked close up on me. His face was inches away. "No problem. Anytime. It was good just to be in your presence again, Maiya."

I backed up; sure I would have kissed him if I waited a moment longer to back up. He straightened, noticing my discomfort.

"And I'll send you the jazz concert info as soon as I get to the office. Can I call you tonight?" he asked.

"Sure, that's cool." I smiled.

He raised an eyebrow as he looked at me. "What's that smile for?"

"You don't have to ask me if you can call me. That is perfectly fine with me."

"Okay, Maiya," he relaxed. "You know I have to check and ask. You always letting me know how you're Miss Independent. I'm not trying to take for granted what I feel is happening between us right now. A brotha has to be sure, you know?" He pulled me closer by my hands and leaned close. "I'll talk to you later. Have a good day." He kissed me on my cheek, slow and soft and then released my hands as he backed up. I was floating. I swallowed hard.

"You do the same, Malachi. Bye." I turned and walked out of the gym and across the parking lot, sprinting a bit as my heart fluttered in my chest. My condo was right across the way from the Arena. I could feel Malachi watching me leave. This time, I turned around and smiled at him for one last time before sprinting to my place.

*   *   *

When I got to work, I was in an exuberant mood. Kari greeted me with news that Kendra called to cancel on Thursday and wanted to know if she could come in today.

I told her, "Call her and have her come in at eleven."

"Yes, ma'am."

I wanted to check my email and give Malachi a response to his invitation. After spending more time with him today and vowing to myself that I would take things slow with him, I decided that I definitely would not be passing up the chance to enjoy jazz and good company. I already knew what my answer would be before checking my messages. I just needed to be sure there was nothing planned that I needed to attend that week. I was looking forward to it. I also wanted to ask Malachi if he would be interested in being the contractor for the project in New Orleans.

"Ms. Vaughn, Mr. Taylor is on line one."

"Good morning, Malachi. Thanks again for the workout."

"Anytime, just say the word. What's up? Did you get my email?"

"As a matter of fact I was just checking it. Give me a sec and let me pull up the June schedule to see if that will work. Okay, looks like I am available, so yes, I accept your invitation. But, where will I be staying?"

He laughed. "I knew you would ask. My Aunt Marie has a duplex condo in Hampton, and she has the upstairs vacant. It's fully furnished, has two bedrooms, full kitchen, balcony with hot tub; a really nice layout. You can stay there, and I'll be in the downstairs condo with her. How does that sound?"

"It sounds like you have a date, but give me by the end of the day to be sure." I paused. "Malachi, how busy is your schedule for the next few months? I have a project you may be interested in, if you are taking on anything new at this time."

"My schedule is not tight at all, actually. I pulled that all-nighter and that put me ahead of schedule. What do you have in mind?"

"Milan and I are working on an office in New Orleans, trying to expand our business, and I was wondering if we could get some ideas from you and possibly hire you to design it. We want to keep a similar basic layout of what we presently have here, but we really need fresh ideas. After the work I have seen you do, I am very impressed."

"I would be honored. If you could give me some time next week, I will be able to meet with you."

"Great! Tell me what would work for you and I will make sure we get you in here. I will have Kari, my office assistant, call you to confirm. You'll get to meet Milan, and we can go from there."

"Wow. You're something else." His laugh was gentle and washed over me. I didn't know what he meant though.

"Something else? Is that a good thing?" I asked. With men, you could never tell what was going through their minds.

"It's a great thing," he said. "When I first saw you, and checked you out, I admit, I was instantly attracted to you because, and you know this, you are beautiful. Even with a swim cap on smashing your eyes, you were stunning to me. But, now, spending the morning with you, seeing your discipline as an athlete and then seeing how driven and focused on your work you are, like me, it just makes me even more impressed with the woman you are, Maiya. You're incredible."

His words lifted me up in a way that I never felt before. I had never been complimented by a man on my work ethic or discipline. Yes, I always got the comments about how cute or sexy I was, but Malachi seemed to see me beyond looks. It touched me and made me want to open to him even further. I cautiously thanked him.

"Thanks, Malachi. What a nice thing to say. I have to admit, though. You impress me each day I get to know you. You're almost too good to be true. I'll talk to you later, ok?"

"Ok. Bye, Maiya. And thanks for thinking of me for the job."

"You're welcome. Good bye."

*   *   *

I sent an email to Milan to let her know of an upcoming meeting with Taylor Made Construction Inc. to design the office in New Orleans, and inquiring of any available days next week. Since I was given the job to find a contractor, I knew my decision would not be met with resistance, especially since I was the one who had secured the small business loan that was paying for all of this. Milan and I have a good working relationship and trusted one another's judgment. We are honest with one another, and always keep it real.

Since Kendra cancelled for Thursday, I was hoping we could meet then, but would wait to get confirmation from Malachi and Milan. If that day wouldn't work, I could use the day to do more field research for the new office. There was an agency in the process of recruiting technicians and therapists, and would even pay travel and relocation expenses if anyone was interested. So far, they received thirty-four applications, but only four wanted to work full time. I wanted to host a job fair to encourage people to transfer. We would even consider hiring new graduates and offer a stipend or sign-on bonus to transfer. I had some good ideas; I just hoped that I would be able to pull it off.

Kendra showed up at ten-thirty, and I was ready for her. I took Kendra on a tour of the facility, and showed her the vacant rooms for rent. Kendra was in need of a suite with a separate shower room, and a private office adjacent to it. The suite was available, but there was no room for a shower.

"I'm sorry, Kendra, but this is all we have right now. None of the rooms have showers in them. This one has a private bathroom, but no shower."

"Is there any way that a shower could be added? You could include the price of that in the monthly rent."

"I would have to get the original plans to see what adjustments can be made, and I don't know how long that could take. What are you willing to work out in the meantime?"

"That's just it. I really need the shower room, especially with the different services that I offer. How long do you think it would take to get the plans in order?"

"First, I need to run this past Milan, since this is our building and decisions are based upon our agreement. Secondly, we would have to set up a meeting to have the contractors come in and give estimates. But, we won't make any revisions and then you back out. This is a business, and we need to know where your loyalty lies. If we go all out to do this, a stipulation would be included in the contract, before construction, that would pretty much confirm that you will agree to a contract of at least two years leasing the suite."

"Oh, I understand," Kendra said. "That would only make sense. This is the most space I have seen in a long time, and I really want to make my business here. The location couldn't be better. I want to make this work. What do you need from me?"

"Well, let's go over the cost to rent the space for now, as is. You will have to also be willing to sign a two-year contract and accept penalties for reneging. There will, of course, be an increase on the rent once renovations are made. You do understand that?"

"I understand."

"Well, then why don't we go in my office and finish up. I will need to see your certifications and what services you are permitted to provide." Kendra nodded, and followed me down the corridor. I pointed to a chair next to my desk. "Please, have a seat."

"I have everything you need right here in my portfolio. I can leave a copy of this with you to look at and discuss with Milan at your leisure."

"Let me buzz Milan and fill her in on what we discussed. Just give me a moment."

Milan answered on the first ring. I told her the plan and asked for her input. Milan agreed that the estimate for the upgrades was necessary before deciding upon accepting Kendra's lease application. We did not want to be caught up in an amount that Kendra would not be able to afford nor be stuck with a newly renovated suite with no interested renter. Milan agreed that everything should be drawn up on contract and signed once the estimates were within reason. I shared this with Kendra.

"Milan has agreed with what we discussed. We will need time to gather the estimates, but in the meantime, if you are willing to start working without the shower room that is fine by us. It's your call. We can do a month-to-month lease until the estimates are drawn up, or you can wait and see what difference the estimates will make to your rent. And I'm not sure if you will be able to function during the renovation. This may put a damper on your business momentarily, but it's up to you."

"Is it alright if I take some time and think it over, and then get back to you?"

"That's perfectly fine. How much time do you need?"

"Can you give me two weeks?"

"I can do that. This will allow me time to get a few estimates. Keep in mind, Kendra; if I don't hear back from you in exactly two weeks, the space will be vacant again. What are you willing to do so I can hold it for you and ensure no one else gives us an offer?"

"How does a thousand dollars sound?"

"Sounds like I will hold your suite for two weeks. If you change your mind or make a decision before then, do not hesitate to contact me right away. Here is my card. Until March first, take care. And if I get the figures before then, do you have an email or fax that I can send it to?"

"Yes," replied Kendra. "It's here on my card. Thanks for all your help. I'll be in touch."

"Have a good afternoon. Bye now."

I paged Kari. "Can you get our top three contractors' information for me and call to set up appointments. I need estimates for a renovation. Oh, and add a fourth one, too. Call Taylor Made Construction. Mr. Taylor may be interested and have someone we can use."

"Okay, Ms. Vaughn. Would you prefer it to be days that both you and Ms. Douglass are here?"

"No, as long as one of us is here, that's fine. I know what is generally needed, and I'll leave a copy in a folder for you in case I'm not here. Email it to Milan as well. Thanks, Kari."

"You're welcome. How'd it go with my cousin?"

"Well, nothing final yet. We should know in a few weeks."

"That's it?" asked Kari.

"Kari, you know I can't discuss details with you about your cousin. That would be unprofessional. What I can say is that I like her, and I want her to have a lucrative business, and if we can help her out along the way, I will be pleased."

"Understood. I'll make those calls now."

I tied up some loose ends and phoned Milan. I wanted to know if Milan could meet me at Martini's. "Sure thing, girlfriend. My last appointment is at three o'clock, so I will call you when I am finished," said Milan.

"I'm leaving early to take Chloe to the groomer, around six. Just come by and get me and we can leave out together."

"Alright. I'll see you then."

*   *   *

By the time I got home, I was broke down. Though I knew I had had a long day, I had been extremely tired over the past two months, and my doctor had been monitoring my lab values due to my anemia.

My irregular menstrual cycles and heavy clotting, not to mention the endometriosis, left me sluggish. I was taking iron pills, and pretty soon I would need to take Epogen or be faced with a blood transfusion. This always scared me, since the unknown consequences left me wondering my fate of being able to have children. I thought about that hot bath that Malachi recommended and headed for the bathroom until I was greeted by my dog Chloe.

"Hey there, Chloe. Come here girl." Chloe came willingly, walking very slow and careful. I scooped her up and noticed that her nails needed cutting, and her coat needed a trim. *Uh oh, my bath will have to wait*, as I remembered Chloe's grooming appointment. The groomer was ten minutes up the street, so I'd be back in time to get a quick nap before Milan came knocking at the door. I sent a text message to tell Milan that I left and to meet me at home. No sooner was I putting the key in the door than my phone was ringing.

The caller ID showed it was Milan. "Hey girl, what's up?"

"Girl, I'm beat. Can I get a rain check on Martini's? I just wanna chill."

"Yeah, girl, that's fine. I actually wanted to rest, too and take a hot bath. How 'bout you come over here and I fix us some daiquiris later?"

"Okay, see you in about an hour."

"Works for me. Just let yourself in."

The phone rang as soon as I hung up. This time it was Malachi. "Hello."

"Hey, Maiya, it's Malachi. How ya doin?"

"I'm okay; just a bit tired that's all. How are you?"

"Fine now that I'm talking to you. Just wanted to tell you that I will be seeing you next week for the New Orleans project and also for an estimate to do renovations. Kari was very professional when she contacted me. Seems like you all run a tight ship over there."

"Well, we do try to keep the place in line. We aim to please." I yawned. "Oh, please excuse me. I gotta run and pick up my dog in a little bit, and then Milan's coming over. Can I talk to you later or maybe tomorrow?"

"Cool. If it's not too late, you can give me a call back tonight. Or just call me tomorrow. What is your schedule like for lunch? Will you be free?"

"I am available around one? Where would you like to go?"

"Do you like Mexican food? I can pick you up at the office and we can ride to Waldorf for lunch at the restaurant called Mexico. Does that sound alright?"

"I love Mexican food. I'll be waiting for you."

"Okay, until then, good night. Get some rest."

"Good night." I felt weird about my attraction to this man. It was all just too fast. I curled up on my bed with him on my mind and before I knew it, I had drifted into a dream state. An hour later, Milan was walking through the door. "Hey, girl, where's my drink?"

"I'm sorry. I was interrupted by a call from Malachi, and then I dozed off. Come with me to pick up Chloe and then we'll do daiquiris," I suggested. Milan was down.

We picked up Chloe who looked and smelled fresh. She was happy to see Milan. She jumped and ran around in circles when we got back to my place. Milan and I headed to the kitchen where Milan started mixing the daiquiris.

"Hey there, little girl. You missed your auntie?" Chloe sat and wagged her tail. Chloe was a Yorkshire terrier that I got a year ago. She was the smartest, most obedient puppy I could ask for.

"Okay, girlfriend," Milan began. "So, tell me, what's up? That rose festival in the office was out of this world. What in the world did you two do on your first date? I thought you were just going out for tea!" She poured vodka, rum and some other liquor in the blender.

"Girl, when I tell you that is all we did; I am telling you the truth. We just did tea. We talked. It was nice. It was good. No, better than good. We talked for a long time, and I really like him. Then we got together for a workout and talked a whole lot more. He told me about his fiancée, the break up, his construction business, what he wants in a woman… girl, he went on forever." I paused and watched Milan. "Is dark liquor supposed to go in daiquiris? What are you doing?"

"Girl, this is my own recipe. Chill. Go on now. Whatchu gonna do?"

"About what? I mean, we just met. I'd like to get to know him better. He asked me to go to Hampton to a jazz concert. For a weekend."

"Girl, whaaaaat? Are you gonna go? I mean, but you hardly know him. Where will you stay?"

"His aunt has a condo that I will stay in, and he'll stay with her. I'm actually excited about going, but I'm just hesitant."

"Hesitant. Girl, bye. Even if nothing comes of it, you will at least have made a friend. He's a successful, handsome, down-to-earth man who obviously knows what he wants. Don't look for something to fail. Just be friends and enjoy yourself." She poured me a daiquiri in one of my cute glass tumblers and then poured the rest of the blended drink in her beer glass. "Let the past stay in the past. You will never find the love you deserve if you don't let go of the hurt. It is better to have loved and lost, than never to have loved at all. How many times must I tell you that? It's time to do you. And if Malachi is showing an interest in you, you should get to know him. Life is too short. It's all about you being happy. I say go for it."

"I know you're right. Sometimes I feel it is too good to be true."

"Maiya, have you not been in love before? Have you not been hurt before? Didn't you fall down and pick yourself right back up?"

"Yeah, but…"

"But nothing. Where is your faith? Did you not make your request known to God? You have to be patient and wait on Him. He knows the desires of your heart. You must let go and let God."

"I hear you. I'm gonna do me. And I'm gonna have fun."

"You go girl. Be happy. You deserve it. And there is still time to know him better. The concert is months away. I am sure you two will have made that love connection by then."

"Alright, Dr. Love," I said, joking her. She had all the answers for me. As I watched her drink her drink in almost one swallow, I decided to turn the questions on her.

"So, I noticed at our girl's gathering the other night that you were pretty quiet when it came to you and David and your upcoming marriage," I began.

"Oh, there you go," Milan said, getting visibly uncomfortable.

"What, Milan? Look, you better not be keeping secrets."

This didn't appear to be a good sign to me. I know my best friend.

Milan and I are very close, but a lot of times she can be secretive about things in her personal life. She will act like everything is all good, when it really isn't. Then, when things get out of control, like it sometimes does, she falls apart. When we were in college, Milan became stressed out and began smoking and drinking. She even began sleeping around with men she didn't even know so she could forget her problems—problems she didn't even share with me. At one point, her behavior was such that I just couldn't relate to her anymore and we actually drifted apart, mostly because her choice of company was not for me. But, we both missed each other so much and it appeared that she grew out of that wild phase, so we reconnected as if we never were apart. Later, she rededicated her life to Christ-- but there was still a lot she was going through that she still didn't share with me. When she met David and less than a year after meeting him said she was marrying him, I grew worried that she was probably rushing things. David is nice and everything, but, he just doesn't seem like he's for her.

David lived in Bowie, a suburb in Maryland, and spent a few nights a week with Milan, but not too often. He had dreams of opening up his own accounting firm in Washington, DC, which is where he wanted to move to. He spent a lot of time at business meetings and was out of town quite a bit doing business seminars and seeking to employ a myriad of personnel. I saw happiness in her eyes when she talked about him, but there was something missing that I could not quite put my finger on. Milan has always loved living the simple life, and David just seemed bent on turning her into a socialite. She felt he spent too much money on her and he got mad whenever she made a big deal out of it. Their disagreements always seemed to revolve around money and lifestyle and I was doubtful they would be resolved before the wedding. But, I knew David loved her. So, I wanted to know why the reluctance to talk about her wedding to him.

"Milan, is something going on with you and David? Are you two having problems?" I gently asked again.

"Oh no," Milan started. "David and I are fine. There is nothing wrong with us. Look…," she trailed off. "Never mind."

I could tell she had a lot on her mind. She drank the daiquiri so fast that it was gone in no time. I had barely touched my own drink. It was way too strong.

"Girl, what do you have planned for this weekend? How about we go for a girl's day out and go to Robert Andrew Salon and Spa for massages and facials. It will be my treat."

"That sounds good, Mai. Then maybe you can help me pick out a ring for David. He says whatever I want for him is fine. He says it like it is so easy. But you know he wants something flashy. I just can't believe he really puts up with me. I can really be something else."

"Yes, you can, but he knows that you are extra special. And he is a bit special, too. He sees something good in you, just like I do. You are the sister I always dreamed of, and I hope that you two have a wonderful life together. You deserve it. I really mean it. I love you girl. And as often as I say it, you know that you can come to me about anything that is ever on your mind."

"I love you, too, sistah! You always know just what to say. And I do know that I can talk to you about anything. But, I am good. Don't worry about me. So, anyway, are you running in the morning?"

"No, Lani. I'm swimming tomorrow. But I'll catch you at work. Good night."

"Good night, Mai."

* * *

After my bath, my head hit the pillow with the quickness. I was dog tired. The phone woke me out of my sleep. When I looked at the clock, it read 11:00 p.m.

Who in the world is calling me this late? "Hello?" I answered, sleepily.

"Maiya, sorry to call so late, it's Malachi. I just needed to hear your voice again, and I couldn't wait to talk to you tomorrow. I know this may be a bit premature since we don't know each other that well, but I would really like to move past all of the hurt we succumbed to in our lives and move forward. I guess what I am trying to say is, ever since I first saw you at the Arena that day, I feel like God answered my prayers. I prayed for you. Everything about you. Your personality, the way you smile, laugh, roll your eyes; just all of it. You make me feel good about meeting someone and starting to love again. Well, not love love, cuz we hardly know each other, but, um, well…..," Malachi stammered.

I laughed out loud. "I'm sorry, Malachi. I'm not laughing at you. It's just that I have been feeling the same way. I have been beating myself up over my past, and then you come along and share so much of my similar qualities that it is almost scary. You make me want to love again, and I know it may be a bit early, but I am feeling you, too. I just need to take my time. I wanna get it right this time, you know. Make sure all of the bases are covered, and there's no stone untouched."

"Thanks for being on the same page with me. You give me a comfort. And I really don't want to scare you off or anything, but I just can't let you get away."

Despite how tired I was, I couldn't hang up the phone. We talked for two more hours about everything, from favorite foods to places to travel, and family history to religion. I learned that he grew up in an A.M.E. church, and although his mother was a devout Catholic, she converted. I also learned about his dream to open a catering business because he really loves to cook. I shared with him my upbringing in a Baptist church and that my dream was to take up cooking as well, mostly baking. I told him all about my arts and crafts, and how I loved to create photo albums. We talked for what seemed like an eternity, and promised to meet for lunch the next day.

"Maiya, it is such a pleasure to be able to talk to a woman who actually knows what she wants out of life. And it feels good to be in the company of an intelligent, beautiful person, inside and out. You are such a blessing to have, and if given the chance, I will stop at nothing to make you happy."

"Well, Malachi, that's really sweet of you to say. And it means a lot to know that you are genuine. It is just refreshing to know that I can say what I really feel. It is also refreshing to not be met with resistance. I am glad you called me that first day. And I am glad you called me tonight. You have got to join me at church some time."

"I would like that very much. Well, I know it's late, so get some rest. And I will see you for lunch later today."

"Good night."

"Good night, Maiya."

Maybe all one can do is hope to end up with the right regrets.
~Arthur Miller

SEVEN

MALACHI

At the end of my first date with Maiya, I knew there was something special about her. The way she could relate to me when I talked about how Tia and Fred played me, the way she looked at me when she spoke about her life and her passions. I just couldn't stop thinking about her. As I watched her walk to her car, I had to tell Ms. Janet how I felt about Maiya.

"You know what Ms. Janet?"

"What's that, baby?"

"That woman is going to be Mrs. Taylor. Mark my words!"

"Okay, now. Slow your roll baby boy. It hasn't even been a year yet since you got out of something. Take your time, honey. It will happen. I ain't gonna lie though. She seems really nice. I feel good vibes about her. I want you to be happy either way," Ms. Janet had said.

And here we were, a week had passed, and I still had Maiya in every thought. We had been in contact via email and texting, but we had not seen each other all week. I was extremely busy, but wanted to make sure I put the time in to date Maiya. I had really enjoyed Maiya's company the week we met, so I wanted to go out again. Not only was she beautiful, but she loved to work out, enjoyed listening to jazz, and she had a wonderful sense of humor. I wanted this woman in my life. But, I could not erase Tia from my mind. Especially now since she told me last week that she is pregnant.

71

Yes. Out of the things to tell me, out of all of the times to be told that I am about to be a new father, nothing could be more inconvenient, or questionable. I enjoyed children a lot, and even if Tia was having my baby, I would be there for my child. But, given Tia's history with Fred and her past record of being a liar, I was not one hundred percent sure that I was the baby's father. Her news messed me up so much that I missed my swim date with Maiya.

All I can do now is wait.

As I pushed thoughts of Tia from my mind, I thought about my plans for the weekend. I was hoping that Maiya would be interested in coming to my set at the Birchmere. I had to rehearse tonight and tomorrow, and my band was performing both Friday and Saturday nights. I could join Maiya for church on Sunday, then head for Virginia that evening to visit Momma. My cousin Benjamin and his wife Lindsay were expecting their first baby, and they wanted me to be the godfather. I was excited about being there for them and looked forward to travelling in a few weeks when the baby was born.

As I set off to rehearse with the members of the band, I was not looking forward to seeing Fred. I was hoping that Doug would be there tonight, since Fred usually filled in for Doug whenever Doug was playing with Kim Waters. I wasn't even trying to have a face-off with him. But I knew it was only a matter of time. Especially once the baby issue with Tia surfaced.

The phone rang just as I was heading out the door. I looked at caller ID, and saw that it was Tia. *Damn.*

"Tia, I can't talk right now; I'm walking out the door, late for a set."

"This won't take long. Since you won't return my calls, I gotta catch you whenever I can."

"Alright, Tia, what is it? I really gotta go."

"I just wanted to call to tell you that I made an appointment to see the doctor on Friday, so I'll let you know what happens. Look, I know it's been over for us, but I just need to know one thing."

"What's that?"

"Will you at least be there for the baby?"

"How could you even ask me that, Tia? You know I will be there for my child. *If* it is even mine. I know you are still screwing around with Fred, and that he stays with you now since Jasmine put him out. So, you can't be sure whose baby it is. I just want a paternity test as soon as you can get one."

"Look, I know the baby is yours, but I have no problem getting a paternity test. Just be ready to take care of your baby!"

"No need to get nasty! With all of the dirt you've been doing, who can blame me for being a bit distrustful of anything you tell me? I wouldn't be surprised if you made the whole pregnancy thing up. Look. I gotta go."

"Whatever, Malachi. Pretending to be pregnant is not my style. I'm not desperate for you or any man, thank you very much. No one was begging you to make love to me like you did, clearly after you found out about me and Fred. So, don't try to make me out like a slut because you can't control your lust. Look, just make sure you tell your little girlfriend about your bones that are about to fall out of the closet. I don't want no mess once this baby is born."

"Girl, what are you even talking about? Bones? I don't have anything that I regret in my life other than thinking that you were good enough to marry."

"Whatever, Malachi. You're just mad because you couldn't satisfy me. You would have married me if you didn't find out about Fred. Also, whoever you've been sending flowers to over at the professional building, you need to make sure you hip her to the fact that you're gonna be a Daddy soon. You won't be able to keep this baby a secret for too long."

Good Lord, I thought. *Was she stalking me now, too?*

"Don't make me have to call a favor in to the police station and have a restraining order put on you. Stay away from that building, and stay away from me," I yelled.

"You weren't telling me to stay away from you a month ago. Last I recall, you couldn't keep your hands off me."

"I'm out." I slammed the phone down, grabbed my guitar, and headed for rehearsal. I was not going to let Tia get into my head again.

* * *

I dialed Maiya's number on my cell phone. She answered on the first ring.

"Hey, Malachi. I was just thinking about you. What's up?"

I know she wanted to ask where I had been for the past week, but she kept the question to herself. Her restraint was appreciated. I wasn't ready to share the news about Tia's pregnancy yet.

"Glad I was on your mind. Look, I am on my way to rehearse for our performance this weekend, and I wanted to know if you would join me. Did I catch you at a bad time?"

"Oh, no, not at all. I would love to come listen to you play. How soon do I need to be ready?"

"I can be there in about twenty minutes, if that's okay."

"Yeah, that's fine. You know where Waterfront Street is at the Harbor? I am around the corner in building 32, on the second floor, G. I'll be ready."

"Ok. See you in a few."

On the ride to rehearsal, we talked about music and how I was glad she came along.

"Don't pay the guys any mind while on set. Sometimes they like to tease when they see a new face."

"Trust me. I can hold my own."

"And I already know this." We both laughed out loud.

On set, I was a force to be reckoned with, in a world of my own. Luckily Fred wasn't there, so there was no awkwardness and I was able to just be in the music. The band seemed to really like Maiya.

On the way back from rehearsal, we stopped by Latté Dah to order some hot drinks. Janet was just about to clean up.

"Hey. What brings you guys out this evening?"

"Maiya came with me to rehearse on set for this gig on Friday. You are still coming right?"

"You know I will be there, Malachi. Tell me that your man Doug will be there. I am bringing my girls, and they just love to hear him get down."

"Now, Ms. Janet. I thought you were partial for the bass player?'

"I think you have a new admirer now. I am sure she can speak on that," Janet responded, as she winked at Maiya.

"You're right, Ms. Janet. Doug is bad on those drums, but I will place my bets on the bass player." Maiya winked back at Janet.

"And I didn't even tell her to say that!" I put my arm around Maiya's waist and pulled her close to me. "She will have a large chai tea with rice milk, and I will have a large cappuccino. Any muffins left?"

"Take what's in the dish right there. Help yourself."

We sat by the window while Janet made the drinks. I told Maiya how much I was glad she enjoyed our music, and wanted her to come to one of the shows this weekend.

"If you come out on Friday night, we can go grab some drinks afterwards. Denise, the lead singer, usually invites us to come over to her place to hang out. She and her husband have a nice house in Indian Head, if you wanna join us."

"I would love to come."

"You can ride with me and sit with Janet and her friends during the concert, and then we can leave together. I have to be at the Birchmere by five. Will that be a problem?"

"Um, no. I can leave work early and be ready."

"Sorry to interrupt, but here are your drinks. I gotta close up so I will see you two Friday night. Be safe," said Janet.

"Good night."

*   *   *

I dropped Maiya off afterward and walked her to the door.

"I am glad you could join me tonight. Now you have seen me in a different light."

"I was impressed. You've got skills."

I stepped towards Maiya and gave her a hug. I looked down at her and moved her hair out of her face. "Would it be alright if I kissed you, Maiya?"

Maiya looked up at me and smiled. "You don't have to ask my permission."

I gently placed my hands around her face and leaned in to her. I kissed her lips softly, and she returned my kisses.

"You smell so good, Maiya." I buried my face in her neck. She exhaled and breathed me in. I pulled away and placed a kiss to her forehead. "Good night, Maiya. I'll call you tomorrow."

Driving home, I smiled to myself.

I plan to make her my wife, I thought.

Life's not always fair. Sometimes you can get a splinter even sliding down a rainbow. -Terri Guillemets

EIGHT

MAIYA

I got to work around eight o'clock. I did an early swim at six this morning so I could relax after work this evening. My thoughts began to drift to Malachi while swimming. I recalled our evening watching him rehearse with his band. The way he handled that guitar and got into his music was a joy to watch. It turned me on.

I thought about the two of us being together. I really wanted to go with him to Virginia, but my insecurities kept eating at me. The encouraging words that Milan spoke to me quelled my uncertainty at first, but something kept gnawing at me. I really wanted to be sure that I was taking my time moving forward. But, I couldn't get the feel of his lips out of my mind. When he kissed me, I felt ready to love again.

But, then, my mind instantly did a flashback to all of my past failed relationships. It had been a year since Joaquin and I split up. And when Carlos and I parted ways, there was unfinished business that neither he nor I have addressed. He never found out that I had been pregnant with his baby.

The last time Carlos and I had been together, I was still in a relationship with Joaquin and just felt like I was making a mess out of everything I touched. I rationalized to myself that Carlos and I had a "would-be" relationship that "would never be". When I finally got up the nerve to tell him about the pregnancy, I couldn't do it, even when he confessed his love for me. At the time, I was in a relationship with another man who was making me miserable and I just wasn't emotionally strong enough to go through this again. Despite my love for Carlos, I didn't trust it. I decided not to tell Carlos about the baby.

Things got crazy after that. My hormones, it seemed, were all over the place. Of course, I broke up with Joaquin and, when Carlos continued to call me, I ignored his calls at first until I thought I was strong enough to interact with him and possibly tell him about the baby this time. But, one day when I asked him of a future together, he just talked about getting himself "situated". I guess he was being protective of himself since I never told him I loved him back when he professed his love for me, but, it didn't matter. I couldn't handle his nonchalance. I think my continued worry and increased stress level played a part in the miscarriage I eventually wound up having. I was devastated and don't think I recovered wholly from it. But, I accepted it for what it was: it just wasn't meant to be.

After the miscarriage, after Carlos, Joaquin and my bad track record of love, I focused more on the business and helping to rebuild and expand our practice in Louisiana. I wanted to give back to the community, so I consumed myself with work. Our business was doing well, and pretty soon the building would be paid for. I was pleased.

But something about Malachi was different. He was spiritual, worked for himself and had a successful business, loved his family, took care of himself physically, and was a genuine, caring man. And let me not forget he is fine! OKAY! I laughed out loud. *What did I have to lose by accepting his offer for the weekend*, I asked myself. He was giving me a separate place to stay, so it wasn't like he was openly trying to get some, although I would be tempted to give him some. We both loved jazz, and I would also be in the presence of his aunt. What harm was in that?

I sent a text message to Malachi to 'pick me up at 11:30 instead of 12:30'. I decided I would let him know over lunch that I definitely planned to go to Virginia with him. Then, I called Milan and asked her to stop by my office. I wanted to show her the plans for the renovations, and to keep her abreast of the upcoming estimates.

"Can you come around here for a few moments? I have some updates to share with you," I said.

"Be there in ten minutes."

I called Kendra and left a message in regards to the upcoming contractors, letting her know the plans were in place. I was really impressed with Kendra and wanted her small business to flourish. I was a big supporter of entrepreneurs, and if I could help a young sister out, I would do it.

"Hey, girlfriend. Whatchu got for me?" asked Milan, as she walked in.

"Oh, here are the proposed plans that came across today, and I should have the final numbers by Friday. If you like, we can get together then to discuss them, and have the weekend to make a final decision."

"That may not work. I am supposed to be going to David's mother's house for dinner. She wants me to meet her after work to help her pick out a dress for the wedding, and I promised him I would go. What do you have planned for Saturday, or even Sunday after church? Do you have time either of those days?" She had her thermos again.

"I scheduled our spa appointments for this Saturday, remember? Then we can go over the plans at lunch afterwards."

"Ok. That'll work." She took some of the liquid from her thermos to the head.

"What you got in there, more brandy?" I asked trying to smell it. She pulled it away from me.

"Naw, it's just juice," she lied. I could smell the odor of Remy waft out before she closed the top.

"Hmm, juice and Remy," I muttered, as I straightened papers on my desk.

"What's up for lunch today?"

"I am meeting Malachi for lunch," I said, grinning.

"Wow. I guess my pep talk helped."

"Yes, it did, Milan. Thank you so much. We actually talked on the phone for two hours last night, and it was so refreshing and fun. He sounded really serious about getting to know me and wanting to spend some time together, so I'm gonna go for it. I'm excited about hanging out with him. I am going to tell him that I will go with him to Virginia."

"Well, well. I'm happy that you're happy. Enjoy your lunch. Don't forget we have lunch on Wednesday. Where you wanna go?"

"I don't know. I'm in the mood for Italian."

"Excuse me, Ms. Vaughn," Kari interrupted on the intercom. "I need to go over my next semester's schedule with you. Do you have a minute?"

"Okay, sure." I turned to Milan, "Sorry Milan, let me get with Kari. I'll call you tonight. Maybe we can get over to Martini's after all, around seven."

"Alright. Call me later girl."

"Okay." We said in unison, laughing.

*   *   *

At the restaurant Mexico, I enjoyed every moment talking to Malachi. I opened up the conversation first.

"I was wondering if your offer was still open for the jazz concert, or have you written me off and found another date?" I laughed.

"I told you, Maiya. I like you. I wanna get to know you better, and I really would like for you to join me. If you weren't going to come, my cousin Carmen and her fiancé were going to take my place. Listen, I am not tryna run game on you, and I know you've been hurt in the past. Let's just do this, have a good time, and see how things go. You already know I'm feeling you, but I can go at your pace. I ain't going nowhere, okay?"

"Okay."

He shared with me all the times he spent with his Aunt Marie when he was growing up, and how he enjoyed every summer with her and his cousins. They spent time at the beach, and he was always collecting sea shells which he would later turn into some form of creation. He laughed when he told me the summer he turned seventeen, he found all the shells he had collected over the years and made a small end table for his aunt's living room.

"And you know what is funny, Maiya, is that she still has that table! I will show it to you when we go there. You will like her. She loves to cook so you better bring your appetite. She does not take no for an answer!"

"Oh, I will surely eat; just make sure you show me the nearest trail so I can run it off!"

"That is not a problem. She lives near one of the high schools, so we can go to the track and run." Malachi smiled at me. "You know what, Maiya?"

"What's that?"

"I am really enjoying this time with you, and I cannot wait to have you all to myself when we get to Virginia. You know what they say about Virginia, right?"

"No, but I am sure you are about to tell me."

"Virginia is for lovers. But I am hoping to be more than just a lover to you. Of course, if that's alright with you. No pressure, though." Malachi smiled again.

"Right. No pressure. You are funny. You know, we will just have to see how things go. I am enjoying the time we spend together, and it is a bit premature for us. Come to church with me first."

"Oh, so you have a test for me, is that it?" Malachi asked.

"Well, not really. But you see a person in a different light when they are in the presence of the Lord. Praise and worship can take you to a whole different level, and the Holy Spirit can do some things to you that you just don't expect. Why don't you join me this Sunday? The second Sunday is always family and friends day, so you will feel right at home. My pastor will really bring you the Word. Your spirit will be filled."

'You know what, Maiya? I will join you at church on Sunday. Shall I pick you up or do you want to meet me there?"

"I would very much like it if you picked me up. I usually go to the early service, but we can go later if you like."

"Early service is fine with me. I would like to be anywhere you are."

"You are such a big flirt," I said, laughing.

"But you like it, Maiya. Admit it. I know you do."

"Let's eat and get back to work. We can talk more later."

"Alright, I will let you off easy this time, but not next time. Enjoy your lunch."

We sat for another forty-five minutes eating and talking about everything. He made me laugh and we shared more childhood stories. He missed his father tremendously, and he could not wait to have children of his own. He had lots of cousins and he longed to be a part of their lives. I told him how much I wished that I had my mother, but it was different because I never knew her. Milan's mother was like a mother to me, and my Aunt Rocsi raised me to be the woman I am today. When we left the restaurant, it was pouring rain and we had no umbrellas. It was a bit chilly, so Malachi ran to get the car and pulled up in front of the restaurant so I could jump in. We rode back to my office listening to Jill Scott and talking some more. I found myself thinking how glad I was that I gave him a chance to get to know me. Malachi was very attentive, and I knew that if nothing came of this connection, we would be friends for life. But I would be a fool if I let him get away.

We pulled up in front of my building and I thanked him for lunch. He got out of the car and opened my door for me.

"It was my pleasure. Give me a call later, if you are not too busy."

"I'm actually meeting my trainer at four-thirty and won't be free until six o'clock. After that I will be going over to Martini's with Milan for a much needed break. We shouldn't be out too late, so I will call you when I get home, if that's okay."

"That's fine by me. I'll talk to you later."

"Bye." Before we parted, I looked up and saw Milan walking towards the front door, right in my direction.

"Hey, girl, I see you are back from lunch. I know you're not gonna

get away without introducing me to Mr. Taylor Made Construction?"
Milan said, laughing.

I turned to Malachi and rolled my eyes, laughing. "Malachi, this
is my best friend in the whole wide world and protector of my life,
Milan."

"Nice to meet you, Malachi. I have heard so much about you. All
good, of course, from both my girl here and your uncle. It is nice to put
a face with a name," said Milan.

"The pleasure is mine. I feel like I know you already from all that
I have heard about you. It's uncanny how much you two look alike,"
he said, looking at me first and then Milan. "I'm not surprised folks
confuse you as sisters. Could almost be twins."

Milan and I grinned at each other with knowing looks. Folks told
us that all the time.

"You will be seeing me around more often, so you are gonna have
to share your girl's time with me." Malachi looked down at me at that
moment and wrapped his arms around me. The rain fell on top of my
head but I didn't care.

"I know that's right!" Milan replied. "Well, Malachi, it was nice
meeting you. Hope to see you again soon. I gotta go. I have patients
to see." Milan turned to me. "Maiya, I will catch you later. I gotta go."
She winked at me.

"Likewise. Take care now," Malachi said to Milan.

"See you later, Malachi."

Still wrapped in his arms, I moved my arms around his neck and
peered into his face. "So, you've met my best friend and it seems like she
liked you. She doesn't like anyone when it comes to men I date."

"Ah, so I'm a winner then, huh?" he asked, laughing.

"I guess so. You're a keeper, I suppose," I said playfully.

"Well, good then. I hope you keep me around, so I can do stuff
like this," and before I could stop him, he had begun kissing me full
in the mouth in front of my job. Instantly, I forgot everything and
kissed him back, a small kiss deepening into a passionate one. Deep

and breathtaking, the kiss lasted longer than I could count. When I pulled away, I was flushed, despite the rain. Malachi caressed my face, kissing my cheeks.

"I will talk to you later, right?" he asked, while hugging me tight and extra long. I took a moment to breathe him in. He smelled so good and his arms felt good around me.

"You bet," I assured him.

I reluctantly pulled away at that moment.

At this rate, we would be standing out there in the rain until midnight.

"Good-bye, Malachi. Thank you for everything." I turned and ran inside.

Life is like a coin. You can spend it any way you wish, but you only spend it once. ~Lillian Dickson

NINE

I had a few messages waiting for me. One was from my dad, another was from a contractor interested in the spa, and the last one was from Joaquin. I frowned and wondered what in the world could he possibly want as I read the message. It was concerning his son Noah. It read URGENT. I decided to call him after returning my other calls. I changed out of my wet clothes and pulled on a sweat suit I had in my office closet.

"Hey, daddy, what's up? How's the business going?"

"Hey, Princess. All is well. Business is really moving, so I can't complain. There is never a dull moment until the Fall. Look, I was calling you because your aunt is having a big cookout for the 4th of July and she wants to have it here at the house. I won't be back in town until the sixth and Consuela will be on vacation. Can you coordinate with her and check on the house while I'm gone? Will you be available?"

"Not a problem. But, Dad, that's not until summer. Why are you planning so early? And, doesn't she still have a key? Are people staying over while you're away? I can get another housekeeper during that time if you like. You don't think Consuela would mind if her niece stays in her guesthouse, do you?"

"Rocsi should still have a key. You know I don't like a lot of folk all up in my house. But she wants all of your cousins from Texas to come and I have a job to do in Atlanta then. I'm coordinating this early so there won't be problems. Your cousins Brandon and Jackson and their families will stay at the house. Everybody else is staying at your Aunt

Flora's or Aunt Jeannette's houses. And, Consuela shouldn't mind about her niece staying at the guesthouse, since she has been here before. Consuela won't be back until the end of August."

"Okay, well, I will call Aunt Rocsi and talk to her. I have plenty of time; it's only five months away," I said looking at my calendar. "I haven't seen my cousins in almost ten years. They are all grown up and married with families now and here I am still unmarried and the odd person out. Who'd have guessed it," I said absently as I flipped through my rolodex and found the number I was looking for. "Found it. I'll get Consuela's niece Lucy to help out."

"That's fine, baby. I'll leave some money for you to pay her, too. And Maiya, there's nothing wrong with not being married yet. You just haven't found the right one. Finding true love sometimes takes time. Keep your head up, baby girl. And thanks for helping me. I'll call you next week. Love you."

"I love you, too, daddy. Thanks for that."

"You know I love you, Maiya. You're my baby girl. Talk to you later, now."

I hung up the phone and laughed. My dad was a trip. In the midst of all of his craziness, he always managed to lift my spirits if he thought I was downing myself. When momma died, Aunt Rocsi moved in to help her baby brother, my father, raise me when I was just a baby. Rocsi was raising her own identical twin boys-- cousins Brandon and Jackson by herself while helping dad raise me. It was like having big brothers in the house. Four years older than I am, they always treated me like their baby sister while Aunt Rocsi nurtured me like a mother.

As I reflected on my family, I realized that Milan would be pleased to know that they were coming to visit-- especially Jackson. She always had a crush on him, and they even had a relationship when we were teenagers that lasted for a while. I remember how they secretly said they would run off and get married. But something happened that led to them breaking up; something that I never fully understood and Milan kept to herself. I knew for a fact, though, that Milan's mother couldn't stand Jackson and was always phony nice to my Aunt Rocsi. I never understood why Milan never talked to me about her relationship with my cousin. I just assumed she didn't want to put me in the middle, especially since Jackson was not just my cousin, but like a brother to me.

They kept in touch while we were in college, but drifted apart once he returned home from the Navy. Jackson once shared with me how Milan had changed, and I knew that to be true. She became more distant and seemed to be in this state of unrest when Jackson asked her to give their relationship a try again. Jackson had every intention of marrying Milan, but he said she gave him an ultimatum, and they broke up over it. I don't know what the ultimatum was, but I do know that he married a naval officer that he met while on tour in Guam less than a year after leaving Milan again. I don't think she really got over it, even though she claims she has and tries to say that David is proof that she has. But, who knows?

I remembered my cousins fondly and looked forward to seeing them again. It had been a while since both of them relocated to Texas. Jackson and Brandon expanded my dad's landscape business into a larger company in Houston, Texas where they each raised their families. Brandon has twin daughters while Jackson has a girl and a boy separated in age by nine months. I could not wait to see them. I put a reminder in my cell phone to call everyone for my dad and then continued to sort through my messages.

Now let me see what Joaquin wanted to talk to me about.

I haven't spoken to Joaquin in more than six months now, after he got upset that there was no chance of reconciliation. As I dialed the number that Joaquin left, an uneasy feeling came over me. Something is not right about this. I could just feel it.

Joaquin answered on the first ring. "Hello?'

"Hey, Joaquin, it's Maiya. I got your message. What's going on?" I asked harshly. I couldn't help it. I kind of resented the fact that he had called me and didn't have time for this if it was a game.

"I'm actually right across the street at the hospital. Can you come over? It's Noah. There's been an accident."

My heart sank. "I can be there in ten minutes. Is he alright?'

"He will be fine, Maiya. At least he's stable. I'll fill you in when you get here. I'll wait for you in the lobby."

"Okay, I'll be right over." I walked quickly next door and into the main entrance. I saw Joaquin right away. He looked stressed and his eyes were bloodshot like he had been crying. "Hey, Maiya. Thanks for coming. I didn't know who else to call."

"Where's your mother? You didn't call her? Or your sisters?" I asked, rolling my eyes. "Joaquin, you have a lot of family in the area. I should have been the last person to call."

"Don't start, Maiya. My parents and Gabi went to North Carolina to see my grandparents, I couldn't get in touch with Leah, and Noah's mother isn't answering her phone. I really didn't have anyone else."

"Just tell me what happened."

"Noah was on his way to school this afternoon when he was hit by a car. He has a broken arm and leg, and a lot of internal injuries. His face is swollen like a watermelon and he is all black and blue. The man who hit him swerved to avoid an oncoming car. Noah's gonna need a blood transfusion."

I hugged him, horrified to hear the news. "Oh, Joaquin, I'm so sorry," I sad sadly.

"Actually, the doctors say Noah will need a few transfusions," he continued. "I offered to donate and they said I could. When they typed my blood, they said it was not compatible with Noah's. I told them it was not possible because he's my son. I told them to run it again. They did. They said it is impossible for him to be my child. I am not his father, Maiya. How could this be?" He put his head down and just sobbed. His body heaved as his cries grew audible. I had never seen him like this. He sat down in a chair and I sat beside him and wrapped my arm around him.

"Oh my gosh. I am so sorry."

"How could Nicole do this to me? That trick! I have raised that boy since he was five years old. He knows me as his dad. I gave that girl child support for him, I took care of him. I moved him out of that bad neighborhood and got him in a stable environment. Why? And for what? That boy is NOT even my son!" Joaquin shouted.

"You need to calm down and lower your voice. I know this is upsetting and devastating news, but he still needs you. Biology or not, he is still your child, and what he needs right now is for you to be strong and to be there for him. This is not his mistake; it's Nicole's. Maybe she knew, maybe she didn't. You are all Noah's got in this world. You've got to keep it together for him."

Joaquin reached for me and I just hugged him. He held on to me so tight that I thought he would never let me go. When he let go slightly, he moved towards my face, like he was about to kiss me.

"Whoa, hold up now. We can't EVEN go there," I said.

"I need you Maiya, I really do. I need you back in my life. I miss you. A lot."

"It's not even about us, Joaquin. I'm not gonna address this right now. I'd like to see Noah."

"Oh, so it's like that. Don't you care about me?"

"That's a stupid question. I wouldn't be here if I didn't care. But, I've moved on, and I think it's time you did, too," I responded, walking away from him towards the information desk.

"Excuse me, sir. Can you please tell me where I can find Noah Ramirez? He was taken to surgery," I asked the clerk at the desk.

"Are you family, ma'am?" Before I could answer, Joaquin was standing next to me, answering, "Yes, she's his stepmother."

"Okay, well, looks like he's on the surgical ward and that's on the second floor. Before sending you there, let me call to see if he's actually there yet. Do you know when his surgery was scheduled?"

Joaquin answered, "He was in a motor vehicle accident. He came through as an emergency about an hour ago. The nurse said someone would page me overhead and tell me where to go."

"Then you must go straight to the surgical waiting area. Go right down this corridor and through the double doors. Make a left at the first corridor and you'll see the waiting area to your right."

"Thank you, sir," I said. I looked at Joaquin as we walked down the hall. "What's the stepmother thing all about? Are you smoking somethin'?'

"Nah, I just know what I want now that I've seen you again. I need you, Maiya."

"Oh, please," I said, shrugging off his hands as he tried to draw me close. "Please have the decency not to use your son's injuries as a way to worm your way back into my life. Right now, deal with this tragedy that's in front of you. Your son is in there dying. He will soon find out that his mother lied about who his real father is. This is not the time, nor place, for you to try and push up on me. Come on now, get it together, man." I folded my arms and looked at him. He bowed his head and I felt bad enough to hold his hand and lead him to the surgery wing.

"It is good seeing you, Maiya," he said as we walked. "You look beautiful as ever. I like what you've done with your hair."

"Thank you. I will take the compliment. Especially since you never liked the way I wore my hair. It was too "black" for you, remember?"

"Maiya, if I could take back a lot of things, I would. I can apologize until I am tongue tied, and it still won't matter. I messed up."

I stopped walking and pulled my hand out of his hold.

"Yes, you messed up. Please, spare me. This is not the time, Joaquin. Just give it a rest, man."

"Oh, is this your way of telling me you have a man? Okay. I guess I'll just have to steal you away from this dude, then," Joaquin said, laughing.

"Ha, ha," I said, turning down the hallway where the arrow pointed. "That's not gonna happen," I muttered. "Oh, here we are, right through this door."

Joaquin walked over to the woman at the desk. "Excuse me, ma'am. Good afternoon. My name is Mr. Ramirez and they took my son into surgery. Can you tell me who I can speak to about him?"

"Was he scheduled or an emergency?" the woman asked.

"Emergency. They told us to wait here."

"Yes, sir, let me call back there. One moment please."

While we waited, I noticed how calm and neatly put together the waiting room was. The furniture was ornate and very warm in earth tones. I glanced over at Joaquin to catch him staring at me. It's funny, but if this were three years earlier and I was in love with Joaquin as I had been, finding him staring at me would have made me feel all giddy inside. Instead, I was just annoyed. I was particularly disgusted at how he could focus on trying to get with me when his son was lying in the hospital. His priorities were so screwed up. Once I knew Noah would be alright, I was going back to work.

Just then, my thoughts were interrupted. "Maiya, she said we could go back to the recovery room area and they can give us more information there," said Joaquin.

"Oh, okay."

In the recovery room area, we were shown to a separate room for families. It looked like a cozy den, with large lounge chairs and a small table with a lamp in its center. The window overlooked the Emergency Room entrance with the Harbor as its backdrop. We waited for half an hour before the surgeon came in.

"Is the family of Ramirez here?"

Joaquin and I stood up and walked towards a tall, thin doctor in pale blue scrubs.

"Here we are, sir," answered Joaquin.

"Mr. and Mrs. Ramirez, I am Dr. Katz. Let me tell you about your son. Please, have a seat." He motioned us over to where we had been sitting. As we sat down, I grew nervous with dread. *Please don't let Noah die*, I thought.

"So let me start off by saying that he is stable, and he did fine during surgery."

Joaquin and I, relieved, hugged each other as Joaquin cried a bit out of relief.

The doctor continued, "But, he lost a lot of blood, which is why he needed a blood transfusion. I had to reset his femur, the large bone in the upper leg, as well as the two bones in the right arm. Noah is a very lucky young man, very strong, and a fighter. We transfused a total of four units of blood, and we will monitor his labs over the next few hours to determine if he may require more. We will be transferring him to the ICU and keep him there for a few days, then transfer him out to the surgical ward. Do you have any questions for me?"

"How long will he be in the casts? And what about the recovery period?" asked Joaquin.

"The casts will be on for about eight weeks. I will see him in two weeks to evaluate him, but I will be following him while he is in here. He may need physical therapy and I can recommend a good therapist just across the street in the glass building. Her name is Milan Douglass. I will set it up for an evaluation, and then follow-up as an outpatient. He needs all the support he can get. That young man is really shaken up, and he will be happy to see his parents."

"Well, you're right, Milan will be the perfect PT to work with him to get him back to his old self," I confirmed.

"Oh, so you know Milan Douglass?" the doctor asked

"Why, yes. She's my business partner. I'm Maiya Vaughn." I put emphasis on my last name.

"What a small world. Nice to meet you. You're Ms. Vaughan?" asked Dr. Katz. "I didn't know you were married."

"I'm not." I looked over at Joaquin. "Mr. Ramirez and I are no longer in a relationship. I have, however, known Noah for six years and he is the closest thing I've had to a son," I responded.

"Oh, well then, I don't have to tell you, Mr. Ramirez, I am sure you know that you will get the best treatment over there with Ms. Douglass. These young women are highly recommended," said Dr. Katz.

Joaquin looked at me and said, "Oh, I know. I know, doctor." He grabbed my hand and squeezed it while I did my best to pull away.

"Well, if there are no more questions, I will excuse myself. I will be in the ICU to check on Noah this evening during rounds. Take care, and it was nice meeting you both. Take my card. The nurses on the unit will take good care of him, and make sure they have your contact numbers. Have a good evening. Give them about another forty-five minutes or so, and Noah should be in the unit. It's located on the first floor. And tell Milan I said hello."

"I will. Thank you."

"Thanks again," said Joaquin. He turned to me. "Wow, you ladies are 'highly recommended'. That's great. Beautiful and successful. I shoulda never let you go."

I just sucked my teeth and rolled my eyes. "Ugh, boy, get outta my face. I gotta step out and answer these calls. I'll meet you downstairs. Go and see your son." I walked down the hall and out of the hospital front doors to call my office.

*   *   *

My phone was ringing just as I was hanging it up from listening to messages.

"Hey pretty lady, you're hard to catch. Whassup?" It was Malachi.

"Hey there, yourself. I'm over here at National Harbor Medical Center with a friend."

"Everything alright? You need me to come down?"

"Oh, no, I'm good. It's Joaquin. His son was in a really bad car accident and he called me panicking. I just couldn't leave him hanging. Noah is not doing too well."

Malachi paused. "Oh, I see. Well, I hope the little man heals up quick. I'm sure his family is pulling for him right now." Before I could respond, Malachi continued. "Look, Maiya. I'm no dummy. You were with the man for six years. You were in love with him. And now, he's got this tragedy on his hands and you're the first person he calls? I hope this isn't a message to me that you two are going to get back together because…well, look. If he wants you back, you don't owe me anything; we're just friends right? But, just don't play games with m…"

I cut him off. This was not the time for him to be in his feelings and jumping to conclusions so quickly. "Hold up Malachi. I am NOT playing games with you. I'm being honest with you. I loved him, yes. Past tense. Been there, done that. I have no feelings for him like that, and he knows it. I'm not the same person I was when we were together, and I don't want him. I wanna be..." I had to stop myself. I just couldn't reveal too much of my feelings to this man, not like this. Not so soon.

"You wanna be what, Maiya?"

I wanted to scream **I WANNA BE WITH YOU**, but instead I said, "I wanna be happy, Malachi, that's all. I just can't turn my back on a friend. I was around his son for six years, so cut me some slack, okay?"

"I'm sorry, Maiya, I just know how men are. I am one, remember. And if I messed up and could have a fighting chance to get back the one that got away, I would try my best and use all avenues, stopping at nothing until I succeeded. If you wanna roll with dude, let me know. I'm not about to compete. I am finally in a place where I can settle down and be happy and I wanna be with only you. Look, I got another call I need to take. Just think about what I said and call me later when you get a chance."

"Alright, then. I'll call you later. And Malachi."

"Yes, Maiya."

"For what it's worth, I don't wanna be with him. I wanna be with you." Then I hung up. I couldn't believe I was just that bold.

But I was not about to miss out on what could be the love of my life.

Life loves to be taken by the lapel and told: "I am with you kid. Let's go."
~Maya Angelou

TEN

Milan and I sat in Topolino's for lunch, after what seemed like months. The weeks had flown by after Noah's accident and the busy action at the office had kept us pretty much focused on work when we were together. I hadn't had time to catch Milan up on what I had been up to with Malachi, nor Noah's accident and Joaquin's behavior at the hospital. This lunch was our first time to talk about all of that. I told her of the time I had been spending with Malachi, our upcoming trip to Virginia for the jazz fest and the drama with Joaquin and Noah at the hospital.

"I don't even know why you went to the hospital," Milan said.

I sipped my sweet tea, and then said, "You know I have never been one to turn my back on anyone-- especially not Noah. I was around him for so long, and I care about that boy as if he was my child. He is gonna need your services as an outpatient, so I am sure Joaquin will be bringing him to his appointments. So be nice."

"Girl, I ain't trippin' off that man. I just don't want him to start nothing. I don't trust him and he will stop at nothing to get you back. You better stop being so gullible," she finished off the martini she had, chomping on the olive.

"Trust me, Lani. He ain't got nothing coming. Malachi is who I wanna be with. I am looking forward to spending time away with him. So, you gotta help me plan my wardrobe. I was thinking I would wear something comfortable and cute for the afternoon concert, maybe some Capri pants and a cute top and leave the cool, midnight blue dress for that evening. How about that?"

"Sounds cute. With that pretty beaded necklace that Heather made. Wear your strappy silver thongs, too. And pull your hair up on top of your head. You sure you don't want me to surprisingly show up and check y'all out?'

"Girl, please. I'm a big girl. You just tryna be nosey."

"You know I gotta make sure you do like I told you. Just keep it grown and sexy." We both laughed. Milan motioned to the waiter to refill her drink.

"Speaking of keeping it grown and sexy. What's up with you and my cousin, Jackson? He left a message for you on my phone and he sounded desperate to get in touch with you. You keeping something from me, Lani?"

"Girl, please, he has been trying to talk me out of this wedding, that's all."

"I thought you hadn't been in touch with him for awhile. What is really going on?"

Milan paused, and then looked away. "Look, I didn't say anything to you because I didn't want you to judge me. Jackson and I have been seeing each other off and on for the past year. We have always been in touch. He claims that he is leaving his wife, but I don't want him to do that. I am happy with how we are. I know it sounds crazy, but we have a history Maiya, and I can't just let it go."

"What about David? Hello? You are getting married."

"And I still will. I just can't stop seeing Jackson, at least not right now."

"I know you just didn't say that! Are you tripping? David loves you. What is this going to do to him?"

"Girl, please, David and I have been so far apart that it's like the Red Sea parting ways all over again. He doesn't care about anything but his interns and his business. This union is all for business purposes and nothing else. And stop looking at me like that. Your cousin is a grown ass man and he…"

"…is married and has a family to take care of," I completed for her. "Lani, you know that this is all wrong. How can you be the other woman and be okay with that? And why didn't you say something to me before?"

"Because, girl, you are so happy with Malachi, and it's your time to shine. Look, there is some more to it, but I'm going to work it out. Don't worry about me, I'll be fine. Have a good time away and enjoy being in a real relationship. I do not want to trouble you with all my drama. I can handle your cousin, and I can handle David."

"It's not Jackson that I am worried about but his crazy wife Leesa. She is psycho and you know it."

"I can whip her in my sleep. So let it go. I am not talking about it again, so let's drop it. Go have your fun and I will get Chloe in the morning."

I was quiet for a minute.

"Stop looking like that, Mai. I will be fine. Trust me." Changing the subject, she said, "You ready? I have a new therapist that is teaching his water class and I have to do an evaluation and observation. Plus, I don't wanna miss seeing him in his swim trunks."

"You are not right, girl. You know that man is a tambourine shaker anyway. He ain't even thinking about you!"

"He is NOT gay! Stop playing. He's just a bit more manicured and neat than what comes through that door. Don't hate on a brotha. A lot of men get mistaken for being homosexual just because they speak intelligent and dress with a bit more style."

"Not hatin'. And that boy is gay, mark my words. You just better watch it. Innocent flirting can turn into sexual harassment, and we are not about to have that all up in here. You know what I'm saying?"

"I got this, and yes, I feel you. Don't get me wrong. I'll be good."

"That's what I'm afraid of."

* * *

Heading back to the office, I got back into the flurry of work that was waiting for me. Apparently, I was so caught up that I didn't realize I had been missing calls on my cell.

There was a missed call on my cell phone from Malachi. He left a message to apologize for getting upset about the hospital visit with Noah. I called him back and accepted his apology, and reassured him that there was nothing for him to worry about. I had a strong connection to my ex-boyfriend's son, and I could not turn my back on him just because I was no longer with his father. Malachi said he understood, but I had to let him know that I did not have time for a jealous man. I had no intentions of hurting anyone, and I needed him to know that.

"I believe you, and I just wanted you to know how I felt. I am gonna have a problem if y'all are gonna be hanging out like old buddies, especially with all that he put you through."

"I understand where you are coming from. But, trust me; we are not hanging out like that. I am still friends with his sisters, but I haven't even spoken to them in a bit. I have no reason to keep anything from you. And I wouldn't put you in an uncomfortable situation. You have NO reason to feel threatened by Joaquin."

"Maiya, I want us to have a nice time this weekend and I don't wanna be unclear with my feelings. I just needed you to know that I understand. And I don't plan on dictating the choices you make or try to control any situation. You understand where I'm coming from?"

"I most certainly do. I hope that you will be as honest with me as I am with you."

Malachi mumbled an "of course" before we said good-bye.

* * *

The trip to the jazz fest in Virginia finally arrived. Malachi arrived to pick me up around nine a.m., since I told him I wanted to get in my early swim before going out of town. My bags were packed and sitting by the door when he arrived. Milan was coming by after work to get

Chloe and keep her while I was away. As the doorbell rang, I thought to myself, *he is so punctual.*

"Coming," I yelled out.

I opened the door to a smiling Malachi, holding a hot beverage in one hand and a book in the other. "Good morning, Maiya. This is for you. Vanilla spice chai tea latté, two sugars, rice milk. Did I get it right?"

I laughed out loud. "Let me find out you know what a sistah likes! That's cute. You get some points for that."

"Can I get a kiss, too?"

"You sure can." I grabbed him and kissed him hard on the mouth.

"You better watch out girl. Don't take advantage of me already."

"Oh, you like it. What's this?" I reached for the book he had in his hand.

"Compliments of Ms. Janet. This is *Liberated Muse Volume I: How I Freed My Soul* by some folks from around the world. The editor went to school with my cousin Carmen. I read it and thought you might like it, too. I know you love to read, so maybe you can check it out on the way to VA."

"Thanks so much. Now, can you help me with my bags?" I asked, pointing to the door. There were three plaid Dooney & Bourke pieces of luggage. His smile froze on his face when he saw my pile of luggage.

"Dag, girl, I said a weekend. Why you gotta bring your whole wardrobe?" Malachi laughed. I shoved him playfully and fake punched his arm.

"You know I need my workout gear, plus my shoes, a few dresses, hair products, makeup. Whatever! Just help me so we can go already."

Malachi drove a black Dodge Charger with tinted windows and a license plate that read 2BLK4U. The drive to Virginia was smooth and the morning proved to be warm and welcoming. We drove with the sunroof open, and the breeze was wonderful. I was excited that this was our first getaway. Malachi and I had been seeing each other for four months now, and there was nothing more intimate between us than sharing hugs and kisses.

"You're so quiet, Maiya. What's on your mind?"

"I'm just thinking about this moment. This is our first REAL trip together, and it feels good. I enjoy being with you. It's been awhile since I've shared good company, and I like it."

"Me too. I hope we can keep this thing going. I would like to take you all around the world. Show you where I grew up, where I've travelled to, my family, and friends. All that." He smiled at me and held my hand.

"Sounds alright with me. I like that idea."

We talked a lot more about our childhood and how we both wished we had siblings. Although we had cousins that were close to our own ages, it just wasn't the same. Our conversation was interrupted by my cell phone.

"Hello?"

"Hey girl, you on your way outta town?"

I covered the phone and whispered to Malachi "it's Milan," before continuing. "Yes, Lani, we already left. Just don't forget about my dog. And water my plants, please. I gave Rosa the week off, so if you could help a sistah out, I would appreciate it."

"I gotchu girl, don't worry. Just have fun. Loosen up a bit. I'd like to see you guys have more getaways. He's good for you, Mai. Call me to let me know you got there."

"I will, Lani. Smooches." I closed my phone and looked at Malachi. "She told me to have fun and enjoy ourselves."

"And so we will do just that. Can you grab the CD case and load up the player for me? There's a variety of music in there, so whatever you wanna hear."

I chose Wayman Tisdale, Kem, Jonathan Butler, Brian Culbertson, and Alicia Keys. It was weird listening to Wayman and remembering him in concert just two years ago, and now he was gone. He had lost his battle to cancer, and I was devastated. We listened to the music, and I read the book Malachi bought me. We stopped for breakfast at IHOP after driving for about an hour.

Back on the road, we talked more and he told me about his mother and that he wanted me to meet her.

"Don't you think that's a bit premature?"

"Not really, Maiya. I mean, we are friends, right? You not scared are you?"

"No, it's cool, I guess. I'd like to meet her. She can tell me the kind of child you were growing up. I bet you were a bad boy," I laughed.

"Ha, ha, very funny. I'll have you know that I was a good kid. Never gave my parents any problems. Ask her. She'll tell you. I played Little League baseball, swam for my high school team, studied Aikido, played football, sang in my uncle's church choir, volunteered at the local Boys and Girls Club. You name it, I did it."

"Wow. Just an all around American boy. Very active, huh? So, what got you into your business, besides not really having a choice?"

"Funny again. Well, my mother swears I could make anything out of my LEGO blocks and that I always liked to draw. I studied architecture and art in high school, and got a scholarship for college. I spent my summers practically all over the world, taking photographs of dilapidated buildings. My dream was to restructure and bring life back to what was abandoned. What better way to use my own drawings and plans than with my dad's company. I love it."

"I hear you. That sounds amazing. It makes a difference when you really like what you do. I've been meaning to ask you if you have decided to go with us to New Orleans. We could really use your talent."

"I would love to go. We can plan it around the next Habitat for Humanity project. I think there's one either next month or August. That would be great."

"My girlfriend is getting married next month, so let me know what works for you."

We were having such a good talk that we didn't realize we had arrived. The neighborhood Malachi's aunt lives in was quiet and there was a pond at the entrance. The condominiums looked fairly new and the landscape was beautiful. There was a community pool, tennis court, and golf course towards the back of the development.

When we arrived at her building, his aunt was very welcoming. She met us at the front door, and gave Malachi a hug.

"Aunt Marie, I would like for you to meet Maiya." He turned to me and said, "Maiya, this is my aunt Marie."

"Pleased to meet you, Maiya. What a lovely name for such a beautiful girl."

"Thank you, ma'am. Nice to meet you as well."

"Please, chile, call me Aunt Marie." She grabbed me and gave me a hug. "We are very loving around here. I hope I am not invading your space." She laughed heartily.

I laughed. "No, ma'am. I mean, Aunt Marie."

"That's more like it. Now Christian, go unload the car and come back to enjoy lunch. I am sure you all are hungry after that long drive, yes?"

"Yes, ma'am, I'll be right back."

"Come, Maiya, help me with the table. I hope you like pasta and seafood salad. And I made some fresh lemonade."

"Oh, that sounds good. I can eat a whole bowl of pasta!" I followed her inside.

"Well, dear, there is plenty. Tell me. How was your trip? Has Christian been treating you well?"

"The drive was nice, yes. Malachi has been very nice to me. Really nice. He is so very thoughtful and pays attention to me. He is a good listener."

"He got that from his father. Now, he was a good man. And he took good care of his family. Christian is very fond of you, young lady, and he talks about you all the time. I was excited when he told me that you were coming along this weekend. Our family is very close, and we want nothing but the best for him."

"Truth be told, Aunt Marie, I am very fond of him as well.

We have spent quite a bit of time together, and he truly makes me happy."

"I'm glad to hear that. Maiya, dear, make yourself at home. The bathroom is the first door to your left. There is fresh linen on the table just inside. When you're done, just meet us in the sunroom."

"Okay."

The condo was very well decorated, and I felt at home immediately. Inside the bathroom, I washed my face and hands, and pulled my hair back into a ponytail. I could hear Malachi and Aunt Marie down the hall.

"She's a sweet girl, Christian. I really like her. Nothing at all like that ghetto girl, what was her name?"

"Tia. Don't go there, please. And yes, Maiya is sweet. I plan to keep her around."

I smiled to myself as I listened. I met them in the sunroom and helped to set the table. There was a marvelous view to the back of the sunroom with a lake surrounded by a trail. "Your home is beautiful. And the view is amazing. It kind of reminds me of home."

"Thank you, sweet pea. It's just perfect for me. You know the designer, of course," she said, looking at Malachi.

"I should have known."

"Yours truly, that would be me. I designed it so that the upstairs remained a part of the main floor, but like a separate guest house. It made it easier when my cousin Benjamin lived here, so that Aunt Marie could have her privacy."

"I love it. So is that where I'll be staying? The guest house?"

"Yes, you will. I already took your things upstairs and Aunt Marie has it set up quite nice for you. I'll show you around after we eat, then maybe we can catch a movie later."

"I'd like that."

"Christian, please honey, would you say grace?"

"Sure." We held hands. "Most heavenly and gracious Father, we thank you for this day. We thank you for this food prepared before us and ask that you bless it. We thank you for granting us travelling mercies and we are blessed to have family join together. Amen."

"Amen," we said in unison.

* * *

We ate our fill of seafood sandwiches and pasta salad, sipped on freshly squeezed lemonade, and shared our versions of how we met with Aunt Marie.

"Christian tells me you are a swimmer. He was checking you out at the gym, I understand?"

"Before you respond, Maiya let me first explain why she calls me Christian. I saw your puzzled expression when she first said it."

"I just figured it was a nickname."

"Sort of, but it's actually my middle name. It's my father's name, and since I look exactly as he did, Aunt Marie has always called me that."

"It's my term of endearment for him, sweet pea, and I can remember his father as if he were right here with us. He got his dad's talented gift of graphics and drawing, and used his gift just as his father did."

"How sweet. Well, to answer your question, yes, I am a swimmer and very active in the gym. Malachi may have been checking me out, but I was checking him out just the same," I said, laughing out loud.

"What's even funnier is that Maiya's swim cap was so tight that her eyes were squashed down and barely visible. But she was the sexiest in her one piece swimsuit, I must admit. And ATTITUDE! My, oh my!"

"You are so wrong," I responded.

We laughed.

"Well, it sounds as if you two like each other well enough. And I'm glad. Christian is a really good man, and he will make some lady a wonderful husband some day. Well, you two, I hate to run, but I gotta get to the market. Take whatever is left upstairs with you."

Our brief lunch ended as Aunt Marie began to clear the table. She had some errands to run and would be back much later. She had to gather all of her organic and natural hair and skin care products and other paraphernalia to sell at the jazz festival on Saturday. We promised to finish cleaning up and Malachi agreed to show me around her home.

"Have fun and if I don't see you tonight Maiya, make yourself comfortable. And if you need anything, and I do mean anything, do not hesitate to ask. See you later."

We exchanged hugs and then she left. Malachi showed me around downstairs, and then we were off up the stairs to my suite. There was a door that we passed on the way in that I paid no attention to. It looked like a door to someone else's apartment. There was even a doorbell and door knocker, with numbers above the door, 1170, in gold. Malachi used a key to open the door, and then handed it to me. On the other side of the door was a staircase that led to a small foyer and French doors.

It was gorgeous inside. The living room area had white leather furniture and deep rust walls that blended well with the amber-colored bamboo flooring. The kitchen had an island with bar stools and a subzero refrigerator. Down the hallway were two bedrooms, each with individual bathrooms. One of the bedrooms had a balcony that faced the lake. I couldn't wait to run around that. I was so excited as I looked around, I almost forgot Malachi was there. He came up behind me and wrapped his arms around my waist.

"Your speechlessness means you like it?"

"I love it! It's amazing. You did wonders with this place. And the bathroom. It's absolutely beautiful."

Malachi buried his face in my neck. "Mmm, you smell so good. Let me show you the balcony." He took my hand and led me towards the French doors. We stepped outside and onto plush chocolate carpet. It was a patio enclosure with a Jacuzzi tub off to one side. This could be my Shangri-la.

"How did you manage all this? This place is huge."

"It's about twenty-four hundred square feet, and I designed it with the well-deserved people in mind. It's low maintenance, and has everything a single person or couple could dream of."

"You are so talented. I'm very impressed. But who keeps the place up since your aunt lives downstairs? Does she rent it out?"

"She actually takes care of it herself. In the summer, she rents out to referrals only, but it has been vacant since last February. It's been paid for, so she likes to keep it available mostly for family and close friends. My cousin Benjamin lived here before he got married two years ago and his younger brother Jonathan stays here when he comes to visit. Aunt Marie is VERY particular about who stays here. And as you see, she has really put her time into decorating."

"I can see that. She has done a great job. And the location is great; not in a congested area at all. I like this place. I hope you'll bring me back here one day."

"Oh, I plan to, Maiya. Trust me on that. Now come over here." He reached for my hand and enveloped me into a strong hold. He kissed me, and I didn't want him to stop. When he released me, looking into my eyes, he said, "I am so glad I met you. It's like you are the missing piece to my puzzle of life. I don't know what our future holds, but I do know that I want you in it. I don't wanna pressure you, Maiya, but I would like for our friendship to be more. I wanna take this to another level."

"I don't really know what to say to that. I mean, things with us are so good right now, and I don't wanna mess up our friendship. I like you, Malachi. A lot. Sometimes I just get scared of not being able to make a relationship work. How about this: let's just go with the flow and see where that takes us. No expectations."

"That sounds alright to me. Sort of like dating with a purpose, somewhere down the road?"

"Yes, pretty much."

"Well, Maiya, I do play for keeps. And I do wanna be married some day. We will go with the flow and see where that leads. No pressure."

"It's a deal." I gave him a peck on the lips, and then said, "Now let's find a movie to go see!"

"I'll check right now and we can decide."

The phone was ringing in the next room.

"Maiya, can you get that?'

"Sure," I said, walking into the guest room.

"Hello?"

"Hey, girl, whassup? You were supposed to call me when y'all got there." It was Milan.

"How did you get the number here?"

"Malachi called me last week to ask me about some things to get for you to keep at the condo and he gave it to me then. Don't be mad. I called your phone twice, but your voicemail came on. So how was the drive? And what's the condo like?"

"Oh, girl, you would love it. Malachi is so talented. You've gotta come see this place. I feel like this could be my home away from home."

I heard Malachi call out to me from the next room. "Hey, Maiya. *Avatar* starts at six thirty-five. You wanna see that? Oh, sorry, I didn't know you were still on the phone."

"Excuse me, Lani. I'm a have to call you back."

"Okay, tell Malachi I said hello. Have fun. And you better not give him none. Keep that pocketbook closed."

"Girl, shut up. You need to be worrying about giving your own man some. Bye."

"We can see that movie, that's fine," I yelled to Malachi. "Let me grab a sweater and I'll meet you downstairs."

"Ok."

We drove to the mall and walked around holding hands until the movie was about to start. We shared a bag of popcorn and cherry Icees. We had a great time, and back at the condo, Malachi walked me to the door of my suite and kissed me. "I had a great time today. Get some rest 'cause we have a busy day tomorrow. Here's the house number so you can call me if you need to. I'll be right down here."

"I had fun, too. I'll be getting up early to run around the lake. Join me?"

"You bet. Good night."

"Good night." I closed the door and he turned to go downstairs. Left alone, I took in my surroundings. I took time to look through all the cabinets and closets and found lavender and vanilla scented candles. I lit them and brewed a mug of chai tea, after taking a long, hot shower. I wanted to be near Malachi tonight. For some reason, I just didn't want to be alone. I called him on the number he left me, and he answered on the first ring.

"Hello?"

"Hey you. I was wondering if you could show me how to work this stereo. I don't wanna mess up your aunt's stuff."

He laughed. "You sound so pitiful, Maiya. You are a trip, you know that? Why you just can't say that you wanted me to stay with you?'

I laughed. "I guess you got me. So, you coming or what?"

"Be right there."

Ten minutes later, there was a knock at the door and I ran to open it. Malachi had changed into some grey sweatpants and a white tee shirt and he smelled so good. Like he just stepped out of the shower. I was smiling so much on the inside, my face was beaming.

"What are you smiling so much about? Your damsel in distress story worked on a brotha." He followed me into the living room.

"I just didn't wanna end the night, honestly. I wanted more time with you."

"Well, I don't see anything wrong with that. So, what's the 'problem' with the stereo?"

"There's like two remote controls and all I get are these lights and nothing else."

"Give me a few minutes and I'll have it all set up. Anything in particular you wanna listen to?"

"You know how I love my jazz."

"Okay, cool. It smells good in here. What's that?"

"These candles I found in the linen closet. Lavender and vanilla. The scent is for calming and relaxing moods. You like?"

"I do. How 'bout Jonathan Butler or Gerald Albright?"

"Either one is good for me. You want something to drink? I have cranberry or apple juice, water, tea, lemonade. Dessert?"

"I prefer something hot to drink. Got anymore chai tea?"

"Sure. I can make you some." I walked over to the kitchen counter and set up another individual serving on the Tassimo. Malachi talked to me from the living room.

"So, Maiya, what more do you wanna know about me? I'm thinking you wanted to spend time with me for a reason. Whassup?"

"I like being around you. Your vibe just gets me. I enjoy your company and I wanna know everything about you."

"Hope you got some caffeine in your cup. Cuz I'm about to have you up all night long." We both laughed.

I walked into the living room with our cups of tea, and sat down on the floor near one of the speakers. Gerald Albright was playing and I was so relaxed. Malachi moved over to me and sat next to me. He put his face into my neck and inhaled. He kissed my neck and I could feel myself getting moist. Damn!

I turned to him and said, "What are you, like a vampire? You're always on my neck."

"I just love the way you smell, and your skin is always so soft. You're beautiful." He touched my chin and turned my face towards him, leaned in, and kissed me. His soft, full lips covered my mouth and we were lip-locked for a few minutes, with our tongues playing Follow the Leader.

Our breathing became rhythmic.

Intense.

He pulled me closer into his body and we lay back on the floor. I followed his lead and climbed on top of him, kissing him more passionate and stronger. His hands massaged my back and followed my spine down to my hips. I could feel him getting excited, and I was not ready for what could happen next.

I slowed down my kisses, and pulled away. I rested my head on his chest and exhaled.

"You okay, Maiya?"

"I'm good. Just wanna lay here with you."

We just sat and stared into one another's eyes, listening to the music. I could feel Malachi's heart through his chest, beating against my own. I didn't want him to leave, so I asked him to stay with me. We walked together to the bedroom, and the music continued through the speakers down the hall. We lay down and I fell asleep in his arms. Malachi kissed my forehead and held me tight as I fell asleep first.

We literally slept together that night.

In everyone's life, at some time, our inner fire goes out. It is then burst into flame by an encounter with another human being. We should all be thankful for those people who rekindle the inner spirit.
~Albert Schweitzer

ELEVEN

When I woke up in the morning, Malachi was already gone, but there was a note on the dresser.

RAN TO THE STORE TO GET YOUR RICE MILK. BRB. –
Malachi

I smiled. I got up and washed my face and brushed my teeth, and then put on my sweat shorts and tank top. I went through my bag and found my iPod and went to the kitchen to get a bottle of water and an Access bar. Walking back to the bathroom, I heard the doorbell ring and ran down the stairs. Peeking through the hole, I could see Malachi ready to work out. Damn, he is so fine.

Opening the door, I said "Good morning. How come you didn't take the key?"

"I didn't wanna invade your space or walk in while you were indisposed," he answered, laughing.

"We've been closer than close. You can invade my space anytime. I'll put the milk away and get my stuff. You ready to run?"

"Yep, let's go. I'll meet you out front."

I ran to put the milk in the fridge and grabbed my iPod and water bottle. My phone rang, but I ignored it. *It's nobody but Milan anyway, and I can catch her later*, I thought.

Outside, it was quite warm even so early in the morning.

"Okay, Maiya, show me whatchu got?"

"Oh, trust me, I got this. You've seen how I work out. Don't get it twisted; I ain't no punk!"

"Miss Tude. Gotta love it."

We walked to the back of the complex to run the course around the lake. I wanted to clarify my conversation with Malachi about a relationship so he would know where I was coming from. I was very much attracted to him, but I didn't want him to think I was a tease. Oh, I planned on giving him some, no doubt. But I just wanted to be in control of my cookies. OKAY!

"Malachi, I want to clear something up with you. I know I told you I wanted us to go with the flow, and whatever happens, happens. You are a perfect gentleman, and you are very sweet to me. So, it's okay to invade my space. I want you in it. You are welcome in my space."

"That's crystal clear to me."

"Like Ludacris says, 'when I move, you move.'"

"You're funny Maiya. Now let me see you move it around this lake. C'mon, let's go." He took off running as I fumbled with my music. Once situated, I caught up to him and ran at his pace. We ran for thirty minutes, and then walked over to the nearby lawn to do push-ups and sit-ups. Sweat was glistening all over his face and shoulders, and he took off his tank top to wipe his face. The six pack abs and defined triceps and biceps looked as if they were drawn by an artist. All I could think about was when we finally come together intimately, I would be whipped. Indeed.

*   *   *

Back at Aunt Marie's, we agreed to get showered and have breakfast. I wanted to know about our busy day and how I should dress, so Malachi just told me to dress casual.

"Where are we going?"

"Ever been fishing?"

"Eww, no. Gross!"

"Oh, come on Maiya. Stop being so prissy. It will be fun. Trust me. You said you were willing to try new things. I wanna take you to the pier, and then we can get some jet skis. What do you say?"

"I guess so. We'll talk over breakfast. What time are we leaving?'

"It's seven now, so how about nine, nine-thirty? I can whip up something quick for breakfast. You want me to come up or you wanna come downstairs?"

"I'll meet you downstairs. I can be ready by eight."

"Don't forget to bring your suit. I'll see you in a little bit."

*   *   *

The sun was beaming down on us as I sat on the cooler watching Malachi bait my line. We stopped earlier to get bloodworms and I begged him for rubber gloves. Even with them on, I still can't get past the sliminess of it. The worms reminded me of an old movie that Milan and I watched as little girls. SQUIRM. It was disgusting, and I just wouldn't touch it.

"C'mon Maiya, it'll be fun."

"Not. That's okay, I'll pass," I said, walking over to the edge of the pier. "I like watching you anyway." I smiled and stuck out my tongue.

He laughed. "Girl, you are so crazy. You better be nice to me before I throw this worm at you!"

"Oh, no, you wouldn't dare!"

"Then behave and follow along. Let me show you how to do this," he said, walking towards me with the tackle box and rods.

We spent the next few hours fishing. And although I was not interested at first, I had a great time. Malachi was a good teacher. And I caught two rockfish! Malachi promised to clean the fish so we could have it for dinner. He caught a good amount of fish and I couldn't wait to taste it.

After fishing, we got cleaned up at the boathouse and changed into our swim gear. Malachi bought wetsuits for us and we rented jet skis. We had so much fun on the water, racing and riding the waves. It was still early in the afternoon and we were getting hungry. By the time we got back to Aunt Marie's, we were famished. Aunt Marie made grilled chicken salads and corn chowder. It was delicious. We sat out in the sunroom after showering and enjoyed lunch.

"If you don't mind, I need to make some phone calls and relax for a bit. What time do we need to leave for the concert?" I asked.

"I wanted to clean the fish anyway. The concert isn't until eight, and we should leave around seven. Just call me. You know where I'll be." He leaned over to give me a peck on the lips and I cleaned up the dishes.

Upstairs I checked my phone for missed calls and messages. "You have three new messages. To listen to your messages, press one."

"First message. Hey Mai, it's me, Milan. Hope you guys are having a good time. I took Chloe to the park and we went to see my parents. Dad isn't looking too good, but he swears he's fine. Call me when you get a chance.

"Second message. Hey cousin, it's Jack. Did you give Milan my message? I'm up here this weekend to see her and she's not around. When you get this, call me. I'm staying at the Gaylord, room 420." *What is up with them*, I thought. I pressed 3 for delete.

"Third message. Hey, girrrrrl, it's me, Tion. I know you are out having your wonderful weekend with your man and all, but I really need to talk to you. There might not be a wedding after all. I think he's cheating on me. Call me."

Damn! I do not have time for all of this. I am tired of pulling out my psych lounge chair. I decide to dial Milan's number first. "Hey, girl, I got your message. What's up?"

"Oh, hey. Just visiting with mom and dad. Chloe wouldn't leave his side. Dad isn't looking too good. Mom says he's been sick for awhile, but he won't go to the doctor. I told her to make the appointment and I would go with him. He looks really bad."

"I'm sorry to hear that, Lani. I can't do much here, but let me know what you find out."

"Thanks girlfriend. I may take some time off next week anyway. Jackson wants me to come to Houston and…"

"Hold up, Lani," I cut her off. "Why are you even doing this? He's there in Maryland looking for you now anyway. He left a message on my phone!" I yelled at her.

"Oh, he is? I didn't know. I left my cell in the car. Maiya, look, please don't start with me and don't trip. I gotta take care of some things and I'll explain later. I told you, don't worry about me. Go have your fun and we'll talk when you get back. K?"

"Yeah, whatever. What about Tion? Have you talked to her?'

"Yeah, but I'll let her tell you what that's all about. It's that man of hers and she's stressing because he's been hanging out a lot lately. Look. Turn your phone off and do you. I've waited a long time to see my sister finally happy. So enjoy it. Now get off the phone. Tell Malachi I said hello."

"Bye."

"Buh-bye."

I shut my phone. I couldn't believe my ears. Milan is still seeing Jackson. And why did he fly all the way here to see her and she not know anything about it? Or at least that's what she wants me to believe. Something is up, for real. I know she's good at keeping secrets, but this is some scandalous mess. And why is Jackson tryna get me involved? And Tion ready to cancel wedding plans? I can't stand the rain! After listening to all that drama, I needed to relax in the hot tub. I changed into my bikini swimsuit and turned on the tub out on the balcony. I put on an old Maxwell CD and listened to him sing to me in Dolby surround sound, while sipping grape sparkling cider. I turned my cell phone off and drifted into relaxation mode. This is exactly what I needed. Relax. Exhale. Just be.

While relaxing and soaking in the hot tub, I thought about how much fun I was having here. It was calm and quiet; peaceful and serene.

I thought about Milan and the mess she was getting into--or had already gotten into. I always knew she had a thing for Jackson, but to go as far as having an affair. I don't get it. I just can't understand it. And I really don't want to try to, truthfully. Milan is a grown woman and she knows better, so I'ma just leave that alone. As for my cousin, well, I will tell him to leave me out of their scandalous affair. If he knows what's good for him, he would do what's best and leave BOTH women alone. Milan is crazy, but his wife Leesa is worse! And drama with Tion and Jabari. I'm afraid to even call her back, but if I don't, she'll keep calling until she finally reaches me. In the meantime, I gotta do me.

Listening to Maxwell put me in my zone. Before I knew it, I drank almost the entire bottle. I looked up to see Malachi through the French doors. I waved for him to step out.

"Well, aren't you all mellowed out? How is it?"

"Very nice. You should join me."

He gave me a naughty smile. "I don't have my swim trunks with me."

"Well, you can either go get them or just go without. It's up to you," I answered with a smirk.

"I guess the fish will still be there tomorrow." I watched him pull his shirt over his head, revealing the beautifully defined body I tried hard not to stare at this morning. He unbuttoned his jeans and let them fall to the floor. He stood before me in black boxer briefs, and I raised my eyebrows in excitement. As he entered the whirlpool, I moved toward him, standing front and center of his body. He moved in close to me, wrapping his arms around my waist until our bodies were skin-to-skin. His mouth overtook mine hungrily, and I swallowed hard. When we finally came up for air, beads of sweat had formed on his forehead.

We sank down into the tub together, and he came behind me so that my back was against his chest. I relaxed in his arms, feeling his heart beating against my back, while he hummed along with Maxwell singing *This Woman's Work*. I got lost in the moments and enjoyed this shared intimacy.

I didn't want this moment to end, but knew we had a concert to get to.

Malachi broke the silence between us when he spoke. "A penny for your thoughts, Maiya."

His words tickled me, and all I could do was smile and respond with, "I am just living in the moment here with you. If anyone would have told me a year ago that I would be right here, as happy as I am with you, I would have called them a liar. This is nice. I am just taking it all in."

He held me even tighter, and I could feel the strength of his arms holding on to me with such force. I knew we would be pressed for time for the concert tonight, so I asked what time would we be leaving. As much as I hated for this to end, I knew we had to leave. It would just make the curiosity in me peak for what our lovemaking would be when we finally had our time.

"I guess we should start getting ready, huh?" I asked, with a bit of hesitation.

He sighed, still holding on to me. "Yeah, I guess we should."

"Who is on the lineup for tonight?"

"The theme is 'For Lovers Only' and the performers include Gary Taylor, Will Downing, Kirk Whalum, and Mike Phillips. There's supposed to be a special guest appearance by Teena Marie."

"Looks like we are in for a treat."

"I would have to agree with you there. I guess we will have to get dinner there since we had appetizers at home. I didn't get a chance to fix you dinner like I wanted to."

"Mmm. I will let you make it up to me later."

"And trust me, I will make it up to you, and you won't be disappointed." He licked his lips like LL Cool J and I thought I would lose it.

Soul-mates are people who bring out the best in you. They are not perfect but are always perfect for you. ~Author Unknown

TWELVE

Tonight's concert was the absolute best I have been to in awhile. And it was definitely for the grown and sexy. The last time I saw Gary Taylor perform was at Constitution Hall, and Milan had gone with me. It was supposed to be a romantic night that turned into a girl's night out. Joaquin and I had an argument, and I didn't want the tickets to go to waste.

Romance was in the air tonight, and I was up for whatever the universe had for me and Malachi.

Riding in the car, Malachi reached for my hand and kissed it. I smiled at him as we drove to the Cheesecake Factory.

"I hope you enjoyed the show. That Teena Marie really showed off," he said.

"Indeed, she did. I know you wanted to be up there playing with the rest of the musicians. I could see it in your eyes."

"I was exactly where I wanted to be. Sitting right next to you." He smiled at me.

The rest of the evening we enjoyed more conversation and delicious cheesecake until I could stand it no more. I was so tired I could barely keep my eyes open. All I wanted to do was sip a cup of chai tea and go to sleep. Malachi walked me to my door, gave me a big hug and a kiss on the forehead.

"I see the sleep all in your face, baby girl. Get some rest. We don't have to be at the pavilion until ten. If you wanna run in the morning, let me know."

"What happened to you making it up to me?"

"Oh, my bad…I thought you were too tired for an all nighter, but I would love to stay with you tonight. Just waiting on you to let me know I can pass through the green light. Or proceed with caution with a yellow light," he teased.

"The light is green. You can move forward," I smiled up at him.

"Let me change my clothes and I'll be right up."

"You bet. See ya in a minute."

*   *   *

When we got inside, I did some quick thinking on how to get Malachi to make a move and take our intimacy one step further. After being so close to him in the hot tub earlier, I just had to have him. I knew that he didn't want to rush anything, but our chemistry was like fireworks on the fourth of July! Plus, he said he was gonna make it up to me, so I figured there was no time like the present. I didn't want him to think I was teasing him, because I wasn't. What I felt was for real. I was ready.

Malachi changed his clothes downstairs in his aunt's condo, leaving me upstairs to brainstorm. I called him on his cell to tell him to bring some fresh linen upstairs with him. While waiting for Malachi to return, I turned on the shower and began to disrobe. I caught a glimpse of his shadow in the doorway and put my plan into action.

"Oh, sorry, Maiya. I didn't know you weren't dressed. I brought your linen."

"Oh, it's okay, you just startled me." When I reached for the towels, I let my robe fall open and Malachi got an eyeful of my birthday suit.

"Oops! Didn't mean to do that," I said, pretending to be embarrassed. But, Malachi didn't look away.

Instead, he reached for my robe while pushing the door open the rest of the way and brushing the side of my breast. I was instantly aroused, as evidenced by my hardened nipples. As he pulled my robe off my shoulders, he looked me right in my eyes. He moved closer to me, and I met him halfway. Without hesitation, Malachi took my face between his hands and kissed me ever so gently, soft at first, then a bit more aggressive. He opened his mouth over my lips and very smoothly licked my lips before placing his tongue inside my mouth. I took in his tongue and we kissed for what seemed like forever. He pulled my body in close to his, and I could feel his heart beating against my breasts. He dropped my robe to the floor.

He first massaged my hips, waist and buttocks then took off his T-shirt and revealed the most beautiful pecs I ever laid eyes on. His flawless skin smelled of Burberry and sweat. He was turning me on, and I wanted him badly. The bathroom was beginning to fill with steam, and this made our bodies even hotter. I put my arms around his neck, caressing his head and playing in his hair, while kissing him. Malachi began sucking on my neck and caressing my breasts. I could feel his instant erection and got even more excited.

His breathing got even heavier and he whispered in my ear, "Maiya, I want you."

All I could do was moan in response because I knew I wanted him, too and would be giving in to him any minute. Malachi pulled away from me to unbutton his jeans and let them fall to the floor. He stood before me totally nude, and he was a sight to behold.

My mouth fell open when I saw how large he was. His Mr. Feel Good was the thickest and longest I had ever seen. *There is no way I would be taking all of that,* I thought.

He must have been reading my mind because he said, "Maiya, it's okay. I'll give it to you slowly, but you can handle it. I promise I won't hurt you."

He led me to the shower. He took my hair down and let it fall down my back. "You are absolutely beautiful," he said, and began kissing me again. I moved in to his body and started kissing him all over his mouth, neck, chest, and teased his ear with my tongue. He pushed into my body and I felt his thickness trying to part my legs. I wasn't quite ready to give in just yet, so I continued kissing and sucking his mouth. He grabbed my hips and butt and then took my breasts in both of his hands. Malachi began to suck and play with my nipples, and I moaned. I loved every minute of it. I wrapped my arms around his neck and he sucked even harder. I was getting so caught up in the moment that I almost forgot about protection. I pulled away.

"What's wrong, baby?" he asked.

"We don't have any condoms."

"Don't worry, baby, I got this. Just let me take care of everything. Relax." Then Malachi reached for my loofah sponge and creamy body wash. He washed my body from head to toe, shampooing my hair and massaging my scalp. He sat me down on the bench and took time with my feet and legs. He drizzled soap down my breasts and rubbed it in, and then stood me up to wash my back. He turned me to face the shower jets to rinse me off and he leaned into my back and I felt his thick hardness against my back. After he rinsed me off, I grabbed a soap bar and massaged his chest with it to work up lather. Then I used my soapy hands to rub his body down, making sure I gave special attention to his soldier. He moaned and breathed deeply as he became more excited. I got behind him and allowed him to stand in front of the water jets. I massaged his chest while standing behind him, running my hands down his six pack abs. Malachi turned around to me and picked me up. I straddled his waist as he kissed me and pushed me against the shower wall. I let out a sigh as we continued to tongue wrestle. I was almost done with the appetizer and was ready for the main course!

Malachi turned the shower off and got a towel. He dried my body off and pulled my hair back out of my face. I dried him off and ran to the bedroom. He picked up our clothes on the bathroom floor and was right behind me.

I turned to face him as he walked towards me, ready to pounce on me and take control. He pulled me into his arms and began kissing me again. He got my juices flowing. He walked me backward to the bed and slowly we were on top of it.

Malachi whispered to me, "Turn over."

On my stomach, he massaged my shoulders and back, down to my lower back and buttocks, then on to my legs and feet. Slowly, he parted my thighs and massaged my innermost part: the kitten. I couldn't help myself as I let out a low moan. Malachi began to slowly insert two and then three fingers inside of me. He turned me over on my back and I found myself opening my legs wider, inviting him to take control. Malachi was in between them, ready to enter. He leaned forward, and pulled a condom from his jeans on the floor. He took my hand to guide it to his rock solid penis. He was irresistible and I had to have it all.

Once he had the condom in place, he pulled my hips up toward his body. He leaned forward slowly and gently entered me. I winced at the initial thrust.

"Are you okay, Maiya? Do you want me to stop?"

"I'm okay. Don't stop."

"I'll go slowly, I promise. Just tell me if you want me to stop."

I placed my fingers over his mouth to quiet him, and pulled him closer on top of my body until we were skin-to-skin. When he was finally inside, I thought I would cry. It was a pain and pleasure all at once. I could feel myself tearing down below, but I didn't want him to stop. Malachi moved slowly and we found our perfect rhythm.

The moon shone through the window and exposed his perfect body in the light. Malachi buried his face in my neck and gave me pure ecstasy. We made love for a long hour. Malachi gave me pleasure I had never known, and for the first time in my life, I experienced an orgasm. My entire body shook and it felt so good that I cried. Malachi climaxed right after I did, and he held me so tight.

"You alright? I didn't hurt you, did I?"

"No, baby, I'm alright. That's never happened to me before."

"Don't worry about crying. I understand."

"Not that silly. THAT has never happened to my before!" I was referring to the orgasm.

"Oh. Oh, I get it. Are you serious? Never?"

"No. Never."

"Well, I'm glad I could be the man to take you there. In fact, I wanna be the ONLY man to take you there. Can you handle that?'

"What are you saying?'

"Like I said earlier at dinner. I only wanna be with you, Maiya. I wanna be your man. You know how I feel about you, and this is it for me. I wanna be where you are."

"That sounds really good and all, but how do you know for sure? I play for keeps."

"And so do I, Maiya. I wanna be kept by only you." I just loved the way he said my name.

And so it was decided on this evening that Malachi and I would be a couple.

Serious.

For keeps.

We kissed to agree on it.

And for the first time in a long time in my life, I was happy and ready to love and be loved.

*   *   *

Later the following morning, I got dressed and grabbed my water bottle and backpack. I left a note on the door to let Malachi know I was going to the high school for a quick workout. The school was about a half mile up the street from the condo, so I could do three miles in less than a half hour. We were going to part two of the jazz fest this morning and I didn't wanna miss a day of exercise.

It was a bit breezy outside, but the sun was shining. Quite a few people were out walking their dogs, and they nodded friendly in my direction. There were a few people already on the track when I arrived, but it wasn't congested. I put my earphones in, turned on my iPod, and did a few warm-up stretches. I jogged a warm-up lap at a quick pace, and then picked it up at the start of lap two. There was an interracial couple running together, and the woman was pushing a jogging stroller. I lapped them once around, then noticed the man sprint off ahead of the woman. I was done in twenty-seven minutes and thirty-two seconds flat, and then walked a lap to cool down. I noticed the couple again, and realized that they were staring at me. Finally, the young woman approached me, but I couldn't hear what she was saying so I removed one of the earphones.

"Good morning. I'm sorry, I don't mean to stare, but my husband swears that we know you from a site we worked on in Texas. Are you affiliated with Habitat for Humanity?" she asked.

"Good morning. And yes ma'am. I've been volunteering since I was in college. I worked on a site in Texas just last year. It was in San Antonio. My best friend and I came down," I answered.

The woman turned away to yell for her husband. "Honey, she was there. You were right." She beckoned for him to come over.

"I'm Lindsay, by the way, and this is my husband Benjamin. And this sleeping baby is our son Nicholas." She leaned over to the newborn baby in the stroller that barely looked a few months old.

"Nice to meet you both. My name's Maiya."

"Maiya, do you live around here? We've never seen you before today. And we would know. We're here running every day and we would remember a runner as good as yourself," said Lindsay.

"I don't live here, no. I'm just visiting from Maryland. A friend invited me here for the jazz festival this weekend and he told me about this track because I love to run. I really like it here, though. It's so quiet. And your son is adorable."

"Thank you. Honey, we should have Maiya over for the barbecue tomorrow," she said to Benjamin. "Our friends from Habitat will be there, and mom would just love you."

"Lindsay, we don't know her plans." He turned to me. "Excuse my wife, Maiya. She can be a bit pushy. Although I'm sure Momma would love to introduce you to my cousin. He just happens to be from Maryland, too, and he's planning to be here this weekend."

I couldn't help but burst into laughter. "Wait a minute. Lindsay and Benjamin? Your cousin wouldn't happen to be Malachi Taylor?"

They looked at each other with puzzled faces, and then turned to face me. "Yes," they said in unison. "How do you know him?" Lindsay inquired.

"That's the friend who invited me for the weekend. We came up Thursday night and we're staying at Aunt Marie's."

"Now, what a coincidence! He told me he was coming but he didn't mention a lady friend. Wait till I see him. You two are coming to the barbecue, right?" Benjamin asked, with a sly smile on his face.

Why does he keep looking at me like that? I thought.

"He has the whole weekend planned out, so I have no idea what's on the agenda for tomorrow. But, I would love to. As long as you promise to let me hold that beautiful baby of yours!"

"Well, I'm sure we are on his agenda. And you bet you can hold Nicholas. We'll be glad to have you. Here, Maiya, take our number and give us a call. And Aunt Marie would have matched you two up if it had not already happened," said Lindsay, as she handed me her business card.

"Thanks so much. I'll tell Malachi that I met you. And we'll definitely give you a call. Whatever plans he has, we will add you to them."

"Great! Can't wait to hear from you. Talk to you soon."

"It was nice meeting you both. I'll be in touch."

"It was nice meeting you, Maiya. I'm sure you and Lindsay will get along just fine. Just watch out, cuz she's a talker," said Benjamin, laughing.

I laughed too.

"Hey you better watch it Ben," screamed Lindsay as she punched his arm. "We'll see you later. Tell Malachi to call us."

"Okay, I will."

*   *   *

Malachi was in the shower when I returned, so I decided to join him. I fixed us cheese omelets and English muffins with a mug of Constant Comment tea. He said Aunt Marie had already left to pick up her friends to help her set up the tables at the pavilion. I told him about running into his cousin Benjamin, and his wife Lindsay.

"That is too funny! It's a small world. Did they tell you about the barbecue tomorrow? All the family is gonna be there. I'd like for you to meet them. My mother will be there too."

"Sure, I'd love to meet your family. I just hope your mom likes me, cuz I ain't got time for no momma drama," I said, laughing.

"Oh, girl, stop it. Momma will love you. She's really sweet. You'll get along just fine, you'll see. Trust me. I love my momma, but I'm not a momma's boy."

"Yeah, we'll see. So, what time does the show start?"

"The gates open at ten, but we have theater seats by the stage. My boys from SOUL will be there. Well, let me get the stuff that Aunt Marie left in the picnic basket, and then we can roll out."

"Okay, I'm right behind you."

While we gathered things to take with us, Malachi shared with me about his summers with his cousins Benjamin and Jonathan, and all the fun they had at camp. When Malachi moved to Maryland, he called every weekend to speak to his cousins. They grew up like brothers, and they stayed close over the years, even pledging the fraternity of Kappa Alpha Psi. Benjamin's son Nicholas is Malachi's godson, so this weekend was great because he had not seen the baby since he came up for his birth a few months ago. He loved Lindsay and Benjamin. After all the woman-chasing his cousin had done, Malachi was glad that Lindsay was the one to get him to settle down and change his ways.

"Don't get me wrong. I love my cousin dearly, but he was a straight up man-whore! Just a dirty dog."

"Seriously?"

"In the worst way. Jonathan and I were positive he always had at least three women at a time. And never got caught. He was a player, for real.

It was sickening. These women used to call me looking for him. Can you believe that he would tell me to lie and say he was working a project with me? I couldn't do it. We stopped speaking for a while over it."

"Really? How did you finally reconnect?"

"Aunt Marie called me when Benjamin got caught up in some drama. Some young girl tried to kill him and committed suicide after she found out he was cheating and got the other girl pregnant. He got stabbed pretty badly, and he asked for me to come down. I went to see him in the hospital and we talked. He apologized for everything and I forgave him. I asked him to go to church with me and he did. He rededicated his life to Christ and got baptized. Soon after, he met Lindsay and they started dating. They married a year later and the rest is history."

"He looks really happy." *Despite the sly smirks he was giving me today*, I thought. "I'm glad he got it together. His situation could have been fatal. I guess somebody prayed for him."

"And you know it. It was nobody but my Aunt Marie, that's the truth. I'm glad he made the change. He and Lindsay are personal trainers and owners of *HOT Body Fitness*. I'll take you there before we head back home."

"I would really like that. I guess we should get going."

"Okay, pretty lady, after you."

* * *

We had front row seats, and all of his friends from SOUL were there with us. The line-up was amazing: Boney James, Candy Dulfer, Eric Roberson, Lalah Hathaway, Rahsaan Patterson, Norman Brown, Kem, and Ledisi. We walked around and looked at art exhibits and found Aunt Marie's booth. I bought some natural soaps and bath salts from her (well, she wouldn't think about taking my money, so I put it in her apron when she wasn't looking!) We bought matching tee shirts and enjoyed our picnic lunch of turkey sandwiches, fresh fruit, cheese, and wine. We stayed all day, until about seven in the evening, then picked up some takeout Chinese food and went back to the condo to watch old Alfred Hitchcock shows.

We shared a bottle of White Zinfandel and Malachi massaged my feet. We relaxed in the hot tub on the balcony, listening to the latest Eric Roberson CD, with my favorite song he sings with Lalah Hathaway, *Dealing.* They had performed that song today. He signed the CD for us, and everyone thought we made the cutest couple.

Since we planned to go to church in the morning, Malachi didn't want to stay up late. We listened to the rest of the CD, and shared glimpses of the moon shining so bright on this night. I found myself smiling on the inside.

I was in bed and out as soon as my head hit the pillow.

What a day I had.

I was falling in love with this man and it felt so good.

I know God will not give me anything I can't handle. I just wish that He didn't trust me so much. ~Mother Teresa

THIRTEEN

The smell of freshly brewed coffee and baked biscuits permeated the vents and I was awakened by my voracious appetite. I washed up and grabbed my robe and slippers, heading down the stairs to meet Malachi and Aunt Marie for breakfast. I walked into the kitchen, following my nose.

"Good morning. It smells delicious in here."

"I hope you're hungry, sweet pea, cuz I have plenty to eat. I made biscuits, sausage, bacon, French toast, fresh fruit, fried potatoes, and grits. Freshly squeezed orange juice and a pot of coffee on the counter. Help yourself."

"You sure know how to ruin a woman's figure!" I laughed.

"Chile, please. I see how much you work out. Your figure is just fine. And I am sure you get no complaints from this man right here."

"You sure don't, auntie. Good morning Maiya. I hope you slept well last night," Malachi said, while walking over to me and kissing me on the cheek.

"I slept just fine, thank you. What time does service start?"

"It starts at ten, so you better eat up so we won't be late. You gotta be on time to hear my choir sing," said Aunt Marie.

"Aunt Marie directs the Women's choir, so we gotta get a move on since she needs to be there a bit earlier before the service starts."

"Well, let me grab something and take it upstairs, if you don't mind. I need to shower and I don't wanna rush."

"Just go get started and I will fix you a plate and bring it up. Is that alright?"

"That's just fine, ma'am, and thank you."

"Now, Maiya, I told you about that ma'am stuff. I insist you call me Aunt Marie."

"Yes, Aunt Marie."

"Now that's more like it. Hurry along now, we can't be late."

The ride to church was about twenty minutes up the street. Aunt Marie insisted I sit up front with Malachi. She told us she could see how we were making eyes at each other this morning. We pulled up to the church and let Aunt Marie out at the front door so she didn't have far to walk. While Malachi and I walked towards the church, I told him not to be offended because I preferred not to sit with him.

"It allows me to really focus and worship God and acknowledge His presence. We are friends and there is our attraction, and that takes away from what I am here to do. I'm not perfect and I do get convicted. I hope you understand."

"I respect that. I've never heard it put that way, but it makes sense to me. Whatever you prefer. I'll just meet you in the lobby after the service."

The service was great. Aunt Marie directed the choir and the pastor was eloquent and spirit-filled. It is a non-denomination church, and we worshipped like only a southern Baptist church could do. It was not traditional and I really enjoyed the Word. As I looked up, I saw Lindsay and Benjamin, both singing in the choir, and I was welcomed along with other first time visitors. We were out of church by eleven-thirty and I was introduced to the pastor, who is Marie's younger brother Felix. I also met Malachi's mother, who is very petite and soft spoken. She looked like she could be a bit saucy, though.

"It is nice to finally meet you, Maiya. My son has had nothing but good things to say about you. You are exactly how he described you. Absolutely beautiful."

"It is nice meeting you as well, Mrs. Taylor. Malachi didn't tell me that I would be meeting his family on this trip. But I'm glad I did."

"I'll let you in on a little secret. Malachi doesn't bring a woman home often to meet the family, so you must be some kind of special."

"Momma, please, don't embarrass me. We gotta get going anyway." He leaned down and kissed his mother on the cheek, and held her hands tightly. "I'll see you at Ben and Lindsay's, okay ma? Love you."

"Okay, son. Love you, too. Maiya, we must talk later dear."

"Oh, yes, ma'am. I look forward to it."

Lindsay walked over to us and gave me a hug. "You have the most beautiful voice I have ever heard! I love to hear you sing," I said to her.

"Oh, thank you. I have loved music all my life. It's what I do, besides run the business. It's enough to keep me busy."

"Do you need us to bring anything today?"

"Oh, no thank you. It's all taken care of." She turned to Benjamin. "Honey, can you get Nicholas for me?"

"Sure thing, babe. Maiya, good seeing you again. Christian, we'll talk later."

"Yeah, we'll see y'all later," said Malachi.

You can't run away from trouble. There ain't no place that far.
~Uncle Remus

FOURTEEN

MALACHI

I took the time after church to chill out before the barbecue, so I decided to make some smoothies and reflect on the morning service. What I really enjoyed about Maiya was how she listened attentively to my stories. I was open about being saved and living for the glory of God, and I wanted her to see that I had gotten through many valleys.

And having been down in life's valleys is how I learned to lean on God.

It was eating me up that I still did not know the truth to this baby with Tia, and I didn't wanna scare Maiya away. But I also didn't want her to think I was just tryna play her. I knew that being honest is the best answer. I just couldn't find a way to get the words out and explain it to her.

Aunt Marie walked in my room and knocked on the door. "Hey, baby, you doing alright in here? What's on your mind, son?"

"Nothing much. Just enjoying my time here with you and the family. I really hope that the family likes Maiya."

"You don't have to worry about that. She's a sweet girl, Christian, and seems to really be into you. Don't rush anything. Just have fun."

"Yeah, but you know how Momma can be sometimes."

"Your momma just wants you to be happy. Don't you pay her no mind about all this rushing to get married and have babies. She is looking out for her baby, and you know that, right?"

"I do know that, auntie, but Momma can be very pushy."

"And you should know that Maiya will be able to hold her own. Trust me on that. I have picked up on a lot of things, and I know you want to settle down, so give love a chance again. You can't dwell on the past, Christian. What's done is done. That is Tia's loss, and I am sorry you went through that. Your day will come."

"I know. Well, I'm gonna take a quick nap before we go to the cookout. Are you gonna ride with us?'

"No, baby. Lindsay wants me to help her with the baby while she sets up, so I am about to head over there in a few. I'll see you over there."

*   *   *

Two hours later, I was getting dressed when my phone rang.

"Hello."

"Hey you. I guess you don't plan on checking on me, huh?"

It was Tia.

"What do you want? And why are you calling me?"

"Don't you wanna know when the baby is due?"

"Girl, stop playin' games. I don't have time to be talking about this with you. What is Fred saying about all this?"

"Don't worry about what I told Fred. Just worry about you," Tia barked.

"You think this is some kind of game? This ain't even funny, Tia. You know just like I know that Fred can be the father of this baby. Look, I gotta go."

"Whatever, Malachi. Your little secret won't stay quiet forever. I can be sure of that." At that moment, Maiya called for me from upstairs. I tried to cover the phone so Tia wouldn't hear, but it was too late.

"Oh look at you with your new boo. How cute," Tia said sarcastically.

"Mind your business," I snarled.

"Well, did you tell your new boo about your baby on the way?" Tia asked.

"Girl, don't trip. Mind your business. And, stop calling my phone." I hung up.

I finished getting ready and ran upstairs to see if Maiya was ready. The door was ajar, so I let myself in and called out, "Maiya, you ready?"

"Hey, I'm in the bathroom. I'll be right out, give me a sec."

When Maiya emerged from the bathroom, I couldn't help but stare. She was wearing a white one-piece jumpsuit with the back out and strappy white sandals. Her hair was pulled back in a bun with a few strands framing her face. Her makeup was flawless and she smelled like strawberries.

"Wow, you look great, Maiya! But I said we are going to a cookout, not a restaurant," I teased.

Maiya laughed. "I know that, silly. But if you haven't paid attention to anything about me, you should know this is just me. If this is too much, though, I can change."

"No, no. You're fine. Don't pay me any mind. You ready?"

"Yep, let's go. Where's Aunt Marie?"

"Oh, she left not too long after we got home to help Lindsay set up..."

My cell phone interrupted me. I looked down. It was Tia.

"Well, aren't you going to answer it?" Maiya asked as she looked at herself in the mirror, smoothing down her hair.

"Um, yeah, give me a second." I stepped into the hallway.

"What!?" I barked into the phone with a ferocity I hadn't felt in a while. Tia was getting on my nerves.

"Don't hang up on me. Remember one thing, Malachi. You ain't running this. I am."

I almost lost my mind. This girl was tripping.

"You heard me. Hang up on me again, and see what's gon' happen. You got one more time, Malachi." And, she hung up on me. I was stunned.

"What's wrong?" Maiya asked, walking into the hallway, ready to go.

"Uh, nothing," I lied. There was no way I could tell her about Tia now. As we got in the car and headed towards Ben's house, my mind was racing. Would Tia really try to destroy my happiness in an attempt to get me back for not forgiving her and believing this baby is mine? I don't know. But, what I do know is that Tia is waging a war and if I have to fight, I'm bringing her down with me.

The thing about family disasters is that you never have to wait long before the next one puts the previous one into perspective.
~**Robert Brault**

FIFTEEN

MAIYA

The drive to Lindsay and Benjamin's house was about thirty-five minutes. Their home was situated close to the water, and their neighbors were a ways down the road. Malachi pointed out their *HOT Bodies* gym along the way. There were a lot of cars there when we arrived, and I felt a bit nervous not knowing anyone besides Aunt Marie and Lindsay. But I wore a happy face, and Malachi held me close to his side.

Once inside, Aunt Marie asked me to help them in the kitchen. Malachi excused himself and went out back to speak to his family, whom he hadn't seen in awhile. Lindsay came from the back and gave me a big hug. "Thanks for coming. I just put Nicholas back down, so he should be sleep for a bit. Let me show you around really quick. And introduce you to everybody."

"Okay," I said.

Lindsay took me on a tour of their home. It was gorgeous and huge. They had a gym in the basement, where they sometimes did personal training when not at work. There was a theater room with brown leather reclining chairs and a popcorn popper and mini bar. There were also a pool table and bar stools and tables all around. Her décor was very modern and I just loved it. There was a play area for the baby and an adjacent office.

"I have to keep busy and be able to watch the baby all at once, so this works out for me."

"How are you able to manage it all: home, work, everything?"

"It can be hectic, but Ben and I split up our work time. I set my own work schedule so that I can be at home with the baby during the week, and have my clients come here on the weekends. It works out great, especially since I am nursing Nicholas and I get to be home with him. Being in business for yourself is the best that you can do."

"You are right about that. I love being my own boss."

"That's right. You work for yourself as well. I am certain it will be perfect for you whenever you decide to settle down." She gave me a smirk.

"What's that look about?"

"Come on, Maiya. Everyone can see the way you and Christian look at each other. You two are perfect. He really likes you. And it's written all over your face as well. Admit it."

"Well, we are still getting to know each other, and our time together is very valuable. I do like him, that's for real. But..."

"No buts. Just go with the flow and see where you end up. Look, I went through drama. I think most women have. I got it bad because people thought I was just a dumb white girl looking for a successful black man. I grew up in a very diverse neighborhood, so I never judged anyone. Girls always thought I was tryna take their man. You live and you learn. And the Taylors are good people. You can't help who you love."

"I do know that. We should be getting back upstairs to help."

"I just want you to enjoy yourself. You are a guest, so just mingle. I will introduce you to everyone. And there are a couple of my friends from Habitat that are here, too."

Back upstairs, Lindsay and Malachi introduced me to everyone, and I helped put some of the food out. The backyard was large, and there was a pool surrounded by lawn furniture. Behind the pool was the barbecue pit and bar. I enjoyed myself tremendously, but still felt very awkward every time Benjamin looked my way. It was like he was flirting with me and undressing me with his eyes. One of his friends from Habitat shook my hand and remembered me at the site in Texas as well, but there were so many people I couldn't recall who he was.

The food was so good and I had to admit to Lindsay that I was surprised she cooked so well. She cooked better than some black folks I know! Even her deviled eggs tasted like my Aunt Rocsi's. She made her own barbecue sauce and did not accept help from anyone.

"I guess this white girl surprised you with her cooking, huh?" Lindsay teased me, walking in the house to check on the baby.

"Yeah, girl. You got me there. I am very impressed." I excused myself to the kitchen to get a bottle of water. No sooner had I come inside did I realize Benjamin was right up on me when I turned around.

"Hey, girl, let me help you with that."

"Um, that's okay, I can handle it. Thanks."

"Yeah, um, so listen. I was checking you out in service this morning. You looked really nice. Just as beautiful as I remember."

"What are you talking about?" I said, stepping back away from him.

"Why you acting like you don't remember? Texas? The hot tub? Me and my boys? We were gettin' down with the get down," he whispered. He leaned in and grabbed my arm. I could tell he had been drinking.

I backed away and looked out to see if Malachi or someone could see me, just to rescue me from this madness. "Get your damn hands off of me!" I screamed. "GET OFF OF ME!"

"Girl, quit playing. You know you want this. Just like you did in Texas!"

My mind was in a whirlwind. What was he talking about? I had never met him before in my life. Why was he so adamant that he knew me?

When I looked up, Malachi was coming through the sliding doors. "What the hell is going on in here? Ben, what is wrong with you?" Malachi shoved Benjamin so hard he stumbled backwards.

Benjamin let go of my arm and I moved away from him. "That's what I wanted to talk to you about man! She was the girl I told you about when we went to Texas that week. Remember?"

Malachi looked at me with a puzzled expression. "Maiya, what is he talking about?"

"I don't know what he's talking about. I don't even remember meeting him in Texas."

Another guy named Antwan walked in the kitchen. Benjamin turned to him. "Hey, Twan, don't you remember that hottie in Texas. Pretty eyes, jet black hair, named Maiya. That night in the hot tub with me, you, and Nate."

Antwan took off his sunglasses and stared at me. He looked me up and down and so long and hard that I felt uncomfortable.

"Man we was all pretty buzzed but I can tell you, that ain't her. She sure does look like lil shawty, but that ain't her. The other girl didn't seem this innocent, neither. She was a freak."

Benjamin looked at me, then at Malachi. "Christian, man, I don't know what this girl has told you, but it was her. She's a real freak. Man she let us do her all kinds of ways. Me and my boys. Matter of fact, she got a tattoo of a butterfly on her lower back. I can't forget looking at that when I was getting her from behind and...."

"Hold up, dog. You are NOT about to stand here and talk about my girl like that," said Malachi.

"C'mon, Twan, help a brotha out! Tell him!" yelled Benjamin, looking at his friend Antwan.

"Yeah, Twan, tell him and while you're at it, tell me about it, too!" It was Lindsay, shouting from the doorway. She had been in the back checking on the baby. We all just froze.

"Baby, that was a while ago. That was college."

"But, Benjamin, you were trying to get her to have sex with you now. I friggin' heard you! You are such a liar! How could you do this to me?" She ran out of the room.

"Baby, I would have asked you to join us but you were indisposed," Benjamin yelled after his wife. I was grossed out. His drunken behavior was embarrassing. I felt so bad for Lindsey and was totally humiliated. He wouldn't quit. "Just ask her man, look, Christian, I am sure you hit it by now. Don't she have a butterfly tattoo and the fattest ass--She moves fast!" Malachi hit him in the mouth so fast that before Antwan and I could blink, Benjamin was on the floor holding his face.

I ran out with tears streaming down my face. I had never been so embarrassed in my life. I bumped into Malachi's mother on my way to the bathroom. "Sweetheart, what's wrong?"

"I'm sorry Mrs. Taylor. I have gotta get outta here. Please, I am so sorry. Where's the bathroom?"

"Christian, what is going on in here?" Mrs. Taylor asked Malachi who was running after me. He grabbed my arm and pulled me into his arms. I began crying and just couldn't stop. Malachi hugged me protectively and rubbed my back. He explained to his mother what happened.

"It's Ben, Momma. He is back to his drama again, always stirring up trouble. And, drinking. He is a drunken mess, already."

I pulled back and dried off my face. I couldn't believe that this was happening.

"Hey, all you gotta do is look at the tat. It was her, man. It was her," Benjamin yelled from the kitchen.

The fury in Malachi's face was easy to detect. I pulled his arm so he wouldn't do any more damage to his cousin's face, even though Benjamin deserved having his teeth stomped in. Malachi restrained himself from going back into the kitchen and turned towards his mother.

"We gotta go, Momma. I'll call you later. Please tell Lindsay I'm sorry." He kissed his mother's cheek.

"Just take care of each other. I'm so sorry this happened. We will clean up this mess," his mother said. Malachi and I held hands and walked towards the car.

We rode back to the condo in silence. Rather, Malachi spoke and I just listened and nodded in response. I was really hurt. And embarrassed. The only thing I could think of was getting on the phone to call one person.

Milan.

I just cried until my eyes hurt. Malachi broke the deadening silence, touching my hand and apologizing. "I am so sorry Maiya. I had no idea he was coming on to you like that."

"It's not your fault that your cousin is a dog. I just knew something was up with the way he kept looking at me funny."

There was the silence again, and then he continued, "So, I guess from the description he gave that Benjamin was talking about Milan?"

"Yeah. She must have told him that her name was Maiya. We worked different crews and my ex was with me on the afternoon shift. We hardly saw Milan at night. I had no idea what she was up to."

"Again, Maiya, I'm sorry for all that."

"I guess your mother will REALLY write me off now."

"Momma's not like that. Trust me." His cell phone rang. "Hey ma." He turned to me and smiled, and I stuck my tongue out. "No, she's okay. I'll tell her. Okay. Call you later. Bye."

"What did she say?"

"She apologized for the drama. She wants us to have breakfast with her before we leave tomorrow. Is that okay?" He smiled at me again.

I smiled back at him. "That would be fine. Damn, I didn't even get to bring a plate of food home."

Malachi looked at me and laughed. "Don't worry. When Aunt Marie cleans up, she'll bring plenty of leftovers."

"Do you think it would be alright if I called to check on Lindsay? I mean, with everything that she heard, she may think that I really did mess with her husband."

"I don't think she'll mind. I do believe she heard the whole thing. Unfortunately, Benjamin hasn't changed his dirty ways. But, they will have to work that out. Maiya, I have a question for you."

"What's that?"

"You seemed to be a bit surprised about what you heard about Milan. How are the two of you so close yet you don't really know her at all?'

"I don't know how to answer that, honestly. It's apparent that Milan has a side that I never knew. I mean, she had her moments in college, but she got better. She changed." I was quiet for a moment, and then continued, "I guess she never really did change after all. This is madness."

"Well, I'm sure she'll give you a story on that. Just listen to her Maiya and try not to judge. There may be something underlying that needs to come to the surface. She will have to explain the situation with Ben."

"I know, but my thing is this: how do I know that she hasn't done that with somebody else? That really bothers me. Will someone else mistake me for the hottie who was gettin' down with the get down?" I got quiet and turned to look out the window. Tears rolled down and stained my face with mascara, and I folded my arms across my chest.

Malachi spoke softly, "It's okay, Maiya. Everything is gonna be okay. Trust me. Hey, you wanna go get some Cold Stone ice cream. It usually makes me feel better when I wanna take my mind off things."

He was a man after my own heart. "You bet I do." Nothing that a Love It portion of Mint Mint Chocolate Chocolate Chip couldn't help to ease my mind.

I looked over at him and smiled.

And I did believe that everything was gonna be okay.

Eating ice cream and laughing outside of the Cold Stone Creamery, Malachi and I moved on from the drama at the barbecue and looked forward to more time together. I had to admit to him that I was glad that I decided to get away from home and come down here with him. He promised to bring me back for Hampton's homecoming in the fall.

We decided to walk around the lake once we got back to the condo and just people watch. "This has been a great trip for me, too. I have really enjoyed your company, and the band can't wait to see us together again real soon. You can really hold your own. And just for the record, I didn't think for a second that you and Ben had hooked up. I am just sorry that I did not pick up on his subtle hints of flirtation."

"Thanks for the compliment. And let's not talk about him anymore. I plan to speak to Milan about him once we get back home. I had to turn my phone off so my girls would stop calling and bugging me with all their drama. It makes me wanna stay here another whole week!"

"I wouldn't mind that at all. How about you make that call to Lindsay and check on her. I'm gonna give momma a call back and come see you before I go to bed, if that's alright."

"Sounds good to me. See you in a bit."

You don't choose your family. They are God's gift to you, as you are to them. ~Desmond Tutu

SIXTEEN

I dialed Lindsay's number and she picked up on the first ring. "Hello."

"Hey, Lindsay, it's Maiya."

"Oh, hey, Maiya. I thought you were Ben calling. He left out and hasn't come back. It got really ugly after you guys left."

"I am really sorry about all that. Look. I just wanted to call to thank you for having us over and to apologize for the drama. I never got involved with Benjamin, Lindsay, and to be honest with you, I don't even remember him at the Habitat trip last summer. My ex-boyfriend was with me on that trip, and I had enough drama with him that I didn't even think about going out with anyone else. I don't know what else to say."

"Unfortunately, I always knew Ben loves women. And I did not think you were involved with him. He is just not a one-woman man. He has to have his hands in all of the cookie jars. We have built so much together, and with the baby now, I just don't know what to do. Counseling. Separation. Child support. Divorce. It's just all too much right now."

"Look. I have never been married before, so I can't give you any advice on that. What I will say is you have to decide if your marriage is worth saving. Do you love your husband enough to try to get through all of this? Plus, Ben seems to have a drinking problem. How much of this is alcohol related? No one knows your heart but you. Trust in God and ask Him to guide you. He won't steer you in the wrong direction. I don't even know you but I can sense you have a sweet spirit and you know the Lord. He will work it out, if you let Him. I'm not gonna keep you. I've got to finish packing since I leave to go home tomorrow, but do not hesitate to call me and I promise to come back for a visit."

"Thanks for calling to check on me Maiya. You are a good person. Malachi picked a good friend in you. I wish you two the best with whatever happens. And if a love connection does not happen, you will always have a good friend in him. He is very special. And I will pray. If there is one thing I do know, it is the power of prayer. Have a safe trip and I will be in touch. Goodnight."

"Goodnight."

After hanging up, I started packing up my things and fixed a pot of chai tea. I knew Malachi would be up here, and he would share some with me. I turned on Rahsaan Patterson's *After Hours* CD. I just needed to hear *The One for Me*. That was how I was feeling about Malachi. It may seem a bit fast, but why fight what I am feeling? I cannot deny my attraction to him, and his obvious attraction to me. Who can put a time limit on love?

I decided to put on my bathing suit and relax in the hot tub. I brought my mug of tea on the balcony with me, and turned to see Malachi coming through the door. Our eyes met and I asked him, "Are you joining me out here?" He held out his shorts in confirmation and I reached for his hand to take and he followed me.

He and I sat back in the hot tub and didn't speak at all as the music filled the air. This time, I closed my eyes and swayed as Malachi's hands explored my body in the hot tub. He slid his strong hands down my shoulders, pulling the straps of my bathing suit down. His mouth began kissing my neck first then sucking on my nipples as the water jets pulsed around us and the darkness outside covered us softly. I ran my fingers through his hair as he pulled me onto his lap, opening my legs so I could straddle him as his face nestled at my breasts. I reached down to pull his face up, lips finding lips as we hungrily kissed each other, finding solace in each other's sweetness. As we moved our lovemaking from the hot tub to the bedroom, our release powerfully ignited an energy that made me feel even closer than I could have ever imagined being with anyone ever before.

Another night in his arms was just the remedy to my crazy day.

*   *   *

I had planned on getting up early to go running, especially with all the drama from the afternoon before, but decided against it and slept in instead, with Malachi's arms wrapped around me. I sent Milan a text to let her know that I would be home this evening and that she could bring Chloe back to my place. She never responded. I showered and got dressed, and placed all of my bags by the door.

"Morning, babe. You ready to go?"

"Yep. As ready as I'm gonna be. Is Aunt Marie around? I wanted to tell her goodbye."

"She wanted to ride with us over to mom's. I'm gonna drop her off at Lindsay's to watch Nicholas. She's waiting downstairs for us now."

On the ride to Lindsay's, Aunt Marie welcomed me to come and stay with her whenever I needed to. "My home is your home, Maiya, whenever you need a place. Think of it as your home away from home. I hope you enjoyed your stay and I hope to see you again real soon." She got out of the car and I followed.

I gave her a hug and she whispered in my ear, "That nephew of mine is very fond of you, sweet pea. Don't let him get away." She kissed my cheek.

"Thanks for everything, Aunt Marie. I will be back to see you real soon."

Malachi hugged Aunt Marie. "Thanks, auntie. You sure know how to make us not wanna leave."

"I'll see you soon, Christian. Take care of that young lady there. She's one to hold on to."

"Oh, trust me. I plan on it." He turned to me and smiled and we were off down the road to his mother's house.

We arrived for breakfast around nine a.m. Malachi let us in. "I still have my house keys as you can see. I wouldn't have it any other way." He laughed.

"And I'm sure neither would your mom."

"Hey, ma, we're here," he yelled out.

"I'm out here on the patio. Be right there."

It smelled delicious in the kitchen. And I was so hungry. Malachi pulled a stool out for me to sit at the kitchen counter, and then sat right next to me.

Mrs. Taylor came in with a basket of fruit in her arms. "Good morning lovebirds. How are you two doing this fine day?"

"Momma, let me help you with that?" Malachi took the basket from her. "Lovebirds, momma. Come on now." She grabbed my hands and squeezed tight, turned to Malachi and kissed him on the cheek.

"Christian, I just call it like I see it. It's written all over this young lady's face. Stevie Wonder can even see that!"

I couldn't even hold back my laughter. And I also knew I was blushing.

Malachi turned to me and said, "I told you not to pay her any mind. She just likes to hear herself talk."

"Now, you stop it, chile. I only speak the truth. And I can always see through people. You can't deny it, sweetie. You've got feelings for my son."

"Momma, don't put Maiya on the spot like this. You always…"

I interrupted him. "No, it's okay. Your mother's right about me. I am fond of you, and you know that. It doesn't embarrass me at all." I smiled at him.

"See. I told you. Can't fool me. Just like you couldn't fool me with that ole scalawag you were about to marry."

"Momma. Don't do this now!"

"Oh, sorry baby. Don't mean any harm, Maiya. Please forgive me." She turned away from Malachi and rolled her eyes. "Now," she continued, "I made some waffles, and I have fresh strawberries and blueberries from my garden. I was picking them before y'all came. So, get washed up and I'll clean the berries and then we can eat."

Malachi walked me down the hall to the bathroom. I stopped along the way to look at photos on the wall. There were pictures of Malachi in his youth playing baseball with a man, who I later found out was his father; in his ROTC uniform as part of the color guard; in his high chair with food all over his face; and a photo of him kneeling at his father's headstone. There were other photos of him all the way up through college, with his fraternity brothers at a step show, and on a boat in the Caribbean. He was such a handsome young man.

"There's the bathroom. Later, I'm sure Momma will talk to you in detail about these photos."

At the breakfast table, Mrs. Taylor reached for our hands. "Before we bless the food, I do want to say to you, Maiya, welcome to my home. It was a pleasure meeting you. I also want to apologize if I offended you or embarrassed you in any way. It's just that….well, how can I put this? I've waited a long time for my son to settle down, and I see something different in you. A special kind of different. So, please don't take it personal. I like you." She squeezed my hand.

"Thanks for having me. And I accept your apology, ma'am, but you have not offended or embarrassed me in any way. Besides, Malachi warned me about you, and honestly, you remind me of my Aunt Rocsi."

"Well, now that we've cleared the air, shall we?"

We bowed our heads and Mrs. Taylor blessed the food. "Gracious Father, on this day we come to you with humble hearts, to say thank you for all that you've done. We thank you for being our Provider and Protector. Right now we ask that you bless this food for the nourishment of our bodies. Amen."

"Amen," Malachi and I repeated in unison.

"So, I've got waffles and fluffy scrambled eggs, fresh fruit and whipped cream, maple turkey sausage, and orange juice. Enjoy."

During breakfast, Mrs. Taylor shared with me a lot of how she

spends her time as a volunteer at the youth community center that
Malachi used to manage. She was responsible for teaching etiquette,
hygiene, and crafts to the younger children and classes on making
responsible decisions, healthy living, avoiding and dealing with peer
pressure, and teenage pregnancy and STDs for the older children. She
had also invited Lindsay to start a music program for those who were
interested in singing. Mrs. Taylor was very instrumental in the lives of
the youth, and was genuinely concerned for their welfare.

She also shared with me a program she worked on with a dynamic
life coach and motivational speaker out of New York named Nathan
Seven Scott. He is responsible for G.O.A.L., Girls Only Academy for
Leadership, a program established to empower young women. Within
that program, DIAMONDS emerged. Following teen women through
their pregnancy and allowing them to discuss issues they deal with
on a daily basis, the end result is to be recorded and shared among
YouTube.

"It is just getting started, but Nathan has really been instrumental
in getting this together, and I believe in it. The other children in our
afterschool program don't necessarily come from a hard knock life or
broken homes, per se. They simply have nothing to do afterschool and
would normally fall prey to drugs and sex due to lack of supervision. I
love these kids and look forward to my time with them."

"That is really awesome, Mrs. Taylor. How do you get your funding
with all that you offer?'

She pointed to Malachi. "Christian was a part of the center as a
child and he always said he would be a part. As a volunteer when he
was in high school, he started a sports program. He keeps the center
together financially."

"It's my way of giving back. Momma always said 'you can't take it
with you.' My dad and I always enjoyed our time with the children, and
I knew I would always belong here."

"Yep, and Christian found a way to keep the older children interested
by starting a mentoring program. We started a teen job summit that

prepares them for the workforce, helps them interview, write resumes, etc. A lot of them even come back after they have gone away to college to speak on different topics. It gives back to the community ten-fold." She paused. "So, Maiya, tell me more about your work with Habitat for Humanity. Christian says you are a volunteer."

"My friends from college get together and volunteer our time with Habitat. We started when we were pledging a sorority at Grambling State University and still make time to help out. We even teamed up with the Red Cross for disaster preparedness training. It's our way of giving back to the community that so richly welcomed us and helped us learn a lot about culture in Louisiana. That's how Lindsay recognized me. We did some work in Texas last year."

"Oh, I see. You sound like a very busy woman. Yet Christian here was able to steal you away for a few days." She winked at Malachi.

I looked at him and saw him wink back at his mother. All I could do was laugh. "You two are a team. I can see that. And nothing can pretty much keep me away from jazz and Rahsaan Patterson." I winked at both of them, and we all laughed. I enjoyed breakfast with Malachi and his mother, and she too, apologized for Benjamin's behavior.

"Now I love my sister-in-law Marie dearly, but I have always told her that boy of hers was nothing but trouble. Been chasing after women since I can remember. Women just going crazy over him. I swear he must have a gold mine in his drawls!"

I could not help but laugh at her. "You are too much, Mrs. Taylor."

"Yes, she is, isn't she? Benjamin just loves women. All women. He just can't get enough of them. I always told him to slow down, or one day it would catch up to him. He has had much drama in the past; you would have thought he learned his lesson. He still hasn't learned ma, and that's too bad."

"Yeah, well, some people just weren't meant to be married. He also has a drinking problem. He's not too different from people I know," I said, thinking of Milan.

Malachi's mom turned to me and said, "Well, I hope breakfast was enough for you Maiya. You can take the rest of the berries home with you, if you like."

"Thank you, ma'am. Everything was wonderful."

"Christian, do you mind loading the dishwasher for your mother? And take the small cooler to put the fruit in. I'd like to take Maiya out to the backyard and show her my garden."

"No problem, momma."

Mrs. Taylor led me out the sliding glass doors to an enclosed patio. We walked straight through to another set of French doors and outside to her garden. There were roses, blackberry and canna lilies, hyacinths, tulips, dahlias, shrubs and trees; it was an arboretum. Stone pavers adorned a pathway and a hammock attached to two large maple trees. Off to one side was where her berries grew. Strawberries, blackberries, raspberries. In her vegetable garden, she had cucumber, tomatoes, onions, sweet potatoes, and cabbage. It was lovely and I didn't want to leave.

Her warm and welcoming spirit gave me a feeling of belonging as I walked through her garden, breathing in all that I could. A stone birdbath and hummingbird nectar sat in the center, separating her vegetable and fruit garden from her flowers. Nestled just to the east of the hammock was a small pond filled with koi. Mrs. Taylor had her own Shangri-la. I could sit back here all afternoon.

She broke the silence. "Lovely, isn't it?"

"It is exactly that. There is such a peace. A calm and quiet that is soothing. All I can say is wow. It makes me never want to leave."

"Maiya, you are welcome here anytime you like. I truly hope you will come back and visit. You are someone I would enjoy having in my son's life."

I was immediately quiet and she must have sensed my uneasiness, so she touched my arm and spoke softly. "Maiya, my son is a good man. I don't meddle in his business, but he is my only child. I see the way he looks at you and you at him. He has good things to say about you and he is very fond of you. And if you could have seen the look in his eyes when my nephew showed off at the cookout…. Well, that was enough for me.

Don't let him get away, Maiya, that's all I'm saying. And I promise. You won't regret it." She smiled and let go of my arm.

"Thanks for sharing that with me Mrs. Taylor. And thanks for having me in your home."

"Do come back soon. We'd love to have you."

We embraced, and I had a feeling that we would see each other again soon. We walked back inside and Malachi was waiting with the cooler in one hand and a bag of mixed berry muffins in the other. I reached into my purse and pulled out a photo. It was the one taken of me and Malachi at the marina. I handed it to Mrs. Taylor.

"Here. I want you to have this. So, when you think of Malachi, you'll look at this picture and smile."

"Thank you, Sweetie." She hugged me, and I whispered, "I'll think about what you said."

"Bye now. Be safe on the road. And Christian, let me know y'all got home safely."

"I will Momma. Love you." He hugged her and she kissed both of his cheeks.

She walked with us out front and mouthed to me 'remember what I told you'. I nodded in the affirmative and waved good bye.

*   *   *

I slept most of the ride home, only opening my eyes to readjust the visor. We made a stop to use the restroom, and then I was back in my seat, fast asleep. I was awakened when Milan sent me a text stating that Chloe was safe in her room at my place and that she would call me later. I rolled my eyes and didn't respond, but shut my phone and went back to sleep. When I awakened, we were in front of my building and I was starving.

"Hey Sleepyhead, you're home."

I yawned. "Excuse me. I must have really been tired."

Malachi took my bags inside and I called out for Chloe. She was in her room and jumped around when she saw me come through her door. I scooped her up and headed for the door to take her out.

"Maiya, wait, I'll walk out with you."

"You're not gonna stay? You don't wanna get a bite to eat?"

"Yeah, that's cool. I just figured you wanted to unwind."

"With all that sleeping I did, I am wound up. You wanna just order some Chinese takeout? I'd really like it if you stayed." I was flirting with him, and he knew it.

He smiled and said, "I would love to stay. Tell me whatchu wanna order and I'll call it in."

"Okay. The menus are in the top middle drawer on the island. I want Singapore noodles with shrimp and chicken, shrimp toast, and a shrimp egg roll. Get me a cherry Coke, too. I wanna take Chloe outside and see if Milan is home. I'll be right back."

"Okay."

Chloe was excited to be out chasing squirrels. I sat on the bench in front of my building and watched her run around. I didn't see Milan's car in the parking lot, so I figured she must still be at work. I dialed her office number.

"Douglass and Vaughn Physical Therapy Services. Shane speaking. How may I assist your call?"

"Hi Shane, it's Maiya. Is Milan around?"

"Hey Miss Girl, how you doing? No, I ain't seen that chile today. She called in saying she was sick and left us with all this work. You know she wrong for that."

"Sorry, Shane. I just got back in town. I'll try her cell. Thanks."

"Unh-unh! Her phone goes straight to voicemail. She is MIA, honey!"

"Shane thanks. I'll be in tomorrow morning. Take the day to rearrange the schedule for the rest of the week, and I will make sure you are taken care of. Thanks for holding down the office."

"You're welcome. That's how I do. Plus, I'm glad you got away. You always are taking care of folks!"

"Thanks, Shane. Just call me if you need me. Here's my cell. 9-4-3, 9-3-0-3. Anytime, Shane. I mean it."

"I will, but we should be alright this evening and tomorrow. I'll see you in the morning. Just hook a brotha up on a nice room when we go to New Orleans."

"I got you."

Malachi was walking to the car as I was coming up the stairs. "Hey, I'm going to pick up the food and stop in to see Janet. I left the door unlocked. See you in a minute?"

I nodded and ran up the stairs with Chloe at my heels and used my spare key to open Milan's door. As soon as I walked inside, the smell of weed hit me like a ton of bricks. The place was a mess. Bottles of cranberry juice and Grey Goose were all over the living room floor. Shells of sunflower seeds were scattered all over the hardwood floors. A trail of clothes led me down the hallway to Milan's bedroom. I could hear the moans and groans of a man and slurping sounds. I didn't need to venture any further. Milan was getting her freak on and I didn't wanna stay around for the show.

I hauled outta there with the quickness and left a Post-It note on the fridge:

I'm home. Call me. Mai.

I couldn't believe Milan would be as careless as to shirk her responsibility as a manager and not show up to work. All for a man! Something is going on with her.

I knew it would take Malachi at least a half hour before he got back, so that gave me enough time to shower and put on my comfort clothes. I decided to throw a load of clothes in the washing machine as well. We had spent the past five days together, and I was enjoying every minute of it.

I could get used to having a man in my life again.

Malachi returned with the food, and also brought me an iced chai tea from Janet. I set up the trays in the living room for us to eat and watch back-to-back episodes of CSI. I asked Malachi if he was due back to work the next day, but he said when he checked the office earlier, nothing was going on.

"Did you need me for something, Maiya?"

"Well, no, not really," I lied.

Malachi knew I wasn't being truthful. "Come on, Maiya. You know you can't lie. What is it?"

"I was just thinking if you didn't need to be at work, maybe you could stay here tonight. I mean, unless you have plans or something."

"You are really something else, you know that?"

"I know. So, you gonna stay or what?"

"I'm not going anywhere unless you tell me to."

I smiled.

Malachi stayed with me, falling asleep on the couch. I covered him with one of my crocheted Afghans, kissed his cheek, and crept off to bed.

Weather is a great metaphor for life - sometimes it's good, sometimes it's bad, and there's nothing much you can do about it but carry an umbrella. ~Terri Guillemets

SEVENTEEN

B ack to work early as usual, I needed to get plans started for the trip to Louisiana. Malachi had his staff making adjustments to the plans they developed and we were travelling in two weeks. There was a gala planned to recognize our team and the mayor and state senator would be there, along with Hollywood celebrities who were instrumental in bringing attention to the horror of Hurricane Katrina.

"Good morning, Miss Vaughn. Glad to have you back. You were missed."

"Thanks, Kari. I got in early to look over the plans for New Orleans. I sent you the details, so you can go ahead with the final list of names and make the travel arrangements."

"Okay, I'll get right on it. Did you have a nice time?"

"Oh, I had a wonderful time Kari. It was so beautiful and the festival was great! I went fishing, got on jet skis, and made new friends. I can't wait to go back!"

"Well, I'm glad you had a good time. You have a glow about you. You look great! Whoever this man is, he's got something on you!"

"Well, Kari, he is special. Now get back to work, young lady. We can talk later."

She laughed and said, "Yes ma'am."

I walked back to my office just as my office phone rang. I could see on the caller ID that it was Malachi.

"Good morning, Mr. Taylor."

"Hey lady, how's it going?"

"Everything is well. You left without saying anything."

"Sorry about that. I got a call from my office manager at five a.m. and he needed assistance so I had to get back home to get some stuff off the computer. I didn't wanna wake you, but I left you a note on the kitchen counter. I guess you didn't get it?"

"No, I didn't."

"I took Chloe out before I left and I saw Milan and her fiancé as I was leaving. She was pretty drunk and they smelled like weed. She didn't recognize me and her fiancé looked upset."

"That doesn't sound like David. Was he tall, brown skinned, with curly hair?"

"Not sure about the hair since he had on a hat, but he was about my height and your complexion."

I got quiet for a moment.

"Maiya. You there?"

"Um, yeah, I'm here. That wasn't her fiancé though. That was my cousin Jackson."

"Oh, I see. Well, I'm gonna get some more of the plans looked at and everything should be completed by Friday. I will be flying out earlier than you guys, but I'll let you know where I'm gonna be staying."

"That's fine. I'll talk to you later then."

"Is everything alright, Maiya? Your whole tone is different."

"Everything's good. Look, I gotta go handle something. Call me later, okay, baby?"

"Okay, then. Bye."

I hung up quickly and dialed Milan's home number.

No answer.

I dialed her cell phone. It went straight to her voice mail. I didn't leave a message. I called upstairs to her office. It rang several times before it was answered.

"Good morning and thank you for calling physical therapy. This is Shane, how may I help you?"

He is always so dramatic.

"Shane, it's Maiya. Is everything alright?"

"Everything is fine thanks to my help in finding agency work. I gave my regular assignments to the PRN staff so I could do hydrotherapy. Have you talked to Miss Milan?"

I couldn't even tell him what I discovered at Milan's condo. "No, Shane. I haven't spoken with her. She's not answering her phone either. If you see her before I do, tell her to call me."

"I will. I gotta run, Maiya. My class begins in twenty minutes."

"Okay, thanks. I'll talk to you later, then. Bye."

I buzzed Kari on the intercom to tell her I was stepping out.

"Kari, I'm going upstairs to see how things are moving along with your cousin's renovations. If Milan calls, tell her I need to see her, please."

"Okay, I will."

Upstairs on the third floor, Kendra was setting up for clients. They agreed to expand larger than originally planned since her clientele had increased. The business was booming. The latest expansion was a spa tub and massage suites. Those rooms would be complete in just under two weeks.

"Hey Kendra, you busy today?"

"Good morning. Yes, busy today and every day, but I love it. I have a full schedule. I had to hire an additional massage therapist and two estheticians. Just let me know when you're ready to be pampered. It's on the house, of course."

"Of course, thank you. I just wanted to check in with you and see how you've been making out."

"It was good to see you. Just let me know when you're ready."

"Alright. Take care now."

I went back to my office and took care of a few things before I ordered lunch for the office. Before long, I realized how fast the time had flown. It was five p.m. I made my way to the Arena for a swim, but was stopped in the parking lot by Milan. She had on dark sunglasses and was leaning up against my car, wearing pink scrubs and a white lab coat.

"Hey, Mai. I didn't see your note until this morning. I was just about to leave you a note on your windshield. Glad you're back safe."

I just cut right to the chase with her.

"Cut the bullshit, Milan. Where have you got the nerve to leave your staff to figure stuff out on their own? What is going on with you?"

"I don't have time for one of your extreme 'how to be classy' lectures. I just came to get a few things from my office. I gotta get outta here."

"What's going on Milan? And where are you going?"

"Look, me and Jackson are taking a trip to Vegas. I need to get away from here for a while. Just try to understand, Maiya, please!"

"Understand what? Wait a minute. What is going on? We're in the middle of this big project and you are planning your wedding. You're going to Las Vegas? Please, what am I missing?" I asked, confused beyond belief.

Milan shrugged and threw her head back, rubbing her temples.

"Shit, I don't know what to say. Everything is happening so fast. I don't know what to say. I love him. I love Jackson, but, most importantly, there is stuff I have to tell him. A whole lot of shit, Maiya. You just can't understand. But, trust me. I got this. Everything will be ok," she said. She sounded like she was trying to convince herself.

"Love? Love? Hmm, I would bet that that is the last thing you have a clue about," I said. I didn't realize how angry I was becoming. "Do you realize that your sexcapades and scandalously slutty behavior has impacted me, out of all people? I just had the worst experience of my life thanks to you and you have the nerve to say you love someone? You cheat on David, fool around with my married cousin and fuck slews of men you don't know and you think you know what love is? Ha!"

Milan stared at me. Her pained look let me know that my words stung her like a needle.

"Maiya, I have no idea what you are talking about. Why are you talking to me like this?"

"Of course, let me explain. How about your past is now affecting me and how about I was totally humiliated and embarrassed at Malachi's family cookout when your sexcapade from Texas attacked me? How he thought I was you because you told him your name is Maiya?" Milan's face dropped in shock. I continued. "How could you be so careless and shiftless? How could you do that to me?"

"I'm so sorry, Maiya. I never meant for you to get mixed up in any of my messes," she said.

"But you did. Look at you now. We have a business to run, Lani. Where are your priorities?"

Milan got very quiet and took off her sunglasses. She revealed a bruised left eye and tears rolled down her face. "You have no idea what I have been going through. I am trying so hard, and I just can't get it right." She sobbed.

Her face looked terrible. I grabbed her and hugged her close. "I have known something has not been quite right with you for awhile now. You can talk to me, girl; you know that. Whatever it is, we can get you help. I came by yesterday to check on you after Shane told me you abandoned them. Your place was a mess. And it was apparent that you had company. Malachi told me that he saw you coming in this morning, very drunk and very high. From his description of your escort, it sounds like Jackson."

She looked at me. "I love him, Mai. And he loves me, too. We are gonna be together, you'll see. A family. Finally." I let her go. Was she losing it? My cousin would never leave his wife and kids. Though he was as reckless as Milan, he had a lot more to lose.

"Lani, don't. Don't do this to yourself. And you can't go inside like this. Let me take you home. We can talk and figure out something. Please, let me help you."

"I can't. My flight leaves in a couple hours. Just give my keys to Shane. He'll know what to do."

"Wait. What happened to your face?"

"I got in a fight with some broad last night at the club. You should have seen her face! Ha ha ha!"

"A drunken bar fight, Milan," I said disgusted. "Milan, that is not a good look."

"Don't lecture. So, tell me, what was Malachi doing at your place this morning, huh?"

"Well, if you had time to talk I'd love to share. Please?" I begged.

"Maybe some other time. I gotta go. I'll call you when we get to Vegas. Oh, tell Rosa I left an extra five hundred dollars to get the cranberry juice outta my carpet." Then she was gone.

I got in my car and sat in the parking lot and cried for my best friend. I was starting to move forward in my life and with our business, and she was struggling and chasing after a hope that would never come to pass. She was self-destructing right before my eyes. How could this happen? Tears filled my eyes on the drive to the Arena. All I could do is pray for her.

She was in trouble in a really bad way.

And it was beyond my control.

And hers.

*   *   *

Milan didn't call that night or the night after that. She turned off her cell phone and the mailbox was full, so I couldn't leave any messages. Rosa cleaned up her place and made it look like new. It looked like a model home. At work, I covered for Milan as if she were away on business. I couldn't let Milan's actions affect what we built and I knew I needed to move forward. Yet, I couldn't let go of the visual in my mind of Milan's bruised eye and her erratic behavior. I wish I had some idea what was going on. I was just as unlucky getting in touch with Jackson.

Malachi could sense something was wrong with me and tried to get me to tell him what was going on, but I told him that I wish I knew. "Milan is just not herself," I told him. As we left my place on the third day of not hearing anything from Milan, Malachi and I ran into David as he was walking up to Milan's door. I tried unsuccessfully to pull Malachi back towards my place so David would pass us. But, he saw us.

"Hey, Maiya," David called. "How are you these days?"

"Fine, thanks, and yourself?"

"I'm good. Is my girl home?"

"No, she isn't. You haven't spoken to her?"

"No, why?"

I looked at Malachi, then back at David. "Sorry, Malachi, this is David, Maiya's fiancé." They shook hands. "Nice to meet you man."

"Yeah, same here," said David. He looked at me. "So, Maiya, where's Milan? She left me a crazy message about needing to get away and that she needed to talk about us. I called her back, but her voice mailbox is full."

I looked at Malachi again and said, "I'll see you later, okay?"

He nodded and gave me a wink, then waved good bye.

"Why don't we go inside and talk?"

He opened the door with his keys, and held the door open for me to enter.

"I really don't know much except the she left to go to Vegas. She never called after I saw her a few days ago. She was really upset about a lot of things, but refused to talk to me." I hesitated for a moment, and looked away.

"What is it Maiya?"

"I don't wanna get in the middle of this. You really need to talk to her."

"She is your best friend and she is about to be my wife. I know she's upset because I'm always gone, but I'm doing this for our future. I just put a down payment on a penthouse in DC at the Madrigal Lofts. Help me out here, Maiya."

"All I can say is that something is troubling her. I just don't know her story."

"Let me ask you this: is she alone?"

Without hesitation, I answered, "No, she isn't."

"That's all I needed to know. Thanks for your help." David stood up and walked toward the door, opening it for me—a sign he wanted me to leave.

"I'm sorry, David. I really am."

"I'll be fine, don't worry. I'm gonna stay here tonight in case she calls. If I hear anything, I'll let you know."

"Alright then, and I'll do the same if she calls me. I gotta run." I gave him a hug.

"One last thing," David said, looking me squarely in the face.

I knew what it was before he said it.

"Yes," I said. "She's with Jackson."

* * *

I left David and went next door to put some things together since I was staying with Malachi that night. I gathered Chloe's bed and toys and packed up my car. I went for a quick run around the complex and then showered and got dressed. I sat down to read a few more chapters of Ananda's book and drink an iced chai tea out on my balcony. The warm breeze and smell of the rain that was soon to come put me in a relaxed state of mind.

I exhaled.

I looked up to see David standing on the balcony, looking out towards the harbor. He was startled to see me sitting outside. He had a joint in his hand, and he had a look on his face of being caught with his hand in the cookie jar.

"Don't mind me, Maiya. I just happened to find this stash of weed in Milan's nightstand drawer. She left her engagement ring in there." He put his head down. I could tell he had been crying. I always saw the tough, rugged, go-getter side of David who exemplified the business mogul. Seeing him like this made my heart sink. I just listened.

"I spend a lot of time away from her. I'm always travelling on business, wanting to give her the world. She always begs me to stay here with her, to cut back my workload. All she wants is my time. There is nothing I can do to fix this."

"I believe that you love her David. And she knows it, too. I just really feel that she is going through something and doesn't know how to ask for help. And she doesn't know how to explain herself. And you can't change someone who doesn't wanna be changed. We can't push her so much. Or she'll be gone forever."

He looked right at me and said, "She's with Jackson. She's already gone." He went inside and closed the door.

I went inside and phoned Malachi to let him know that I was on my way. I had been to his home a few times since we had been seeing each other, but I wasn't too good with directions. I put Chloe on the backseat of my car in her traveler and programmed his address into my GPS.

"I'll see you when you get here," he said.

On the drive over to Malachi's house, I thought about what David said about Milan being "already gone" and I wondered what he knew about Jackson and Milan. Milan told me a while ago that she shared with David everything about her past and her relationship with Jackson, but I wonder just how much he knew. Also, I remember how Milan said before she left that her marriage with David was just a business arrangement. What the heck was going on? I decided then that I would check in with her parents before the weekend was over to see how Mr. Douglass was getting along. Milan was very close to her father and I figured maybe he could help me reach her.

I wasn't ready to give up on my friend.

*   *   *

Getting to Malachi's house, my mind rested on how in just a few short months, so much was changing in my world. My love life was infused with so much life with Malachi right in the center of it. And, my best friend—my sistah friend Milan—was slowly self-destructing as I watched helplessly on the sidelines. I took a deep breath. *Enough of that already*, I thought. *Time to spend time with my man.*

I rang the doorbell after parking in the driveway and setting

Chloe down on the step in her Louis Vuitton duffel. I could hear Malachi's dogs barking inside, and he yelled at them to quiet down. When Malachi opened the door, I could smell the food right away. He was wearing a white Tee shirt and jeans covered with a black apron with a white embroidered building and the words TAYLOR MADE CONSTRUCTION in red. He greeted me with his signature smile and kisses on my cheek, and said, "I hope you're hungry."

"I am starving. Mmm, it smells wonderful. Where can I put Chloe?"

"She is free to roam around. My dogs are in the basement, so she's safe. Can I pour you a glass of wine?"

"That would be nice, thank you." I walked into the living room and put Chloe's bed on the floor. I followed Malachi into the kitchen.

"Here you are. It's one of my favorites. Hope you like it."

I took a sip. "Mmm. That's nice. Real nice."

"Let me put your things in my room and then we can eat. Just follow me." He led me down the hallway to a bedroom. "I hope you like it."

"Oh, it's just fine. But, Chloe is gonna wanna be wherever I am," I laughed.

There was a window seat and small mahogany desk on one side of the room, which was decorated in rich, warm shades of beige walls and walnut and peach accents. It wasn't too masculine or too feminine. It was pleasing to anyone's eyes.

"This is very warm."

"Glad you like it. The bathroom is over there. I'll give you a few minutes and meet you in the dining room."

Dinner consisted of mini crab cakes, rice pilaf, steamed asparagus and carrots in a butter sauce, and a tossed salad. He even served fresh rolls and sweet peach tea.

"So, how's everything? You like?"

"It's delicious. I see that your mom taught you well." I smiled. "The vegetables are very fresh, cooked to perfection. I must say, I am impressed."

"Thank you. I go to the Amish market for my produce and they have fresh baked goods also. You should come with me some time."

I nodded yes, while my mouth was full, then swallowed. "I'd like that. Nothing like fresh produce." I took a sip of wine.

He smiled at me. "Here is a toast. To us." He held his glass up and touched mine.

"To us."

At that moment, his cell phone rang. He ignored it like he seemed to do a lot lately when we were together. Though I liked him focusing on me, I couldn't shake the feeling that the calls weren't just from his work associates and family. I pushed my suspicions aside as I bit into the flaky crab cake he served me.

After downing the delicious meal, we washed and dried the dishes, and then relaxed in the living room in front of the big screen television. There was a rack of DVDs in the entertainment unit, so I looked for recent movies that I hadn't had a chance to see. "Have you seen this one, yet?" I asked, while holding up *Law Abiding Citizen*.

"No, I haven't. I have a bad habit of buying movies and then don't get a chance to watch them until after they are no longer a hot topic." He got up and headed towards the kitchen and was soon in the freezer. He laid out different containers of Cold Stone Creamery ice cream. "Hey, Maiya, I decided to bring the ice cream to you this time. Come and see what flavor you want. I got a few different ones."

"Did you get Founder's Favorite?"

He laughed. "Of course, but I thought you liked the Mint Mint Chocolate Chocolate Chip? I got that, too."

"Can I get a little bit of both?" I asked, as I walked over to the island counter.

"Where do you put it all and still find a way to stay in shape?"

"I indulge every so often. But you know I will work it off at the gym, either way. It's all about moderation, that's all."

We ate our ice cream and enjoyed the movie. Chloe balled up at my feet and fell asleep. Malachi excused himself to the basement to check on Samson and Apollo and let them out before retiring for the night. I decided to check my phone for any messages from Milan or David before getting ready for bed. As I sat in the living room, I could hear Malachi's voice in his backyard. At first, I thought he was talking to the dogs. Listening closer, I realized he was on the phone.

"For the last time, I don't want you calling here again," he yelled into the phone. *Who was he talking to like that?* I thought. I got up and went to the window in the kitchen. I looked down and could see him from the side. He looked furious. I had never seen this side of him before. As he angrily turned his phone off and yelled for his dogs to come back inside, I ran to the bathroom to avoid being seen spying on him. I took a deep breath. *Should I be worried,* I wondered. I told myself to stop jumping to conclusions.

I checked out my surroundings. The bathroom was beautiful. The bathroom walls were painted honey except one wall that was double espresso, and the ceramic tile that adorned the shower was in varying shades of brown: hazelnut, amber, tweed, and sepia. Ivory seashells sat on the sink counter. The bathtub and shower were on the other side of a frosted glass door. There was a bench inside of the shower and three jets. The bathtub was quite large and also had jets. It smelled of ocean breeze and I felt right at home. I took a shower, luxuriating in the mist with Malachi's phone call conversation on my mind. *What was up with that?* After mulling over it for a while, I decided to drop it. He would tell me if it mattered, I'm sure. All I wanted was a good night's rest in the arms of my man. When I came out of the bathroom, Malachi was sitting by the window, reading.

"Hey, do you have your Mike Phillips CD we got at the jazz concert? Can you put that on?"

"Yeah, I got it." He left out and as I watched him walk out of the room, I smiled to myself and thought how glad I was that we had our time in Virginia. That had started something special between us. We spent most of our time in public, which didn't leave much time alone.

But, when we were alone, our lovemaking was like the first time, each and every time. Malachi was the best lover I had ever had. His touch ignited passions in me that I never knew could exist. He took the time to explore my body, mind and emotions and catered to each part when we made love. And, he taught me how to please him, too. That girl Tia that he was engaged to must have been a fool. Malachi was a gentle and skilled lover.

Despite our ravenous sex life, we were able to build a very spiritual side to our relationship. Before our Virginia trip, Malachi spent time with me at church, and he even talked about joining, too. Unlike my conversations with Joaquin that always ended in bitter disagreement about Bible scripture, Malachi and I discussed our interpretations of the Bible together and when we disagreed, we respectfully tried to see the other person's point of view. Malachi really inspired me to be less judgmental and see all sides of an argument.

My thoughts about Malachi made me smile as I pinned up my hair and I got ready for bed. As I reached for a bobby pin, I almost yelped aloud as I felt a needle-sharp pain in my abdomen and uterine area. The pains in my abdomen were starting again, but I didn't want Malachi to think something was wrong, so when I got in bed, I turned to my side and got in the fetal position, covering up with the comforter. Malachi came back in the room and walked over to the stereo in the corner of the room. He also brought the pictures we took while we were in Hampton. He had them put nicely in a photo album. He commented about one of the photos, saying, "Wow, that's a handsome couple, don't you think? You looked so pretty in that dress."

"We are a handsome couple. You didn't look so bad yourself!"

"Can you imagine what our kids would look like?"

I just looked away and got quiet. Why did he have to go and mention children? I wasn't ready to go there with him.

"What's wrong? Did I say something wrong, Maiya?"

"I'm not gonna lie to you. Everything is good with us and all that. I love everything about you, but…"

"But, what?"

"I'm not so sure that I can have babies," I sat up, wincing as the comforter slid down my chest. "Like right now, I'm in pain because I have endometriosis that is so bad that I've been tested to find out if I'll need a hysterectomy," I stopped. I couldn't believe I was telling him this. I hadn't even told Milan this. But, I realized then the truth. I loved him and wanted him to know everything about me.

He came and sat on the bed, pulling me close to him. He looked me in the face and spoke softly. "Maiya, why you gotta be so dead serious all the time? Don't you know how much I love you?"

My breath paused at the very instant. It was like we were suspended in time. Tears dropped slowly from my eyes as he held me.

"I love you, too," I whispered.

"Remember when your pastor said 'what God has for me, it is for me.' We pray about it, and leave it to Him."

I nodded.

"Well, I've always experienced that as the truth. And you and I were destined by God. I love you and I love all that is you. Your ability to have children has nothing to do with the love I have for who you are. With God, all things are possible. You believe that, right?'

"Yes, I absolutely believe it."

"Then stop doubting and start living. Right now. Starting today. You promise?"

"I promise."

He grabbed me and we embraced. Then he kissed me ever so softly again.

I love this man, I thought to myself.

We fell asleep in each other's arms, listening to the smooth sounds of Mike Phillips. When he rolled over on his back, I rested my head on his chest, and stayed there until the sun, and Chloe, woke us in the morning.

Love is an act of endless forgiveness, a tender look which becomes a habit. ~Peter Ustinov

EIGHTEEN

MALACHI

M aking love to Maiya was better than I could have ever dreamed it to be.

I knew that she wanted to take things slow, but I also knew from the first time I laid eyes on her that she would be Mrs. Taylor.

The time we spent together in Virginia with my family was a wonderful time, and I had even told her that it was hard for me to be so near to her and not be able to make love to her. But, after being so close to her in the hot tub that day, I could not resist. We had perfect opportunities on many different occasions. And, yes, we had fallen asleep together in a bed before.

But nothing happened.

As much as I wanted to, I wasn't gonna press her.

Like I said, I wanted her to give me the signal to move forward. And the evening after seeing Gary Taylor in concert…..whew! We both knew it was about to be on!

I thought it was cute how she asked me to bring her some bath towels, and conveniently, rather accidentally on purpose, left the bathroom door ajar. She was clever. And seductive.

She had the most beautiful light brown eyes and her hair, with its wild, bushy look was so exotic to me and it turned me on. She always had a certain confidence and sex appeal about her.

I caught a glimpse of her as I stood outside the bathroom door. I didn't mean to sneak a peek, but I am a man. I was not expecting to see her half naked, but I was pleased with what I saw. And when she didn't turn away, but welcomed me to come inside, I didn't hesitate to give her a sensual experience right there in the shower.

Her body was perfect.

From her perky melon-sized breasts down to her slender waist, and thick, muscular thighs.

Her eyes almost popped out of her head when she saw how large I was. But I knew I would take my time with her. I had a large package to work with, but I knew how to handle my business.

I brought along my HIV and hepatitis results to show her just in case anything jumped off. I needed her to know that I do practice safe sex and had no intention of jeopardizing my life or hers. Surprisingly enough, she had the same lab results to share with me, and we laughed about it.

Maiya had shared with me that she had not lost her virginity until her freshman year in college. Ironically for me, I lost mine during my sophomore year in college.

When we made love, Maiya was uninhibited. She moved her hips right along with mine, after she got past the initial phase. I took my time with her, and was as gentle as I could be. When she reached her peak of ecstasy, she cried.

Unsure of where the tears came from, I thought it was because I had hurt her. To my surprise, Maiya admitted to never having experienced an orgasm before. I promised to always bring her such pleasure, and we became an official couple.

I had already made up in my mind what my intentions were, but it continued to bother me how to break the news of Tia and the baby to her. It seemed that the closer Maiya and I got, the more time passed before I was telling her the truth about Tia. I was getting a bit nervous that things could get out of hand at any possible moment.

With Tia continuing to call and harass me, I was beginning to question whether she would threaten Maiya as well. She was becoming relentless in her attempts to get money from me. First, it was to help pay for doctor visits since she was uninsured. Then it was money to buy things that the baby was going to need. I gave it to her each time with the hope it would be the last, but it wasn't. Eventually, she started asking me to go with her to the doctor to hear the baby's heartbeat. Against my better judgment, I went. As much as I wanted to hate Tia, the reality was that she may be carrying my child. And, I was nobody's deadbeat daddy. If this baby was mine, I was going to be there for him or her, despite having contempt in my heart for Tia. I was going to be a good father. But how do you explain this to a woman who you just met and have fallen in love with—especially when you know she loves you, too? Maiya would be devastated. So, if it means I have to keep this a secret for now to avoid causing Maiya pain, then that is what I have to do. But I hate feeling like I'm lying.

After returning from Virginia, our relationship got pretty heavy pretty fast. I could tell that she was amazed herself with how open she has been with me. I admit that even though I was attracted to Maiya from day one because she was so damn fine, I am amazed each day with how kind, ambitious, responsible and loving she is. When my asshole cousin disrespected her in Virginia and she cried on my shoulder, not for herself, but for her best friend, I knew that she was probably the most caring person I knew. With all of this stuff going on right now with her friend Milan, I just want to make sure Maiya knows how much I care about her. Damn, for real, she needs to know that I am in love with her. When I told her that I loved her and she professed her love for me, too, I admit, I almost cried like she did. My feelings for Maiya were so deep that it didn't matter if we couldn't have children. But, I know I had to tell Maiya, as soon as possible, about Tia and her pregnancy. I just don't know how to bring up the subject especially now. I hope keeping a secret as big as this one wouldn't ruin the start of the good thing Maiya and I have.

Character is doing the right thing when nobody's looking. There are too many people who think that the only thing that's right is to get by, and the only thing that's wrong is to get caught. ~J.C. Watts

NINETEEN

MILAN

Although I didn't call Maiya like I said I would, I called my mother instead, even though I never really had that wonderful mother-daughter relationship with her. My dad had been sick, and I promised to check in on them. I was a daddy's girl, and I wanted to make sure he was getting better.

"Hey, mom. I was just calling to check on daddy. Is he doing any better?"

"He's still a bit weak, but he says he's alright. He doesn't have much appetite lately and says everything I cook tastes funny. He's missed quite a bit of work, and I'm worried about him. He still won't see a doctor."

"I'll come by to see him next week. How have you been? You know you can't worry yourself with your high blood pressure."

"I know, you're right. Where are you? Can you come tonight?"

"I'm not home right now. I'll come see you on Sunday. I promise."

"Milan, where are you? Maiya called here worried about you. Is everything okay?"

"I'm fine, just fine. I just needed to get away for a little bit. I am with Jackson. He wanted to take me to Vegas, so here we are," I injected in my voice enthusiasm that I didn't feel.

The phone went silent.

"Mom, you there?"

"Milan, why are you with Jackson? I hope you are keeping your mouth shut and leaving well enough alone. I just don't like you with him. He has hurt you so much, yet you always want him. He will go back to his family and you know it. Why do you do this?"

"I didn't call for a lecture. Tell daddy I love him and give him a kiss for me, too."

"Milan, please be careful. I can't fix any more of your problems anymore. It's not like before, you know. You're not a little girl anymore where a trip can rid you of the consequences of your actions."

"My phone is about to die, mom. We're at the Bellagio in case you need to reach me. I gotta charge my phone." My phone died and I was left looking at the phone.

I knew exactly what mom meant about a trip getting rid of my consequences. We promised never to talk about it. But I knew that it would eventually come back up. It was the reason I had agreed to come to Las Vegas with Jackson. I had to tell him the truth. I had to tell him about Nadia. I knew what was best. I was tired of all of these lies.

*   *   *

Jackson and I have a long sordid history that is full of drama that you'd only find in a soap opera. We met when we were kids and we instantly became attached, exploring each other's bodies and having sex by the time we were twelve. We would sneak off and do it anywhere we could be alone—a closet, a park or under the porch where my mother stored old things. By the time I was fourteen, I got pregnant, scared out of my mind and afraid my mother would kill me or Jackson. At eighteen, Jackson could have gone to jail for making love to me. I wasn't having it. I vowed I wouldn't tell her until I had the baby and she couldn't be mad anymore once she saw its little face smiling back at her. I didn't tell Jackson, either. The hardest part was not telling Maiya. She knew all of my secrets until then. But, my mom found out before I knew it.

I was barely two months pregnant before she picked up on my changes in eating, sleeping and mood due to the pregnancy. She took me to the doctor to confirm. She cried. She hollered. She slapped me. But, she didn't make me get an abortion. After all, she said, it was her grandbaby. But, she refused to let me raise my baby.

"Ain't nothing a fourteen year-old baby knows that is worth teaching a child," she would say. She rendered me incompetent to raise my own child from day one. Also, she threatened me, making me swear that Jackson was never to know.

"That fool boy is about as worthless as you are when it comes to raising a baby," she had said. "It is in everyone's best interest if the baby and your pregnancy is our little secret."

So, that's what happened. She took me away for nine months where I delivered my baby I named Nadia and we came back as if nothing happened. I gave birth in Germany the summer between my ninth and tenth grades of high school.

It was our family secret, and I had never even told Maiya.

Neither David nor Jackson knew.

I was expected to spend each year as if I was not a mama. It poisoned my heart. My mother and I visited her in Germany every year where she was being raised by my maternal grandmother and aunts. My mother wanted it so my baby would know me, but it was hard enough having to come back to Maryland after Nadia turned a year old. She was a beautiful girl, with long curly locks, oatmeal skin, and hazel eyes. My relationship with Jackson soured while I was in high school and before I went off to college, we were basically over. He knew something had changed, but, since I wouldn't tell him about Nadia, he could only attribute it to me not loving him like I used to. He left for the Navy and my heart left with him. When we reconnected after he got back from the Navy and I told him I never stopped loving him, he asked me right then to marry him. But, ashamed at how I had kept the secret of Nadia away from him, I said no and he left, marrying someone he didn't love to spite me. I always wondered if he would have left me if he knew about Nadia. I loved Jackson and I always felt he would hate me if he found out how I kept our daughter away from him. I hated myself for keeping that secret.

I kept a wallet-sized photo of Nadia hidden in the visor of my car, and on my nightstand. In the closet, I kept hidden a photo album of Nadia ever since she was born.

Each year, she grew even more stunning, yet looking like her father all the more. It killed me when I visited Nadia on her fourteenth birthday. My baby begged me to let her come back with me. But, with so much time having gone by and no one back home even knowing she existed, I didn't know if that would be the best thing. Also, I didn't want her to have the same thing happen to her, so I told her yet again, "Next year, baby. I promise."

"You always promise, and every year you change your mind. Don't you want me with you?" Nadia pleaded.

"Of course I do, sweetie, but you need to finish school there."

"But I told you I want to be a model. I want to try out for Tyra Banks' *America's Next Top Model*. She is coming to D.C. this summer, Milan, please!" I hated that she called me by my name.

"No, Nadia. You need to wait another year. And even then you need to be eighteen. I promise, just be patient."

But, what I really wanted was for her to stop asking. I didn't want to face the day when I had to introduce Jackson to his daughter and see on his face the pain I caused by keeping him in the dark about her birth. I also didn't want me or Nadia to be the reason he left his family if he found out. I knew he never stopped loving me, as I have never stopped loving him. But, there were so many lives at stake. I was so scared. I didn't want to be the cause of so many worlds collapsing.

My impending marriage to David encouraged me to want to come clean to both Jackson and David about Nadia. I called Jackson first to break the news and things spiraled out of control before I even got one word out about Nadia. We were making love and meeting as clandestine lovers as soon as we said "hello" on the phone. It was insane. Our sexual chemistry seemed to have magnified since our time away from each other. One visit turned into weekly visits and before I knew it, Jackson was flying from Texas to National airport in DC once a week to see me. With David busy and working just about every night, I wasn't at risk of getting caught. But, it was getting tougher to stay focused at work. Jackson was becoming my obsession again and I was losing focus on why I connected with him in the first place. Nadia.

So, when he suggested we hit Las Vegas, I was down. What better place to break the news than in the town where secrets don't leave? Because I knew that Jackson had a temper, I didn't wanna break news like that to him in the privacy of our suite. He would most likely resort to shouting and throwing things around. So I decided to tell him over dinner after he had a couple of drinks. In our suite, I repeated in my mind how I was going to break this to him as I tweezed my eyebrows.

"Hey, baby, you almost ready?" Jackson called. "You know it takes you forever to put all your makeup on and to fix your hair."

"Real funny, Jack. I can be ready in about forty-five minutes." I peeked outside of the bathroom and asked him, "What time are the reservations?"

"Not until seven, so you better get a move on. Here. I got something for you." He pulled out a strapless red dress. "How about you put this on tonight. It's perfect."

The dress was slinky. I liked it immediately.

"It's beautiful, thank you. I won't disappoint, I promise." The same words I had said to our daughter just last summer.

I promise.

I was never good at keeping promises.

* * *

At dinner, I clumsily tried to make small talk, but it was no use. I literally just came out with it as the bread was placed on the table.

"Jackson," I started. "There is something I have to tell you." And, I just blurted it out. I told him everything—from how my mother operated so expertly in making sure no one here in the US knew that I was pregnant to how I had to be quiet lest Nadia be given away.

Jackson handled the news quite well, to my surprise. He got quiet and looked sad for a few moments. As tears rolled down his face, he asked me, "Why? Why couldn't you just tell me?"

I looked at him, with pain on my face, knowing how much this hurt him. "Would it have changed anything? You were in school, and I didn't wanna keep you from your dreams of being in the Navy."

"It wasn't for you to decide."

"I didn't decide. The decision was made for me!" I looked away as tears streaked my makeup. "I was only fourteen, and my mother wouldn't even think about an abortion. When they sent me away, it tore me apart, knowing I couldn't be with you. The one thing I could have of you all to myself was the baby. I am so sorry. I just couldn't keep this secret from you any longer."

"What's her name? How old is she, like thirteen? Fourteen? When can I see her?"

"Her name is Nadia Michele Vaughn, she's fourteen-and-a-half years old, and she is so beautiful! Here, I have a photo that I keep in my car, but I brought it along with me." I dug in my wallet and handed it to him.

His mouth fell open. And he cried. "Can I keep it?"

I nodded. I covered his hand with mine and he looked at me and said, "I'm sorry, too. I just wished I had known so I could have been there for the both of you."

"It's okay, Jackson. Our daughter turned out just fine. As a matter of fact, she wants to pursue acting and modeling. I am planning on sending for her to stay the rest of the summer. You can see her then."

"I would like that very much."

* * *

Contrary to what I thought would happen, news of our daughter made Jackson realize how much he had been in love with me practically all his life. We made love that night. And I cried, confessing my love to him, as I always had, after all these years. "You never answered my question, Jackson."

"What question is that?"

"Would it have changed anything? Your knowing about the baby?"

"Yes, it would. I would have tried to make things work with us. Especially for Nadia. I have always loved you, Lani, and you know that. But you were so stubborn! The cards were just read to us differently."

He turned my face towards his and looked in my eyes. "I'm about to be completely honest with you, here and now. And I need you to listen. I'm not happy at home with Leesa. We've been miserable for some time now. I love her, but it's more out of obligation. She's the mother of my children. But, I'm not in love with her. That's what I came all the way from Texas to tell you. I am filing for a divorce. I am leaving this time. For real."

"I've heard you sing that song before. Why should I believe you this time? It's time you face the music, not just hum the tune, Jack."

"Because it's true. I only married Leesa because I was lonely. After you left me, she was there for me when I didn't have you. And when the children came…well, it just complicated things. I guess I stayed because I love my children so much."

Silence fell between us, and then he continued. "But, I love you, too. I always have. You've been my passion for as long as I can remember. I can't say that we will be together and everything's gonna be like it was. We both need to get our lives back. But, now, with Nadia in the picture, our relationship is much different as we look at it together."

"I know. You're right. I just don't know how. Where do we begin? We've made a total mess of our lives."

"We seek professional help, Lani. We both need it."

I sucked my teeth. "This change. Where did all of this come from all of a sudden? You've been just as much as the life of the party as I have."

"I have been thinking about making a change for awhile. The crazy time back at your place….that was just a last chance to play my Wild Card. And now that you told me about my baby girl. We have to set the example. When I get back home, I'm moving out and bringing the kids to Mom's for the summer. It would be great for Nadia to meet her siblings."

"I think so, too. I have a lot of people I need to apologize to. Maiya, for starters. David and my parents. I would like you to be there when I tell Maiya about Nadia. And if you need me when you tell your mom, I'm there."

"I am here whenever you need me. We will get through this, I promise." He kissed me and watched me fall asleep. Jackson stayed awake, lying on his back and thinking about the changes he needed to make. He crept out of bed when he thought I was asleep. He closed the bedroom door behind him. He needed to speak to the only woman who knew him better than he knew himself.

His mother.

Rocsi.

The measure of a man's real character is what he would do if he knew he never would be found out. -Thomas Babington Macaulay

TWENTY

JACKSON

It was midnight when the phone rang. It startled Rocsi Vaughn from her sleep and she scrambled to answer it.

"Hello?"

"Ma? It's Jackson. Sorry to wake you. I couldn't sleep."

"What's wrong, son? The babies okay? Is it Leesa?"

"No, no. Everybody's fine. It's me. I'm what's wrong."

Rocsi sat up in bed and cleared her throat. One thing was for sure. Of her two boys, Jackson was always the more sensitive twin. More off-the-hook, as the kids said these days. I heard her exhale. "Talk to me. What is it?'

"I don't know where to start." I sobbed into the phone. Once I collected myself, all I could muster up was "I'm sorry ma. I'm a mess. My life is a mess."

"Well, let's talk about it. Where are you?"

"Milan and I ....we're in Vegas. It's not what you think."

"And what DO I think?"

"That we've run off, and that...."

"Look, son, you called me to talk. I'm here to listen, not pass judgment. I've always been here for you and your brother. Talk to me, Jackson."

"My marriage is a mess; it's falling apart. I've dragged Milan into my world of drama and I haven't been a good person. Listen, Ma. I'm going back home to file for a divorce, but I'm coming to see you first. I'm gonna bring the kids back next week like we planned. I just….um, well…I'm sorry, Ma. I'm sorry." I began to sob again.

"Oh, Jackson, it's gonna be alright. Come stay with me. Go to church with me on Sunday."

I smiled. "I would like that. And Ma?"

"Yes?"

"Do you still pray for me? Like you did when me and Brandon were little?"

"I never stopped praying for you, Jack. Now, get some rest and I'll see you when you get here. Y'all be safe now. I love you, son. Everything will be alright. You'll see."

"I love you, too, momma. See you soon." I hung up.

I decided to call my wife next. The phone rang three times before I got an answer.

"Jello?" Marisol's thick accent spoke clearly as she answered. Marisol was my housekeeper and nanny. She was sweet as pie, and she loved my children. Marisol had been living with our family since before Nicholas, my eldest son, was born. She was great with the children. This was the weekend she was going to Corpus Christi, so I was surprised when she answered the phone.

"Hello? Marisol, is that you?"

"Yes, Meester Jackson?" Marisol questioned in her thick, Salvadoran-accented-broken English. "Miss Leesa went out and she ask me to stay wit de children. Is okay, no?"

"No, no, it's fine. Did she say when she'll be back?"

"She no say, Meester Jackson. When you come back? Soon, yes?"

"Are you alright there? Do I need to be back soon?"

"Oh, no, Meester Jackson, we okay here. I call you if problem, yes?"

"That's fine, Marisol. I'll be back on Tuesday. You can take your vacation early and the kids will come to stay at my mother's for the summer."

"Yes, is good. She will like, yes? I will miss my babies. I see you Tuesday. You pay for me to take early, yes?"

"Yes, I will pay you."

"Okay, good night."

I dialed Leesa's cell phone but only got her voicemail. "Hey, it's me. You know the drill."

"Hey, Leesa, it's Jack. I am flying back either Monday or Tuesday. I'm going to Momma's first, so I'll call you on Sunday. It's been crazy, and we need to talk." I hung up. I did not want to discuss our problems over the phone. It bothered me that Leesa called Marisol to stay with the kids, when she didn't even hang out anymore. She had pretty much cut her family off and she didn't have any friends. I decided not to make a big deal out of it, especially with all the drama I had going on right in front of my face. And to think I was only miles away from my daughter when I was stationed in Landstuhl for three years! I could have seen my baby girl then.

All the years I missed out on.

Milan and I had really made a mess of things.

I knew I couldn't make up for lost time, but I made a promise to do everything to be in Nadia's life. I may be bad at making love relationships work, but I was a good father, and truly loved my children.

I walked back into the bedroom and climbed back in bed with Milan.

Families are like fudge - mostly sweet with a few nuts.
~Author Unknown

TWENTY-ONE

MAIYA

I had almost forgotten about the family meeting with Noah today, when my phone showed a message waiting for me. "Hey, Miss Maiya. It's Noah. Don't forget we are supposed to meet today with the family. You said you would be there for me, remember? We are gonna be at Granny's house at 2 p.m. I hope you can come. Bye."

Noah had called me while I was in Virginia with Malachi to ask questions about his dad. I didn't want to tell him the truth of what Joaquin discovered in the hospital, but I agreed to support him. I wasn't looking forward to seeing Noah's grandmother, but it wasn't about me. I truly cared for that young man, and wanted to be there for him.

I got up and showered and took Chloe outside. Malachi was in the backyard with Samson and Apollo. "Hey, Sleeping Beauty. I thought you would never get up."

"You should have awakened me." It was only nine a.m. but I was usually up by seven o'clock, even on the weekend.

"I figured we could go over to Allen Pond Park and run the trail with the dogs. Later, we could go down to Baltimore and hang out at the Harbor, maybe go to Phillips for some seafood?"

"I forgot that I had somewhere to be at two, so can we make it much later?"

"That's totally fine with me. What time do you think you'll be back? I can come and pick you up."

"I'm not sure, so I will have to call you when I'm done. If it's too late, maybe we can just go to National Harbor instead. Is that okay?"

"Yeah, that's cool. Did you want something to eat before you go? I can fix you something really quick?"

"No, really, I'm fine. I gotta get going." He followed me inside the house while I gathered up my things. I picked Chloe up and Malachi took my bag to the car.

"Looks like your car could use a washing, too. You can leave your car and take mine if you like. The registration is in the glove box."

"Okay, that's fine with me."

He put everything in his car, and then opened the driver side for me. He gave me a hug and a kiss, handed me his car keys, and I told him I would call him later.

* * *

I got home early enough to go for a run. I did the five mile course, and then went to the Arena to lift weights. I was back home by twelve noon, so I decided to wash a load of clothes while I ate my Greek chicken salad and sipped my passion fruit tea on the balcony. I finished up some work with the schedules that Shane had sent me for the remaining appointments to close out this month. I was in bad need of an office manager since Kari would be gone for the summer. I needed to review applicants and set up interviews before we left for New Orleans. Just then, I saw an email from Milan.

Maiya, sorry I haven't called. We got here safely. I will be back late Saturday, so maybe I'll see you at church. I'm a real HOT MESS as you say and I owe you an explanation. Talk to you soon. – Lani

I decided not to reply to her email. If I ran into her at church or when she got back Saturday, I would deal with the situation then. I refused to let Milan's actions get to me. As much as I loved and worried about Milan, I would wait for her explanation. The phone rang and interrupted my thoughts.

"Hello?"

"Hey, Maiya, it's Gabi. Noah told me that he asked you to come to mom's today. I was just checking to see if you are still coming."

"Hey, Gabi. Yes, I'll be there. I know your mother is not gonna be pleased to see me, but I'm coming to support Noah. It will be nice to see you again, too. It's been a long time."

"Yes it has; too long. I look forward to seeing you. Joaquin doesn't know that you are coming. I guess Noah conveniently left that out."

"Thanks for the heads up. But, I'll be just fine. See you later."

"Okay, see you in a bit, Maiya."

Joaquin's parents lived near me in Indian Head on Metropolitan Church Road, and it would only take me about twenty minutes to get there. I got myself together and headed out the door.

When I got to the Ramirez residence, Gabi was getting out of her car. She turned to me and waved. Waiting outside on the porch for me as I walked up, she looked happy to see me.

"Hey, girl. How you been?"

"I'm good. How 'bout yourself?" I answered, giving her a hug.

"I've been busy trying to keep those kids of my sister's entertained. And that has not been easy. Daddy will be so glad to see you, Maiya. You look great!" She let us in the front door, and I followed her. "It looks like Joaquin and Noah aren't here yet, so come out back with me," she continued.

I followed her to the backyard patio, where Mr. Ramirez was reading and smoking a cigar. "Well, well, well. Look what the cat dragged in! Where have you been young lady?" he asked, while getting up from his chair.

"I've been around. Just really busy on the job. Same old stuff, different day, that's all."

"That's my girl. Come over here and give me a hug."

We embraced. "Let me just look atcha for a minute. You are still looking good, girl. I have really missed seeing you around."

I smiled. "I miss seeing you, too. But, it wasn't always pleasantries with me when I came around, if you know what I mean."

"Now, Maiya, you know that wife of mine has not always been wrapped too tight. No one was ever gonna be good enough for our son, you know that. I always liked you and I thought he made a big mistake, so …"

"Papa, please," Gabi cut in. "Maiya did not come here to reminisce, so let's not go there, okay?"

"You are absolutely right, honey." He looked up and I saw Mrs. Ramirez walk through the doors.

"Hello, Maiya. It's nice to see you again."

"Nice seeing you as well, ma'am."

"The boys are just a few minutes up the street. Would you like something to drink? Water, lemonade, tea?'

"Water is fine, thank you."

"Mama, I'll get it. You stay put."

Gabi went inside to get the water, leaving me outside on the patio with her parents. It was an awkward silence that neither of us knew how to break. I looked around the backyard and remembered the many family cookouts we had where I chased her grandkids and enjoyed quiet family evenings by the fireplace on holidays.

Mrs. Ramirez interrupted the silence. "So, Maiya, do you have any idea why Noah would have wanted YOU here? This is a FAMILY meeting, you know?"

"I do know that. As a matter of fact, Noah called me and asked me to come, and that is why I am here," I responded curtly.

Mrs. Ramirez wasn't finished. "Look, if this is too much and you need to leave, I am sure Noah will understand," she said.

"Noah will understand what?" asked Noah.

We all looked up as Noah and Joaquin walked onto the patio. Noah limped as he maneuvered carefully with a crutch.

"Nothing, sweetie. Nothing," Mrs. Ramirez responded, walking over to him and giving him a hug.

Noah looked at me and smiled. "You came. Thank you, Maiya."

I winked at him. "No problem. I keep my word."

"It's good to see you again, Maiya. You look great," Joaquin said. "It's a surprise to see you here. Does anyone wanna tell me what's going on?"

"Thanks. I think your son can explain that better than I can," I answered.

Joaquin turned to Noah with a puzzled look on his face. "Noah, you wanna tell me what's going on?"

"Why don't we all sit down? Shall we?" asked Mrs. Ramirez.

We sat down and Noah began speaking. He explained his feelings of confusion ever since his recuperation began after the accident, the hushed conversations regarding his mother, and simply being left out of his own life. Noah told his family the closeness he felt towards me and how he wished I was still in his and his dad's life. He also wanted his family to know that he knew the truth about his mother: she didn't know who his real father was.

He turned to Joaquin. "Dad, you have always told me to be honest and you have not been honest with me. You have kept this information from me since the accident, and I am tired of being treated like a little boy. It isn't fair. I want you to tell me the truth about my existence."

"Unfortunately, son, I have to admit that I am not your biological father. I found that out when I wanted to donate my blood to you at the hospital. There is no mistake in what we discovered. Your mother was not honest with me, and I wasn't honest with you. I am sorry. I don't love you any less. And although you may not have my blood running through your veins, I am still your father. And you are my son. I should have told you. But I didn't know how. I AM sorry. Please forgive me."

Noah looked at me, and I nodded for him to move forward. "I accept your apology. I love you, dad." They embraced.

When they let go of one another, Noah looked over at me again. "Thank you for being here for me, Maiya. It means a lot to me."

"You didn't need me to say what was in your heart. Your dad has done a great job raising you to be a wonderful young man. I am proud of you, Noah."

I gave him a hug, and asked him if he needed anything else. My phone rang, and I excused myself to answer. It was Malachi.

"Hey, baby, I just wanted to tell you that I needed to run out for a bit and wouldn't be back for another hour, in case you tried to reach me at the house."

"Okay, well, I should be back home within the hour, so just call me when you are on your way."

"Alright, then. I'll do that."

"Bye." I turned back to Noah. "So, is everybody good?"

"Everybody except for me, Maiya," answered Joaquin. "You got a minute?"

"Sure, what's up?"

"Do you mind if we go inside?" He extended his hand as if ushering me to a seat in the theater. I followed his gesture and walked inside the house.

"Look. I just wanna thank you for being here for Noah. For me. It means a lot. I know this is probably as hard for you as it is for me."

"Actually, it isn't. Seeing you isn't hard for me at all, Joaquin. Like I told you when the accident happened, I am doing fine. I have moved on from what we had, and you should, too. It wasn't all bad between us, just know that. We just weren't meant to be together."

"So, what should I do with the ring I got for you?"

"What do you mean? What ring?"

"I was planning to propose when we were in Miami. But things didn't quite work out. I thought maybe after our time apart that maybe, well, that we would make up and get back together."

"Wow, I was so NOT expecting that at all! Are you serious? Do you have any idea how long I waited for you to give me just what you gave me? You are just a little bit too late. Sorry. I guess you need to get your money back for that ring of yours."

There was a dead silence that fell on the room. An uncomfortable silence that lingered for almost a minute. I decided to break it. "Joaquin, it just didn't work out for us. And I am doing just fine. I am happy now."

"I am happy to hear that, Maiya. You deserve to be happy. I know that I messed up. I know this. I just, well, um…."

"It's okay. And it's all good. It is what it is. Hey, I gotta get going, so I'm gonna say my good-byes to your family."

"It was nice seeing you again."

I smiled and walked outside to excuse myself. Gabi promised to call me and keep in touch. I told her to have Leah call me so we could get together for a girl's day out.

"I promise, I will. That would be great for us. And you can tell me all about your new man!"

"Girl, how did you know?"

"Honey, you are glowing. That has got to be love. And I know that's not your ride!" She pointed to Malachi's ride. We both laughed and hugged one another. We parted and promised to keep in touch. I gave Mr. Ramirez a hug and said farewell to the dragon lady of the house. She scoffed and rolled her eyes, and I just laughed and walked myself out the front door.

I was on my way back home to relax and hang out with my man. Malachi.

* * *

I decided to stop in and see Janet at the shop instead of going straight home. It was hot, and I wanted her to fix me up with my usual. As I walked in, I think I walked in on the end of an argument between Janet and a woman who looked like she had a little gut or she was in the early stages of pregnancy. She was very pretty but her face was screwed up with an attitude. When she saw me, she stopped and gritted on me so hard, I thought her neck was going to break. I was pissed.

"Um, can I help you? You are all in my space," I said, letting it be clear that her behavior was not cute.

"Don't nobody need your help. What you need to do is move out of my way, Miss Thang," she said.

Janet interrupted.

"Maiya, don't even waste your breath. She was leaving. Good-bye, Tia," Janet said.

Tia rolled her eyes at Janet and stared hard at me before passing and walking out of the door. Both Janet and I looked at each other and frowned.

"She is a mess. I have no idea what is wrong with her," Janet said. "Hey Maiya, how you doing? What can I get you today?"

"I'm good, Janet. I will have the usual iced chai tea. And do you have any of those honey pretzels?"

"Sure thing, lady. Anything else?"

"That will do it. Do you know her? Is that Malachi's ex- fiancée, Tia?"

"Yes, that's her. I met her a long time ago, she came in here once or twice, but she just was in here expecting me to give her a hook-up like I do for Malachi and I told her I don't know her like that. She talked to me like trash when I told her that. I finally told her to get the hell on up out of here."

"Wow. What a mess. Well, on to better things. What you got planned this weekend?"

"Me and my girls are gonna check out the club over at the Gaylord tonight and just hang out at the National Harbor. How about you? I'm sure that man of yours has your time taken up."

I laughed. "You're right. I'm just about to text him to see what we're gonna get into. He cooked for me last night. I'm very excited about spending time with him. It just feels good when you just connect with someone, you know?"

"It's written all over your face, girl. You've been bitten by the love bug. It's a good thing. Malachi deserves a genuine person like you. I can see the union between the two of you. Tia was not a fit for him."

"Thanks. I'm just gonna sit over there by the window. Have fun later."

"I will, darling. If I'm gone before you leave, you two have fun and I'll see you next time. Tell your man to hook me up the next time he opens for Ledisi."

"Will do. I'll talk to you later."

I sat off by the window in a comfortable chair, and began to text Malachi. We sent back-and-forth messages for a few minutes, and he wanted to know if I was available. I told him I saw Tia and he sent me three messages asking did she say something to me. I assured him that I don't think she knew who I was. He seemed relieved.

He made reservations at Grace's Mandarin at the National Harbor for seven p.m. I told him I would be ready when he came to pick me up. This would be my first time there, and having heard about it from my girl Jordan, I was glad my first experience there would be shared with Malachi. I stayed at Latté Dah for another thirty minutes and then left to go visit my aunt Rocsi. I missed her the last few times I visited daddy and I knew she wanted my help with the 4th of July cookout she was planning.

I let myself in once I got to daddy's house, and walked through the kitchen toward the backyard. The house smelled lemony fresh, and I knew Rosa had been here.

I called out to my auntie. "Rocsi, where are you?"

"Maiya, is that you? What brings you here?" she answered me from the other side of the deck. "I'm down here, pulling weeds from my flower bed."

I walked to the railing of the deck and looked down. "I just hadn't seen you in awhile and wanted to check on you. Is that alright?"

"Yes, it is smarty pants! I'll be inside in just a minute. Go inside and pour us some tea. I made a lemon pound cake. Help yourself."

I went inside and got the tea from inside the fridge. I got two large tumblers, poured to the top of each, and looked for a knife to slice the cake. Rocsi baked the best cakes you ever tasted. They melted in your mouth. She was planning on enrolling in school to become a pastry chef, but never got around to it. Most of her time was spent exercising her green thumb, which is why she helped my dad down at the nursery.

As I sat down to eat my cake, my cell phone rang and aunt Rocsi walked through the door. I looked at the caller ID and since I didn't recognize the number, decided against answering it. "Hey auntie, how've you been?"

"Busy at the nursery. We had a clearance sale last weekend so I could make room for the new shrubs coming in. My greenhouses are full!"

"That's a good thing. I knew you were busy because every time I came through to see you, you were never home. I've missed you."

"And I've missed you. Been to church lately?"

"Yes, ma'am, I have. Early service, as usual."

"You know I'm at the late morning service since I'm in the kitchen preparing meals for the choir and ushers. You know you can always come and eat anytime."

I nodded in affirmation.

We sat and talked for another hour, and she shared with me the concerns she had about Jackson. He and Milan were in Vegas; this I already knew. She had a feeling something was up, but not quite sure. Aunt Rocsi told me that Jackson was coming here tonight and would be at church in the morning. I didn't share any extra information, especially since I knew about as much as she did. It wasn't my place to let all of their business out. She is his mother and I'm sure she knows him better than I do.

Rocsi went on to tell me about her grandchildren, Joshua and Rocsan, and how excited she was that they were coming for the summer. She talked about Leesa and how withdrawn she was the last time Rocsi was visiting them. I always knew her elevator was stuck in between floors, but that was my cousin's choice to marry her. Leesa's father never really liked the fact that she left her military career to marry "one of them", so she lived her life with Jackson, being cut off from her family. But, every Christmas since they were married, Leesa's mother would send a card and a check for one thousand dollars. I remember Jack telling me how they opened up a savings account and put the money aside for the children, when they came along. One year later after their small church wedding, Joshua was born, followed by Rocsan a year after.

Aunt Rocsi recognized the differences in her identical twin boys and always said Jackson was her "wild child" who thrived for a lot of attention, although he was more sensitive. Brandon was the opposite, being more mild-mannered and focused. "Don't get me wrong," she once assured me, "there ain't no good twin, bad twin here. Both my boys were always good. Good in school, good in sports; just plain good. And even though their daddy wasn't about nothing, your daddy made sure they had a father figure. And they turned out just fine."

Rocsi went on and on about how she wanted Jackson and Milan to work on their individual issues before continuing this "farce of an affair." She wasn't about to pass judgment. That wasn't her nature. She just wanted her son to think about his family when making decisions that would affect them. She said Jackson was a lot like my Dad.

"No, can't be true," I said.

"Yup," Rocsi said. "Your dad was a wild one, too. Most of the men in our family were. Brandon is the most quiet."

I couldn't imagine my dad being like Jackson, sleeping around on my mom and bringing kids in the world with no game plan or respect for their mother. Rocsi looked in my eyes.

"So, Princess Mai, you must wanna talk to me about something. Your eyes could never lie to me. Your face has that glow. Tell me. What's his name?"

All I could do was smile. I told her all about Malachi, how we met, the time we've been spending together, the trip to Hampton, the jazz festival, his family. Everything. Even the drama with his cousin.

She listened attentively and told me how happy she was for me. "I can remember how sad and broken you were when you left Joaquin. You can't make someone be who you want them to be. Love isn't hard work, darling. And it's a good feeling. Remember what I always told you: people come into your life for a reason, season, or a lifetime." She put her hand on top of mine. "I think you just found your love for a lifetime."

"I don't know that I love him, love him."

"Chile, please. You ain't fooling nobody. Like the Rude Boys used to sing… 'It's written all over your face…..you don't have to say a word?'" We laughed. "No, but seriously Maiya, all jokes aside. It's okay to love and be loved. And be IN love. It's about time you broke the wall down. You don't wanna miss out on your blessing."

"I know, you're right."

"So, when do I get to meet this young man?"

"We leave for New Orleans next week, but he will be coming to the cookout on the 4th. He should be coming to church with me tomorrow, too."

"How about you come to dinner tomorrow? Jackson will be here, and probably Milan. It will be nice."

"Um, I don't know about all that. Milan is still keeping secrets from me and I don't know what's going on with her. And she is being irresponsible when it comes to our business."

"We all have our faults. Talk to her. Trust me, it will all work out."

"We'll see. I guess we will be here for dinner."

We stood up from the table and embraced. She stepped back for a moment and smiled, nodding as in affirmation of a thought.

"What is it, Auntie?"

"I was thinking how much you look like your momma. She would be so proud of you. Just as I feel right now." Tears welled in her eyes. "I love you, girl. Just like my own daughter."

"You taught me everything I know, and I love you, too."

She touched my cheek, and I covered her hand with mine. I said good-bye, and then left to go home. I needed to find an evening outfit to wear for my dinner date.

* * *

The missed call that was on my phone began to bother me. I decided against calling it back. Whoever it was would have left a message if it was of any importance. Since I felt sweaty while riding home, I took a quick shower and pulled my hair back so I could cleanse and exfoliate my face.

Using my mint facial scrub and chamomile calming mask, I began my beautification ritual. I searched my bag of make-up to coordinate my colors with my dress. I chose a silky red, black, orange and gold A-line dress with choker neckline. I decided to wear my black, four-inch Kenneth Cole sandals and my black shawl. To set it off, I chose to wear my gold jewelry ensemble that Milan bought when she went to the Caribbean last year. Bangles, a thumb ring, and spiral earrings. I dabbed a few spots of DKNY Cashmere Mist on the parts that matter: neck, wrists, and in between my thighs. It was a subtle scent that I adored.

Malachi arrived at six-thirty with a bunch of exotic flowers, and wearing a crème-colored crewneck dress shirt with black slacks. And his signature smile. He smelled of Usher's new fragrance.

"Wow, you look gorgeous!" He handed me the keys to my car.

"Thank you. You're just as handsome as ever." I winked.

We rode in his car and parked in the garage closest to Waterfront Street. It was still warm outside as we walked to the restaurant. Inside, we only had to wait ten minutes before we were taken upstairs to our table. The three-story waterfall and Buddha are an extravagant décor piece. Our table was in the corner of the restaurant in the style of a cozy booth. We faced a view of the waterfront and a large flat screen television.

We sat side-by-side at our table, and Malachi kissed me on the cheek. "You smell nice."

I smiled and said thank you.

I was really impressed with the ambiance of Grace's. It boasted of Asian décor and the food was wonderfully pleasing to my palate. We ordered sushi and shared seaweed salad, crab Rangoon, and crabmeat spring rolls for appetizers. I decided to try a bowl of Korean seafood soup. It was delicious. For my main course, I settled on Teppanyaki Atlantic salmon with brown rice with a raspberry margarita, and Malachi chose the seafood medley with Pellegrino. We passed on dessert and decided to walk the waterfront to see the boats. The air was warm and the moon was full. The lights that dressed up the street were colorful and bright, like a pre-lit Christmas tree. We held hands and walked by the dock enjoying one another's company. He asked me about David, and I told him what happened after he left. I also told him that Milan may be at church in the morning, and that I wasn't sure how I would react towards her.

"You will treat her as you always have….with love and respect. We all make mistakes, Maiya. She may have lost her way and will need you." He sounded like he understood more than I thought he could.

"I know. It just hurts, like always."

He squeezed my hand and I squeezed back.

"Oh, my aunt Rocsi wants us over for dinner tomorrow. Can you join us?'

"I would love to. Will your dad be there?"

"He is out of town with the business, but my cousin Jackson will be here."

"I will be there."

"I'm not gonna be able to walk another step in these," I said, pointing to my feet.

Malachi laughed at me saying, "Want me to carry the pretty Princess the rest of the way?"

I nodded and smiled. He lifted me up and carried me to the car. I giggled the whole time like a schoolgirl.

At my home, Malachi walked me to my door and we said good

night. We kissed and he said he would see me tomorrow. As much as I wanted to invite him to stay and make love, my mind was elsewhere.

"I'll call you after church," I said.

And then I closed my door.

As I walked to my room, I remembered I had left my cell phone in Malachi's car. I ran outside barefoot to catch him before he left but I saw him by his car, on the phone enraged. Creeping closer, I could hear his rage.

"Tia, don't call me and I don't want you near Maiya again, do you hear me?"

My skin got chills as I heard him say Tia and my name. What were they talking about? Malachi turned a bit and saw me out of the corner of his eye. He dropped his phone on the pavement, startled.

"Oh baby, I'm sorry, I didn't mean to scare you," I said.

"Oh, no, oh no, you good," he stammered. I saw him turn his phone off. I opened his car door and pulled my cell phone out and held it up.

"Cell phone. I forgot mine."

I kissed his cheek and sprinted back upstairs. What was Malachi hiding from me?

Remember, if you're headed in the wrong direction, God allows U-turns! ~**Allison Gappa Bottke**

TWENTY-TWO

"The Lord is in His holy temple. Let all the earth keep silent before Him."

Aunt Rocsi sat on the third pew from the altar, dressed in a peach-colored suit that complimented her creamy peanut butter brown skin. She wore a matching hat with lace covering the front of her face. Next to her sat Jackson, clad in a tan Armani suit with white shirt and orange tie. A matching handkerchief was tucked neatly in his left breast pocket.

As the choir sang Donnie McClurkin's *We Fall Down*, tears rolled down my cousin Jackson's face. He rocked from side to side, and his mother held his hand. She sang along. "We fall down, but we get up….. For a saint is just a sinner who fell down, and got up." She praised the Lord and was thankful that He answered her prayers and brought her wayward son back to worship. Jackson turned to his mother, and she smiled and whispered, "See, I told you I never stopped praying for you. He hears our cries." Jackson nodded in the affirmative, enjoying the rest of early morning service.

In the middle of a pew, about ten rows back, Milan sat next to me. She held onto my arm like a lost child in Macy's department store, crying nonstop during service. Many times, I thought she would lose it and break out into a convulsive crying spell. I just let the Spirit move her and offered my handkerchief. She didn't look like her usual self. Her face wasn't made up and she looked very pale. Her hair was slicked back in a pony tail that hung down her back. You could see the sadness in her eyes and my heart ached for her. Her mother sat in stoic silence on the other side of her. There was something going on that I was clearly out of the loop about.

The sermon was powerful and by the end, we were gathered at the altar for intercessory prayer. Jackson was in a way that I hadn't seen before. He was visibly shaken and when he stood to rededicate his life to Christ, I felt I was witnessing something powerful happening. He and Milan were changed and they were transitioning into different people right before my eyes, it seemed. I was overwhelmed with the Holy Spirit. Tears filled my eyes, and I gave Him all the praise. "Thank you, Jesus." As I walked back to my seat, I saw Malachi on the opposite side of the church. He nodded to me and I smiled. After greeting the pastor, I waited in the vestibule for Aunt Rocsi and Jackson. Mrs. Douglass wore an uneasy look on her face as Jackson walked through the church doors. When I looked at her, she rolled her eyes at Jackson and walked away abruptly, leaving Milan, and me standing together. *What was going on?*

When I saw Jackson, I rushed to him and embraced him anxiously since I hadn't seen him in years. I felt a sense of peace in him I hadn't sensed before and I wanted to acknowledge his transition.

"I'm proud of you," I whispered in his ear. He smiled at me and kissed my cheek before reaching for Milan. They locked into an embrace that seemed to last for minutes. I heard her say to him "I'm so sorry" over and over again while he whispered back, "It's okay. We're okay. We're in God's hands, now."

I walked outside, giving them their moment. Outside in the parking lot, Aunt Rocsi waved me over, and as I walked toward her, Malachi swooped up behind me, embracing me from behind. He kissed me on the cheek and then fell in step beside me. I paused and turned to him, wrapping my arms around his waist. Surprised, he stopped and encircled his arms around me, gently squeezing.

"Wow, Maiya, what's this for?" he asked.

"I just love you, that's all," I said, laying my head on his chest.

Aunt Rocsi walked over to us, coughing dramatically to interrupt.

"Uh, look lovebirds, we are still in front of the church," she playfully admonished. I blushed as Malachi and I reluctantly pulled apart and held hands.

"This must be the lovely Aunt Rocsi I've heard so much about," Malachi said, reaching to shake Rocsi's hand with the hand I wasn't holding.

She smiled. "Yes it is, but a handshake just won't do, young man. We give hugs around here." They embraced. "You must be Malachi. It's nice to finally meet you." She turned as Milan and Jackson approached us. "And this is my son, Jackson."

The two men shook hands.

"Good to meet you, my man," Jackson said. "I can tell already that you and Maiya have a powerful thing going on." He looked at me and winked. I couldn't stop blushing.

"Well, Maiya is a very special part of my life," Malachi shared. "I am so grateful that we have each other." He leaned down to kiss me and then said, "Well, I'm gonna head on home. I just wanted to come over and meet you all." Turning to me, he said, "I will see you this afternoon."

I nodded yes. Aunt Rocsi looked at me and gave me a wink and thumbs up. I laughed.

"So, dinner is tonight at your dad's house. I take it you will be bringing Mr. Malachi? Shoot, who am I kidding, of course you are," Aunt Rocsi laughed at her own question. She turned to Milan.

"And you, miss lady, will your parents be joining us?"

"I don't know Auntie. Dad's not been feeling well and mom...well, you know how she is." Milan looked away, trying to avoid eye contact. I saw the tears well in her eyes. I touched her arm, and she said, "I'm sorry. There's just so much I need to tell you."

"It's okay, Lani," I said, rubbing her arm. "Let's not do this right now. We can talk at home."

She nodded. "Okay."

I grabbed her hand while Jackson wrapped his arm around her and we headed to my car. At my car, Jackson kissed Milan on her check and went to catch a ride with his mother. As I unlocked the door, I could see Milan's mother drive past us in her car, looking straight ahead as if she didn't see us. Milan saw, too. She tried not to show that her mom's dismissal of her hurt her feelings, but it was too late. I saw the pain streak across her face as she bent down to get in my car.

On the drive home, we listened to an old CD of Virtue, *Virtuosity*, and the songs just touched our spirit. Milan continued to cry as she had done in church and I just drove us in silence, willing to just wait until she felt comfortable to speak. Eventually, she did.

"I've made some mistakes, Mai. And I've kept secrets from you, David, and Jackson. I'm talking about secrets that have a hold on me. I know I've been freaking you out with my behavior as of late, but, things have just been overwhelming for me. The secrets have just been taking their toll. I guess with this wedding coming up and all of this, I just broke down knowing that I was adding yet another false moment to my life résumé." She sat up and turned to me. "Look, I'd rather not do this in the car. Can we stop somewhere? Oh, there, let's go there. That's that spot you like, Latté Dah, right?"

She pointed to my special place with Malachi. I turned into the parking lot and stopped the car.

"Sure, Lani, whatever you want. But, you're scaring me. What is it?"

Milan shook her head no. "Not here. Please. Wait until we are inside and facing each other. I have so much to tell you, girl. So much."

Inside the café, we found a table by the window, and I ordered two large raspberry chai teas with rice milk, and a banana nut muffin for Milan. Ms. Janet wasn't in sight, so I accepted my carrot raisin muffin from one of her employees. When we sat down, Milan looked at me with sad eyes.

"All I ask is that you listen. Please be patient. This is not easy for me."

I nodded. "Go on."

She exhaled, and looked straight in my eyes.

"This secret has been tearing me up for years. I know you always wondered what was it that made me stay connected to Jackson."

"Well, I just assumed you were attached to him because he was the person you lost your virginity to," I said while sipping my tea.

"True. Yes. He was my first with everything. He was my first love. He was the person who first told me he loved me. He was my first crush. He was my first boy best friend. He...," she trailed off. "He is the father of my child, Maiya."

I almost choked. *Child? Milan was pregnant?*

"You're pregnant? You are having a baby! Oh my God, Milan. That's great, I mean, isn't it?" I was elated. Then I remembered. Jackson was married. Milan's sadness started to make sense. Milan watched me closely and watched how my face brightened then grew cloudy. She looked down when she realized I was judging her.

"I know what you're thinking. You're wondering how I could get pregnant by Jackson when he's married to someone else," she said.

"Well, that's not all I was thinking, but c'mon Milan, you knew his situation..."

"I'm not pregnant, Maiya."

"What? But, you said..."

"I said he was the father of my child. He is. My child, Nadia. She is 14 years old."

Her news stunned me. I was so at a loss for words that my mouth fell open. She couldn't help but laugh as she reached in her purse and pulled out a picture of one of the loveliest girls I'd ever seen. She looked like a perfect blend of Milan and Jackson. Tears welled up in my eyes as Milan began her story.

"That's my baby. My big girl, Nadia. It's my...our...we have a child. A daughter, Maiya. She's in Germany. She's fourteen-and-a-half. I got pregnant when we were kids. Remember the summer I left and went to Germany and came back in the middle of tenth grade?"

I nodded yes. I remembered quite well, because we volunteered to be camp counselors that summer. I went without her that year and then started the fall semester of tenth grade without her by my side. I remember thinking how strange it was that Milan's family was vacationing past the start of the school year. And I remember having to catch Milan up with her classes so she wouldn't fall behind.

She continued. "Mom and Dad sent me away to my grandparent's home in Germany where I had Nadia at home. It was the most painful yet extraordinary moment in my life. My mother didn't want anyone to know. She didn't want my life ruined, she said. We promised to keep it a secret. I didn't wanna leave my baby girl, but Momma said that was the only way she was going to let Nadia stay in the family and not be put up for adoption. I was so afraid of that threat-- that she would be given away, that I agreed to keep secret about her birth.

"So, every summer I spent with her and my grandparents in Germany. And as she got older, it got harder and harder for me to come back here and pretend she didn't exist. I mean, what kind of mother pretends her baby doesn't exist? I couldn't tell you, of all people, and then to look at Jackson and not be able to tell him about his baby, to share the news that we created life together...well, it was just too much. Momma told me to break up with Jackson and focus on my studies at school and when Jackson and I were over, my life felt like it was over. I started acting out in college, getting drunk and stuff, sleeping around. That kink fest I had with Malachi's cousin was just one of many nights like it. I'm so sorry what happened to you, Maiya, but understand where my head was at that time. I wasn't thinking. I was just trying to numb the pain.

"My mother tried getting me therapy, someone to talk to, but the only help I wanted was to have my daughter and Jackson with me. That's when I started going to church regularly; around the time you started having your issues with Joaquin. I thought I was doing well until I started realizing that I was living a lie. My daughter didn't look at me as her mother. I was more of a sister or aunt to her, not a mother. My grandparents are her parents in her eyes, not me." She started to weep. I rubbed her arm.

"Oh Lani, but you don't know that. You don't know what she thinks. She's a teenager. Their thoughts are all over the place. Does Jackson know he has a daughter?"

Milan nodded yes. "I had to tell Jackson. That's what that trip to Las Vegas was—my way of coming clean. Jackson thought I was trying to rekindle a sexual relationship with him, but I had been trying to find the courage to be honest with him. My mother had me scared for a long time that if he or anyone else found out, they would judge me, but no one has judged me harder than I've judged myself. I've done some really self-destructive things to myself over the years out of guilt about not being there for my baby and telling those I love the truth. But, now, in God's name, I've found strength. I love my mom, but her rules are not for me anymore."

My mind was reeling. This news was not what I expected at all. Milan—who was, at least I thought, almost perfect in every aspect—was going through this tortuous existence all this time. Here I was, worrying about finding a man and trivial stuff like how I looked in my new clothes and my best friend was trying to keep it together as she hid from us that she was a teen mother forced to break up with the love of her life. I felt terrible.

"I don't know what to say except that that was a helluva story. I'm sorry. I really am," I began. "I wish I had known. And you didn't make a mistake. Nadia is a gift. And she'll be fine. We are family. I can't wait to meet her. And she will love her little brother and sister, I'm sure."

"I know," Milan said, grateful I was not judging her. "Both of Jackson's children will be here for the summer, so it should be great. Looks like it'll be a family reunion at last." She beamed at me, finally free from her secrets. I could tell she had something else to say, though.

"So, Maiya. I wanted to apologize about work, too. I've let a lot of stuff slip, I know."

As non-judgmental as I wanted to be, my frustration with her and her slack at work started to surface in my mind. I couldn't stop the words from coming out.

"Lani, you really have been slack with your stuff at work. You really left your staff hangin' and Shane came through. He held it down for your team. And it made us look bad with you just taking off and not caring about anyone else," I said honestly. "But, I know you feel bad about your secret and all, but damn. You could have let a sistah know."

"I know, I know. But, I just had to take care of this mess before I focused on work or anything else."

"Well, are you sure that's it? I mean, when you left, you weren't just distraught, you were boozed up, high and bruised up from a bar fight. I mean, it was like you had started having a substance abuse problem, too."

"Maiya, c'mon now. It's not that dramatic. I wasn't that bad."

"Oh, no? Well why don't you tell me what happened to lead you into a bar fight?"

Milan scrunched up her face and tried to think hard. I could tell she couldn't even remember.

"You don't remember, do you?" I asked.

She sheepishly looked and me and shook her head. "No," she said.

"I'm not trying to make you feel worse. You know I love you and I'm here for you. But, you have got to start by being completely honest. You've been spending years of trying to self-medicate to hide the pain of your secrets; do you think that one admission is going to get you off of being hooked? You have to be all the way honest. What can I do to help?"

She smiled at me. "You can help me get rid of all the liquor in my house. And help me find a twelve-step program."

"Well, the first step you have just taken. You are acknowledging that you have a problem and need help. I am here for you-- just like you've been here for me." I stood up and walked to her side of the table, wrapping her in my arms. We both cried as we held on to each other.

*   *   *

It was after eleven a.m. when we left and drove home. We decided to change our clothes and go for a walk on the trail. I told Milan all about my trip with Malachi and how sweet his family is. She asked me to join her and Nadia for a girl's day out when she comes here in July. I told her that I didn't wanna impose on a mother-daughter bonding, but she insisted. She talked to me about David and how she needed to talk to him. I told her about the conversation I had with him, and how hurt he looked when he found the engagement ring she left behind. I also told her about the condo he bought in D.C. for them to start their new lives together, and that he knew she was with another man. We spent an hour walking and talking, and when we returned, I helped her rid her place of anything with alcohol in it. I asked her if she still planned on going to New Orleans, and she said she was unsure.

"I have a lot of cleaning up to do in my life, and I don't think I would be any good right now. I have groomed Shane for the position. I will stay behind and clean up things here. Plus, I wanna keep an eye on daddy."

I told her that I understood. She said she would grant me authority to make decisions in her absence and would have a notarized document stating such. As we said good-bye, she thanked me again for listening. I went to my apartment drained yet reflective. What a day.

PART TWO
THE FUTURE FORWARD

Our future lies chiefly in our own hands. ~Paul Robeson

Instead of always looking at the past, I put myself ahead twenty years and try to look at what I need to do now in order to get there then. ~Diana Ross

TWENTY-THREE

JACKSON

B ack in the comfort of her home, Mom began preparing her famous Sunday dinner-- a meal that would consist of baked ham with pineapple dressing, fried chicken, potato salad, sweet potatoes, macaroni and cheese, collard greens, green beans, corn pudding, mashed potatoes and gravy, and her famous homemade biscuits with honey butter. I was full just thinking of it. It had been a while since she cooked like this, and oh, how I loved it. Being home was a good feeling, and in a couple of weeks, my twin brother Brandon would be here with his family.

As Momma walked to the kitchen to get started, she stopped past my room and peeked her head in. "Everything alright in there, son?"

"Yes, Momma. You need any help in the kitchen?'

"I could use your company if you don't mind."

I followed Momma into the kitchen and sat at the table. I was ready to bare my soul to her, and be freed of the burdens I had been carrying. I let out a sigh, and then began. "Momma, I am sorry about calling you like that from Vegas. I had just received some news and I really needed to hear your voice. What I am about to tell you, I couldn't say over the phone."

I hesitated.

"What is it, Jackson?"

"For starters, I had no business carrying on with Milan as I have all this time. Leesa and I have been apart for some time now, and I guess neither one of us wants to be the first to say good-bye. Things have changed with us. With her. It's like she doesn't wanna be around the kids, and Marisol spends more time with them as it is. I always had a connection with Milan, and even though I know we would always be friends, a part of me just always loved her. But, that's really no excuse for my actions. I've pretty much been reckless all of my life, and only now have I had the courage to admit to the mess I've caused mostly everyone in my life."

I stopped and put my head down. Covering my face with my hands, I wondered if I could continue. I could hear Momma put down her spoon she had stirring her collards and walk over to me.

"Jackson. Go on," she said. I lifted my head and took a deep breath.

"Well, you know Milan was the first person I loved. I mean, ever. I'm pretty sure that you know that she and I were having sex as early as twelve and thirteen."

Momma frowned and shook her head. "Oh Jackson, no, I didn't know all that. Good Lord. Why on earth are you telling me that now? You afraid I'm going to judge you for something you did more than fifteen years ago? Boy, that's water under the bridge. You can't tell me that Leesa is mad about what you did as a boy."

"No Momma," I interrupted. "Leesa is mad and has every right to be mad about what I've been doing ever since she and I got married, ever since I was a boy. Seeing Milan. Loving Milan. I never really let go of Milan. Never. And to make matters worse, there are now children involved."

"Are you worried Leesa won't give you custody?" Momma asked me.

"Well, Leesa has been very distant lately and leaving the kids, our kids with Marisol, our housekeeper more times than not. But, they aren't the only children I'm talking about."

Momma frowned again. "I'm not following," she said.

"Well, while I was in Vegas with Milan, right before I called you, Milan shared with me that we have a daughter."

My mother almost fainted. I moved her to a chair where she sat down.

"A daughter? What? How old? Where? I haven't seen Milan with any baby."

"She lives in Germany with Milan's grandparents, and she is fourteen years old; well, soon to be fifteen. She showed me her picture." I passed the photo to my mother.

My mother Rocsi stared at the picture and tears filled her eyes. She was quiet for a moment, just taking it all in. When she looked up, I was staring at her.

"Momma, she was sent to Germany to give birth because her mother didn't want a baby to ruin her life. Plus, I guess, I wasn't the most ideal baby daddy for their daughter. I can imagine how disgusted she was to learn that I was having sex with their fourteen year-old daughter when I was old enough to know better.

"I never even knew about the pregnancy. Milan said she didn't say anything because she didn't want to make me choose between the Navy and being with them, and her mother threatened to put the baby up for adoption if she told anyone."

I finished talking then, exhausted from all that I had shared. It sounded unreal, even as I knew it to be true. Momma was still dazed, but found strength to speak.

"Jackson, you know we always had a problem because of the age difference between the two of you, and her mother was always very strict. I knew you would do the right thing, but hormones on a growing teenage boy and girl are raging. You took a risk when you got involved with her, but you two have been inseparable for as long as I can remember. The both of you were the wildest children around here, but we always surrounded you with love." She walked over to me and rested her hand on my shoulder. "It's alright son. God will work it out. Doesn't He always?"

"I know Momma, but it hurts. I missed out on my baby girl growing up, she missed out on having a father; Joshua and Rocsan would have loved having an older sister. I can't help but wonder what would have been different if I had made different choices. "

"If you knew about your daughter, you wouldn't have had Joshua and Rocsan, son."

"What do you mean?"

"Who is to say that Leesa would have married you, knowing you had a child already. Then, you may not have had the children with her. You had to go through life the way you did. You can't change the past. You can only make decisions differently from this point forward. It is what it is. We accept it and move on. I am sorry you missed out on this child, but Milan has to deal with the way she and her family handled that situation. So, tell me. What is my granddaughter's name?" she asked, smiling.

"Nadia Michele. She wants to be a model and actress. She is coming here this summer to stay with Milan, so it will be perfect that she will be able to meet her little brother and sister. I will have my children altogether."

"And I can't wait to spoil them all." We laughed until the doorbell interrupted us. "You mind getting that so I can get this dinner started? It is still early, so I don't know who it could be."

I walked to the front door and peeked out the side window. I looked right into the eyes of Milan. "Hey you," I said, opening the door. Leaning down to kiss her cheek, I asked, "You okay?"

"I'm good, I guess. Now that I talked everything out with Maiya. That was really hard, but she was very accepting. She is going to support me with going to AA meetings."

"It's a good thing. I am glad you made that move. I actually was planning on searching for one as soon as I got back to Texas."

Milan looked away and walked ahead of me into the kitchen. I grabbed her arm to stop her. "Lani, wait. You have to know that I am going back for my children. I have to settle things with Leesa."

"I know, I just wished things were different, you know?"

"Yeah, well, you still have to talk to your fiancé, too. You can't make this about us anymore. Our connection is too tight for me to walk away from anything, but you know we gotta get our lives back in order. We can't be selfish anymore. It's not about us; it's about them."

She nodded and then followed me into the kitchen. "Hey, Aunt Rocsi. I decided to come early to talk to you before the others got here."

Rocsi looked up from peeling her potatoes and pointed to a chair across from her. "Have a seat and grab some potatoes."

Milan sat down and started peeling.

"So, um, did Jackson talk to you?"

"Yes," Momma said. "Jackson told me everything."

Milan burst into tears and put down the potato she was peeling. She and my mother embraced. Through sobs, Milan apologized. "I am sorry for robbing you of getting to know your grandchild. I can only start with the present and clean up everything. I am really, really sorry."

My mother pulled back and looked at Milan. "I know darling. I was once young and in love, too. You have always been attached to Jackson. Always. I couldn't keep you two apart if I wanted to. I just wished you had told us. I would have made sure that baby of yours was taken care of. You know it was nothing for me to take care of Maiya. I would have welcomed you both with open arms." She smiled at Milan.

"Do you accept my apology?"

"Of course I do, baby. Of course."

I interrupted. "Okay, now, enough with this stuff. We are moving forward, yes?"

"Of course, son. Now, if you don't mind, you can leave us to talk, thank you very much."

"Yes, ma'am."

It's not that some people have willpower and some don't. It's that some people are ready to change and others are not.
~ James Gordon, M.D.

TWENTY-FOUR

MILAN

Rocsi and I talked about Nadia. I promised that after dinner I would share the photo albums of her childhood. I told Rocsi of my plans to join AA and that I was going to make a change in my life. I talked to Rocsi of how devastated David would be, but that I would not be able to go through with the marriage.

"I really do feel bad about the way I treated him. But, we had no business getting married in the first place. Our love is like the love between friends, not soul mates."

"Have you spoken to him?"

"No, I haven't. I don't know where to start."

"How about starting with a phone call? Avoidance is only gonna make matters worse. You have wedding plans to cancel. And you have a lot to explain to him. I don't know that much about David, but what I do know is that he is human. All of this is going to be a lot to take in, but you have got to start with a clean slate. I am here for you if you need me."

"I think I will be alright. I have to make the changes not only for me, but for Nadia. She is at that age when I got pregnant and I want to be a good role model for her. Wait until you meet her, aunt Rocsi. You will love her."

"I already do love her, because I love her momma." She winked at me.

When Malachi and Maiya arrived, Rocsi was just taking the biscuits out of the oven.

"Mmm, it smells delicious in here, Ms. Vaughn," said Malachi.

"Why, thank you very much. Hope you brought that appetite, because there is plenty to eat and more to take home with you!"

We all gathered in the living room, while Jackson finished setting the table.

"So, Malachi, Maiya tells me that you are in the construction business. You designed the Arena, huh?"

"Yes, ma'am, that's correct. It's a family business that I have always dreamed of being a part of. My father died and my uncles and I kept it going. We have done alright."

"Oh, auntie, he is being modest. They have done VERY well. He is going to head the construction project in New Orleans, which is why this trip is very important. It means a lot to us that he can help out," said Maiya.

"Well, that is just wonderful."

I remained quiet. I knew my choice to stay behind was necessary, and I had other things in mind. I was planning on selling my half of the business or having Maiya buy me out. I just didn't know when would be a good time to approach the subject. I had only recently made up with Maiya, and didn't want to rock the boat again so soon. Maybe with Malachi distracting her, Maiya really would not mind the change.

"I'm done in here. You all can get washed up and join us in the dining room." Aunt Rocsi dried her hands on her apron and walked in the kitchen to take it off.

"Where's the bathroom, Maiya?" asked Malachi.

"Down the hall and second door on your left."

Get rid of all bitterness, rage and anger, brawling and slander, along with every form of malice. Be kind and compassionate to one another, forgiving each other, just as in Christ God forgave you.
~ **Ephesians 4:31-32**

TWENTY-FIVE

FREIDA

"I don't know why you just won't talk to the boy. It isn't his fault," my husband said to me.

"Oh, so now it's Milan's fault, huh? She got herself pregnant. Doesn't it disgust you to think of the abomination they created?"

We were arguing about Milan and Jackson, as if they were still children and Milan was still fourteen, knocked up, about to have my grandchild, Nadia. May the Lord forgive them for that sin.

"You just never liked the boy, admit it."

I rolled my eyes at my husband. He always had to be right.

"Honey, you have to let the past go. We have a beautiful grandchild out of all of this—despite the biological risk. Nadia is not disabled, deformed or anything. No one could possibly know or suspect. It is time to let what you feel about him go. He is a good young man. He and Milan have always had that connection. And it ain't anything you can do about it. If you hadn't kept the secret from her and let the truth out, none of this mess would be happening," he scoffed.

I shrugged my shoulders and left the room. I gathered the family photo albums and stacked them on the table. I went to get my purse and keys.

"You were going somewhere?" he asked.

"Well, I thought if maybe we left now, we could make it for dessert."

"Freida, they only live down the street. We don't have to go far. And, why on earth are you going to dinner when you know you can't stand Jackson or Rocsi?"

* * *

I decided that we would join our daughter at Rocsi's after all. Milan had begged me on our way to church this morning, but I would not agree when I found out Jackson would be there. I couldn't stand him. He ruined everything. But, I reconsidered when I realized Milan had told our secret and now just about everyone knew that she had been a teenage mother. How humiliating. At least they don't know the whole truth. Milan doesn't even know everything. How many other people knew, I couldn't say, but I was not going to let Rocsi and her good-for-nothing son think that I was going to let this hold me down. Uh-uh. I don't get knocked down so easily. As we rang the bell, I exhaled deeply and put a fake smile on my face.

"Just be nice," my husband pleaded. I had dragged him with me and he looked haggard and tired, hunched over gripping his cane with all of his strength. *I sure hope he doesn't fall out*, I thought.

"I will be nice," I said through gritted teeth as I rolled my eyes at my husband, and exhaled again.

Rocsi was surprised to see us, but welcomed us with open arms.

"Please, come in. You can have a seat in the living room. Can I get you anything? I was just about to serve dessert."

"No thank you. We just really want to apologize," I said.

"What do you mean we?"

I elbowed my husband, but he continued. "It was your decision not to tell her about the baby. If it was up to me, she woulda known a long time ago," he continued.

"Oh, shut up." I looked at Rocsi. "I don't know where to start. Please, may I sit down?'

Rocsi pointed us to the sofa. She sat in the chair across from us.

"Look, I first want to apologize for the way I acted at church. And then, for the way I have been towards Jackson. I know that our daughter has loved him since they were little, and I knew we could not keep them apart. But when she got pregnant. Oh! What was I to do? How would it look?"

Rocsi interrupted. "Freida, please. They were only teenagers. You should have been able to talk to me. We should have sat down and had a family meeting. You took that away from us and have had the joys of seeing your granddaughter grow up before your eyes. My sons grew up without their father. And you allowed Jackson's daughter to grow up without hers."

"I am sorry, Rocsi, I really am. Cochise and I battled over this for years. He wanted to speak up long before it would come to this. I can't take it back. I want to move forward, I really do, but….."

"Hey, Momma, you gotta come hear these stories Malachi is telling. He is really something….." Jackson stopped as he neared the top steps, looking straight at me. "Oh, sorry. I didn't know you had company."

"No, wait, Jackson. I need to say something to you," I responded.

He turned to face me. It took all the strength I had to utter this lie.

"I apologize for being rude to you. And for keeping this secret about your child from you. We thought we were doing the right thing, but we have hurt a lot of people along the way. I know that I can't make it up to you, but please forgive us. Forgive me?"

"I accept your apology, and I forgive you. You must understand that I always loved your daughter, and never meant to hurt her. I just wished I had been given the choice back then. At least Nadia would have had a chance to know her daddy." He turned to walk away.

"Please, wait. I want to share these with you. Come, sit down."

Jackson looked at his mother, and she gave him a loving nod. I thought I puked a little in my mouth. They made me sick. But, I had to make it seem like I was apologetic. I mean, really, I was not going to be outclassed here.

I began opening the albums to share the photos with Jackson and Rocsi. Milan and Maiya joined everyone in the living room to view the family photo albums that included Nadia as a baby and teenaged Milan as a new mother. They listened as I shared memories of bittersweet farewells between my daughter and granddaughter.

We were so wrapped up that no one noticed, not even me, that Cochise had paled over and began sweating, and passed out.

"Honey you remember the year Nadia turned two and you had her in the backyard with her pool, and …." My words trailed off as I turned to my husband who was covered in sweat and appeared lifeless on the sofa. As we all looked, Milan began shouting.

"Daddy? Daddy! What's wrong?" Milan cried. "Please, someone call 9-1-1!"

I felt for a pulse, which was present, but weak. Malachi and Jackson loosened Cochise's shirt while Rocsi phoned for an ambulance. Paramedics arrived within ten minutes, after which he started coming around. His blood sugar was only 46. His skin felt cool and clammy. An IV line was started and I gave his medical history without flaw or hesitation.

"Ma'am, we will be taking him to National. If you can bring a list of his medications, along with his history, that would be helpful."

"Mom, I'll get it. You go on to the hospital, and I'll meet you there."

"Do you need us to do anything here?" asked Rocsi.

"No, thank you. We'll call you as soon as we get him situated," I responded. I was all my husband needed. *Those low class fools were probably the reason my husband was in this condition*, I thought.

At the hospital, I was being asked a lot of questions and filling out paperwork for my husband. I felt bad since I had been begging him to go to the doctor for some time now. He had always been stubborn when it came to managing his high blood pressure and diabetes. And now his stubbornness had caused him to be in this situation. *Look what you have done,* I thought.

*   *   *

"Can you please fill out the information highlighted? Does your husband have an Advance Directive or Living Will?" the ER secretary questioned.

All of the paperwork made me nervous. What is all of this? *I wish Milan would hurry up,* I thought.

The secretary interrupted my scrambled thoughts. "Excuse me, ma'am? Advance Directive?"

"Um, yes. No. I don't know. My daughter is bringing all that stuff. When can I see him?"

"They need to stabilize him. As soon as I see the doctor, I will let you talk to him. Try to be calm and as soon as your daughter comes, send her back to my desk."

"Okay, okay, okay. Um, thank you." *Try to be calm, my ass,* I thought.

My husband was given a dextrose solution in his IV to bring his blood sugar up, and continuous fluids were infusing. His heart was in bad shape and his blood results revealed that his kidneys had failed. They explained to me about kidney failure, saying something about his blood tests could determine it. With a BUN of 116 and a creatinine of 18.2, they told me that he was uremic and needed to start hemodialysis immediately. As Milan and I listened to the nephrologist ramble on and on about congestive heart failure, diabetes, and temporary catheters, he was fighting for his life.

"What would Daddy want, Mom? Does he want this?" Milan questioned me as she fought back tears.

"I don't know. Why can't we see him?"

Dr. Paul Richards, a nephrologist on call at the National Harbor Medical Center, spoke calmly and clearly to us. He explained the entire process of hemodialysis and how it would rid the body of toxins while removing fluid to help him breathe easier.

"I need to know if you want everything done to save your husband's life. If his breathing worsens, we will have to put a tube down his throat to help him breathe better; thus, putting less stress on other organs. You can go see him but we must do this quickly. The sooner, the better. Can you sign for him giving us permission?"

"Yes, yes I can," I answered.

"And if his heart stops, do you want us to do everything for him?"

"Oh, absolutely. Everything."

I went to my husband. Looking down at him, I couldn't accept how weak and pale he looked. He peered at me and spoke softly in between gasps of short breaths, and agreed to start dialysis. When Milan stepped out of the room, he used this time to address me.

"If I get really bad off, promise me that you will tell her the truth, Freida. Promise me. You must tell her everything. Please," he pleaded.

I shook my head no. "I don't know if I can do it. She'll never forgive me. Or you."

"We can't keep it from her any longer. Please," he begged. "Promise me you'll do it."

I began to cry. "You will get through this, and then we can tell her together. You can't check out on me yet." I held his hand tightly. I leaned over and kissed his forehead. *He can't die on me,* I thought.

But I knew that if he died, then I would make sure the secret died with him.

Other things may change us, but we start and end with family.
~Anthony Brandt

TWENTY-SIX

MAIYA

I helped Aunt Rocsi clean up and put away the last of the dishes, while Jackson and Malachi finished watching the Celtics whoop up on the Mavericks. You could hear their excitement from the basement.

"Today was something else, huh?" Aunt Rocsi asked.

"Yes, ma'am it sure was. You discovered you have another grandchild, your son rededicated his life to Christ, and poor Mr. Douglass is in the hospital. I sure hope Milan keeps it together. She is so vulnerable right now, and I know she needs to be strong."

"We have to pray for all of their strength, baby. I will go see Freida and Milan tomorrow. God will work it out. You will see."

I smiled at her. "You want me to put on a pot of tea?"

"Sure thang, baby girl. That would be nice."

We sat and drank our tea, and when Malachi came up to say good-bye, I walked with him outside.

"Thanks for having me over to meet your family. I had a nice time. Is Milan's dad alright?"

"They are gonna start him on dialysis right away. I'm planning on going to see him tomorrow at some point."

"Well, baby, I'm gonna go on home. So, call me to let me know you got home okay."

"I will."

* * *

I stayed and looked at the photos of Nadia with Jackson and Aunt Rocsi. Milan looked like a baby herself giving birth. You could see the happiness on her face as she played with Nadia as a toddler. Jackson made comments about the similarities between Nadia and his baby girl, Rocsan, noting the deep dimples and green eyes. Their only difference was the color of their skin.

Jackson revealed to me the connection that he and Milan shared; a bond between them that was more than just their daughter. He told me how much he loved her, but that he couldn't turn back the hands of time. Their paths in life crossed in the way they were supposed to.

"We really have no business being together and I know she thinks we will reconcile. I couldn't get her outta my system, but I have been convicted." He paused for a moment. "I have to get myself together. Get my life in order. I don't know what's gonna happen with me and Leesa. Our marriage is pretty much over."

I touched his shoulder. "It's gonna be alright."

"I just wish Milan could see what I see. I don't think she gets it."

"She told me that she wants to get help and asked me to help her get through AA. A part of me wants to believe her, but…I don't know. I'm trying to stay positive. I just have a gut feeling that something isn't quite right."

"I know what you mean. We just have to give her our support."

"You can say that again. She's been through more than we could have ever known. But, I'm worried. You can't just recover that quickly from years of self-medicating and engaging in harmful things to take your mind off of your problems. Can you?"

"I know her behavior all too well, since we did it together. The drinking, smoking weed….all of it. But, that was me, too. I was reckless and irresponsible and hurt. I was really thinking that Milan only wanted me for fun and sex and nothing more. I could never have imagined that she was hiding her true self to protect our baby from being put up for adoption." He paused. "I guess, to be real, I will need you to give me your support as well. Man. What kind of life have I been living? I apologize, Mai, for everything. I feel bad about dragging you in our mess. And I'm sorry she wasn't there for you. I'm glad you finally found someone. I like Malachi for you."

"No apology needed. I'm happy and in love. God has given me strength and serenity so I can offer support to you all as you endure this challenging time. Your lives will never be the same."

He grabbed me and gave me a hug. "But, everything is gonna be alright. I know it is." He smiled. I hoped he was right.

*   *   *

The week flew by until it had been a week since I last saw Malachi at Aunt Rocsi's. Thankfully, there was email and cell phones to keep us connected. My flight to New Orleans was scheduled for Thursday, and he would be there on Tuesday, so I was looking forward to us reuniting. My staff would be staying at the Four Points by Sheraton, but I planned to stay at the West New Orleans in the French Quarter with Malachi. I did not need the folk from the job all in my personal business. I made that mistake when I dated Joaquin, and I would not go down that road again.

Milan would not be joining me and our team on this trip, especially with her dad's recent illness. I met her every day to visit with him, and he appeared to be getting better. He smiled when he saw the two of us together, and he said, "Promise me that you two will always be close. Always."

We told him that we would.

He nodded, and then drifted off to sleep.

When I asked Milan about her dad's plan and what the doctors suggested, she told me that he needed to continue on dialysis for three times a week for the rest of his life. Or get a kidney transplant. Mr. Douglass did not want to continue on dialysis, and he wasn't sure he wanted to undergo a surgical procedure either. Ultimately, it was his decision. And since he had all his mental faculties, he could make the decision.

Milan recalled their conversation.

"Daddy, if you don't stay on dialysis, you will die. I'm not ready for that. Please think about it."

"I have, angel. This isn't about you. I have lived a good life, and I watched you grow up. You have your daughter to raise now. I am ready to leave this place and go on to glory. Please don't fight me on this."

Milan cried, but she promised to grant his wish. Her mother accepted his decision as well.

"All you can do is keep him comfortable, and love him all the way till the end. Spend time with him. I know this is hard for you, letting go. You're a daddy's girl, but you will have to respect his wishes." I hugged her tightly and told her that I would visit as much as I could.

Mr. Douglass was transferred out of the unit and onto a regular floor in the hospital. He would be discharged home in a few days, before I was leaving out of town. I told Milan that I would come to the house on Tuesday when he came home. She seemed to be staying strong, but it was hard to read her sometimes. Milan wanted to move back home, but Mr. Douglass insisted she not do that.

"Continue to live your life, angel. Just visit me when you can. Your mother and I will be fine. I'm okay, really. I don't need a babysitter."

I gave Milan a hug and promised to call her from New Orleans. "Call me if you need me."

A lie has speed, but truth has endurance. ~Edgar J. Mohn

TWENTY-SEVEN

MALACHI

My cell phone rang on Wednesday afternoon, the day before Maiya was to arrive. The number on the caller ID was from Douglass & Vaughn. I knew Maiya wasn't at work since I had just talked to her. I figured it may be Milan and that something was wrong concerning her father, so I answered without hesitation.

"Hello, Malachi speaking."

"Yes, I know it is and how ARE you, Malachi?"

"Who is this?" I said, irritated.

"It's your future baby momma. Or did you forget already?"

"Tia? Dammit, girl. What is it with you? What do you want?"

"Oh, I'm getting exactly what I want. I just started my new job. Recognize the number?"

"What are you doing there?"

"I work here now. As a temp receptionist. Right outside of your sweet little Maiya's office," she answered, with sarcasm in her voice.

"I will have you fired!" I screamed into the phone. Good Lord. Tia was the temp that Maiya had been talking about coming in to replace Kari for the season. I'm sure Maiya had no idea who she was.

"You wouldn't! Unless of course you want Maiya to know about the baby. Our baby."

"Girl, you musta forgot who you're messing with. I will have that baby taken away from you and your dusty ass boyfriend. I told you, that's NOT my baby."

"Yeah, well, we will see about that. Oh, and enjoy your time in New Orleans. Knock 'em dead at the gala." I had no idea what she was talking about as she laughed out loud.

I could hear on her end Kari ask her what was going on. "Tia, we're not supposed to make personal calls at the front desk. Ms. Vaughn put a phone in the break room for us to use," I heard Kari say.

"Well, she ain't here now, is she? So, it looks like I can use the phone right where I am. Whatchu gonna do?" I almost choked as I listened to Tia disrespect Maiya's assistant.

"Now, look," I heard Kari say to Tia, "you just got here and you are already stirring up trouble. And for the record, this IS my business. So, unless you wanna go there with me, I suggest you acknowledge the rules and know your place!"

"Bitch, I will knock your ass out and mop the floor with your Asian ass. You don't know me. And you don't know how I roll!" Tia challenged her. I listened to this drama helplessly. I was too afraid to hang up but felt guilty listening without doing something. Tia had lost her mind.

"You apparently don't know me," I heard Kari say. "Look at you. Carrying a child and you acting like you ready to fight. I'm not even gonna waste my time on you. But I will tell you this….your temporary position here will be terminated."

"What? You threatening me?" Tia yelled. At this point, the phone had been dropped and I could imagine Tia standing there, looking at Kari with her hands on her hips.

"Let me just say this…You better not be here when we get back next week. That's all I'm saying."

And, at that point, I assumed Kari left because Tia picked up the phone again.

"I assume you heard all of that," she snarled.

"Tia, get your things and get out of there now. You have no business being at Maiya's office. This thing, this baby thing, it's between us. Maiya has nothing to do with it."

"Oh, that's what you think," Tia said. "What I'm realizing is that it might take longer than I thought, but I'm going to do what I gotta do, baby. Alright?"

And, with that, she hung up. The fear in my heart lingered well into the night.

We tell lies when we are afraid... afraid of what we don't know, afraid of what others will think, afraid of what will be found out about us. But every time we tell a lie, the thing that we fear grows stronger. ~Tad Williams

TWENTY-EIGHT

TIA

I left Douglass & Vaughn and headed to my condo in Tribeca of Camp Springs, next to the Branch Avenue Metro station. I waited to make the phone call to Maiya after she left the office, blocking my number so Maiya couldn't call it back. I wanted to get the girl to start questioning the validity of her new relationship with Malachi. But, that bitch still ain't answering her phone.

I was hoping that Fred wouldn't be home so I wouldn't have to put up with his lazy ass and his triflin' friends. If I had known before that Fred was such a waste of space, I never would have ruined what I had with Malachi by screwing him. But, hindsight is a bitch and I'm a quick learner.

Things fell apart pretty fast when Malachi found out I was sleeping with Fred. My mother always said I had a big mouth, but calling into the Wendy Williams show was so tempting since I really didn't have too many people to talk to about my affair with Fred. I mean, my closest friend at the time was Jasmine, Fred's ex, so it wasn't like I could very well tell her how much I enjoyed screwing her man. And, Wendy is so similar to me, I had to be on that show and dish it with my girl.

No one understands why I would have cheated on Malachi, but

it's simple. He's way too square and boring and really not my kind of guy. Granted, he is very handsome, is paid out the wazoo and has some physical equipment most men would pay to have, but, all in all, he's not my type. Not like Fred. Fred is daring, wild and crazy like me. But, as I learned, that does not cancel out the fact that he is lazy, has awful taste in friends and is broke as all hell. At least, that's what he says. I know he's a dealer. He just don't give me none of his money. Asshole. What sucks now, too, is that he isn't performing onstage like he used to, thanks to Malachi.

Since he and Malachi stopped talking altogether, Fred has not had any chances playing with SOUL. I knew Malachi was the reason Fred didn't play, but I really couldn't blame him. I couldn't possibly expect the two of them to be boys like they used to be. But, it really dampened the sexy factor that Fred had going on.

I would have been ok with being pregnant and being with Fred if I didn't realize how quickly Malachi was able to get over me. I mean, who did he think he was? I'm unforgettable. I realized that he really hadn't gotten over me as much as I thought when I was able to get him to sleep with me one last time.

I was already pregnant when Malachi came over that night. I got him pissy drunk, and I poked holes in the condom to make it seem like it broke by accident. At first, I didn't think my scheme would work, but apparently it did. Malachi fell for it, especially when he saw the torn condom.

I just didn't expect him to ask for a paternity test.

Nor did I anticipate him moving on to the arms of another woman.

I was running out of options, and I only had a few more months before my baby was born.

Fred's baby.

But, the Lord knows that Fred could barely support himself and the baby he has with Jasmine without having to set aside even more money for an extra mouth on the way to feed. Uh-uh. I needed another baby daddy fast and Malachi was the sucker for the job. That new girlfriend of his was not going to mess up me hitting my jackpot. I would get rid of her if I had to.

When I got to the door, I could hear laughter on the inside. *Damn.*

I opened the door and instantly inhaled the marijuana.

"Hey, baby. How did the new job go?" Fred asked.

I rolled my eyes. "It went."

I looked at one guy who had his feet on my coffee table.

"'Scuse me. Get your feet off my table!"

He set his feet on the floor and sat up.

"You ain't gotta holler. All you gotta do is axe nicely."

"The word is ask, not axe. And I do gotta holler. That's the only way you'll get it."

Fred stood up to embrace me, but I shooed him away and put my purse down.

"Hey, hey, baby. Calm down. Don't get all worked up. You got my baby and all," said Fred.

"Whatever, Fred. Your company needs to leave. I'm tired and I just wanna take a bath and go to bed."

"Girl, stop trippin'. They just got here. You need to chill out. Go on and lay down and I'll bring you a little something. You know daddy gon' take care of you."

"Ugh. I'll pass."

His friends started laughing. He turned to them and yelled, "Y'all can bounce. You ain't gon' disrespect me in my own house," he yelled.

"Why not? Your woman just did," said one of the guys. They burst out into laughter again and high-fived each other.

"Alright then. We'll see who's laughing when I make that paper and y'all want in on some of the action."

It got quiet very fast. "Yeah. That's what I thought," Fred continued.

He turned back to me and I threw up my hands and walked up the stairs.

"Baby, don't be mad. They not stayin' all night long," he called out.

"Hey, you want me to come up and make that kitty purr? You know you do!"

"Leave me alone. And get those bammas outta my house!" I yelled.

They laughed again and I slammed the upstairs bedroom door. Once in my room, I ran my bath water and made a phone call. I knew it would be no use, but I wanted to try to make things better. I dialed the number, but only got the answering machine.

"Hey, it's Jazz. I'm not able to come to the phone right now, so leave me a message, and I'll call you back."

"Jazz, it's me, Tia. Look, I've left you three messages. I know you're mad, but I'm really, really sorry. I have something to tell you, and I..... well, I need you. Please call me. Please."

I hung up. Oh well. I tried. Jasmine knows she can't be mad at me forever. I've known that girl for almost all my life. I didn't blame her for not returning my calls. I was wrong for sleeping with her man. And to be pregnant having his baby, too. It was a bit much for Jasmine to take. I guess, it did sound a bit more trifling the more I thought about it but, shit, what was I supposed to do?

Love has no desire but to fulfill itself. To melt and be like a running brook that sings its melody to the night. To wake at dawn with a winged heart and give thanks for another day of loving.
~Kahlil Gibran

TWENTY-NINE

MAIYA

It was hard leaving my hometown when so many things were happening. Milan needed me, and I wanted to be there in case Mr. Douglass didn't make it. But, one of us—either me or Milan had to make an appearance in New Orleans and head our team. When Thursday came and I landed in New Orleans, Malachi picked me up from the airport. We fell into each other's arms as if we hadn't seen each other in months.

I could not stop thinking about Malachi on the ride to the hotel and anticipated our lovemaking. I needed it for stress release. I could barely get my key in the door before we were in each other's faces. When he started kissing me, I immediately put my tongue in his mouth and he received it with a sense of urgency. I could feel his breathing become heavier and he pulled me closer to his chest, his heart beating faster.

He helped me out of my dress and it fell to the floor. He reached behind me and unsnapped my bra. I was eager to have him inside me and began unbuckling his belt. His slacks dropped to his ankles, and he stepped out of them. I could see his bulge through his boxer briefs and slid my hand inside to massage him. He moaned and grabbed me by the waist, lifting me up in the air and pushing me against the wall. He kissed my neck and my breasts, teasing my nipples with his tongue.

I moaned and begged him to take me.

He carried me to the bed and laid me down. He climbed on top of the bed and pulled my panties down, then massaged my clitoris with his tongue until I climaxed and my legs trembled. He knelt on the bed and took off his briefs. His penis was at full attention, and I was ready for him to "forward march."

Malachi got on top of me, licking and sucking and kissing me all over. He took my hand and placed it on his penis, and I squeezed and massaged until he moaned and his eyes rolled back in his head. He pressed his body on top of me, and I could feel his penis trying to make its way inside by itself. I eased up just a little bit closer to him, lifting my backside off the bed.

"Maiya, wait." Malachi hesitated. "I don't have any condoms."

I sucked my teeth and replied, "Neither do I. And you know I'm not on the pill."

"Look, baby, we can wait. It's no rush. I can run to the store right quick."

I shook my head no. "I don't wanna wait. I can't wait. I need to have you now. Right now." I pulled him on top of me and kissed him forcefully and passionately. I wanted to please him as much as I wanted to be pleased.

Malachi followed my lead and entered me slowly and deeply. I arched my back and moaned with pleasure. He took his time with me, as he had in the past, and filled me with a new pleasure. This was the second time I had made love to Malachi without a condom and the sensation was like no other.

We climaxed simultaneously and I begged him not to pull out, as my orgasm was at its peak. I held on to him tightly, and kept my legs wrapped around his waist. I could feel him pulsing inside me as he relaxed, then exhaled deeply. Malachi buried his face in my neck and, like he always does, said, "You smell so good."

He kissed me, giving me a sweet peck on my lips and rolled to the side of me. I turned on my side towards him, and rested my head on his chest.

"I love you, Maiya."

I felt the same for him, too. "I love you, Malachi."

We fell asleep, not regretting anything that happened.

* * *

Kari called me my first mid-morning in New Orleans and shared with me the drama that occurred with Tia after I left work on Wednesday, and reassured me that she would not be there working upon my return.

"That girl tried to get cute with me, and I just wasn't gonna have it."

I was shocked. "Wow, Kari. I knew you had a saucy side to you, but I would not have thought you were THAT saucy!"

"I just don't like drama. And people are always underestimating me because of my stature and my culture. Just push the wrong button, and you will be surprised."

"I see."

We both laughed.

It was still early morning, too soon for lunch, so I decided to sit off in a quiet place to finish reading a few more chapters of my book. Malachi was with his team in town and I was still waiting for all of my folks to arrive. Malachi sent me a text saying he had ordered lunch to be delivered by room service and would arrive before it got there. I smiled. *My baby thinks of everything*, I thought.

I sent a quick text to Milan to let her know where I was and that I had arrived safely in Louisiana. She let me know that all was well at home, and her dad was enjoying the company of Chloe.

When I hung up with her, I surveyed my room; I hadn't really gotten a good look when Malachi and I had christened it with our lovemaking the night before. The room was elegant and I really did feel like a Princess in my very own castle. Enjoying my surroundings, I must have fallen asleep because the next thing I felt was a long, hard passionate kiss that almost made me come on myself. *Was I dreaming?*

I opened my eyes and Malachi was above me with his work polo on. I smiled and pulled him closer, kissing him deeply.

Does he ever know how to push my buttons? I was hungry, but I could see that Malachi was, too. And I seemed to be on the menu.

There was a knock at the door, and in the waiter came with our food on a cart. He set my food up at the table, and told us to call if we needed anything else. While, just moments before, I had just wanted to eat and have a shower and a nap, but with my man waking me up so passionately, *I could add some other things to the agenda*, I thought seductively. But, first things first. I was starving.

I ate like I hadn't eaten in days. I was ravenous and couldn't understand why. I figured it was because I was getting close to my menstrual cycle, but that was still more than two weeks away. Malachi sat and watched me eat.

"Did you want any of this?" I asked, hoping that he would say no.

"Naw, babe, I'm good. I had some hot wings before you called me. So, how was your day?"

"It was good. Quiet. Kari told me there was drama with Tia after I left. She also said that Tia wouldn't be back once we returned to work next week. I did want to ask you something," I had just thought of this as I recounted the story.

Malachi, who was reading his phone, looked up.

"Yeah, baby. What is it?" he asked.

"This assistant. Her name is Tia Jamison. Is this the same Tia that you were engaged, to?

Malachi's face drained of color.

"Well, yes. Yes, that's the name of my ex-fiancé."

I put the chicken down.

"Why is she working in my office? I know it's a small world, but that seems too much like a coincidence."

Malachi didn't say anything. He looked guilty.

"You knew about this, didn't you? I really wish you had told me about this."

"I really didn't foresee it being a problem, Maiya. And I had no idea that she would seek you out to cause more drama. All I know is that I am with you. That is all that matters to me now. That chapter in my life is complete. It's done. There is nothing you need to be concerned about."

I felt a bit uncomfortable about this. Malachi knew his ex was working for me and didn't say anything? What else did he know and not tell me?

"Well, ok. I guess. But, for real, I will need for you to handle it. The next incident may not allow for Tia to walk away without a beat down."

"Let's not talk about it anymore. What is on the agenda for the rest of the day?"

"Well, we are supposed to meet with everyone that flew in today for a dinner tonight, and then tomorrow morning we have nothing planned. I have left everything up to the event planners, so all we have to do is show up. How did your meeting go with the team of guys out here?"

"It was productive, and we should be breaking ground in the next couple of weeks. With the Essence music festival the weekend of July 4th, we have to wait until the following week or so, but everything is going on as planned. I am getting very excited. Too bad Milan couldn't be here. How is her dad doing, anyway?"

I was in the middle of chewing, and held up my hand to excuse myself. "Um, his spirit hasn't changed. He has already planned his funeral, and I sat and talked with him for a bit the other day. He kept saying something about promising that Milan and I would always be close and to not be mad at her. He was really confusing me. He has accepted the change that is going on in his life, and he is at peace with death. He is pretty much ready to die."

"In a way, that is sad."

"It is but it isn't. You have to respect what a person asks, so I just told Milan to give him what he asks of them. I told her to call me if anything happens, but she said she didn't want to disturb us." I gulped down my root beer, and let out a belch that was so unladylike, I was embarrassed. "Please excuse me. That was really nasty."

Malachi just laughed.

I told him to reach in my bag and get the CD of the Secret Society. I wanted him to turn it on so we could listen to it. He played it, and bobbed his head to the beat. I could tell that he liked it. I cleared my empty plates to the side, and Malachi sat them on a tray by the door. I excused myself to the bathroom to put my toiletries away and brush my teeth. I found myself falling asleep on the chaise lounge while listening to the music in between Malachi talking to me. Before I realized it, I was sound asleep with a blanket wrapped around me.

When I woke up, it was after five p.m. and Malachi was in the sitting room watching television. "Hey, sleepyhead. You really must've been tired. You snored so loud that I had to come out here to watch TV!"

"Shut up," I tossed a pillow at him. "What time are we supposed to meet everyone?"

"I told them around six. They are setting up everything in the Red Room at the Sheraton. It is only a few blocks away, so we can walk over, if that's alright with you."

"I have a driver for the whole time we are here. He will be taking us, if that's alright with you," I said with a fake attitude and hands on my hips.

"Ah, of course. You in New Orleans now and getting lazy. What happened to the woman who walks and runs everywhere every day? Huh, huh?" he started tickling me and I fell on the bed laughing. Of course tickles turned to touches and before we could stop, we had begun another sexy romp before dinner that was even better than the one from the night before.

*   *   *

The remainder of the weekend went by too fast. Funny how time flies when you're having fun. Nobody can say it better than Janet. Miss Jackson, if you're nasty!

Dinner at the Four Points Sheraton turned out to be nice. Malachi's staff was very excited about the project and couldn't wait for it to get under way. I didn't eat much, since I was stuffed from lunch earlier, but I had a couple of glasses of wine and a slice of cheesecake in plum raspberry sauce. I felt overdressed, but eased up a bit when I saw that my female staff was similarly clad in dressy attire of slacks or skirts and flowing blouses. Malachi and I didn't stay long, and I was knocked out once we got back to the room. It poured rain that night and the thunder and lightning practically ripped through our window. I slept like a baby.

But our time spent in New Orleans wasn't all about sleeping, no. On Friday, Malachi and I took a tour of the French Quarter and received much education. The culture is rich with much history, and I was amazed at the hospitality with which we were greeted.

We later rode to Bourbon Street, and I fancied the many shops with their exotic and bright colors, and friendly business owners. We shared with them the construction that would take place in a few weeks to enhance the existing medical facilities that were destroyed by Katrina. Many were ecstatic to hear of the work we planned to do. One gentleman, a carpenter, hugged both of us and gave us many well wishes and "God bless you's".

We were done with our sightseeing just as the sky darkened and clouds opened up. The air was warm and moist. The wind was picking up and lightning began to streak the sky. The rain poured down heavily, and we ran for the closest awning. It was still eighty degrees outside, so the rain was a welcomed coolness. As we stood waiting for the rain to lighten up, Malachi pulled me close to him and turned my chin to his face. He kissed me hard and very forceful. He pulled away from me just as his cell phone vibrated in his pocket. It was the limo driver looking to pick us up. Malachi told him where to find us, and we ran, in the rain, to find shelter in the limo.

Once inside, I unbuttoned my shirt and threw it on the limousine floor. My hair, wet from the rain, whipped behind me as I flung my head back. I was feeling like the Nasty Girl that only Vanity 6 could sing about. *"I'm looking for a man that'll do it anywhere, even on a limousine floor."* I straddled Malachi who, surprised at first, was up to the naughtiness of making love in a limo. While he buried his face between my breasts, I grabbed his head between my hands, loving every minute that he gave my body the attention it craved. I wanted him to take me right then and there, but I also wanted to pleasure him first to get the party on and popping. I pulled out his long, thick Mr. Feel Good and wrapped my tongue around him in such a slow, soft and tantalizing way that Malachi almost hollered aloud. I covered his mouth with my hand to muffle his moans as I flicked with my tongue. As I saw the awning of our hotel up ahead, I realized I would have to wait to get to our room to finish what I had started. But, Malachi begged me not to stop.

Large raindrops began to beat down on the roof of the limo, making sounds of Congo drums, and turning me on the faster it came down. Foreplay with Malachi was intense, and it was enough to whet my appetite until I could get to the main course. Malachi grabbed my hair, still dripping wet from the rain, as my tongue slid up and down Mr. Feel Good. I could feel Malachi shudder with pleasure and it wasn't long before he pulled me from off of my knees and tore off my panties. He pulled me on top of him and my body filled quickly with him inside, thrusting as I bounced up and down. My hair fell in his face and he pulled it back with a forceful tug, making me moan with pleasure. He soon pushed me onto my back, making me lie down with his body on top of mine. Using his legs to move open mine, he pulled down my bra straps and sucked my nipples until they were erect. He reached down under my skirt to feel the warm wetness, before inserting Mr. Feel Good into my kitten again. I was literally purring. The rain continued to beat down with force. Thunder ripped through the clouds. Lightning illuminated the sky.

We were so into one another until a voice interrupted us through the speakers. "Excuse me, Mr. Taylor. Should I drive around longer or go straight to the hotel?"

Malachi looked down at me, as if to ask me to answer the question. I raised my eyebrows, and nodded yes.

"Um, you can just drive around some more," Malachi answered.

I whispered to him, "You know he's watching us."

"Well, then, let's give him a show worth looking at."

He sat up, and pulled his shirt over his head and tossed it to the floor of the limo. He took his time with me, as he always did, and gave me maximum pleasure. I came right before him, and we collapsed in each other's arms. He wrapped his arms around me and held me tight. We rode around for another half hour before arriving at the hotel. We dressed back into our wet clothing and made it inside to continue with part two in the shower.

What happens to a dream deferred? Does it dry up like a raisin in the sun? ~ **Langston Hughes**

THIRTY

An evening of elegance and fun awaited us Saturday night in New Orleans. Malachi was dressed in a black tuxedo and I wore a black strapless evening gown. My hair was pulled to the side in a chignon, and my accessories included diamonds and onyx. We were the most handsome couple there. When we arrived at the ballroom, we were greeted and escorted to our table near the front of the room. The evening was spectacular and I was pleased that all of this was in celebration of us being able to give back to the community.

The total program time was set for four hours, and allowed for us to mingle, dance, and network. Malachi and I sat at a table with Shane and his partner, Matt, along with some members of Malachi's team. I realized that I did not have my speech with me, and quickly became a basket case.

"You're going to do just fine, Maiya. Don't worry. You have it memorized, so just calm down." Malachi kissed my forehead. "Speak from your heart; those words will always be your best bet if you forget something."

Prominent figures from the area were in attendance to show support of our cause. Such individuals included Tyler Perry, Ellen DeGeneres, Carl Weathers, Bryant Gumbel, Reese Witherspoon, Raquel "Rocsi" Diaz, Harry Connick, Jr., District Attorney Jim Garrison, Mayor Ray Nagin, United States Senator David Vitter, Clyde Drexler, Lee Collins, Richard Simmons, Wynton Marsalis and New Orleans Saints owner Tom Benson with players Drew Brees, Jermon Bushrod, and Reggie Bush.

I was pleased to see all of my staff, and they all came over to congratulate me. I was so nervous that I could hardly eat, so I just nibbled on a garden salad and some sushi that was set before me. Malachi had me mingle with him and walked with me to introduce me to his staff working on the New Orleans contract that sat at other tables. After a glass of wine or two, I loosened up a bit. Kari introduced me to the crowded room, and I made my way to the podium with less nervousness than when I first arrived.

"Good evening everyone, and thanks for coming. This night would not be successful without all of the love and support that you have given to this project. Although I have since moved away from New Orleans, it still plays a major part in my life. Having attended Grambling State University, I spent four years learning of the rich history of Louisiana and loved this place as my second home. My best friend and partner in this business, Milan Douglass, could not be here with me tonight due to her father's illness, but she sends her gratitude and appreciation to you as well. Just to give you a brief history of our company, Douglass & Vaughn, I want to share with you the dream that we had of being in business for ourselves, to serve the people and our community. We provide physical therapy services on an out-patient basis as well as other rehabilitative services. We would be remiss in our duties if we didn't give the best we have to offer, and since we have been able to live our dream, Milan and I wanted to come back to what we call our home away from home. We are continuing to expand, which is why we are here tonight. At this time, I would like my staff to please stand and be acknowledged for all of their hard work."

In the ballroom, applause rang out as my staff stood.

"I want to thank each and every one of you for your hard work and dedication. Without you, we would not be able to provide the services that we do, and keep the satisfied customers coming back. You may be seated.

"In 2005, Hurricane Katrina rocked the south, rearing her ugly head along the Gulf coast and causing destruction from Central Florida through Texas. She was one of the five deadliest hurricanes in the history of the United States, claiming the lives of over eighteen hundred people. Katrina was the largest natural disaster in history alone. The total damage was over eighty billion dollars and Milan and I knew that we wanted to be a part of rebuilding a place we still call home. And we also knew there was a need for better healthcare. Our dream is now becoming a reality thanks to all of you. But the construction would not at all be possible without Taylor Made Construction, Inc. I proposed my idea to this gentleman, and without hesitation, he agreed to help me with this project. Please help me in recognizing Mr. Malachi Taylor, architect and designer of the new building, set to break ground in a few weeks."

Malachi stood to be recognized and blew kisses to me, and then sat down.

I continued. "I could stand up here all night rambling on and on, but I won't. There are a lot of you that I would like to name personally, and forgive me if I forget anyone. The one person I want to recognize as being the one man who actually returned my calls and spoke to me directly and not through his assistant, is Mayor Ray Nagin. Thank you from the bottom of my heart for turning my team on to the right people and for allowing us to invade your space to make this happen. Much appreciation goes out to, and this is in no particular order, Tyler Perry, Reese Witherspoon, Harry Connick, Jr., Wynton Marsalis, Branford Marsalis, Carl Weathers, and Richard Simmons. There are many others that I may be forgetting, but please charge it to my head and not my heart. Please enjoy the rest of your evening, and I hope to have each and every one of you come visit the new building once it is complete. Thank you."

I received much applause and a standing ovation in the room. I was overcome with emotion and could not hold back the tears as they streaked down my cheeks. Malachi gave me an enormous hug and kissed me. He whispered in my ear, "You were fabulous. I love you."

I smiled at him and said, "I love you, too, Mr. Taylor."

The rest of the evening included more celebrities to tell of their involvement and their history with Louisiana and Hurricane Katrina. We spent all night getting introduced to a lot of them, taking pictures and sharing stories about how tragedy brings people together, regardless of race or stature.

By the end of the night, I felt like I was on cloud nine and didn't want the night to end. Malachi must have been reading my mind, because he told me that there was some place he wanted to show me.

We rode in the limousine to the front of a place called Brennan's on Royal Street, and I waited for my surprise. I waited inside the limo while Malachi got lost inside the restaurant. When he returned, he thanked our driver and told him that we would see him in the morning. The driver let us out on Royal Street, and a carriage was waiting there for us.

Malachi helped me up into the carriage and climbed up behind me, sitting very close to me. There was a bottle of chilled champagne with two wine glasses. The night air began to chill me and I was glad that I brought my shawl. Malachi saw the chills on my arms, and took off his jacket and put it around my shoulders.

"How's that? Better?"

"Much better. Thanks."

"Tonight, you were absolutely in your shine. It was wonderful. I think you did a great job, Miss I-forgot-my-speech-and-don't-know-what-to-say." He laughed.

"Ha, ha. You got jokes, hunh? But thanks, anyway. It was great to see the room filled with people for a good cause. Did you see Kanye West, and how about the Saints' players? Oh, and what about Taraji P. Henson? She was gorgeous! I was so excited. It was like my dream come true. I was so in love with the connection. It was so…"

Malachi cut me off and kissed me ever so passionately that I wanted to cry. He took me by surprise, and I gave in to him. When we finally came up for air, he took my hand in his. "Just as you were in love with the connection tonight, I could not stop thinking about how much in love with you I am. This is my dream come true-- being with someone who absolutely complements me in all that I do. I am not perfect, Maiya, and I will never act like I am. What I do know is that we are a perfect match."

The carriage was taking us through Woldenberg Park, near the Mississippi river. There were street performers and local musicians entertaining those of us who chose to be out this late. I noticed that the carriage stopped and we were in front of the most beautiful skyline view of the city. Malachi reached into his pocket and pulled out a small box. He got down on one knee and, taking my left hand in his, said to me, "Maiya, I have loved you from the first time we had coffee and conversation back in February. I go to bed thinking about you and I wake up hoping you have the most blessed of days. I cannot see myself without having you in my life. Will you please do me the honor of being my wife?"

I was speechless. I just couldn't find the words to say. Is this really happening to me? Tears rolled down my face again. Damn, I didn't mean to be a crybaby!

"Your silence is scaring me, Maiya. Please say something."

"Wow, Malachi. I was not expecting this at all! Yes, I will marry you. Yes!"

He placed the ring on my finger and then got up off his knee. He grabbed my face between his hands, and kissed me. He wiped the tears from my face, and handed me a glass. He popped the bottle of champagne and we toasted our engagement. I had never felt like this before. Of course, I thought everything was going up from here, but how sadly mistaken was I.

To us, family means putting your arms around each other and being there. ~Barbara Bush

THIRTY-ONE

"Thank you for flying US Airways flight 626. And welcome to our nation's capital. Please be careful when opening up the overhead luggage compartment, as bags may have shifted during the flight. Have a great day. We hope you fly with us again."

"Come on, baby, we're here," Malachi nudged me gently, causing me to awaken.

"Wow, I must have slept the entire flight."

He smiled and grabbed my bags. Our driver was waiting for us as we rode down the escalator. As I neared the door, a sharp pain attacked my abdomen, causing me to double over and drop my purse.

Malachi ran back to where I stood. "Maiya, what's wrong? You alright?"

"I'll be fine. I just got a pain that shocked me. Just gimme a minute and I'll be alright."

"You sure? There's no rush, you know?"

"No, really, I'm alright. Really."

Malachi didn't look convinced.

It took me a few minutes to get myself together and I faked a smile in between the twinges of pain that continued until we arrived at my condo. Malachi's car was parked at my house from when I drove him to the airport. He took my luggage inside, as well as his.

"I'm not leaving you like this. Let me get you inside so you can lie down. You need me to go get Chloe?"

"No, she's at the Douglass'. I can call later. What about Apollo and Samson?"

"My man Kevin has them, so I will let him keep them until I can get there to pick them up. Don't worry. I'm gonna stay with you for awhile."

Once inside, I took eight hundred milligrams of Motrin with a sip of water. I asked Malachi to get my heating pad from the closet. I got undressed and put on shorts and a tank top.

"You need anything else?"

"No thanks, baby. I'm okay now. I just need to rest."

But I knew that wasn't true. My endometriosis was rearing its ugly head this time harder than it ever had. This pain was unlike any I had ever felt before. I slept for two hours and woke up starving. Malachi was down the hall washing clothes and didn't hear me come up behind him.

"Hey baby, did I wake you?"

"No, the hunger pangs woke me. I'm starving."

"Well, you have nothing in the fridge. I can go pick up something or do you wanna have something delivered?"

"I'm in the mood for pizza. The number to Ledo's is in the kitchen."

"Veggie pizza, right?"

"Right. And some barbecue wings and mozzarella sticks."

"Okay, just let me put this last load in the washer."

"I got it babe, go ahead."

"You sure?"

"Will you go already?"

When Malachi left to get the food, I placed a call to my doctor's office.

"Hi, it's Maiya Vaughn. I need Dr. Woods to call in a prescription for me?"

"Hold on one second, ma'am."

A few moments went by, and my doctor came on the line.

"Maiya, what is it? Are the pains back?"

"Un-hunh, with a vengeance. I need something."

"Listen, Maiya, you're gonna have to make a decision soon. You can't go on like this. Surgery is your best option. We've talked about it. We can help fix this."

"I'll think about it. Can you help me in the meantime?"

"I will call in Motrin and give you enough Percocet for two days. Come see me on Thursday. Can you come at nine?"

"I can make it."

"Okay, get some rest and I'll see you on Thursday."

Next, I called Milan to check in on Chloe and Mr. Douglass. She answered on the first ring.

"Hello?"

"Hey, Lani, it's me. We got back this afternoon. How is everything? Did Chloe behave herself? When do you need me to...?"

Milan cut me off. "Maiya, Daddy died. Chloe was the one who found him."

"I am so sorry. I thought he was getting better. What happened?"

"He must have died in his sleep. She fell asleep in his lap, and in the morning he usually gets up to walk her to the door. When he didn't get up, she kept barking until she came in my room to get me, and that's when I found him."

"Are you doing alright? How is your mom?"

"We are doing okay. We knew it was just a matter of time, though. And at least he wasn't in pain, and he's not suffering anymore. We are working out the funeral arrangements now, and I am trying to get Nadia and my grandparents to come in a few days. Jackson is flying out in the morning and bringing his children back. Your aunt is here with mom now, and she is helping put together the program."

"Man, Lani, this is terrible. It sounds like if it's not one thing, it's another."

"You can say that again. I'm beat down, Maiya. Daddy dying is tougher than I thought it would be."

"Did you want me to come and help out? I can be there in a flash."

"No, actually I wanna come home. I need to get outta here. I will be on my way there soon, and I'm bringing your baby home."

"Okay, I will see you when you get here."

* * *

By the time Milan got to my place, I was in the middle of licking the barbecue sauce from my fingers, sitting across from Malachi at the table, and laughing about how funny Shane and Matt were at the gala on Saturday evening.

"You have to admit it, Maiya, they are an interesting couple."

"I have to agree with you on that one," I answered, as I got up to answer the door. "Hey, Lani. It's good to see you." We exchanged hugs, and she was handing my terrier to me, who was very quiet. "Let me wash my hands; I got barbecue sauce just about everywhere."

Malachi stood up and hugged Milan as I washed my hands.

"Let me know what you need from us, Milan," he told her. "My dad died when I least expected, too, so I know exactly what you are going through. Just let me know if you need anything."

"Thanks very much; that's kind of you," Milan said. Her eyes were red-rimmed. I prayed she hadn't relapsed and started drinking or smoking again.

"Mai, I'll be right back," she said before dashing out.

Malachi and I looked at each other, stunned by her quick exit.

"Did you get a chance to tell her about us?" Malachi asked me.

"No, I didn't. When I called she just started telling me about her dad. I didn't feel right, so I figured I would share the news when she got here."

"You finished with this?" he asked, pointing to the pizza box and wings. "Do you have any more room left for anything else?"

"Nah, I'm done."

Milan walked back through the door. "So, please tell me all about New Orleans. I could use some fun, happy news around here."

Malachi and I told Milan all about the city, where we stayed, the gala, and all the celebrities that were there. He bragged about my speech and made me blush. "She is really being modest, Milan. My girl here was awesome! Got all teary-eyed when they gave her a standing ovation!"

"Wow, Maiya that is great! I wish I could have been there with you guys. Wait! Hold up! What is this I see?" she screamed, while grabbing my hand and looking at my engagement ring.

"Oh, yeah, that's what I wanted to call and tell you, but it was so late that night. Malachi proposed to me after we left the event. He took me on a carriage ride and we could see the moon shining down on the Mississippi river. It was beautiful."

"Girl, come here and let me give you some love!" She grabbed me, and hugged me extra tight. "I am so happy for you two. I couldn't have picked a better person for you. Congratulations, Malachi."

"Thanks. Well, look, I'm gonna give you two time to catch up. I have rehearsal tonight, so I won't be back until ten. I'll call you when I'm on my way back." He kissed me and turned to Milan. "It's good seeing you."

"Bye."

Milan was so overwhelmed with emotion, she started to cry.

"I just feel so lost, Maiya. Daddy was so ready for this, but Mom and I were not. We did everything he asked, down to giving him a pipe to smoke and fixing him a rib dinner. I even baked him a sweet potato pie! He was the happiest I had seen in a long time. He kept saying to me over and over to promise him that you and I would be close. 'Promise me, angel.' That's what he kept repeating. What do you think he meant? What do you think that was all about?"

"I don't know, Lani. He said it to me, too, before I left. He also gave me blessings with Malachi, telling us that we would have 'pretty babies'."

We both laughed.

"I'm gonna miss him, Maiya. I really am."

"Me, too, girl. Me too."

Milan didn't wanna be sad and cry anymore, so she asked me more about our trip. I told her about our naughtiness in the limousine, and she almost spit her drink out of her mouth.

"I can't believe y'all got busy in the limo! You are such a freak!"

"Well, I learned it from you, so what does that say about you?"

"Ooh, you skank, no you didn't!"

"Oh, and I forgot to tell you about the new temp that showed up last week. How 'bout she is Malachi's ex and came up in there starting trouble. And you won't even believe who shut it down!"

"Let me guess. One of my wonderful tambourine shaker employees?"

I made a buzzing sound. "Wrong answer. I will take the small Filipino assistant for two hundred, Alex!"

We burst out in laughter.

"Shutchamouth! Are you kidding me? Kari? I would have never guessed it."

"Me neither. She told me everything after it happened."

"And how did you explain that to Mr. Fine? You didn't get all ghetto, did you?"

"No, girl. I didn't. Apparently, she has been stalking him and she used the temp position to get next to me. It's crazy, but I believe he will shut it down. He already has a restraining order against her and he told me he would handle it. I trust him."

"Yeah, okay."

"What, Milan?"

"It just sounds fishy to me, that's all I'm saying. Don't let me have to whoop a bitch's ass now! You know I am quick to put on my red lipstick!"

"Well, you might not wanna do that since she's pregnant, too!"

"Damn, Maiya! You gonna be a stepmom, too?"

"He didn't say anything about the baby."

"And you didn't ask him, did you?"

I shook my head no.

"Girl, what is wrong with you? How do you know that baby ain't his?"

"And how do you know that it is?"

"Maiya. You accepted the man's marriage proposal. Hello? And you didn't even ask him if that is his baby? That doesn't sound smart, if you ask me."

"Well, I didn't ask you," I said. Sensing my attitude, she stood up to leave out.

I stood up and grabbed her arm. "Milan, please don't leave. I really need you right now."

"Well, apparently you just want me to hear you live in a dream world," Milan folded her arms. "Maiya, what has been the common theme with all of the men in your past and the reason why things never worked out?"

I couldn't look at her.

"Maiya?"

"Trust, dammit. Truth. Being honest. None of those mofos could tell the truth to save their life."

"Exactly. Whether it was Derrick lying about his inappropriate relationship with his ex-girlfriend or Joaquin lying about his desire to have kids, all of them lied about something important. Even Carlos lied when he couldn't be upfront about how much he cared about you."

"So, what's your point, Milan?" I wanted to know.

"My point is that you need to be the one to ask questions, Maiya. You have to be the one to demand from your partners that they be upfront with you. If there is something that sounds fishy, you need to speak up and ask about it. If I am suspicious about that baby of Tia's being Malachi's baby, I know that you had that thought cross your mind. Why wouldn't you ask him?"

I couldn't respond. She was right, and I knew it. At that moment, a sharp, gut-ripping pain tore across my pelvic area. I crumpled to the floor.

Milan cried out. "Maiya! What's wrong? Are you having those pains again? Like before?"

I nodded my head yes, and started to cry.

"What should I do? Should I call the ambulance?"

I told her to just help me to the sofa and get me some water. I sipped on it and curled into a ball.

"You didn't tell him, did you?"

"Yes and no. I told him once before that I may not be able to have children, but that didn't bother him. He said we could always adopt."

"But you didn't tell him that the abdominal pains get worse after you have sex?"

"No, I didn't." I started crying again. "I already called my doctor, and I am going to see her on Thursday. She wants me to have the surgical procedure."

"You know I will be here for you. And so will Malachi. Look, I don't know what's behind all this mess with the ex, but just watch your back. And if you have questions, you better ask. Don't be a fool, Maiya. I am not about to sit here and watch you get all broken up over another man! It's obvious that he loves you, but don't let the smooth taste fool you."

"I trust him, Lani. I really do. Just let me handle it."

"Alrighty, then. If you need me, you know I gotchu."

"Yes, I know."

A gentle answer turns away wrath, but a harsh word stirs up anger.
~Proverbs 15:1

THIRTY-TWO

MILAN

I knew if Maiya knew what I was about to do, she would be mad. Who am I fooling? She would be pissed! So I kept it to myself.

I got to the office building and let myself into Kari's office.

The personnel files were kept in a file cabinet behind her reception area, and I went right to it, and found what I was looking for. I didn't have Tia's last name, but it didn't take me long to go through all the files until I found her. Scribbling her address and phone number down on a notepad, I put the files back and stepped into Maiya's office where I made my phone call on a disposable cell phone I had purchased the night before from the corner store.

In a few moments, Tia was gonna wish she never crossed Maiya.

I dialed the number I had written down, and a guy answered the phone.

"Hello."

"Good afternoon, I am trying to reach Tia," I disguised my voice with a southern drawl.

"She ain't here right now. But you can call her on her cell phone. Is this about a job?"

"Actually, it is, but she didn't list an alternate number on her application."

I saw how easy it would be to get her number. After hanging up, I dialed her cell phone. She answered on the first ring.

"Hello?"

"Is this Tia?"

"Yeah, who is this?"

"Someone you don't wanna mess with. I know all about your plans to mess with Malachi's new love interest, Maiya. But, if you know what's best for you, you will stay away from Malachi and Maiya."

"Malachi? Maiya? Look, I don't know who you think…."

I cut her off. "I didn't stutter, Tia. Show up at Maiya's office again or make any attempt to call Maiya and you will be sorry. That baby you carrying. You don't want the truth to come out now, do you?" I was reaching with that threat, but it was worth throwing in there. I continued. "And if you keep it up, I will make sure your baby finds a nice home with a decent family. It's apparent you have time to run around town and harass people. I will have you up on charges for stalking. CPS will take that baby from you quicker than your breast milk can come in. You don't want none of this." I hung up abruptly. *Now,* I thought, *let's see if Ms. Tia runs to Malachi's arms for solace or, if Maiya was right, and it's over between them and that's not his baby.*

If you have health, you probably will be happy, and if you have health and happiness, you have all the wealth you need, even if it is not all you want. ~Elbert Hubbard

THIRTY-THREE

MAIYA

"Ms. Vaughn. The doctor will see you now?"
I decided to come to my appointment alone and talk it over with Milan later. After my examination, Dr. Woods recommended I see another specialist for a second opinion.

"It's just that I am seeing a change in your cells, and I would like for another specialist to provide an opinion before you decide what treatment to take. But you should know that you are pregnant, Maiya. It's an ectopic pregnancy, so we need to operate. The embryo can't grow in your fallopian tubes. I can get you into Dr. Willow's office tomorrow, and he will be able to do both procedures at once. I know this is a lot to take in right now, but you need to take care of the pregnancy first. I am sorry."

Tears welled up in my eyes. Pregnant? And, now, they're telling me I have to abort my baby or I'll die. *God*, I screamed in my head, *why me?*

"Is there something else you are not telling me?"

"I am not so sure that what I saw in your cells was endometriosis. It's as if it may just be a cyst. This is why I need to do another biopsy and get a second opinion. So we can compare notes. I want to send your records to Dr. Willows right away."

"What can I do in the meantime?"

"Continue with the Motrin and Percocet, and abstain from intercourse. The pain you were having was from the ectopic pregnancy; but there appears to be a cyst on the ovary on the side of the same Fallopian tube. I am sure your future husband will understand. If you like, I can explain it to him if you want to bring him back."

"No, that's okay. I can talk to him. I'll be fine."

Malachi would feel horrible if he thought he was any way responsible for what I was going through.

"Good, well, wait for me in the waiting room and let me make that appointment for you. Dr. Willows will probably schedule your surgery sooner than later, so don't make any plans over the next few days."

"Okay, thank you."

"No problem, Maiya. Everything will be fine. And you should be able to get pregnant again, so don't worry." She smiled, and placed her hand on my shoulder.

I accepted the appointment she made with Dr. Willows in the morning, and called my office to tell Kari that I would be out the rest of the week. I also wanted to make sure the staff knew about the death of Mr. Douglass, and that plans would be forthcoming for a funeral.

I was in a daze, operating in slow motion. Pregnancy. Surgery. Death. All of the events of the past few months tumbled in my mind. How could I be happy with getting married when Milan was dealing with her dad's death and here I was, pregnant for a second time with yet another unhappy ending? Just a year ago, I lost the baby from Carlos, and now this. It just seemed like I would never get the baby that I longed for. I felt like I was being punished for whatever reason. My eyes were too dry to cry. I needed a pick-me-up.

I got in my car and just started driving. I had no idea where I was going. As I drove, thoughts flooded my mind. That wench Tia somehow came to the forefront. All the things Milan said came to my mind. Could Malachi be her baby's father? And if so, why wouldn't he say something to me about it? All of a sudden I was beginning to question my trust in him. Could he be playing me?

I got home and climbed in my bed, tired and confused. I slept and then woke, still maddened by all of these things coming at me at once. When Malachi walked through my front door, I was standing on the balcony looking out at the boats at the Harbor, wishing I could be cruising away on one of them.

He opened the door to the balcony.

"Hey."

As soon as I saw him, I just lost it and burst into tears. He embraced me, and I held on tight.

"It's gonna be alright. Just tell me what's wrong."

Once I was able to calm down, I looked up at him.

"I'm pregnant," I whispered.

Malachi raised his eyebrows, as if questioning me. A smile spread across his face.

"Is that why you're upset? It's okay. We said that we wanted a family, right?"

"It's more complicated than that. It's a tubal pregnancy, and I'll have to have surgery. Plus, they want to see what else is wrong with me. I'm really scared."

He held on to me and comforted me until I was calmer.

"Tell me. What is a tubal pregnancy? I'm not sure what that means."

"It's when the fertilized egg implants itself along the Fallopian tube instead of travelling to the uterus, where it is supposed to implant. If it isn't caught soon enough and continues to grow, it can cause more complications and can rupture. That can be deadly."

I decided to tell Malachi what he needed to know about our intimacy and what my doctor suggested about abstaining from intercourse. He was supportive and told me that he wanted to make sure I was taken care of.

"There are many levels of intimacy, Maiya. It doesn't have to always be about intercourse. We will just have to wait until we get the green light from the doctor."

"That's why I love you," I said softly.

"So, what's next? What does the doctor need you to do?"

"I have to go see another specialist tomorrow, and he may want to do the procedure as soon as possible. As soon as Saturday."

"Okay, okay. I'm here, and I'm not going anywhere. We will get through this together. Okay?"

I nodded yes and he wiped my tears from my face.

"I gotta make a few calls to the office, and I'm all yours, baby."

After calling his office, Malachi stayed with me and held me until I drifted off to sleep. He insisted on going with me to my appointment in the morning, and I agreed. In the meantime, we tried to focus on the positive, our upcoming wedding, and discussed how we would tell our families. He told me his family reunion was at the end of July, and that we could tell his mother and the family then. I knew she would be happy for us. Our connection was genuine, and I was looking forward to becoming a part of the Taylor family.

*   *   *

My surgery happened sooner than later. It disrupted much of the family festivities for me that July. We missed my Aunt Rocsi's Fourth of July cookout where Milan's daughter Nadia made her appearance. Though I insisted that Malachi go to the cookout without me, he would not leave my side. A part of me was glad he decided to stay with me. He showed me a lot of attention, and I knew he genuinely loved me.

Jackson, Milan and Brandon came over to visit me, though, bringing the children with them and I was happy to be able to see all of them. Meeting Nadia in person made everything seem surreal to me. My best friend was a mother—to a teenager. Jackson and Milan together beaming at their precious daughter as she played with her younger siblings was a sight to behold. I felt a strange twinge of jealousy that I had never felt towards Milan before. Will I be able to have a family like Jackson and Milan?

Shane and Kari also came to visit me during the time I was recuperating, bringing flowers, Edible Arrangements, balloons, and plenty of food from my staff. Milan had offered Shane a management position before my surgery and he had decided to accept the offer, so he and Kari were pretty much running things back at the office. I asked him fifty million questions about how things were operating at the office but he cut me off immediately.

"I did not mean to come here and discuss work chile, you are here to rest!"

I laughed at him. "It's okay, really. It doesn't bother me a bit. I am glad you came to visit me. Thanks."

"Anything for you, Maiya. You have worked so hard for this company, and we just want you to relax and get better," said Kari. "And Kendra says you didn't have to go and get yourself in the hospital just to get a massage. She was gonna give you one either way!" We all laughed.

"You just tell Kendra to save me a spot," I answered.

Malachi walked in from taking Chloe out for a walk. "How's everybody doing?"

"We are good, thanks," responded Kari.

"Are y'all gonna stay for dinner? I was just about to run over to the Smoke Shack and pick up some ribs and chicken."

"Mmm, that sounds good, but I have a date," said Kari.

"Well, honey, I don't have a date, but I need to go get these tired feet a pedicure. Maybe some other time, but thanks," said Shane, through pursed lips.

"Well, alright then. Maybe some other time." Malachi turned to me. "Babe, I'm gonna go on over and pick up the food. You need me to pick up anything else?"

"Some ginger ale is really all I want. But we don't need any more food. Did you see what was in the kitchen? Kari's mom fixed pancit and lumpia."

"Okay, but I really had a taste for some barbecue. If y'all are gone when I get back, it was good seeing you and thanks for coming to see Maiya. She is always talking about you both and can't wait to get back to work!"

"Honey, don't rush to get back. Take your time. You got this fine ass man taking care of you, too. Whew!" Shane said, fanning himself with his hand.

Kari laughed. "I just never know what will come outta your mouth. Come on, let's get outta here."

"If y'all are ever interested in hearing my band play, let me know and I will get you some tickets. We have a show coming up next weekend, and I would love to have you come and listen."

"Sounds good. Matt is going to New Orleans to look at a few apartments next weekend and I will be by myself. I got somewhere to go now." He leaned down to kiss my forehead. "Bye, Maiya. Feel better now."

"See you, Maiya. We will hold down the fort, don't you worry," said Kari.

"Thanks for coming by," I said.

They followed Malachi out the door.

* * *

Six weeks had elapsed, and I was recuperating one day at a time. I still was not back to work, but was able to get things done from home.

Dr. Herbert Willows performed a biopsy during my procedure, and the tissue was not indicative of endometriosis. At my follow-up appointment, he gave me a clean bill of health, and told me that when I planned to conceive, I should have no problems. I was told to return in a few months to see if my menstrual cycles became more regular and to take further action if necessary. I already had one irregular menstrual cycle, then another cycle of spotting, and Dr. Willows told me that was normal.

I was pleased with the news, especially since I was horny as hell.

For the first two weeks after my procedure, Malachi insisted I stay with him. He was able to manage his employees in Louisiana from home, and didn't have to go in to the office. The rest of my recuperation time was spent at my place. I knew it was a sacrifice for him to leave his dogs, but his friend kept them at his house.

He did everything for me that I could possibly need. He made me feel so secure. I was miserable that I couldn't work out yet so when I just needed to get outside, we walked the trail down to the waterfront.

It was hard seeing him every day and having him lie next to me in bed every night. I watched him shower, getting dressed and undressed. Damn! He was just as sexy as could be, and I could not wait to give him what I knew he had to be missing as much as I was.

After eating breakfast at my place one morning, I helped clean up the kitchen. I went to the bedroom to gather clothes to do laundry, but was sexually frustrated and just sat down on the bed. When Malachi came and sat down next to me, he looked at me and asked me what was wrong. I told him that I missed him and that I really wanted him to make love to me. He gave me a naughty look and his lip curled in a sexy grin.

I leaned over and kissed him hungrily and with so much force that I pushed him down on the bed. I climbed on top of him, kissing his neck and unbuttoning his shirt. My heart began to race and my breathing was heavy, matching his breaths as he returned the passion. I wanted him badly. I needed to feel him inside me. I reached down to feel his erect penis and he moaned with pleasure. Then, without warning, Malachi stopped me, pushing me off of him and sitting up.

"What is it? What's wrong?"

"I don't wanna hurt you, Maiya. We need to take things slow."

"But I'm fine. The doctor says everything's fine. I need to have you inside me. Don't you want me?" I pleaded.

"You know I do, that's not even a question. I wanna make sure you are ready. I think we should wait."

"Wait until when? Until the cobwebs begin to fall out of my

coochie? Damn! Just forget it." I got up and walked out of the bedroom, slamming the door.

He followed after me, and grabbed my arm.

"Get off me! You know what Malachi? This has been really hard for me. It's been almost two months, and I am going crazy. Seeing you everyday here with me, having you next to me in my bed. I am horny outta my mind! And now I'm pissed off! Why don't you just go? Get out and go home!" I yelled at him, scaring Chloe as she ran into the living room.

He grabbed me by the arm again, turning my body to face his. He took my face in his hands, and kissed me with so much hunger I swear my panties were moist. He pushed his body into mine and I could feel his erection coming alive again, pulsing against my pelvis. He pulled my tee shirt over my head and unsnapped my bra, allowing my breasts to fall into his hands. He kissed and sucked with so much hunger, I moaned. He pushed me up against the wall and pulled my legs up around his waist. He sucked on my neck and my earlobes, and returned his attention back to my breasts.

I returned the favor, sucking his neck, leaving hickeys and causing him to moan and breathe even heavier. I almost couldn't stand it. He carried me back to the bedroom and laid me down on the bed. He took his shirt off and peeled my sweat shorts and thongs off. He hungrily commenced to giving my kitty the much needed attention she craved. He licked and sucked my clit until I came only moments later. My legs almost went numb, and then he went back for seconds.

He assumed his position between my legs; having a feast and making me come two more times. When he came up for air, I sat up and pulled down his pants. He wasn't wearing any boxers or underwear, and I just wanted him.

Badly.

I lied back down, and Malachi was on top of me, ready to enter. He took his time, entering me inch by slow inch.

I moaned in ecstasy. "Ssssss, oooh. Give it all to me."

"You sure you want it all?"

"Mmm-hmm. All of it."

Malachi gave me all of him, and our bodies were in synchronized rhythm. He felt so good that I cried.

"What's wrong, baby? You want me to stop?"

"No, baby, don't stop. You just feel so good."

When I was close to reaching another climax, I wrapped my legs around his as he continued to give me pleasure.

"Maiya, I'm about to come; I gotta pull out."

"No, baby, I am coming too!" We exploded and I could feel him pulsing inside of me, releasing all of his swimmers.

He relaxed, and kissed my neck. "You are so beautiful."

I smiled at him, and kissed his lips. He wrapped his arms around me, and we spooned for a little bit, until I could feel him getting excited again.

"Hey, you. I think somebody is ready for round two. You ready for more?"

"Meet me in the shower!" I jumped up and ran to the bathroom.

Malachi was right behind me.

I turned on all the jets to my shower and while we waited for the water to get hot, he kissed my mouth and reached behind my head to let my hair down. I stepped in the shower and he was behind me. We were face-to-face, continuing with part two of our lovemaking session. He turned me around, massaging my back and buttocks, and poking me from behind with his large penis, Mr. Feel Good. He had to bend down to get right under me and entered me with such force that I screamed with pleasure.

"Ooh, baby."

"You like that?"

"Do I? Give it to me, baby."

As the water ran down our bodies, Malachi gave me such a workout. He was gentle with a little roughness, and it was not much later that we reached our climax, with me coming in first place. He exploded inside of me, and then washed my body. He washed my hair, massaging my scalp and giving my body all the attention. When he massaged my neck and shoulders, he leaned in to my ear and whispered, "I love you so much, Maiya."

I turned around to him. "I love you, too," I whispered.

"I just didn't want to hurt you, Maiya," he started. I quieted him, placing my finger on his lips.

"Baby, you can never hurt me. You have to trust that I know what's best for my body."

"But what if you get pregnant again in your fallopian tubes and need surgery again? I don't want to bring you that kind of pain that you had before. I want us to have babies, yes, but not if you're going to suffer."

My heart melted. He was withholding being intimate because he didn't want to hurt me and get me pregnant again. *Oh, Lord*, I thought, as I held Malachi's head to my chest and ran my fingers through his hair. *Please let this man be as perfect as he seems. I love him more than anything.*

* * *

Six weeks later, I knew something was different with my body. So, I was only mildly surprised when the window of the Clearblue Easy digital indicator read PREGNANT. I had started spotting, but did not get my period this time. I was scared and happy at the same time, if that even makes sense at all. Malachi and I had not even set a date for the wedding, and here I was expecting a baby. But, given our insatiable sexual appetites and constantly going without using a condom, something was bound to happen.

I immediately called him with the news. "Hey, baby, you busy?"

"I have a lot going on, but never too busy for you. Whassup?"

"Well, how soon before you can get here?"

"Whatchu got going on? You know I don't like surprises, Maiya."

"I really need to see you. Like right now."

"Now, I know the sex is good, but damn girl, I got work to do," he said, laughing.

I got quiet and didn't respond.

"Maiya, don't go copping an attitude. I really do have a lot to do, babe. I may need to fly to New Orleans in the morning to take care of some things at the site. I promise to get there as soon as I can. Or why don't you go to my house and wait for me there?"

"This is really important, though. It sort of can't wait."

"Is something wrong?"

"No, nothing like that. It's just...well, never mind. I'll be at your house." I was disappointed that he couldn't come sooner and that he may be leaving tomorrow.

"I hear your emotion through the phone and see your lips pouting. I'll be outta here as fast as I can, okay? Take my boys out. I am sure they will be happy to see you. I'll call you when I am leaving."

"Okay."

He laughed into the phone. "You are so spoiled. I love you."

"Love you, too. Just hurry up."

* * *

I made shrimp scampi and a tossed garden salad with breadsticks for dinner. A bottle of Muscato was on chill, the dogs were in the backyard, except Chloe who was on her sofa. Norman Brown was playing on the stereo. The table was set, and I lit the candles when Malachi called to say he was on his way. I showered and put on my sexy black halter sundress and waited for my future husband in the living room.

When I heard the keys in the door, the butterflies fluttered around in my stomach and I got nervous like I was meeting him for the first time. I took a deep breath and told myself to calm down.

Malachi walked in and I met him at the door. "Mmm, it smells good in here, and you look nice." He put his briefcase on the foyer floor and took me in his arms. I kissed him like he was a soldier just getting back from a deployment. When he let go, he looked at me. "What is all of this?"

"I know, I know. I just wanted to cook you dinner and I needed to talk to you. So, go get washed up and let's have dinner." I kissed his lips and pushed him down the hallway.

When he returned, I watched him fill his plate with scampi. He looked at me puzzled. "Aren't you gonna eat?"

"I feel too nervous to eat." I smiled at him.

"Okay, what's going on? You are acting weird."

"Well, I took a pregnancy test this morning and….," I hesitated. "And?"

"We, Mr. Taylor, are gonna have a baby," I nearly screamed.

Malachi's eyes got large and he almost choked on his food. "Are you serious? For real?"

I nodded yes. "For real. A baby."

He got up from the table, pulling me to my feet and kissing me all over my face. "So, have you made an appointment to see the doctor? What do you need me to do? Are you sure it wasn't a false positive? You know I read somewhere that……"

I covered his mouth with my hand. "Shh. You are sounding like a worry wart. I will call to make an appointment in the morning. We are gonna pray for the best and keep a positive outlook on this. Everything is gonna be fine this time."

"Wait right here, I gotta call Momma."

"No, Malachi, please don't. I don't wanna tell anyone we know until everything is alright this time. Please," I begged.

"Okay, okay. I understand. You're right. I am just so happy. But what about the wedding?"

"I didn't want anything big anyway, so we can just have something small at my dad's. But we should do it before the baby comes, don't you think?"

"Whatever you want, baby, is fine with me."

And when he hugged me, I believed that everything would be alright this time.

Character is much easier kept than recovered. ~Thomas Paine

THIRTY-FOUR

MILAN

The death of my father, Cochise Douglass, took a toll on me. More than what I thought it would.

My relationship with my father was really all I had. I just never felt close to my mother, with her insecurities and misguided perception of reality. The vicissitudes of my daily life made me ponder my past habits, and tore at the inner core of my being, straight through to my soul. Though mostly bad, I could not escape the lost feeling I had now that daddy was gone.

I know my mother spent many years thinking she did the best for me. But, her controlling and devious ways got in between any type of mother-daughter relationship we were to have. The only thing we shared was the secret of Nadia's birth. Love was the last thing that existed freely between us. For years, I worked hard at gaining my mother's attention, but it was of no use. If it wasn't for my dad and the love I found with Jackson, I would have been more lost than I already am.

The secret about Nadia changed me and led me to all kinds of ill vices to ease my shame, yes. But, I realized lately, after all the truth came to light, that there is a part of me that relished many aspects of what I had become over the years. It was easy to blame my promiscuity, drug use and boozing on my controlling mother and the things she made me do when it came to lying to hide my love child. But, I admit, there is another side of me, a part of me that is fighting to come out as I start to be more honest to myself about who I am.

What I didn't anticipate was starting a whole other addiction while getting over my drinking problems. Anxious, I made the call without hesitation.

"Hey, it's me. I need to see you," I whispered in the phone.

There was an evil laugh on the other end.

"Uh-hunh. So you got an itch you need me to scratch?"

"Yeah, in a bad way. So, uh, where can we meet?"

"Whatchu got for me, sweet thang?"

"You know I got the money. That ain't no problem."

"Nah girrrrl," he slurred. "I don't want the money. You know whassup. You owe me."

"Damn, nigga, why you gotta go there? I don't have that much time."

"You want what I got, don't you? And you know you love when I make that kitty purr. So, what's it gonna be?"

I sighed. I knew I couldn't get away with just giving him the money. I was not in the mood for an all night session. Not tonight.

"Hello?" he interrupted my thoughts. "Clock is ticking, and I'ma need for you to get to licking."

"Alright, alright. Where?"

"I'm at the Hilton. Room 602."

"Oh, hell no. You about to get me a fresh room. You know how I roll."

"Yeah, whatever. I'll get that suite you like. I'll leave the info at the front desk." He paused. "Hey, don't play me girl. Show up as Miss Kitty. Cuz you know how I likes it."

"Be there in twenty." I hung up.

I would have preferred to pay with cash instead of ass, but I was desperate and knew my connection could put it down. I took a quick shower, dressed in my crotchless panties and see-through bra, and covered up with my Michael Kors trench coat. I was glad tonight was cool, or else I wouldn't be able to stand it. I pulled my hair back in a ponytail, put on my four-inch Manolos, grabbed my keys, and sped down 210 to my White Horse.

If anybody had the good stuff, Memphis sure did.

* * *

I got to the Hilton in record time. I handed my keys to the valet, and sashayed off on a mission.

"It's a bit warm for a trench coat, don't you think?" asked the attendant.

I just looked at him and rolled my eyes. He couldn't see my eyes through my dark sunglasses that I was wearing. At night. "Mind your bizness," I snapped.

At the front desk, I asked for my room key under Miss Kitty, as directed.

"And how long will you be staying with us, ma'am?" the clerk asked.

"Please, don't call me ma'am. It's Miss. And I will be here the rest of the week. Is that okay, Kelsey?" I responded, with attitude, reading her nametag. I know I can be real stank, but I was not in the mood for twenty questions. I was on a mission. And it involved a Hershey's Special Dark chocolate bar with a side of snow.

"Looks like you are all set. If you need anything, just..."

I held up my hand to stop her. "Save the speech. Heard it all before."

When I got to the suite, it was empty, and that was fine by me. Memphis knew I was gonna be running late, but I was always worth the wait. I needed a minute to touch up my makeup and make sure my girls were in place. I was ready for whatever Memphis was serving up, but he better have my stuff, or it was gonna be hell to pay.

I went to the bar and pulled out a bottle of Moët. I poured myself a glass, and began sipping before Memphis arrived. When I heard a knock at the door, I took my time opening it. I didn't want him to think I was as pressed as I sounded on the phone.

Opening the door slowly so he could take me in from head-to-toe, I stood back and gave a pose.

"Damn, girl, just like I said. Miss Kitty, in the place to be! How you doin'?"

I gave him an evil grin. "How YOU doin'? You got my stuff?"

"And you know this!" He leaned in to kiss me.

"Don't go there. No kissing on the mouth. Take it on over to the bathroom and get in the shower. You musta forgot who were messing with. Ain't a damn thang changed."

He laughed. "Same ole Kitty. Gotta love ya."

"That's right, now act like you know."

While he showered, I found a music channel and turned it to smooth jazz. I was starting to get a buzz, and I couldn't wait for the main attraction.

Memphis stood in the doorway with just a towel wrapped around his waist. I walked over to him and snatched it off. He grabbed my breasts and began kissing me all over, avoiding my mouth, of course. He walked me backwards to the chaise lounge and pushed me down.

"Stay right there. Don't you move. Daddy got a lil sumthin sumthin for ya!"

I rubbed my hands together and smiled at him wickedly, while he grabbed his merchandise from his duffel bag and set it up on the coffee table. I watched him in anticipation, and was getting horny by the minute. I was just as excited about giving him some as I was about scoring my White Horse.

I leaned down and took off my shoes, and unsnapped my bra, allowing my girls to sit up nice and perky, wanting to say hello. Memphis looked at me hungrily, and I returned the look. He motioned for me to come to him, and getting down on all fours, I crawled over to him seductively, licking my lips. I got to the coffee table and sat in front of the mirror. Memphis took his first, and then I followed. We went back and forth until the lines were complete, and my high had me ready to devour his body.

As he gave it to me doggy style, Jackson and Nadia's face flashed before me, but I squeezed my eyes tight, blocking their faces out of my mind. Somehow, though, deep inside of me, the tears that my heart felt would not stay hidden. As my drug-induced mind squealed and tamed Memphis with my merciless pussy skills, tears streamed down my face as my conscience slowly withered inside and died, and my new drug addiction took over.

Giving up doesn't always mean you are weak; sometimes it means that you are strong enough to let go. -Author Unknown

THIRTY-FIVE

MAIYA

I checked my phone to see if I had any missed calls.
There was a message from Milan inviting me to dinner with her and Nadia. They wanted to share some good news with me. I decided to call her back after my ultrasound and join them if I felt up to it. I had been extremely tired and nauseous, and seemed to ache all the time. I had read somewhere that these exaggerated symptoms were sometimes indicative of multiple births. I knew Malachi's father was a twin, but I was unsure if there were any twins on my mother's side of the family.

Arriving at my appointment about twenty minutes early, I checked in and filled out the necessary paperwork. Having realized that I left my ginger gum in my car, I left out and headed for the parking lot. When I got outside, I saw Malachi's car parked in a spot closest to the entrance, about six cars down from mine.

I dialed his cell phone. No answer.

I decided to send him a text message to tell him to come inside the building to suite 107. I knew I left this information yesterday, but felt the need to give it to him again. Just in case I gave the wrong office.

I went back inside, and the technician was ready for me. An uneasy feeling overcame me, and I felt nauseous all of a sudden. I took out a piece of gum and chewed slowly, while taking deep breaths.

"Ms. Vaughn, are you alright? We can wait a moment if you need us to," the technician said.

"No, I'm okay. I'm ready."

Following her directions, I climbed on the table. The gel was warm as she squirted it from a tube onto my abdomen. While she took pictures of various portions of my uterus, Fallopian tubes, and my growing fetus, I couldn't help but worry about Malachi. I had asked the receptionist if a gentleman came in looking for me, and she had told me no one with his description had come in. It puzzled me and I didn't hear what the technician said until she repeated herself.

"Ms. Vaughn, do twins run in your family? Is your mother a twin, perhaps?"

"Not that I know of. Why do you ask?"

She told me to listen, but all I heard was a bunch of convoluted sounds, whooshing and beating into many loud noises. She told me to look at the screen, but I could not decipher what in the world I was looking at. I just saw some white lines jumping around in connection to the beats I could hear.

"There are two separate movements going on. Look here, and here," she said, while pointing to the screen in different spots. "Listen to the beats on this side, and then on this side. Can you hear the difference?"

I nodded yes.

"There are two opposite vibrations. Looks like you are having twins!"

"Excuse me. What did you just say? I thought I heard you say twins."

"That's right. Twins. Here let me get a freeze frame and print out a photo for you."

There was a knock at the door, and the physician stepped inside. "Good afternoon, Maiya. I am Dr. Lloyd. Let me just see what we have here."

Dr. Lloyd took over and explained everything in detail, and repeated what I had just heard about having twins. "Congratulations. It appears as though you are having twins!"

Tears fell from my eyes.

I was happy and sad at the same time.

Happy for the news.

Sad that Malachi was missing all of this.

"Is everything alright? Are they okay?"

"Everything appears to be fine. Now, what I need for you to do is go empty your bladder so we can do one more test. The bathroom is right outside of this door on your left. When you return, please remove everything from the waist down and we can continue."

When I returned from the bathroom and got undressed, a transvaginal ultrasound was done. The doctor wanted to get a better look at all of my reproductive organs, and giving my history of ectopic pregnancy and misdiagnosed endometriosis, it was warranted. Everything went well, and I had pictures of my two speckles which would grow into my babies.

I was given more congratulatory salutes and scheduled for more tests. I fell into a high risk category because of the ectopic and the multiple births, and they wanted to take extra care that I had a smooth pregnancy. While waiting for my future appointments to be scheduled, my phone was vibrating in my purse. I couldn't get to it, and decided to check it once I got to my car. I couldn't wait to tell Malachi the news, but was still confused as to why he never came inside.

As I left the office, I saw something that almost made me lose my breath.

Malachi was walking towards his car with a woman, arguing with her loudly in the parking lot.

A very pregnant woman. I knew immediately who it was.

I watched as Malachi opened the passenger car door, and carefully help her get into the car, despite his obvious anger towards her. I was furious. I pushed through the front door of the building with such force, I swore it could have come off the hinges.

Walking straight up to the hood of his car, my mind kept telling me to stay calm but the other side of my mind told me to go off. I chose the other side.

I banged on the hood of his car. "Malachi! Is this why you couldn't call me back? You're with *her*?" I screamed, pointing at Tia.

He looked up at me with a surprised look on his face. "Maiya? What are you doing here?"

"What am I doing here? What are YOU doing here? And with HER!"

"Baby, please, it's not what it looks like. Let me explain."

Tia looked from me to Malachi, and said, "Yeah, Malachi, why don't you explain?" She looked at me. "Oh no, don't tell me you're pregnant now. Look at you, trying to be me."

I wanted to smack the smirk off of her face.

Malachi looked at Tia. "Tia, just shut up and get in the car!" he yelled.

I just stood there, frozen. I could feel my pulse racing and I started feeling hot all of a sudden. I tried to move, but it was like my feet were stuck. Malachi shut the passenger door, and ran up to me.

"Please, Maiya let me explain. Just hear me out."

"I have been calling you since yesterday to tell you to come here. And here I am thinking you got the wrong office number and you show up here. What is going on? You know what. I don't even want to know." I pushed past him and rushed towards my car, fighting back tears as they clouded my sight.

He grabbed my arm and I tried to snatch away, but his grip was firm on my arm.

"Maiya, please. Baby, hear me out. I know I should have been up front from the jump, but I didn't want to tell you stuff if there was no need for you to know. Maiya, everything is fine. Tia has been lying..."

I cut him off. "Unh unh...you couldn't leave her? But you could leave me, huh? You know that's real smooth. I trusted you and this is how you do me. You knew all along about this baby you had with her and you tried to keep it a secret! How could you?" I lost it and started crying my eyes out.

"Maiya, it's not even like that. She was being hit on by her boyfriend, and…"

I screamed, "Just stop!"

We must have been very loud, because a lady from the office came outside, asking if I needed assistance.

"No, ma'am," I told her. "I am fine. I was just leaving."

Malachi let go of my arm and I ran to my car. He was still standing on the sidewalk when I sped out of the parking lot.

I cried all the way home. I really didn't want to be alone, but I had nowhere else to go. I tried calling Milan, but got her voicemail.

I just needed to get away.

Far away.

So I packed as much of my clothes as I could, put Chloe in my car, and left a note on Milan's door.

I got back in my car and drove all the way to Virginia.

I knew I would be safe there.

And I knew I would be met with open arms.

* * *

I put the address in my GPS and only stopped twice to give Chloe a moment to stretch her legs and use the bathroom.

When I looked in my purse, I cried when I saw the sonogram pictures. My cell phone was blowing up like crazy. Malachi had already called six times. The last time he called, I just turned my phone off. I knew he would keep calling and I didn't wanna talk to him. I replayed it all over in my head, even recalling what Milan had said about the baby being his. I wished I had asked him about the baby. And now I felt stupid that I hadn't asked.

As alone as I felt at this moment, I could not handle the stress. Stress is what caused me to lose my baby with Carlos. And I was not about to let that happen again. I looked down at my stomach and rubbed it softly. I looked at the ring on my finger and took it off, placing it in my cup holder. The tears kept falling from my eyes, and I just prayed that I made it safely to my destination.

I showed up on Aunt Marie's doorstep at eight-thirty in the evening.

I rang her doorbell about three times before she finally answered.

"Maiya? What are you doing here? Is everything alright?"

I lost it when I saw her and cried uncontrollably. I literally fell into her arms, and she held on to me tight.

"Chile, what is it? Please. Come inside. Let me get your things." I walked through the front door and she ran to my car to get my stuff. I held Chloe close to my chest.

"I need…to stay….with you," I said in between sobs. "Malachi…. he…I had…to leave," I tried to say.

Aunt Marie showed me inside, and I sat down on her living room sofa. I still clutched Chloe to me. "Is it okay to have my dog? She's harmless. You're not allergic are you?"

"No, sweet pea. Your dog is fine. Now, Maiya, I can't help you if you don't tell me what happened."

I told her everything, including my surgery, the pregnancy, and even about Tia showing up at my job, her phone call, up to the events about four hours before I got on the road and ended up on her doorstep. She listened attentively, and rubbed my shoulders. I wiped my nose with the back of my hand and she handed me a box of tissues. Aunt Marie told me that she knew Tia was always a slick woman, but she didn't believe that her nephew would deceive me. I shook my head, telling her how they were at the appointment together, how he missed my appointment with me, not calling me or responding to my messages.

I reached down inside my purse and pulled out the sonogram pictures and handed them to her. She looked down at them, and then at me. "Is this what I think it is?"

I nodded yes.

"Baby A AND Baby B? Don't tell me. Twins?"

I nodded again. "Yes, ma'am."

"Does Christian know?"

"He knows that I'm pregnant, but he doesn't know we're having twins. He missed my appointment."

"Sweet pea, you gotta tell him. You know how much he wants children. And with you, too!"

I shook my head no. "I can't. Plus, he's having a baby with her! All I did was trust him! We are supposed to be getting married! What did I do wrong? How could I not see this coming? I was so stupid. To let myself fall in love again!" I sobbed uncontrollably.

"Maiya, please calm down. You are in no condition to handle this right now. Stay down here with me tonight, and tomorrow I can set you up in the upstairs condo. Okay? You want me to fix you some tea?"

"That would be nice." When I looked around the living room while she prepared my tea, I saw the pictures of me and Malachi on the pier before we got on the jet skis. Everywhere I looked, there were pictures of us. I got up and walked into the kitchen with Aunt Marie.

"You know, I just talked to Christian last week. He told me that he wanted to marry you in Louisiana where he proposed. I was so happy....I AM so happy for you. This is not like him at all. There has got to be an explanation. It just doesn't make sense. Did you at least let him explain?"

"No, ma'am. I was too hurt with what was in front of me. You should have seen the way Tia smirked at me. He said something about her boyfriend hitting her and that he needed to help her."

"One thing you should know about Christian, if you don't know already, is that he will not turn his back on anyone, even someone who kicked him while he was down and spat in his face. He is a very giving man. And I do know that he genuinely loves you. Now, I can't explain everything that you told me, but you haven't given him a chance to explain himself. I know it's hard when your heart is in it. Love is love, darling. And you love him. And he loves you." She handed me the cup of tea. "Here. Drink this, and calm down. You got them babies to think about now. The guest bedroom is ready for you. You want me to run you a bath?"

"I can manage. I got it, thanks."

"Okay, well I'll be on the balcony if you need anything. Try to get some rest. Tomorrow you may see a way to give him a chance. Does anyone know where you are?"

"I left my best friend Milan a message. I always told her this could be my home away from home."

"Okay, good night." She kissed my forehead and patted my shoulder. "God will work it out, sweet pea. You will see."

"If he calls you, please don't tell him I am here. I am not ready to see him."

"I won't lie if he asks me if I have talked to you. Y'all are grown folks, and you will need to handle your business. I can give you a place to stay, darling, but I will not get in the middle. Christian is a good man. You know that."

I soaked in the tub and burned some lavender candles to relax. After I put on my pajamas, I crawled under the covers and placed my sonogram pictures on the nightstand. I prayed that my babies would be safe, and that I would remain calm and in a stress-free state of mind to have a healthy pregnancy. I looked down at my empty ring finger on my left hand, remembering that I left my engagement ring in the car.

I had no idea what I was going to do.

Or how long I was gonna stay in Virginia.

The measure of a man's real character is what he would do if he knew he never would be found out. ~Thomas Babington Macaulay

THIRTY-SIX

MALACHI

I sat in the parking lot after watching Maiya speed off. I looked over at Tia with disgust in my eyes. Tia sat looking out of the window with her arms across her chest. All I wanted was for this day to be over. I had just sat through a three-hour long wait of testing and receiving results confirming that I was not the father of Tia's baby. After months of harassment from Tia, at last, this nightmare was over.

Why didn't I just call Maiya and tell her everything? I thought if she really loved me, she would understand.

But I didn't even give her the chance.

And it made me look guilty by not calling her back.

Tia looked at me and whispered, "Sorry." Her sarcasm was sickening.

"You know what, as wicked and nasty as you are, I can't even be mad. You're miserable and are going to stay miserable. You and Fred's baby. That poor kid."

"Well you got your damn paternity test and you're not the father, so what. Your stupid ass was all scared. I almost got away with it."

I looked at her then. How on earth did I ever love this evil person?

"You are a devil," I yelled. "Look, I don't even want you in my car. Get out." I was going to drive her home, but her ass was going to catch a cab after all this. I'll be damned if I put up with her evil ass a second longer. I wanted to go after Maiya.

"Nigga, I gotta get home. Don't play."

"I ain't playing. Get the hell out my ride and call a cab." I tossed her a ten and pulled her out of my car. At seven months pregnant, she was still petite but unstable and bulky. I wasn't rough with her, but I firmly got her the hell out my truck. She stood there looking evicted.

"Well ain't that some shit," she said. She folded the ten and looked at me.

I climbed in the truck and started the engine.

"You made your bed, Tia," I said. "Now lie in it." I sped down the street.

*   *   *

I drove over to Maiya's, hoping to find her at home.

When I knocked and didn't even hear Chloe bark, I decided to try Milan's. To my surprise, Milan had not heard from her all day. When I asked her if she knew about her doctor's appointment and she said she did not, I realized that Maiya had not told her best friend what happened with Tia.

"If you talk to her, please tell her that I stopped by. She is not gonna want to see me, but I really need to talk to her. I made a mistake, Milan, and I need to get my lady back. So, please call me when you hear something."

"Yeah, sure, you know I will let you know."

I knew that Milan would be talking to Maiya real soon, but all I could do was sit and wait.

A few days went by, but it seemed much longer, and I still heard nothing from Maiya. I called Milan every day, and still no word. I had already missed band rehearsal, and I felt bad about not playing with them. But I needed to get my mind right.

When I tried to rehearse tonight, I was all over the place and ended up leaving. We didn't have a show for another couple of weeks, and I was hoping to get myself together by that time. I apologized to the guys and left to go home.

While driving home, my cell phone rang and I recognized my aunt's number.

"Hello."

"Hey, Christian, I was just thinking about you. I believe you need to come down here."

"Why? Is Momma alright? What's going on?" I panicked.

"Calm down, chile. Your momma is fine. All I can say is that there is someone who needs you right now."

I got quiet and let out a sigh.

"Auntie, I don't have time for more of Benjamin's mess, trust me. I have issues of my own right now, and I can't deal with any more drama. Can you just ….."

"Boy, will you just listen for once and stop all your rambling," she cut me off. "Now, I said that I wasn't gonna say anything, but I just can't keep it to myself."

"What is it?"

"It's Maiya."

"Did she call you? Is she there? With you?"

"Mmm-hmm. She needs you, son."

"Is she alright?"

"Well, from the sounds of things, you have some explaining to do. And from what she is telling me, it sounds like you are gonna be a father. I told her that I wouldn't lie to you about where she was, but she felt safe here and you know I don't turn people away. Especially ones that are with child. So, are you coming or what?"

"Let me throw some clothes in a bag and be on my way."

"Christian, did you hear what I said? You don't have time for packing a bag. And you make more than enough money that you can buy whatever it is that you need once you get here. Get your butt down here. Now!"

"Yes, ma'am." I laughed in her ear.

"And drive careful, too. It's about to storm out this way." She hung up.

I stopped to get gas, and got on the road. As much as I wanted to get to my baby, I took my aunt's advice and drove carefully. With the thunderstorm approaching, I wanted to be safe and arrive in Virginia in one piece.

I dialed Maiya's phone one last time, in hopes that she would answer. When I got her voicemail, I decided to leave a message.

"Maiya, it's me. I know you're upset with me, but I really need to explain. I'm really sorry about what happened that day. When you get this, call me back. I do love you and I need you to know that nothing is going on with Tia. Bye."

I pressed PLAY on my car stereo, and welcomed the smooth-sounding voice of Rahsaan Patterson. He was a favorite of Maiya's, and she left the CD on repeat to *The One for Me*. As I listened to the words in the song, I accepted the revelation that she really is the one for me.

I knew I that I couldn't make up the missed appointment for her sonogram. This woman was having my baby, and I was scared and excited all at once.

Visibility was worsening and a couple of times I had to pull over on the side of the road because I couldn't see to drive. By the time I got into Hampton, it was well past midnight. The thunderstorm and traffic caused my commute to be much longer. I was only about forty minutes away and anticipated every mile I cleared to get nearer to my future.

Once I finally arrived and entered Aunt Marie's development, I slowed down to search for a space. Driving past Maiya's car, butterflies swarmed in my stomach, and I felt nervous as a teenage boy asking a girl out on a first date. I wanted Maiya to forgive me, but I also knew she was hurting. When she saw me with Tia, the look in her eyes was enough to kill me dead right on the spot.

I parked a distance away, near the lake around the back, and ran to my aunt's building. I was soaked to the bone when I got inside. My tee shirt clung to me like a second skin, and my jeans felt like heavy duty camouflage cargo pants.

I reached the front door and found the key hidden in a stone turtle by the doormat. I let myself inside, leaving my tennis shoes at the door along with my socks, which were drenched.

I hesitated as I stood in front of the door leading to the upstairs condo. I knew Maiya was still up because I could see the light on from the outside. I didn't have a choice but to ring the bell. And at this hour, I knew she would not be happy to see me.

I took a deep breath, rang the bell and waited.

Nothing.

I rang the bell two more times and could hear footsteps approaching the door upstairs.

"Aunt Marie, is that you?" she asked, in a groggy, solemn voice through the intercom.

"Um, no Maiya, it's me Malachi. Will you come open the door?"

There was silence for a few minutes, so I rang the bell again.

"Please go away; I have nothing to say to you."

"Maiya, please hear me out. I drove all the way, in the storm, to tell you everything. It's important. I've been worried sick about you. I really need for you to let me explain."

"I don't believe you. Just go away."

"Look, baby, just give me ten minutes. If you still want me to leave, I'll go. Just give me a chance. Please." I was begging.

There was silence again, and then the door buzzed. I walked up the stairs, and through the French doors. When I saw her, my heart melted. Her face was wet with tears and her eyes bloodshot red. She was wearing her favorite grey sweat shorts and yellow Victoria's Secret signature PINK tank top. Her nipples poked through, and I couldn't help but stare. She pulled her arms across her chest when she caught me staring. Her hair was pulled back into a large knot. Even when upset and crying, she was beautiful.

"Hey."

"I'm tired and you got ten minutes," she snapped.

That was the attitude I knew and loved. I held on to the smirk that tried to take over my face.

"Okay, first I wanna apologize. I should have called you when I got your message. I had an emergency and I didn't get the message until the morning of your appointment."

"But I called you all day. And left you several messages. And your phone went straight to voicemail. You dissed me, and I…"

I held up my hand. "I only get ten minutes, so please, Maiya. Let me finish."

"I guess so. Go on."

"I was with Tia that day to get the paternity test that proves that I'm not her baby's father." I looked up to see Maiya roll her eyes, and I continued. "She has been harassing me, trying to get to you and doing all crazy things because she is mad that I didn't take her back after she slept with Fred."

"And, why couldn't you have told me all of this before?" she snapped.

"I'm getting to that. Can I get a towel or something? I'm dripping wet over here."

"Yeah, and you're wetting up the wood floors. Be right back."

I laughed on the inside. Attitude 101.

I started to shiver and watched her walk down the hall. When she returned, I could see tears fill her eyes. It killed me to see her hurting like this. I took the towel from her and started to dry off. It was freezing with the air on, so I took off my shirt. She sucked her teeth, and looked at me as if to say, "Hurry up, cuz you got to go."

But her body told me something else as her nipples hardened again, and I smiled.

"The baby isn't mine. I just found out that day. She was pregnant before you and I even got together."

"How do I know it's true?"

"We can call her, Maiya. I have no reason to lie. I kept the baby from you because I was afraid of losing you. It happened in January. Just one time. I suspected the baby wasn't mine, but I was waiting for a blood test." I waited a few moments for her to respond. When she didn't, I continued. "Look, baby, I will understand if you don't forgive me or even if you don't want to give us another chance. I just had to tell my side of the story, and whatever it takes, I will make this all up to you." I pulled out the paternity test results and held them out to her.

I walked towards her, and she turned away from me.

"Maiya, you've gotta believe me. It's been over between me and Tia. For a long time. I only wanna be with you. I love you. I want you to be my wife." I put my hands on her shoulders and turned her around to face me. I placed my hands on her face, and leaned down to kiss her. She looked up at me and tears rolled down her face.

"Believe me?" I pleaded.

She nodded yes. "I believe you. And I accept your apology. I love you, too." She paused. "Promise me you will never keep secrets from me."

"I promise to never keep secrets from you, Maiya."

I kissed her softly at first, and felt her body relax into me. I slipped my tongue in her mouth, and she accepted it hungrily. She pulled away from me when she felt the cold wetness from my jeans.

"I think you can lose these, don't you think?"

I smiled at her. I unbuttoned my jeans and peeled them off, along with my boxers. Standing before Maiya butterball naked, she came close to me and kissed me with much passion. I was so hard that I could have broken a brick in two pieces.

She wrapped her arms around my neck, and I reached down to pull her shirt over her head. I touched her body softly as if it were the first time we were together. I picked her up and carried her to the bedroom, placing her gently on the bed.

She leaned over and picked something off the nightstand, and handed it to me.

"What's this?"

She pointed to the date and the two dots on a black-and-white blob of a photo. I read the words 'Baby A' and 'Baby B', and looked at her confused, with a wrinkled forehead.

"Is this what I think it is?"

"Yup. Twins!"

"No way, Maiya. Are you serious?"

She nodded yes. And then she climbed on top of me and made me a happy man. She had such a voracious appetite for my body that we wore each other out.

I was asleep and snoring after an hour of lovemaking.

With my future wife, pregnant with my twins, lying next to me.

In time of test, family is best. ~**Burmese Proverb**

THIRTY-SEVEN

MAIYA

I had not been prepared for Malachi showing up last night. But every part of me was glad to hear the truth. I had forgiven him and decided to move on. We didn't need to have stress in our lives. I thought about how I had not told him about the family day at Joaquin's house and the time I spent with Joaquin and Noah after Noah's accident and realized that I had done the same thing in a way—withhold information to avoid an argument. I'm not proud of it, but I did the same thing I accused him of doing.

After Malachi drove to Virginia to get me, we spent the next few days together, and went to Lindsay's to work out in her home gym. Nicholas was getting so big, and she told me that Benjamin would be coming back home since they decided to reconcile. Spending time with Nicholas gave me such a sense of motherhood, and I was even more excited to share our news. But we decided against it until I had my next appointment. The only other person we wanted to share the news with was his mother. Driving to his mother's house, Malachi called her to say there was a surprise.

"Oh, Christian, you know I don't like surprises. And when do you plan on setting a date for the wedding?"

"Momma, can we talk about that later? How long are you gonna be home? I have to run out to the store, but wanna talk to you."

"Oh, I'm just gonna be out back in the garden. I'm not going anywhere."

"Alright, well, give me about twenty minutes and then I will call you back."

I looked at Malachi and laughed. "You just have to make a surprise appearance, hunh?"

"Well, it just all goes together with our news, don't you think?" He laughed.

Arriving at his mom's house, Malachi used his key to enter the house. He walked through the kitchen and into the backyard, where his mother was relaxing under one of the weeping willow trees. She jumped up from her wicker chair when she saw him, while I watched from the kitchen window. I watched them embrace then walk towards the house.

"Now how you gonna just come here and not say anything to me? I told you I don't like surprises."

"I know momma, but you're gonna like this one."

As they entered the kitchen, I heard her talk about the wedding and how she was happy. She didn't even notice I was sitting at the table because she went straight for the refrigerator.

"You thirsty? I just made some iced tea, if you want some."

"I would like some, if you don't mind," I said.

She turned to face me and almost broke her neck to get to me.

"Now this is a lovely surprise! I am so glad to see you, Maiya. How have you been?"

"I'm fine, thank you. It's good seeing you, too."

"Okay, now what is going on here? Y'all hiding something from me? Did you get married and not tell me about it?"

"No, momma, not at all. Why don't you have a seat? Please." Malachi pulled out a chair at the kitchen table for his mother to sit down.

"Should I go first? Or do you wanna tell her?" Malachi asked me.

"Um, no. I think that you should tell her."

"Tell me what? Come on, now. What is it?"

Malachi took my hands in his, and turned to his mother. "Now, momma, don't go making a church announcement and all, okay? You promise?"

"Yes, chile, I promise! What is it?"

"You are gonna be a grandmother! But, there is more to it than that."

"Okay, wait a minute! A baby? Y'all don't play with me, now!"

"It's true. But there is a second part to it," I said. "We are having twins."

"Y'all better stop it. Oh my goodness." She started to cry, and Malachi stood up from the table to embrace her.

"I am so happy. I don't know what else to say."

"Well, just don't say it to anyone, since we haven't told anyone just yet. We are still trying to plan a wedding, but Maiya doesn't want anything really big. I wanna take her back to New Orleans and get married there, but we will see."

She stood up to hug me. "You have no idea how happy you just made me. This is the best news ever! Your mother would be so proud of you right now."

"That means a lot to me; you have no idea." I hugged her back.

"Well, how long are y'all gonna stay? Please tell me at least through the weekend. We can throw a small engagement party."

"That's okay, momma. We are gonna be heading back to Maryland in the morning. It was just an impromptu visit, and I didn't wanna give you this news over the phone. Maybe we can have something small at my house in a few weeks and you and Aunt Marie can come down. You can plan that if you like."

Her face beamed with pride. "I'd really like that, Christian. Just send me the names and addresses and I will gladly plan that for you two. Oh, come here and give me another hug." She grabbed us both and embraced us in a group hug.

We stayed for dinner, and then drove back to Aunt Marie's for the night. I called Milan to tell her that everything worked out, and she sighed, saying, "Oh, I knew it was gonna be alright."

I detected something in her voice. "What do you mean, Lani? What did you do?"

"What makes you think I did something?"

"Because I know you and I know that sound in your voice. Now, come clean."

"Promise me that you won't get mad, okay?"

"I won't. Now, spill it."

"Let's just say that I made some inquiries of my own, and let little Miss Tia know that she was barking up the wrong tree, and if she knew what was best for her, she would stay away from you and Malachi."

"No, you didn't. Why you always gotta start something?"

"Because that's what I do. Now, I already knew she was bluffing about that baby. I found out from Cassandra at work. She overheard Tia on the phone talking about her little scheme, so I had to put her on blast. Sorry, Maiya, but I can't have nobody messing with my girl like that. You got a good man there. He was worried sick about you, and…"

"Unh-unh. This won't get you off the hook. That was not called for, and I don't appreciate that at all. You can't just…."

"Look, say whatever you want, but I look out for family. You know how I roll. We been in this for too long, and I was not about to let some scandalous chick mess up your good thing. Now, that doesn't let Malachi off the hook, because he played a part, too. But, he's got a good heart. And he genuinely loves you. I am really happy for you two. This is really happening for you."

I sighed. "Yes, Lani, it is happening. And thanks for looking out for me."

"Not a problem. Just know when you need something to jump off, who you gon' call?"

"You, girl. Nobody but you."

Malachi cleared his throat to get my attention.

"Look, girl, I gotta go. We will be back in the morning."

"Okay. See you tomorrow. Tell Malachi I said hi. And don't let him wear that coochie out. You gotta save some for later!" She burst into laughter that seemed a bit maniacal. I was not amused.

"Bye." I hung up.

* * *

Girls' day out at Robert Andrew Salon and Spa was just what I needed.

After all the drama this week, I just wanted to relax. Nadia, Milan and I sat in the Tranquil Room sipping on hot tea, enjoying the ambiance. When Milan moved to another chair to get a pedicure, Nadia whispered to me about her upcoming photo shoot with the photographer I recommended, Paul Graves. In the middle of the story, she switched topics when her mom was out of earshot.

"Auntie Mai, I met a boy the other day, but I haven't told mom yet. You know she will have a fit," she whispered.

"Well, you have plenty of time to worry about the boys. Focus on your dream right now, because boys can be a distraction. You can go far in this business, so stay focused. And your dad will have you on lockdown with the quickness!"

"I know."

"Let's talk about the rest over lunch, and you can come over later so we can talk in private."

"Okay."

We enjoyed the rest of our Spa day, and had a quick lunch at Chipotle instead of Four Seasons grille. Nadia talked nonstop about her trip next month to New York with Tyra Banks, and Milan just rolled her eyes.

"Lani, what's up with the attitude? I thought you wanted Nadia to go."

"I guess I didn't realize how much travelling she was gonna have to do, and we are swamped at work. I just can't go."

"Mom, it's okay. Nana said she could travel with me until dad got up here. It's no big deal. Really."

"I have been working from home lately, and I can put in some time if you need me to. I told you that I would help you out. Why don't you let me?" I asked.

"I guess so. I just really wanna be there with her. So much can happen on the road and..."

"And so much can happen when I'm not on the road. Mom, please. I'm not a baby anymore. You always tell me how Granny was strict on you and never let you do anything."

"I know, baby. You're absolutely right. So, between your dad, Nana, and Auntie Mai, we will work it out. Don't worry about it, okay. I will try to make it whenever I can."

Milan looked at me and stuck out her tongue. When Nadia got up to go use the restroom, I leaned in to Milan. "You have got to ease up on your daughter. She's a good girl. Stop thinking she is gonna do what you did. Boys are gonna check for her. She's a beautiful, smart girl. You know it takes a village to raise a child. So let us do it."

"I know, okay. I just feel out of sorts. My sponsor was away for a bit. I can't focus at work."

She kept rubbing her nose and gums. Her behavior seemed a bit off.

"Why don't you take some time off and relax? We are way overdue for our monthly gatherings. Let's take it somewhere, like on a retreat or something. There's a nice place in West Virginia if you're up to it. Call up the girls and see what we can do. Kiana still has three more months before she drops that baby, and I know Tion would love to get away. What do you say, Lani?"

"Oh, alright. You twisted my arm. I could use a break. I swear that Shane is trying to take my job from right under my nose."

"Stop thinking like that. He held it down for you for a long time, and he still continues to put his time in. He would make a great partner in the business. You always said you would consider selling your half when you were ready. He is business savvy, has his M.B.A., and is a good people person." I never got around to telling Milan about my idea of having Shane manage the office while she was away. With the death of her father and the start of her AA meetings, I just didn't want to press a nerve and send her over the edge. I would have to find a way to ease my idea into the conversation with her.

"Well, damn, I get the impression you are trying to sell him to me!"

"All I am saying is that if your heart isn't in it anymore, Lani, it's okay to throw in the towel. We built this thing together, but it won't be the end of our dream if we have to move on. I have the wedding coming up, these babies coming next April, and the business in New Orleans. You have to do what you have to do. And if that means walking away, well, what can I say?"

Nadia returned, followed by a young man with a slight limp.

"Mom, auntie Mai, I want you to meet Noah. He's the guy I told you about."

I looked up and almost choked on my soda. "Well, well, well. What a coincidence!"

"You guys know him?" Nadia asked.

"Of course, they know me. Miss Maiya dated my dad for six years! This is so weird."

I stood up to give Noah a hug. I raved at how improved he seemed since I last saw him. He had one crutch now instead of two. Milan scoffed and sucked her teeth. I shoved her and told her to behave.

"Is it okay if we go to a movie, mom? Please?"

"Hold up. How old are you anyway?" Milan asked Noah.

"Eighteen, ma'am. Is something wrong?"

"Yeah, something is wrong. My daughter is only fifteen!"

"Mom, you are always embarrassing me," Nadia screamed. She fled outside, with Noah on her heels.

I looked at Milan. "Wow, look how the tables are turned. You were fourteen and her dad was eighteen and now you wanna judge. I practically raised this boy myself. You know I would not have him around if there was a problem. Nadia is not you, Milan. And until you realize that, you are gonna always be met with resistance."

I got up and went to find Nadia. She was outside crying. I walked over to her and comforted her. "You know she really only wants the best for you."

"She's right." Nadia and I turned to see Milan walking towards us. She continued, "I just don't want you to…"

"I know, I know. You don't want me to get pregnant at a young age," Nadia interrupted. "We talk so much, mom, but sometimes I feel like you're not really listening to me. I like boys, and I'm gonna wanna go out on dates. You can even chaperone. I was raised right, mom. Please. You gotta trust me." She cried, and Milan hugged her.

"I do trust you, sweetie. It's the boys I don't trust."

Never violate the sacredness of your individual self-respect.
~Theodore Parker

THIRTY-EIGHT

MILAN

My habit was becoming expensive. The things I did to feed it are almost too outrageous to admit to. Of course, Memphis was the main one putting me through all kinds of sexual challenges so I could get my blow. After my last session with Memphis, I wasn't quite sure if he would be willing to see me again so soon. I was using so much coke that my habit was bringing me to his doors at least twice a week. I didn't want to wear out my welcome.

Memphis answered on the first ring. "Yo, what up? Talk to me."

"Hey, Sexy Chocolate. Whatchu getting into tonight?"

"Nothing but you, my Kit Kat. Where you at? You want me to scoop you or you wanna hang out over here?"

"That all depends on where over here is."

"Ain't nobody here but me. You can come to my place. I ain't feeling the Hilton tonight. You worth it, but damn I'm staying in."

"Now, hold up. You sayin' that you don't mind me coming to your place? Since when? I know you gotta girl."

"Man, she bounced about a month ago. I ain't seen or heard from her since. Look, you coming or what? I got some good stuff."

"Yeah, give me the address and I can be there in an hour."

"Bet. See you then."

As I dressed in my jean dress and matching heels, I picked up the envelope from my dresser. It was the letter of my daddy's Last Will and Testament, and I still couldn't open it. Mom kept pressing me about it, like she knew what it said. But, I just told her that I would read it when I was good and ready. I just wasn't good and ready yet.

It was a pretty cool night, so I wore my hair out and put on my jean hat. The address Memphis gave me put him right next to the Branch Avenue Metro station, and I could be there in a half hour tops.

I didn't give a damn about his girlfriend. I didn't have feelings for him no how. He was a dealer and I was a buyer. I was just paying with my body; it was really that simple.

With Nadia staying with Maiya, I was able to get high and quell this addiction that was eating me alive. Jackson had already gone back to Texas to handle things, so, even he wouldn't be looking for me.

As I rubbed my gums, imagining the cool buzz that would spread over me when I snorted that line waiting for me at Memphis', my conscience sighed in disgust, ashamed of myself again.

Memphis met me at the Metro so he could let me in the garage under his condo. I couldn't wait to get inside and feel him all over me. With any luck, the quicker we got to screwing, the sooner I could get my blow and be on my way.

"Whassup, ma? You lookin' sexy as ever. You was missin' me, huh?"

I just rolled my eyes. "Whatchu think?"

"Damn that attitude, girl. You the one who want what I got." He grabbed his crotch and licked his lips.

"Whatever!" I had to laugh. He was ridiculous.

I followed him up the garage stairwell to his condo. Once inside, I took off my heels and asked for the bathroom.

"It's right down the hallway. First door on the right."

"Be right back."

Once inside, I came out of my dress and stood in front of the mirror in my red lace bra and thongs. I hung my dress on the back of the door and stepped back in the hallway, turning the light off with the switch on the wall.

"Damn, girl. You really are in the mood. Come see what daddy got for ya!"

After hours of drinking alcohol and snorting coke, I was in no mood for anything but sleep. The last thing I remembered was Memphis carrying me up some stairs to a bedroom, putting me on the bed and covering me up with a blanket. I didn't wake up until about noon the next day.

"Wake up, sexy. Don't sleep the day away." Memphis opened the blinds, causing me to squint from the bright light.

"Hey. What happened?" I asked, yawning.

"You fell the hell out last night. That's what happened. Coming over here looking all sexy, and a brotha didn't even get to hit it. Ain't that some shit!"

"I owe you. You know I'm good for it," I teased, running my hand down his six pack to his crotch.

Licking his lips and looking at me seductively, he said, "Girl, don't start something you can't finish. Plus, I gotta roll out right quick. There are some towels in the linen closet if you wanna take a shower. I cooked some food downstairs in the kitchen if you hungry. You think you'll be aw'ight till I get back?"

"I'm a big girl. I think I can manage, thanks."

"No problem. I gotta work the night shift tonight, so I'm gonna crash after I get back. Should be gone only about an hour. You wait for me?"

"You know I will."

He kissed me on the forehead and then left.

While Memphis was out, I showered and ate what he cooked.

I was impressed. This dude made cheese grits, bacon and biscuits.

When Memphis returned, I gave him the best loving he could handle. I put his ass to sleep, and left without a care in the world. I helped myself to some baggies of blow as well before I left.

My cell phone had been blowing up, and I knew it was either Nadia or Maiya. Smoothing my hair and checking my face, I got my lies together and practiced my walk. No one was going to know I was on drugs this time. My addiction was keeping me sane.

In the time it takes you to understand a 14-year-old, he turns 15.
*~*Robert Brault

THIRTY-NINE

MAIYA

I t was great having Nadia all to myself. It sort of prepared me for my upcoming mother role, even though I played a part in raising Noah. It was easy to mold him, and we bonded well because his mother had abandoned him. He was very hurt when his dad and I split, but he understood that we just couldn't work things out. From the tender age of eleven up until he turned seventeen, I was mother, nurse, confidant, and friend to Noah. Finding out that Joaquin is not his biological father was devastating to them both, but they managed to work it out.

And now that he showed an interest in Nadia, well, it was only natural that I would see the overprotective side of Milan. She was just afraid of the apple-don't-fall-too-far-from-the-tree chapter to be written in her daughter's book.

But, Nadia is a good girl, the sweet and open girl that Milan used to be before she was forced to lie all of those years.

I put on my comfort pajamas and scooped out some ice cream for myself and Nadia.

"Hey, Auntie Mai, I can't have ice cream. You know I gotta watch my weight."

"One scoop won't hurt, now will it? Tyra is not on you like that, is she?"

"Not on me in particular, but I hear how she is with her models,

302

and although I am not there yet, I wanna make sure I stay on top of my game. Is that how you all say it here?"

I laughed at her. "You are so cute. Here. Have one scoop. And if Tyra has something to say, you tell her to call me."

She smiled. "Okay. So, um, what can you tell me about Noah?"

"Well, what is it exactly that you wanna know?"

"Everything you can share with me. What was he like growing up? What does he like to do in his spare time? Does he have a girlfriend?"

"Wow. Sounds like Noah has a true admirer. You really like him, huh?"

Nadia blushed. "I think he's pretty cool, yeah."

"So, where did you meet him?"

"Daddy took me to Arundel Mills Mall with Joshua and Rocsan. He said it was alright for me to go shopping by myself while he took them around. I stopped in this store to get a swimsuit, and these guys were walking by. They were really loud, almost obnoxious, and I just ignored them.

"One of them made eye contact with me and smiled, so I smiled back. I was in the store for awhile trying on swimsuits, and when I came out, there he was. Sitting down on a bench waiting for me. He stood up and smiled, saying hello as he walked up to me. We started talking, and he asked for my number. I said that I was sixteen, because I didn't think he would stay interested if I said I was only fifteen. Anyway, we walked around for another hour until daddy sent me a text to meet him at the movie entrance. We have been talking on the phone ever since. He told me that he was living with his dad, but wants to move out and stay with his grandparents. Where is Indian Head?"

I just smiled and shook my head. "Cute story. Indian Head is about twenty minutes south of here. That's where his grandparents live. Noah was always a good boy, and I never had trouble out of him when we lived under one roof. It was hard when I left because I knew I was leaving him behind. But, I left him with my number, and he called me every once in awhile. He was actually in a really bad accident some months back on his skateboard. He got hit by a car and was really banged up. But, your mom got him back in shape. His favorite color used to be dark green, if I am not mistaken. And as far as I know, he does not have a girlfriend. And you see how fine he's doing."

"And he is very handsome, too."

"Ooh, now don't get cute. So, tell me Michele. What do you know about boys? Has your grandmother talked to you at all about the birds and the bees?"

"My grandmother? Yeah, right. She is such a prude. All that I have learned has been from my friends and their older siblings. But, Nana has shared some stories with me. Made a whole day of it. Just the two of us. We went to have manicures and pedicures, and she made me feel special. I really enjoyed it."

"You know. She did the exact same thing for me and your mom when we started our menstrual cycle. The funny thing is that she told your mom not to say anything to me about it so she wouldn't spoil it for me. We later shared our experiences with each other. It made a difference, especially with me not having my mom and all."

"Oh, I'm sorry, Auntie Mai. What happened to your mom?"

"She died when I was born, and my dad never remarried. Aunt Rocsi raised me as her own. Your mom was like a sister to me, and we were inseparable." I paused, reflecting in my own thoughts of how as we get older, we are drifting apart. "We are here for you and are gonna support you all the way to the top. Now, you know you must stay focused and don't let Noah distract you. He's a good person, but he is a young adult now and he's still a man. He's gonna wanna do what young men do when they are attracted to women. I need to ask you something. And I need you to be honest with me."

"Sure. Anything."

"Are you still a virgin?"

"Of course, auntie! Why would you ask?" she exclaimed, obviously embarrassed.

"Don't be surprised. Most girls your age are already sexually active.

And to be honest….well, your mother gave birth to you at your age. Your dad was the same age as Noah is, and well, you know the rest."

"Well, can I ask you a question, then?"

"Sure thing. Ask away."

"When did you lose your virginity? And how did you know it was the right time?"

I hesitated because I didn't want to give her any ideas. Nadia is a bright girl. Very impressionable. But I didn't want to keep from her what the world would be tempting her with. "I lost my virginity my freshman year in college. I had been dating this guy since tenth grade in high school. We met during a summer internship in Baltimore and kept in touch. He was a year older than me. We wrote letters to each other, and when I told him that I was going to Grambling State, he was ecstatic. I knew it was right for me because I was ready for it. I have no regrets."

"And what happened to him?"

"Well, we stayed together for two more years, but he wanted to get married and I was not about to drop out of school to start a family. We remained friends, but when he graduated, we lost touch. I didn't have another serious relationship until I was out of college. I stayed focused on my grades and graduated magna cum laude. I went on to pursue my Master's degree and here I am."

"I can't talk to mom like I talk to you. She gets all defensive and even suspicious at times. It really hurts my feelings. Daddy is more understanding, and I know he wants to ask me personal stuff, so he usually puts Nana up to it for him. It's actually kind of funny. I know this is an adjustment for us getting to know each other, but I have always wanted to be here growing up with Milan. And I always wanted to know who my father was. I know all about their alcohol problem and he told me that he is getting help. Daddy promised to do everything to make sure that his children are taken care of. And I just promised him that I would do my part as well."

"I am so proud of you. And if no one else says so, I give you my blessing to date Noah. Trust me; your mom will listen to my voice of reason. And your dad will, too. He is a good man, and he will make sure you know everything about these young men. The good and the bad. He never knew about you, Michele, because if he did, he never would have left you and your mom behind."

"I know, Auntie, I know. And I promise to come to you if I ever decide to give it up, is that how you say it?"

I laughed. "Yes, Michele, but let's plan on not giving it up any time soon, okay? Now after all that talking, can we watch *Transformers 2?* I've been dying to see it, but Malachi has been busy with his band a lot lately, and I can't wait any longer."

"Well, scoot over and make room for me!" she giggled, and plopped down on the couch, with my signature blanket wrapped around her and matching socks on her feet.

The friend is the man who knows all about you, and still likes you.
~Elbert Hubbard, *The Notebook*, 1927

FORTY

I t's hard to believe that only two months ago I was ready to pack up and leave Malachi upon seeing him with his pregnant ex-fiancé. And now, here I am, in the middle of September, just approaching the end of my first trimester. They have calculated and recalculated my due dates three times already, and still no one is one hundred percent sure.

All I know is that sometime next March, our boys will be here.

That's right.

We are having boys.

We are still undecided on their names, but we did agree to give them the same middle name as Malachi.

Our girlfriend crew has decided to get together at my dad's house to see the newest addition to our clique. We have all been so busy with our lives that we miss one another tremendously. Kiana's baby girl was born two months ago, and I had not seen them, Tion nor Jordan since the funeral.

Aunt Rocsi was gracious enough to allow me to leave the food last night. We were gonna surprise Kiana with another baby shower.

I arrived early to help Milan and Aunt Rocsi set up, but Milan was M.I.A. Her car wasn't in the parking lot when I left and, as usual, she wasn't answering her phone.

"Hey there, little lady. How are you?" Aunt Rocsi greeted me, with a hug.

"I'm doing fine. Most days I'm tired, but today I'm good."

"Have you talked to Milan? She just dropped off Nadia and never came back."

I followed her in the kitchen to help set up. "No, she didn't come home last night and she's not answering her phone. You know how she gets; I doubt she would miss this, though."

"I hope you're right. I took Nadia out with her boyfriend last night since Milan didn't pick her up."

"She went out with Noah?"

"Mmm-hmm. You know him?"

"I practically raised him. He's Joaquin's son."

"Oh, yeah, that's right. What a small world. He's a respectful young man. And Nadia seems pretty taken by him."

"Yes, he is. His aunts and I stayed on him. I'm proud of how he has turned out. And he is fond of Michele."

"I can definitely see that. I sure hope Milan has had that talk with her. Because Lord knows, my mother didn't talk to me. It was like taboo."

We were interrupted by the doorbell. It was Tion and Jordan. I asked them to come early to help decorate.

"Hey ladies. Oh, how I've missed you guys!" I said as we embraced.

"Step back and let me look at you," said Tion. "You look gorgeous."

"That's what a good man and a belly full of babies will do," said Jordan, laughing. "Come here, girl. I'm so happy for you. So, how much time do we have before the guest of honor arrives?"

"Just under an hour. Looks like most of the decorations are already up, so if y'all just wanna set up the food table, we're done."

Like clockwork, Kiana arrived on time. Her husband Jude dropped her off and we all met them at the door.

"Surprise!" we sang in unison.

"Oh my goodness!" said Kiana. She turned to her husband. "Were you in on this, too?"

Jude nodded yes. "Love you, babe. Gotta go." He kissed her cheek and ran back to their car to get the baby's bag.

We waved and shouted, "Hi Jude. Bye Jude!"

* * *

For the next four hours, we ate, laughed, and shared our latest stories. It felt good to be in the midst of my girlfriends, but Milan was still a no-show. I held the baby practically the entire time. Amara Celeste Stein was born July 12 to proud parents Kiana and Jude Stein. She was beautiful, and I could not wait until I was able to hold my own boys next spring.

Tion admitted to us that she missed Jabari after their breakup and the wedding that never happened, and had even taken him back. "I know y'all think I'm crazy. But we have a history and I couldn't let it go. At least until I realized that Miss Lollipop had a hold on him. He left to go back with her, and we broke it off again. And now…..well, let's just say I totally stepped outside of my box. I met someone new. He's from Sudan and plays for DC United." She couldn't stop smiling.

"Well, we all have had our man drama. So, it's time you finally do you. Take your time. Have fun," said Jordan.

"And keep your pocketbook closed!" I added.

"She says, while sitting front and center with twins in her belly," Kiana said.

We all burst out in laughter.

"Hey, I'll have you to know I made Malachi wait four whole months before he could get it. He made a deposit but I didn't let him cash in right away! Don't y'all hate. I've been through some real jokers, and y'all know it. I had to wait on Him and not lean on my own understanding." I handed Amara over to Tion to hold.

"We just messing with you girl. You know, for the longest time you came to all of us for advice on your man problems, and kept the drama coming. I'm very happy for you and Malachi," said Kiana.

"Yeah, isn't it just like Maiya to be the perfect one?" We all looked up to see Milan busting through the door, with her hair all over her head and clothes all over the place, looking a hot mess! "Leave it to Miss Princess to get everything she wants!" she screamed. She reeked of alcohol and was in need of a shower. I was stunned.

Jordan jumped up and reached for Milan to help steady her, but Milan swatted her away.

"Milan," Kiana started, "Baby, what's going on? Let us help you."

"I'll tell you what the problem is. Y'ALL JUST DON'T GET IT! Maiya likes to paint this pretty picture of her life. Well, it ain't always been so pretty. Has it, Princess Maiya?"

I just stared at her in a confused daze. "What the hell are you talking about, Milan?"

"Oh, quit the Miss Innocent bit. It's old. You ain't nothing but a ho like all the rest of us. Just be a woman and admit it for a change."

"Who she calling a ho?" Jordan asked Tion, with a frown on her face.

I was horrified. Milan was obviously drunk and high, but this anger towards me was new. Had I done something?

I stood up and reached to steady her like Jordan had done before. She hit my hands.

"Get off me, bitch," she yelled. Her breath stung my nose, making my nostril hairs stand on end. I backed up, not trying to have her hit my stomach. She saw me protect my belly with my arm.

"Aw, look at you, all maternal and shit. Hmm, you weren't all maternal when you was messing around with Carlos while you and Joaquin were still together. And….get this, y'all…she got pregnant by Carlos."

She stood in front of me with her arms crossing her chest and head held high. She changed her voice, making it sound like she was whining, and continued. "But, poor, poor little miss Maiya was under so much stress trying to keep her secret a secret, that she lost that baby."

She looked at everyone in the room, and then turned to me. "Didn't you?" she snapped.

"You bitch!" I punched her in the face and she fell backwards, onto a chair.

Tion grabbed me. "Maiya, come on now. She's not worth you getting all worked up. Not in your condition. Plus, she's high. She's not herself now."

Jordan helped Milan to her feet and held onto her. Milan was trying to swing at me.

"Calm your ass down before I knock you out, Lani. You're out of line right now," said Jordan.

"It ain't over, Maiya. You wait and see," said Milan, ignoring Jordan and staring squarely at me. The anger in her eyes chilled me. I didn't know where this was coming from.

"Girl, I wish you would bring it. Don't talk about it. Be about it," I yelled, acting braver than I felt.

Milan glared at me before stomping out of the house in anger. Two minutes later, we heard her car speed off. Aunt Rocsi came from the kitchen to see what the ruckus was all about.

* * *

Once I got home, I was still worked up, thinking about the outburst from Milan. She has some anger towards me that I never knew about before. How long had she harbored this? I was so tired but remembered tonight was a concert with Malachi's band. I had to go to show my support for my man.

I showered and got dressed for the show tonight. Malachi told me that he was leaving my ticket at the booth since I wouldn't be riding with him. I was just about to open the envelope that was left in my purse, when the phone rang.

"Hello?"

"Miss Vaughn. Maiya Vaughn?"

"This is she."

"This is your driver for the show, compliments of SOUL. We should be leaving in the next fifteen minutes in order to make the show on time."

"Okay, I'll be right down." I left the envelope on the counter and walked out the door.

I got to the Birchmere as the staff was setting up, but Malachi was waiting for me as we pulled up, and he led me backstage where the rest of the band was preparing for the show.

"Hey, beautiful. I missed you, babe."

"I missed you, too." He kissed me and held me tight.

"Hey, you two, cut that out. Save all that for later." I looked over and saw members of the band teasing and laughing at us. "All jokes aside, welcome Maiya. It's good seeing you again," said Kevin, the keyboard player. "Malachi, can I steal you for a minute?"

"Baby, I'll be right back."

I waited a few minutes until I saw Janet arrive with a few of her friends. "Hey, Maiya."

"Hi, Janet. How are you?"

We talked for a few moments and she introduced me to her friends. She and the drummer had been seeing one another over the summer, and things were getting pretty serious. She invited me to sit with them, and I was excited about it until Malachi told me he had made other seating arrangements for me.

"Oh, excuse me. I guess we will just see y'all after the show, then." She and her friends laughed and walked to their seats.

"I have something special for you, but right now I need to gather up the guys, okay? I'll see you out there. Love you." He kissed my lips and turned to walk away. "Oh, Maiya, ask for Whitney. She will be taking care of you tonight."

"Okay." I smiled and walked back to where I would be sitting.

The night was magical.

And Malachi was in his glory.

Not only did he play with SOUL, but he was invited to play for Algebra Blessett, who opened the show. When they did the band introductions, he really showed off and played the guitar solo of Michael Jackson's *Beat It*. I was seated in the front row, and enjoyed the evening along with a nice dinner.

When I got up to use the restroom, I ran into Tion.

"Hey, girl, I didn't know you were gonna be here," I said, giving her a hug.

"It was a surprise to me at the last minute. Kwame invited me."

"Kwame? That's your friend, huh?" I said, smiling.

She started to blush. "Yes, that's him. You think you could get us backstage after the show? He loves music and that would really make him happy."

"I'm sitting in the front, so just come down front afterwards. I don't see why not."

"Okay, I'll see you then."

After the show, I met Tion and Kwame and waited for Malachi to come out. He took us backstage and introduced them to everyone. Kwame seemed to really be into the music, and the chemistry between him and my girl was amazing. Kwame promised to get Malachi tickets to his games once the season started up again, and Malachi invited him to come listen to them play anytime.

I started to yawn, and couldn't wait to get home.

"I see you baby. We are about to go." He turned to the guys in the band to say goodnight. "I'll see y'all next week."

On the ride home, Malachi wanted to talk about me selling my condo, or at least renting it out. He was getting tired of us sharing residences, and he had a point. I just wasn't ready to get rid of my place, but I knew we couldn't raise a family in my small condo.

"Maiya, I want you with me, and I think we need to think about it. You at my house some nights, me at your place some nights just don't cut it for me. My dogs are confused. I want all of us together, baby. Can you think about it?"

He had to call me twice because I had stopped listening to him about five minutes ago. My mind was on Milan.

"Hello….Maiya. You didn't even hear a word I've been saying, have you?"

"I heard you baby," I lied. "I'm just sleepy, that's all."

I had decided that I would keep all of this Milan business to myself for now. As far as I'm concerned, Milan was in a bad way, and the less people who knew, the fewer people in my business when I finally gave Milan the tongue lashing that she deserves.

Where you used to be, there is a hole in the world, which I find myself constantly walking around in the daytime, and falling in at night. I miss you like hell. ~Edna St. Vincent Millay

FORTY-ONE

MILAN

I don't know who Maiya thinks she is. Little miss perfect Princess. I can't believe she punched me in my face! And called me a bitch! When she finds out what I know, she won't be all calm and collected as she thinks she is. She better hope the business takes off in Louisiana, because it's about to get ugly with our Maryland office. My high was coming down. My buzz has officially been killed. I wish I was at Memphis' place to get some more blow. I should have stayed there instead of coming here and reading my father's letter.

After I left Memphis at his condo, I came home and actually thought about his girl and their baby. I felt a soft spot for her, knowing that she left before having the baby. It brought back memories of me when I was pregnant with Nadia, and how I used to miss Jackson.

Memphis told me all about their argument some months back and said she never contacted him to say where she had gone. He said the baby was due this month and that was pretty much all he knew. Apparently, his baby mama had changed her number and simply disappeared. She had no family so there was no one who would know where to find her. I told Memphis that he must have really fucked up. Women don't do shit like that unless they hate your ass. Or scared cuz you crazy.

While thinking about their pitiful situation, when I got back home, I kept eyeballing the letter on my dresser. It was just two months ago that we buried my dad and I missed him terribly. Ever since the reading of his Will, I held on to the letter he had written and addressed to me.

There was no time like the present for me to read it.

I opened the letter and immediately felt nostalgic once I saw his handwriting.

June 15

Milan, my Angel,

I have taken this time to tell you what we should have shared with you long ago. While I was in the hospital, I begged your mother to share the secret that we've held on to for so long.

Years ago, while stationed in Germany, I met your mother. She was working in the commissary on the base, and I fell in love with her immediately. Her eyes had such sadness and I wanted to make her smile.

I started shopping there around the time I knew she would be working, and one day, she finally agreed to go out with me. What I would soon learn about her made me love her even more.

She was pregnant with you when we met. Her lover was sent away on orders back to the States. They had been together once; she had hardly a chance to get to know him. At least, that's the story she told me. He was an officer in the Army just like me. We were married before you were born and I adopted you without hesitation.

It wasn't until we finally got orders to come to D.C. that I found out that your biological father was still in the metropolitan area. Your mother sought him out, and even chose the neighborhood to live in. (She was adamant about living in off-base housing.) It took all my strength to not be angry at the fact that she had deceived me and moved next door to her ex-lover, until I realized that he had no recollection of who she was. She was just a hazy one-night stand to him in his mind.

I asked you to promise me that you and Maiya will always remain close. The real reason is because you two have more in common than you know. You and Maiya have the same father. Daniel Vaughn.

What can I say? This is probably the most unlikely news you expected to hear. Believe me when I say that you are my daughter, through and through, even if we aren't blood related. I loved you more than life itself. Please don't be mad with me or your mother. I wanted you to know a long time ago once she told me, but she insisted we wait a bit longer. That is why I hated the fact that we kept Nadia a secret from Jackson. Every man should know whether he has fathered a child or not. A child is not something to keep from any person. It pains me even more to know that he is your cousin and I wasn't given the chance to know this information, or else I would have stopped the two of you from seeing one another.

The bottom line is that you and Maiya are sisters. I am not sure if Danny knows, but I think he had his suspicions all along. Sit down with them and talk about it. And know that you will always be my Angel.

Love Always,
Dad

What in the hell, I thought. *All these years?*
Maiya is my sister? But worse--Jackson is my cousin? Tears rolled down my face. How could they keep that from me? So much hurt and anger came pouring out of me and I acted on impulse and wanted to attack Maiya. That's why I drove to Aunt Rocsi's house to put her on blast. I wanted to make her feel my pain.

Sisters are different flowers from the same garden. ~Author Unknown

FORTY-TWO

MAIYA

I woke up this morning feeling exhausted.

Since I promised to spend some time with Nadia, Malachi drove me home and went back to take the dogs out. He promised to check in on me later. We still had not set a wedding date, and I believe it bothered him. And his mother, too. When we agreed to talk later this evening, my plan was to discuss everything: the wedding, the business, the condo.

I could hear Milan playing music next door. It was so loud I could feel the bass through the walls. That's what she usually does when she's mad or depressed. I wasn't gonna call her nor was I gonna go see her. I had enough drama in my life because of her, and I needed to draw the line.

I'm done with her.

For good this time.

I fixed myself breakfast: turkey sausage, toast with strawberry jam, cheese grits, and scrambled eggs. My appetite had really picked up being pregnant with twins. I drank a tall glass of rice milk and belched like a stuffed newborn baby!

After eating, I made a cup of hot tea and went to sit on my balcony. Walking past the kitchen counter, I recognized the envelope I left there from last night. I grabbed it and took it with me to read outside.

June 15

Dear Maiya,

If you are reading this, it was my desire to make you aware of something you should have known long ago. Hopefully, we will get to talk about it before I leave this world. But, if not, promise not to be angry at me.

Your connection to Milan comes as no surprise. The two of you had an instant bond that has been there since the day we moved to the neighborhood. You are closer than any two people can be. Our move was not by chance. It was on purpose.

Let me explain why.

While stationed in Germany, I met Freida, Milan's mother. It was love at first sight for me. We married two months later, after finding out she was already pregnant with Milan when we met. I adopted her and raised her as my own. We later moved to Maryland after receiving PCS orders and the rest is pretty much history.

I later found out that Milan's biological father was in the area, owner of a lucrative business specializing in landscapes and lawn care. That man happens to be your father, Daniel Vaughn. You and Milan are sisters.
That is why I asked you to promise me that you will always be close. I think your father suspected, though I'm not sure he recognized Freida right away once we moved there. But, he and I never talked about it and we never said anything to your family.

And for that, I am sorry. Milan is special, as you know, and she needs you. Now more than ever.

I have prayed for her and Freida to be close, but they are both stubborn. I could never put my finger on it, but I believe that she resents Milan for your father moving away. I honestly don't believe he would have abandoned her knowing that she was carrying his child. Watching him raise you over the years leads me to believe he really loves you and I know he would have wanted to know about Milan.

And know that I didn't want you to find out this way.

Promise me,
Cochise Douglass

Tears filled my eyes and I wept quietly. It was then that I realized the music from next door ceased. I ran inside to phone Milan. I could hear the phone ringing but she didn't answer. I slipped on my flip flops and ran out the door. Banging on the door and yelling out her name, I cried hysterically.

"Lani, please let me in. I understand everything now. We need to talk. I am soooo sorry!"

There was no answer.

I ran back to my kitchen and scrambled around, looking for her door key that I kept in a top drawer. I found it and went back to Milan's.

Once inside, I called out to her again. "Lani, Lani!"

My heart was racing and I had a bad feeling in the pit of my stomach. My mouth began to water and my palms began to sweat. Running down the hall to her bedroom, I anticipated the worst.

She wasn't there.

I ran across the hall and into her bathroom, stepping into a puddle of water. When I saw her, I screamed so loud I thought that I would pierce my own eardrum. Water was still running into the bathtub and there was an empty pill bottle on the floor and blood dripping from her wrists. I turned the water off and lifted her head out of the water. Back across the hall, I grabbed the phone, dialed 9-1-1 and got back to Milan. "Oh, Lani, please be okay." I felt for a pulse. It was present, but weak. I gave the dispatcher all the information that I could. She moaned softly, and didn't fight me. I drained the tub and covered her in a bath sheet. In less than fifteen minutes, I heard the ambulance in the parking lot.

I got to the door and yelled for them to follow my voice. "Up here. She's up here. Please hurry." Tears blurred my vision.

All I could think about was our fight yesterday.

The last thing I remember seeing was a letter resting on the side of the sink as they lifted my sister on a gurney and carried her away.

* * *

Sometimes we must play the hand of cards we are dealt; we don't always get to choose.

It is what it is.

If you enjoyed *It Is What It Is*, be ready to see what is coming next. The follow up novel, *Promise Me*, is sure to answer the many questions that readers may have. Take a moment to read an excerpt from this author's forthcoming sequel.

FRED

Fred a.k.a. Memphis, that's what they call me. And the ladies say I am a fine specimen of a man.

With skin the color of black licorice, they say I am so black, I could sweat coffee! My locs hang long to my shoulders and are jet black like my skin. My upper body is built like Terry Crews. And women used to line up just to get a taste. They still line up to get with me.

Malachi and I became friends while attending Hampton University, and we were on line together when pledging Kappa Alpha Psi. I am from Memphis, Tennessee; hence the nickname I was given. Plus, I could throw down at a barbecue. My sauce was so good, it will make you wanna slap your momma! I played drums for a local band while in college, but had a dark side that I kept from my best friend, Malachi.

I was a ladies man, and never spent a night alone. I had expensive taste, and still do, which made me want the finer things in life. It wasn't

until the end of my freshman year at Hampton that I began dealing
drugs. My game was so tight that by the time my sophomore year
approached, I was driving a Lexus, fully loaded. I settled down with one
main girl, Sasha, but still kept a few chicks on the side.

Sasha was an exotic beauty, with corkboard tan skin and natural
honeycomb-colored hair. She looked like the actress Michael Michele
from New York Undercover. She was a member of Alpha Kappa Alpha
Sorority, Incorporated, and all the men were anxious to be in her
presence. But, she had a thing for bad boys, so I was the man of her
choice.

Sasha's best friend Hazel had a thing for Malachi, but he only had
eyes for Tia. As much as he pursued Tia, Hazel pursued him even
harder. When Tia continued to ignore his advances, he began to spend
time with Hazel, and realized that they shared common interests. She
loved to sing, and he loved playing his guitar. They quickly became
friends, but Malachi chose not to turn it into something more. He
always had to be this good guy, when I told him all he needed to do
was hit it and quit it. But he was too good for that.

When the four of us got together, it was obvious who was a couple
and who wasn't. Malachi always treated Hazel with respect, but she
wanted to be more than just friends. While Sasha and I were getting
busy in the next room, Malachi and Hazel would spend time talking
or watching television, or playing video games or Uno. He even taught
her how to play Spades one weekend.

Sasha couldn't understand why Malachi didn't wanna be with her
best friend.

"What is it? She's pretty, she's smart, and she's fun to be around. I
know you like her. AND SHE'S CRAZY ABOUT YOU!"

"I don't wanna lead her on. She's a sweet girl, no doubt. But I like
her as a friend."

Sasha sucked her teeth. She knew Malachi was wishing Tia would
eventually come around, and she was getting tired of hearing her
girlfriend complain.

One night when they were at a basketball game, Malachi spotted Tia on the sideline talking to a couple of the players. Normally, he would have broken his neck to get her attention, but not tonight. His days of getting her to notice him were over. Instead, Hazel was the one to make it known whom he was with, and she purposely chose seats directly behind the basketball players.

Malachi's roommate Jarvis played forward and watched us when we sat down. He motioned for Malachi to come over and speak to Tia, and she looked up to see him hand-in-hand with Hazel. After that, Tia made sure she spoke to Malachi every chance she got.

But it didn't matter.

He had long developed feelings for Hazel, and soon thereafter they were a couple.

The only difference between Malachi and me, important as it was, was that Malachi actually cared about women, while I just wanted a dime piece on my arm.

I eventually dropped out of, or was removed from, Hampton University pending an investigation involving an alleged sexual assault on a freshman. It was some bogus claim from a hottie that wanted me.

While attending an after-party following a step show hosted by my fraternity, a young woman claimed that I kept harassing her. She admitted to the flirting we both shared, but it became a bit possessive. Alcohol was involved, along with Rohypnol, and the girl came home with me.

At the end of the night, she was left alone in a wooded area, disheveled and barely clothed. While wandering through a neighborhood, a woman spotted her and drove her to the local hospital.

I denied everything, because it was consensual, but the evidence proved me wrong. They said there were vaginal tears and bruising along her inner thighs, which were proof of an assault. But I was smart enough to wear a condom, so there was no DNA to prove I was the perpetrator. I had no need to drug anyone. Girls throw their panties at me all the time.

The proof came from an eyewitness.

The name of the witness…..Sasha.

Sasha entered the apartment the night after the step show. She and I had argued at the party over another girl who approached her about sleeping with "her man". The girl gave detailed physical descriptions of my genitalia, even down to my well-groomed pubic hair. Sasha confronted me, with the girl standing right there, and I laughed it off, saying, "She let me hit it a few times, but it didn't mean nothing."

The girl, looking embarrassed and with crossed arms, looked at both Sasha and me, rolled her eyes and walked away. Sasha made a scene, and then stormed off. She left the party and went looking for Hazel, only to find she was spending time with Malachi in her dorm room. Hazel and Malachi had left the party a little bit earlier for some quality time.

This would be their first time together.

And I was happy he was gonna finally get some.

Sasha claims that she drove back to my apartment, where she often stayed, and she heard some noises. Now, I ain't gonna lie. Shawty let me hit it that night, but she was into it. I fell asleep and when I woke up, she was gone. Apparently, the bedroom door was wide open, and Sasha saw us getting busy. The bright lamp on the nightstand shone on her face. Sasha claimed to have memorized every facial detail down to the girl's freckles and moles. Her eyes were closed and she looked as if she had passed out from a drunken stupor.

Sasha quickly left out and stayed with one of her sorors.

I moved back home to Tennessee, and then to D.C. I was tryna get my hustle on again, and knew D.C. was where it was at.

Me and Malachi lost touch and later reconnected when returning to Hampton for homecoming weekend. Malachi came with Tia. It was Malachi who introduced me to Tia's friend Jasmine. Tia and Jasmine had comforted Malachi when Hazel died in a car accident during their senior year. The rest is history.

I tried to live a good, clean life, but still found myself drawn to the thug life. I was into dealing cocaine and prescription drugs, and made a fortune. I wore my designer clothes and was very clean cut. A tight fade now replaced the shoulder-length locs I was once known for. I ended up serving no time for that alleged assault. There was no real evidence, and I was found not guilty.

Malachi and I became tight again, and Malachi invited me to play the drums in the jazz band, SOUL. And with our women being best friends, it was just like old times.

I made sure that Malachi knew nothing of my dirty South "Memphis" side.

I lived a double life and would let NO ONE get in the way of my money-making, drug-selling, woman-loving actions.

About the Author

Growing up in Fort Washington, Maryland, Karen shared a love for language arts and reading, along with her sister. She found that her high school English literature assignments were more fun than tedious, and would later express herself in writing. During her freshman year at UMBC, Karen's writing caught the attention of her African American history professor, and she was encouraged to share an assignment in front of her class. Her exposure to Erotique Noir that same semester sparked a greater love for poetry and writing, and she would later embark on a dream: to write a novel. Through much prayer, Karen decided to act on her "to do" list and began her novel in 2007 while sitting on a Bermuda seashore. Doors were opening for her, and Karen found herself in the presence of authors who freely shared advice and writing tips, but most importantly, their support. Before the completion of her first novel, Karen reached out to her college professor, Dr. Acklyn Lynch, to inform him of the impression he made on her writing and he was "moved to tears".

Karen resides in southern Maryland with her husband and their two sons. She is presently at work on her second novel. You can visit her website at www.karenminors.com.